3/2   £5.99

First edition

D1491979

When All is Done

WHEN ALL IS DONE

by

ALISON UTTLEY

"When all is done, human life is at its
greatest and best but like a froward child
that must be played with and humoured
a little till it falls asleep, and then the care
is over."—Sir William Temple.

FABER AND FABER LTD
24 Russell Square
London

First published in Mcmxlv
by Faber and Faber Limited
24 Russell Square London W.C.1
Second impression December Mcmxlv
Printed in Great Britain by
Purnell and Sons Limited
Paulton (Somerset) and London

It is not wholly past, the time enrolled
In registers grown old; those records lie
Outside the playhouse of the inward eye,
And life's a story not so simply told.
We speak of ghosts, as those who from some fold
Of death escape, and as cold shades flit by;
We ponder change, watch in our lifetime die
A multitude of scenes; yet some will hold
These terms of time, ghosts, change and death unmeaning
Compared with that deep presence of all in one
Which through our common notions intervening
Adds magic to the moonlight, gives the sun
Another glory; and quiet place and day
Disclose for a flash the boundless, timeless play.

EDMUND BLUNDEN

Chapter 1

The house stirred in its sleep and stretched its ancient limbs. It slowly awakened and raised the covering of darkness and the web of years from its body. Its old heart beat so loudly that it seemed to be a heavy pulsing rhythm flowing out to the fields, rising to the hills, shaking the trees to music in the surrounding woods. The air vibrated with its waves and a fine dust sifted from the beams of the great barns alongside the building. It breathed deeply, and a sigh came from its antique roots, from those strong foundations that were part of the bedrock of the earth itself. The house opened its eyes and gazed at the windy sky and the wheeling stars, and it recalled past days which were ever present. Slow-moving stars and illimitable sky were part of its own life, for it had spun through space with the earth's motion, conscious of the vast deeps of infinity around it. The house was an entity in that fourth dimension we call eternity. Deep it went, searching in its memory to old days.

The past was ever present in the house's mind. It lived outside the measure of time, and its stones spoke to it and told it of people who had loved it and called it Home, those who had given their lives to serve it. They were part of it too, their minds were in the heavy blocks of chiselled stone, in the shapely doorways and the flat paving stones of floors.

They had builded the house and something of their strength and patience had stayed in the dwelling place. For a house has a personality of its own. Its character is formed by those who have lived within its walls. It is a composite being, remembering the loves and hates, the good and evil deeds, the passions and sorrows of its folk. They are absorbed into its being. The stones of a house are filled with awareness. The long deep silences of nights and the passage of years add to the accumulation of its experience and mould its soul.

The house was a part of the earth, rock and wood and stone-flagged passages and floors, a living tissue, born, growing, harmonious in beauty, embracing the lives of all who had lived there so that it had become immortal. Even in decay, in death, it

7

would live for everlasting, for its spirit was of eternity. The consciousness of other generations was in it, their happiness, their sorrows were in the air, they had lived and loved in the rooms, they had suffered and died, but they were people of strength and faith. The earth around it was kindly, the moss lay in humped cushions of the walls, the ferns sprouted with no human aid and uncurled their green fingers on the steep outside steps, a little ash tree sprang from a rock with no soil and no foothold and clung there like a slender acrobat to amaze the house's eyes. The stream in the yard flowed brilliantly over the stones born from that underground spring that curved like spun glass in the field by the trough and was the cause of the first building of a tiny stone dwelling a thousand years ago.

So there the old farmhouse stood, knowing everything, aware of the thoughts and impulses of the occupants, sending messages to their minds, warnings and encouragements that restrained them from or prompted them to reckonings and adventure. It evoked the past and laughed at the future, for both past and things to come were in its bones. It had celebrated the Defeat of the Armada, and it had rejoiced over Crécy. It had talked of little battles nobody has heard of. It had cheered for Waterloo and Trafalgar, and all these times were as one in its mind.

The house smiled to itself as it recalled only the other day when the kitchen talk was of the Queen of Scotland, lovely as a rose, imprisoned in a Hall across the hills, and the dancing bear and the packmen who came to the farm. The shaggy beast came one night with its bear-leader on the way to the entertainment of the Queen's company. The house remembered everything, the harsh stench of the bear's pelt as the animal stood in the barn and the mooing of the restive cows in the cowhouse beyond. It remembered the wedding of the youngest daughter soon afterwards to one of the Queen's servants and it remembered the Babington plot that stirred the country to a frenzy of hate and fear. It had been wide awake in those times, it scarcely slept at all, for there were bonfires flaring up to the skies on the hills around, warning England of the Armada sailing up the channel. It heard the distant church bells ringing when the Spaniards were defeated, bells that were later destroyed. Chiming bells and hunting horns were its delight, and when the deer were hunted in the woods and moors around, the little old house had vibrated with the sweet clangor of the winding horn. The stout walls had an

8

echo of their own, they were proud that they also could make music.

Once the house had sheltered a fugitive Royalist and hidden him in that upper chamber among the hay. Once it had held soldiers who filled stable and barn and cowhouse on their journey north, following after Prince Charles Stuart. It had no choice, it belonged to the humble who have to obey. The house had comforted the weeping women who had knelt in prayer in the small chamber. Prayers had been its daily portion, petitions said softly in the farm kitchen when the family met in tribulation and anxiety to pour out their troubles to God, prayers recited in powerful moving words by the travelling preachers of John Wesley and the Bible men who stayed the night at the little farm half-way between their open-air meetings in the large villages, and then prayers whispered in faltering broken tones for the sick, the lost ones, the dead.

Its whitewashed walls had heard secrets and kept them, the anguished confessions of some, the death-bed farewells of others. They had heard tales of murders and hangings and miscarriages of justice as men sat in the kitchen and gossiped over their ale.

It had held a pot of money hidden in a hollowed stone in the chimney, and a silver mug brought as the dowry of one wife had been stored for safety under the floor during a rebellion when solders roamed the country and lonely people might be murdered for small riches. A hundred years later, when alterations were made, and a new room was added, a few coins were found and accepted as a miracle, a gift from the house.

So the house stood there, in the valley between the hills, living its own secret life. Kings and queens were born and died. Farm labourers and shepherds and ploughmen also came into the world. They lived their appointed time, they spent their days in toil and tribulation and a few joys and they passed away. The kings were remembered, but the labourers' names were forgotten for they had no tombstones. Their graves were grass-covered mounds in the churchyard, for they were humble people of no account. Only the little house remembered them and cherished their rough graces. It knew their everyday sayings and common talk and plain deeds, their bravery and endurance, their striving in a world that sometimes seemed as if it meant to sweep them away to oblivion before their time was ripe. They were made of strong stuff, and the little old house gave them courage and fortitude from its own store. It helped them so that they bore disaster and bad days uncomplaining, accepting their destiny.

So the house opened its eyes once more on this wild night, and watched the old woman lying in its arms, cradled in the home she loved so much. She was as much a part of it as the rough-hewn stones of the walls, or the blackened timbers of the barns. She was compact of its being, bone of its bone, worn and tired, but enduring. The flame of life flickered like the candle at the bedside. A breath could blow it out, and a touch could make it glow serene and bright as a tiny star in the darkness.

The house opened wide its eyes and regarded her, and the old woman in the wooden bed also opened her faded blue eyes as if she were aware of the scrutiny.

She stared about her, at the shadows hovering like gigantic bats on the walls, swooping over the ceiling of the room, at the stabbing shafts of firelight and the pointed fingers of flame in the sooty chimney. She slowly turned her eyes to the flickering stump of candle on the little round table by the bedside. Its long waxen winding-sheet curled down one side in stiff folds as the oval yellow flame swayed and curtseyed in the draught from the window. Somebody ought to move it, she thought. Somebody should take away that rippling death-sheet and put the candle out of the wind's power. It was her own shroud she saw there, unrolled ready to wrap her for the grave unless somebody moved it.

She tried to raise her arms but there was no strength in them. They refused to do her will. They stayed under the bedclothes like two long bones.

Her being was racked with pain, but her courage and endurance were great and she summoned her powers to resist. Her eyes wandered beyond the thin candlelight with its circular rainbow edge and its cone of deep luminous blue to the fire. Half in the shadows a man was seated. His dark anxious face was lighted now and then as the flames shot up. His strong aquiline features with their bony structure seemed Indian brown and gold in the play of firelight. He sat, leaning forward, staring at the core of heat, frowning at his thoughts, waiting for time to pass. His stained working jacket was opened, a knitted scarf was loose round his neck. The thick hair curled by his ears and hung heavily on his forehead. He looked weary and depressed, unlike the eager, captive sick woman. She looked inquiringly at him, but he was unaware of her gaze. She could neither speak nor move to attract his attention. Her dim blue eyes were over-bright, child-like, glittering with the intensity of her desire for his companion-ship. They were shining with excitement as if she could see something that had been invisible and now was clear. Her thin old face with its hollowed cheeks and high bones lay like an ivory mask on the rumpled pillow as she listened. She made a supreme effort and found words.

"William! William! What's that? What's that sound?" she whispered in low gasps, panting for breath but triumphant that the words had come.

The man started in surprise at her voice. He swung round to his mother and cocked his head to listen.

"It's nothing, Mother. I thought you'd been asleep. How d'ye feel now?" said he, and he slowly stretched his stiff limbs and stood up. The shadows mopped and mowed, and ran about the room on fleet dark toes.

"I hears something," she repeated, and her voice was of the same timbre as the fire's as it licked the bars and whispered in the chimney. "I hears something, I tell 'ee."

"There's nothing, Mother. Keep quiet, now do 'ee. Bide still, will 'ee. It's only the wind rising." He spoke comfortingly and gently as he might have soothed a sick cow.

"It sounded like a sigh, William. It was the house, William. It was the house speaking. It knows I'm going."

The man leaned over her to hide his unease, and patted the pillow.

"Now don't ye be fanciful, Mother. You mustn't imagine things. You'll get well and live for many a year yet."

"Aye, William. I don't want to go yet. Not yet awhile. I'm not ready yet."

She gasped with pain and, "Not yet. Not yet," echoed the house, soft as a dream, but she heard it and smiled.

"Take away that shroud, William," said she, and her voice was stronger.

William removed the long curled wax which fell to the bottom of the candle, with his finger tip. He tossed it in the fire and watched the spurt of flame. Then he lifted the table out of the draught and pulled the curtains closer over the window. He put a horse-rug on the sill, close to the casement, and stopped a moment to look under the blind at the night. It was pitch dark outside, even the stars were hidden, and the wind moaned and ran fleetfoot over the yard, rattling a shutter and shaking a door.

He went back to the fire, and threw on a fresh log. Then he sat watching it, losing himself in the tired contemplation of that piece of wood which he knew quite well. It was elm, grown in the corner by the orchard wall, a bough blown off in the storm at the backend of last year. A gummy tear rolled down it, then fell hissing into the flame that licked it up. His mind dwelt on the grown tree, he lost himself in thoughts among the branches, only his body stayed there by the fire. He forgot his mother, and his troubles, as he watched the gold snakes of fire coil and dart with long tongues at the log, and he summoned the free-growing elm out there under the sky. She lay silent, listening with an acute sense, and the sighing voices floated in the air. She felt the deep pulse of life beating from the walls. It seemed to rock the bed, gently swaying it. It was comforting in that dark abyss of time-lessness that had opened before her like a black pit, where death and eternity dwelt. It was like the clasp of a friend's hand although she wanted no human touch. She looked round the bed-chamber with eyes that could pierce the veil shadowing it. It was strangely illuminated in that hour between life and death. The roses on the faded wallpaper were alive, shaking their velvety petals. She could almost smell their scent. The ancient chintz on the bed-curtains was jewelled with light, and every tiny trellis and bud was distinct in the pattern. The fitful gleam of the cracked china bowl on the medicine cupboard brought to life the Chinese figures painted upon it. A fan of gold rippled along the mahogany chair back, polished by her own hand and that of her mother's. The life of her possessions reassured her. They were fine and old and beautiful these few worldly goods, they were alive too, and how could she die? The inanimate showed its own life to her, with a strange intensity, as if it were revealing its secrets to one who had always known a part of them. In death one shares life more intimately than in life, she thought, as she lay there with the impressions and floods of evocations surging over her.

She spoke again, and her son arose and came to her. She had renewed strength, and she tried to raise herself.

"Take care of Virginia. Mind her. Don't let any harm come to her," she said. "William. Do you hear?"

"Yes, Mother, of course I'll take care of my own niece." He spoke consolingly, and he leaned over and drew the blankets across her clawing hands, but she struggled free again. He pushed the pillows behind her and helped her to a half-sitting position.

"William!" Her voice was suddenly urgent. "Don't you hear it? It's saying something. What does it say?"

She dragged herself higher, and clutched his arm, staring with bright fever-filled eyes around the shadowed room, into the corners, seeking for the whispering voices, the deep breathing of that ancient heart.

"'Courage', it says. 'Courage and Life'," she cried, vehemently.

"Hush ye!" said William roughly. "Hush, Mother!"

"Bring her to me. Bring Jinny to me," she commanded, and she sank back wearied with her silver hair in a cloud on the pillow. Her hollowed eyes were watching the penumbras where the half-shades ebbed and flowed. She lay exhausted, panting.

William left the room and returned in a few minutes with a little girl wrapped in a blanket. The child was asleep. Her long curling lashes shadowed her face, her little fists were clenched over the nightgown strings. Her face was too thin, her forehead too high, her shut eyes were far apart. It was an elfin face, strange and peaked with little pointed chin, but there was a hint of beauty about it, perhaps from the lashes, or the tendrils of damp hair. As the old woman gazed at her, the child opened her dark blue eyes and the beauty was alive.

She woke to full consciousness but she gave no sign. Solemnly she returned the heart-searching gaze of her grandmother, and the old and the very young seemed to exchange some message. They were bound together by an invisible cord, a sensibility which the man didn't possess.

"Can ye hear it too?" asked the grandmother gently. "Can ye hear anything, my little Virginia? Can ye?"

"Mother! Be quiet!" protested William impatiently and he gave the child a shake of annoyance. Her wide lustrous eyes were bright with wonder and excitement. She waited tense, and the long shadows sneeped and swooped from the walls as the little candle-flame flickered. Then she covered her face with small hands and began to weep noiselessly, with choking little sobs which she kept back.

"Mother! You make me fair mad. You shouldn't frighten the bairn. What are you talking about? She ought to be asleep, and you too," cried William, exasperated beyond bearing.

He tried to remove the child, but she clung to her grandmother.

"It's the house speaking. It's awake. I want my Jinny to hear it. Do ye hear it child?" The old woman's voice was sweet and husky as she leaned lovingly to the little girl.

Virginia stopped weeping and raised her head. Her tears glistened on her cheeks, but a smile slowly curved her lips as she nodded. All three listened intently. The man shrugged his shoulders helplessly, angry with all the tribe of womenfolk on earth and in heaven, but he couldn't resist. There it was, they all heard it. A deep sigh came from the heart of the house, a beat like the pulse of a giant. The wind roared and shook the shutters downstairs with sudden force, an owl hooted in an unearthly wail as it flew over the housetop, a sick cow in the cowplace a few yards away moaned in pain, but above all, and deeper, came that insistent stir of an elemental life.

"There's nothing but the wind, Mother," said William, grudgingly. "I must go to that cow of Barley's. Her's due to-night. You lay still Mother and get a sleep. I'll send Hetty to you."

"No! No! I want to be alone," protested the old woman.

"Then come along Virginia. Kiss your Grannie and come back to bed. A nice going on at night."

They kissed with lingering kisses, the grandmother's thin burning lips pressed to the child's smooth cheek.

"Go now, my precious. You've heard it, and don't ever forget. Put her to sleep, William. I'm all right. I don't want nobody, nobody. Leave me alone. Blow out the candle and leave me alone."

William gathered up Virginia and drew the blanket tightly round her body. She sat up in his arms, excited and lively, but her uncle was in no mood for speech.

"I heard it, Uncle Will," she cried in her baby voice. "I heard it."

He pushed the log on the fire with his boot, and glanced round the room at the swaling candle and gliding shades that dipped and bowed over his mother's head. He lighted his own candle at the flame and blew out the other, putting the box of matches carefully near. The thin smoke spired upward like a fine white ghost, and he pinched the glowing wick with his forefingers. Then, balancing the child he stepped heavily and clumsily away and pulled the padded door after him. The landing was icy cold, and he crossed to the double room where his daughter Emmie slept. He put the little girl by her side.

"Go to sleep, Jinny," he whispered, and they smiled at each other in a knowing way. He glanced across the room to the big bed where his wife lay fast asleep, unconscious of the upheaval of the night. He was thankful she hadn't wakened. Two women would have been too much for him. He tucked up Emmie, lying there with her golden curls spread out, and touched Virginia's cheek with his forefinger.

"Go to sleep, Jinny," he repeated. Then he went downstairs to the kitchen, one hand aloft with the candle, the other touching the wall, for the stairs were uneven and crooked even to one who had lived there all his life.

"Her's not bound for the river-crossing yet, thank God," he murmured, and he looked under the dresser for the lantern and went out to the yard. "Her's strong-willed."

He stood by the labouring cow, but his thoughts were on the house. Yes, he had heard something, and it had given him strength. He put his hand on the beast and gave it some of the comfort which filled his own mind. It was a sense of security that had come that night.

Charity Dale lay there, and her mind was new-washed in some crystal elixir of life, so that pictures flowed before her eyes, vivid and bright. She went back through time to her youth. She saw the fields in waves of delicate green at mowing time, the corn-fields gold at reaping time, she saw the threshing when the farm kitchen was full of hungry men and herself cooking a meal for them. She was with the sheep shearers in the great barn, and there was one, a blue-eyed youth, whose name she had forgotten. His frosty blue eyes and raven hair were clear as daylight, and he smiled at her, and then turned to her pretty sister. She saw her husband, Timothy, and the three children, William, and Kate, and Jane, playing round the kitchen table, blind man's buff and turn the trencher. She herself was plump and handsome, gay and light-hearted, filled with happiness and security and carelessness, although she had never been really carefree. The house had wrought the change. Her face lost its deep lines, it was spiritual, beautiful, filled with the serenity of peace. Her breathing became easy, she fell into a deep life-saving sleep.

The house was silent again, watching her, dreaming to itself. It could wait for her company among its many ghosts. What did a few years matter to such an old house? It had seen many a one die, and there had been never a tremor of its stone eyelids, but

Charity was different. She was a part of itself. To those who were aware of its own life, to those who loved with devotion, it gave of its own courage and strength. To the old woman couched in the bedroom over the farm kitchen it gave a draught of life. She slept long and deeply, drawing new strength from its outpouring.

Chapter 2

Shepherd's Fields with its hundred acres of meadow, pasture and ploughland, its little woods and rough stony crofts, had crouched in the hollow between the hills since the time of Queen Elizabeth, but tradition said a cottage had been there long before. It had taken on some of the character of the friendly hills in its centuries, for it had weathered the same storms, it had been bleached in the same droughts. The hills were crowned by woods that rose from the river side and they were part of the house's joy. House and woods regarded each other afresh each morning and passed the time of day.

It was made of the freestone which was the bedrock of those hills, and it had absorbed some of the green-gold colour of the high woods. Three hundred years ago the little old cottage where the shepherd and his wife and many children lived was enlarged and the present farmhouse was built. The tiny cottage remained as the core. One up and one down, oak beamed and strong as a rock, it was now the back kitchen and the loft over it. It had its own door and strip of garden a foot wide where a pink China rose grew round the stone casement and tapped at the glass.

The stout chimneys rose above the ivy that tried to hold them. The gently sloping roof was shingled with flat stones from a quarry which had long been deserted, in a tangle of growth. It was mossy and lichened, tufted with houseleek grown for its medical use.

Charity's ancestors had lived at the little farm for a century before they had had enough to buy the place. Charity's grandfather had saved up for it for many a long year. He bought it for six hundred pounds, which was a lot of money in those days, but he had lived in the house for fifty years before he had saved the sum. Each week he put aside a shilling or two, and he stored his savings in a stocking hidden in the bedroom wall. His wife helped him bravely and kept the secret. There were no banks and money was kept at home, in crannies where no thief could find it. Pence were changed to shillings, silver to gold, and after market day the stocking money was counted. The old house heard the chink and rattle of coins, and listened to the plans with satisfaction. The stocking was filled, and the money was removed to a narrow wall-cupboard, which was pasted over so that nobody knew about it. The stocking went back to its hole, and slowly, surely, the shillings and guineas filled it. Only the old house knew the privations and difficulties overcome, the meals at market resisted, the patched clothes worn, the hard work performed unceasingly, but the house rejoiced that the effort was for love of itself.

The grandfather and his eldest son, put on their Sunday clothes and went off to buy the house from the squire. The squire didn't want to sell, but he at last sent for Lawyer Chettle.

So the grandfather became the owner of Shepherd's Fields, the farmhouse, and the ploughland and meadow and woodland. His son Matthew inherited it, and Charity grew up in the house and loved it intensely, and everything within it. The large white Staffordshire bowl lined with heavenly blue, which stood in the dairy filled with eggs, had belonged to Charity's grandmother. It had been cracked for a hundred years, when a little girl had dropped it on the stone floor, and been soundly slapped for her carelessness. Then it had gone from parlour to dairy and there it had stood ever since, with the great crack like a black pattern in the shining blue and white glaze.

The round stone weights used by the grandfather for weighing, were used as door stops. The quern was in the henchamber for the chickens. Nothing was lost or thrown away from the old days, and now Charity herself was old, and her grandchildren were there to take her place.

This was the farmhouse, Shepherd's Fields. It had comforted Charity in deep sorrow, and shared her joys. Its benignity and warmth had given her strength and fortitude. She was filled with solicitude for it, as for a living person, much-loved. This little low house had sheltered its world of human beings and animals against the storms of nature and of life. It had comforted them in the darkness of death and helped them in the pangs of birth and suffering. Crowns had fallen, wars had swept the country, but the house had stayed secure in the narrow valley, steadfast as the hills it faced. It had acquired something from those centuries of experience. It was nobler than the hills, more sentient than they, aware and alert with its contacts with humanity through the years. Every clod and every stone carried its associations. The paving stones were worn by tired and blistered feet, the earth had been dug and broken and tilled over and over again by clumsy patient hands.

Wherever its children went they took with them something from the house's past. They were different because they had drunk their mother's milk in the house's shadows, breathed its airs and absorbed its life into their blood. They were different too because they had been born to hard work and poverty. They had a stubborn strength, and a hard kernel of common sense, and a flicker of beauty in their remembrances.

Away in the distance were other farms and cottages, hidden in valleys, perched on exposed hilltops. They also had their own sensibilities, they were creatures of immortal flesh and spirit— the flesh of earth and the spirit of those who had lived there. For every house is haunted by the loves and hates, the laughter and tears of its former inhabitants. When the house falls, when ruin and desolation of war or neglect destroy it, the place where it stood holds these entities. They can be felt by a mind tuned in to their own wave-length, they can be caught for a moment and lived again. In a clearing in the wood, by a heap of stones, or by the stream where a ruined mill rears its dark ivy-covered stones, and jackdaws fly to and fro, the spirit of the cottages that once stood there remains, invisible but full of life in the timelessness of eternity.

In spring the hedges were white with may, the orchards were filled with apple blossom, little streams ran down the fields from the springs and hurled themselves recklessly into stone troughs and out again, primroses grew where they had always grown, by the water's edge. Foxgloves stood high in the corners of the fields, they were mown down and they grew again, honeysuckle and wild roses leapt the hedges and walls. Haystacks in the stackyards, horses in the pastures, sheep in the high lands, and the little farms and cottages guarding them, each was a living entity, each a centre of life.

On the whole the farm had prospered, and brought a good life to those who lived there with their kith and kin. Nobody had been rich, or even middling well-off, most of them had been very poor in actual money, but their wealth lay in the land and in the satisfaction of being their own masters. Bad times had come with terrible successions of ills, bringing tears and grief, and partings. They were tided over with such economies and strivings that many folk would scarcely believe possible. Barley bread and nettle broth, porridge and oatcake, with extra work, stone-leading and carting for others, but money was saved. Good times came, and the money went on improvements, better stock, and a well-bred mare, on plough and harrow and a new machine. Bracken-covered slopes were turned up and stony ground cleared and brought into cultivation by immense strength and effort. Bad times came again with more losses but the little farm went on, striving, faithful. Always there would be struggle and a mechanical age would not ease the burden, which was accepted by all who lived there.

The house itself was a long low building of weathered stone, solid and plain, with several doors in a row. The cowhouses and stable were at right angles to the main buildings, but all were under one roof of grey-green stone, mossed and tufted with patches of yellow stonecrop and the ancient houseleek plants. The kitchen door always stood open, even in wild weather, and hens pecked around its sill and stepped indoors with dainty questing foot. It was like the cowhouse door, in two halves, one of which was fastened to the wall by a finely wrought iron latchet curled like a lock of hair. It was graced with a deep porch for shelter while the men knocked the soil from their heavy boots. The doorstep was hollowed by countless feet which had worn the thick paving stone to a curving shell. Floor and passages were scooped out thus by the people of past times who had tramped through, striking flashes from their iron-shod boots. The original shepherd's cottage was the connecting link between the house and farm buildings, and its roof was lower, and sunken like the steps. The greenish hue was more pronounced for the moss and seedling ferns made a shimmering cover of golden green, which was broken by a mansard window and crowned by a thin chimney of twisted stone. Up there the pigeons paraded on their dainty feet, the blackbirds spread their dark fans, and the tits swung on the tufted flowers that grew high above the yard. On this small house front was a grotesquely carved figure, made by the skill of a witty stonemason centuries ago. A large head and small body, arms akimbo, and legs asplay, the little stone man grinned down at the yard in perpetual good humour.

Beyond the cottage were two doors, one above the other, the lower leading to the barn where the great corn bins stood against the roughhewn walls, the upper door high in the side of the farm with no visible means of approach unless the intending visitor possessed a pair of wings. It was the door of the cornchamber where trusses of bought hay were stored, and bags of meal and Indian corn, and linseed cake were heaped. The sweetest-smelling place on the farm, it rivalled the best parlour in the children's minds. Over the door was a pulley half hidden in the stones, and carts stopped underneath while bulging sacks were lifted by tackle and rope to that magical high doorway.

The buildings spread out, cowhouses, stable, barns, cartshed with trellised doors and wooden bolts, great double doors for haybarn and sheds, and finally an open shed for wagons and machines. At each end of the farmhouse and buildings was a flight of stone steps leading to an upper room. These stairways, cut from solid blocks of sandstone and surmounted by square stone platforms from which the doors opened, had a special significance to dwellers at the farm. They were look-outs, where approaching travellers could be viewed, and their identity guessed, where handkerchiefs were waved to friends and curses hurled after enemies. They were little watch towers where the movements of birds and clouds and winds were noted and the weather forecast. They were resting places, for on those broad platforms was tranquillity and safety from the turmoil and danger of loose cattle in the yard. There little Virginia sat, serene and happy, among the ferns that grew in the wall-crannies, watching the horses and cows down below, the cattle going to the watering troughs, shuffling and pushing with long curling horns, the horses frisking as they were set free after work. There Richard flew his kite, with the added height of the steps, and Charity sat with her knitting, looking over the wide domain and then back at the friendly old house, with its doorways and twinkling little windows.

So many doors, all painted the same shade of buff, varying only in degrees of dirt splashes, confused the strangers who occasionally came up the long drive from the cart road to ask for tea, but each door had its own intense and important individuality, its own absolute charm of personality, known only to the dwellers at the farm and invisible to the ordinary wayfarers. For each door led directly into a room, strong-smelling, harsh, with the odour of animals, of sturdy country life, where poverty was unknown because it was unrecognized as such. Food and drink, and a straw mattress for men, feathers for women, limewashed walls, stone floors, steps worn by the hard-working long dead, it was poverty to a townsman, but a rich home life to Charity Dale and her kindred.

The barn door under the meal chamber, had a row of figures scratched or written upon the post, hidden inside the doorway. There were little sums, multiplications and subtractions, a few of them wrong when the sevens and nines were reached, and altered by another hand a generation later. The number of bags of meal, the prices and totals were given but rarely a date. On the cowhouse door were more mysterious hieroglyphics, denoting the times of calving of cows, with names going back a hundred years, Cowslip, Rose and Daisy being the most frequent. The stable door had other figures, for foaling, and pedigree, the number of miles to distant places, notes of special journeys, successes at shows, this written in a good bold hand for it was a record to be handed down to later generations. There were little cures for ailments, salves and herbal drinks, tantalizing to those who tried to decipher the curious symbols and drawings.

Some doors had pairs of interlaced hearts cut in the wood, with initials nobody knew anything about, for the owners were long dead farm men and their girls. Others, especially the doorway of the weighing chamber, had heights and weights of children, and weights of calves and pigs. Charity's own weight and height at the age of five as well as those of her brothers and sisters and her own children were there. Clean white marks cut in the posts showed the attainments of her grandchildren, and ruled lines showed their heights. The doorways were the library, secret to the farm folk. They were personal diaries few could read.

The front door was tightly shut. It was locked and bolted throughout the winter for it was seldom used. There were bushes of rue and sage and lavender close to it, growing nearly across like a barrier, and an iron scraper, painted black each year, and a door knocker of ancient design, so stiff that nobody could lift it. The door was only opened when strangers threaded their way through the thicket of herbs which guarded the step, in the mistaken idea that it was polite to knock at the front door, even when

21

several doors close by were invitingly open. There was such a creaking and groaning of bolts and bars, such a disturbance of the life of spiders and dormant butterflies, the intruder was aghast at the upheaval he had caused. Even the squire knew better, and went to the kitchen door when he called for a chat with Charity and her son William Dale. However it seldom happened that anyone arrived at the front door, for eyes glanced from windows and peepholes in barns and somebody rushed out in apron and print bonnet to welcome the intruder and gently lead him to the kitchen.

The front door led directly to the parlour, a sweet-scented little room, musty and old with memories and fragrance of past events. One could almost smell the wedding feast of William's marriage to Hetty, or the lilies that had lain there when Charity's husband died. The room was panelled, but the wood was papered over, and the oak whitewashed. The tall wall-cupboards, which had been bought from a fine house two hundred years before and put in place by an enterprising member of the family, were the chief decorations. Their arched shelves were filled with bits of Staffordshire china, and some books and an old teaset with bright flowers. It was a room for grace and Sunday cheer, not for everyday use. Scented geranium and fragrant cherry-pie stood on the broad windowsills in gilded saucers. Sometimes a maidenhair joined them, or a hyacinth in a pot. It was Charity's own garden where her cuttings grew into plants and her flowers were tended and admired.

The stone floor was covered with a couple of carpets for warmth, an old carpet handed down from other generations lay on the bare stone, and at the top one whose crudely coloured flowers had at last faded to a soft loveliness. On the walls hung a sampler made by Charity's mother, and one embroidered by herself, with pious motto and stiff birds, and sententious verse.

When you are rich you many friends will find,
But if your riches fail your friends will prove unkind

wrote little Charity's needle when she was seven years old. There was a woolwork picture of Joseph being lowered into the well, and a water-colour painting of the farm done by an artist who offered it in place of food and lodging for a week. They didn't want it, the money was more important, but there he was, in possession, with an empty pocket and a hungry mouth, and they had accepted it as a bad bargain.

The room was no museum of past days, for it was a living part of their lives, it represented the gracious leisurely moments in hard times. Each object in the little room had a story to tell, each had eyes and ears and knowledge, sharing the farm's life, but separated by the painted door and china handle from the worka-day kitchen. The fireplace had small iron hobs on each side, so that cooking could be done in the graceful best room if needed. William's wife, Hetty, wanted to do away with them, they were so common, she said, but Charity refused. At busy times, such as sheep shearing, and harvest and Christmas they came in very useful for extra cooking, and possets and caudles were kept hot on the little round hobs in wintry weather.

Above the fireplace hung an oval mirror, festooned with roses and leaves of gilt. Three candlesticks jutted from the base, each held in a curling leafy golden branch, and ribbon twined about it to the summit. Everybody was proud of the looking-glass. It had reflected the rosy faces of the children in the early days of the nineteenth century when Charity had climbed on a chair to look at herself, and it had showm Charity's cheeks, worn and thin. Charity's uncle, Aaron Woodiwiss, had bought it at an auction at the Squire's hall, when the old squire died in 1790, and it had come from the house of faded grandeur to the plain little farmhouse, bringing an air of past splendour to the dreamy parlour, spinning its web of stories of fine ladies, showing its secret reflections of ancient beauties to the little old room where it hung. All dressmaking and trying-on was per-formed before it. It was the only large glass in the farmhouse, so it had the pleasure of reflecting the home-made fashions and the new bonnets before they appeared at the village church or chapel.

The parlour faced south, like the rest of the house, but there was a west window which gave an added attraction. The golden light came round the gable end, peeping in stealthily as if to catch the room napping. It stretched out its hands and caught those extra sunbeams, and supped them up greedily like a thirsty animal. Some rays it kept to play with on a dark day. For that reason the parlour had a secret dusky glow of gold which it displayed when it was in the humour. Little Virginia knew of it. She crept in when the door was ajar and waited, shy and timid, watchful as the room tossed a light on the ceiling or threw a ball of filigree gold-web on a waterglass. There were pockets of warmth in the room, even in winter's depths, and the butterflies knew

23

about it. They stayed there, wintering like the rich people on the Riviera, and when the first day of spring came, they flew round the room and perched with fluttering, feeble wings on the window, waiting to go out, basking in the scraps of sunshine.

In this room Charity received the vicar's wife when she called once a year for subscriptions, and here she poured out a glass of home-made wine for a visitor. It was here the children came on Sundays, to look at the illustrated volumes on the tall cupboard shelves, to paste Christmas cards in the scrapbook, to listen to Charity read from the pictured Bible. In the corner stood the old walnut piano, soft-toned, with some notes that were dumb, and a mouse nest inside. Here too was the fiddle which young Richard was learning, with much squeaking and anguish for his listeners, to play. It was a room of intimate treasures—a leather-bound volume of Shakespeare which nobody read, a beaded footstool on which no foot must tread, a harp which nobody had played for fifty years.

The parlour was joined to the kitchen by a short passage, alive with whispers and murmurs, a place of hesitations and unease and voices, a windowless spot where a child had stayed in fear, locked out long ago, and a small misery seemed to lurk for ever in that narrow space. Nobody lingered in this cold passage which joined the heavenly beauty of the parlour to the earthly homely kitchen, for there was the well-thumbed old door with its iron latchet waiting to be clicked, with noise and bustle and stir, with all the poetry and prose of intense and full life.

This large room with its stone-flagged floor and low-beamed ceiling was the centre of the farm life and the artery of the house. It stretched across the middle of the farmhouse between the parlour and dairy. Gilt mirror and fiddle and piano at one side, and jingling milkcans and churns at the other, the kitchen was the auditorium of the theatre.

The low ceiling was supported by two oak beams, and as if these were not enough to hold it, there was a stout oak pillar made from a tree trunk resting on the floor a few feet from the house door. So hard was it with centuries of smoke and heat that a nail could scarcely be driven into it, but there were old wooden pegs and iron hooks of rough shape on which the family hung their caps and hats, their mufflers and lanterns. It was a friendly post, round which children played, and against which an old man could lean. "Between the door and the post," was significant, and everything tended to congregate there, as if it were the village pump. It gave off cracks and creaks without warning or reason, except that it was remembering the great oak tree from which it was cut. Then Charity nodded to it, and it was reassured.

Two mullioned windows looked out to the garden and yard, the manure heap in a dark morass with a rainbow glitter on the slime, and the lovely violet hills. One was a workaday window, with leaden sill and a tin of silver-sand for scouring. It was over the long stone sink, and from it the workers looked out for the farmhands' return. The other, on a different level, was a more feminine window, with flowers in scrubbed pots and a cookery book beside them. A tiny peephole of a window looked out at the back of the kitchen on the sloping fields close to the glass, and the hillside that rose from the house's walls with only a narrow channel between. Sometimes a sheep grazing there peered into the farm kitchen, its amber eyes staring close at pots and pans or the horse stood with his nose close to the glass, gazing with interest and contentment, with a flicking of ears and a snuffling of nostrils as he watched his friends within.

In the middle of the room was the heavy oblong table scrubbed till the oak was bleached by soda and hot water, chipped where knives had cut up sides of bacon, hollowed where water had drained down the middle. It was as truly part of the house as the whitewashed walls, for it had been made when the house was built. The fireplace was open, with ovens and boiler, and hook over the flames. Pots and pans dwelt perpetually on the fire, for hot water was always needed and life might depend on a boiling kettle. At the side was the bread oven, unused since the new grate replaced the old open hearth in Charity's youth. Windsor chairs had taken the place of the older rush-bottomed bobbin-backed chairs, now in lofts and attics, or thrown away to decay. At the far end was the important dresser, laden with willow pattern plates and dishes, ready for setting the table, and lustre mugs, one for each child on Sundays, as well as many a treasure of fancy plate with proverb round its rim. There was a grandfather clock with white face and painted flowers in the corners, and a store of boxes of matches on its roof under the ceiling. It was always half an hour fast, so that there were two times, clock time and train time, and the farm went by the clock time.

There were no pictures in the kitchen, although newly-wed wives had brought a picture as dowry now and then. The paper almanac from the grocer was the decoration, changed each January for a new one. Walls were decked with bright tools, harness, horse-collar, and horse-brasses, kept indoors for the sake of the dry room, a leather jack, a powder horn, from old days, and the much-used copper warming-pan. Bunches of herbs hung from the second beam, for Charity was a famous herb-woman. A clothes-line dangled from the first beam near the fire. Over the fireplace were skillets and measures and pans of brass, queer old things once used for cooking. It seemed as if nothing would change there. Everything was as it had been for a hundred years, complained Hetty, and she brought from the market stalls more pans and bits of china to add a modern touch.

The fire beat its flames against the bars, the kettle sang, and the blackbird whistled in the hawthorn bush at the door where the towels were dried. This was the music the house knew, but it remembered other music. The kitchen was pregnant with memories, the song of harvest homes, the hymns and prayers said there, the partings for far lands, the lying down for death, and the first staggering walk of the infant to outstretched arms. The house had listened to the hum of the spinning-wheel and lately to the clatter of the sewing machine, and both were music to its ears. Soon it would hear wireless tunes and accept them along with all its old memories as a part of its life. The spinning wheel had given place to the sewing machine. The long bow and arrows of grey goose feather had been replaced by the musket and then by the double-barrelled gun, which hung on two hooks at the beam.

In a dark corner of the kitchen was the latched door that opened directly upon the crooked staircase. It led to the little bedrooms, long ones and narrow ones, a room poked in a corner, for they were oddly shaped. A wooden wall divided a room that was once too large for a family increasing in size, rooms were tucked over dairy, and larder, an apple chamber here, a cheese room there, each with a little stairway up or down, the doors with wooden pins and iron latchets, with bobbins and strings. One room was entered by the outside stone staircase, and a narrow door had been made in the wall to allow only thin people to creep through to bed. The stout ones had to go outside and climb up the flight of steps from the yard.

Each room had its own character and its own distinctive odour, its tiny cupboards to hold a Bible and a candlestick, and pegs to hang one's wardrobe. Crooked and plain, ugly and beautiful, the farmhouse had grown up from the little shepherd's cottage next door where the churns were kept and apples stored.

This was the farmhouse, Shepherd's Fields. It had comforted Charity in deep sorrow, and shared her joys. Its benignity and warmth had given her strength and fortitude. She was filled with solicitude for it, as for a living person, for it had a soul.

Chapter 3

The children saw their grandmother as an old woman, with a black three-cornered shawl of crocheted wool on her shoulders, and a little lawn cap upon her grey hair. In summer she wore over this a tucked lavender print bonnet from which her quick eyes peered with lively interest at everything that went on. With it she had print dresses with tiny flowers in lavender and grey. In winter the lawn cap was hidden under an ice-wool scarf. She always wore a black dress in winter, buttoned down the front, the bodice tight round her small neat figure, the skirt bunched in thick gathers about her waist under the snowy apron. She was very particular about her aprons, and she had a drawer full of them, starched and ironed to a shiny gloss, finely tucked round the hem. On Sundays she was dressed in grey merino, summer and winter, made in the same style, with a grey Quakerish bonnet. Her clothes seemed part of her and at night when she undressed and hung them on the pegs behind the bedroom door, something of her own personality seemed to be left in them. Virginia thought they climbed down and went off about the house and barns to see that all was safe from fire and danger.

The dresses and coats of all the family hung on long wooden pegs with round knobs, for there were no wardrobes in farmhouses. Charity's garments were well known for they had never changed in anyone's memory. Only the little rooms remembered the blue crinoline and the flower-sprinkled dresses of her girlhood. Sometimes Emmie and Virginia were sent upstairs to feel in the pocket of the Sunday dress, for the bunch of keys, for the packet of lozenges, and for letters, and they knew their grandmother's clothes in the darkness by a faint aroma of some delicate secret herb she used for her personal pleasure.

Charity's hands were thin and curved, hollowed like shells with the sheen of mother-of-pearl in the palms where the skin was polished by seventy years of hard work. The blue veins were knotted like azure cords at the backs of her hands, in the slender fan of bones. The thumbs swept outward in strong arches, and the left forefinger was pricked by a million needle-pricks.

Virginia was entranced by her grandmother's hands, and she took them in her own small soft fingers and examined them carefully, hearing the tale of each finger. Nobody else gave a hand to be gazed at and wondered about, and nobody else had fingers with names of their own.

"This is Tom Thumbkin, and he's my busy workman, Jinny," said the old woman. "And next is Billy Wilkins, and he does the sewing and helps Tom Thumbkin. He is the pointing finger, he shows the way. He's my foreman. Then comes Long Daniel, he's the biggest of the family. He wears a thimble cap, my silver thimble."

"He's got a brass cap too, Granny," interrupted Virginia.

"Yes. He's a rich man. Next is crooked Bess. On my left hand she wears a gold ring and a keeper."

"What does that ring say, Gran?" asked Virginia, touching the gold band with the raised letters.

"Mizpah. That means, 'The Lord watch between me and thee when we are absent one from another.' That's your grandfather and me."

"And does the Lord watch?" asked Virginia.

"Yes. He takes care of us," murmured Charity, softly turning the ring which kept the thin wedding ring from falling off. "And now there's Little Dick, my little finger. He's a jolly fellow. He tastes the soup and dips into the milk, and has a sup of cream from the bowl, and all manner of things." She smiled down at the upturned face beside her. Then she made her fingers dance on her knee to the little girl's delight. It was a wise old hand, an epitome of Charity's life.

Charity's face was golden-brown in her old age, polished like cornstalks in the wheatfield beyond the orchard, reflecting the light in flushed rose on the finely-wrinkled cheeks. It was the face of one who has worked out of doors in all weathers, but the skin was soft and delicate for Charity had some pride in her looks. The cheekbones were high and below them the hollows were faintly shadowed. The nose was severe, the strong hooked nose of an old woman. The lips still held the enchanting curves that had distinguished her youth, and the eyes were brilliant blue, faded but sparkling as if an unquenchable light burned within. It was the face of an old woman who has worked hard, so hard it would be unbelievable if all were known. It was a fine face, handsome, large, masterful, and Charity had lost none of her powers. She was a source of strength to all who met her. She was Charity Dale of the farm Shepherd's Fields, a queen in her own right of field and pasture.

At four years old she began her life's work in the early years of the century, a little bright-eyed eager child who fetched and carried for her mother and father, running on bare feet up and down the cold stone floors with wooden bowls and platters and horn spoons. She was a grand little wench, they said, and that was all the praise she ever got. At ten she was the foster mother of five younger children. She harnessed the horse, and fetched up the cows. She carried the baby to the hills and set it in the flowery grass while she gathered blackberries and mushrooms. She watched over the others as they tumbled about among hens and geese in the yard. She guarded them from harm, from the anger of the flamboyant turkey-cock, from drowning in the trough, from the horns of cattle and sharp hooves of restive horses. She was brave and fearless, independent, impudent and valorous in her small way as she fought her way through those early years. She had taken her mother's place when that valiant woman died from a fever in childbirth, and she sat at the table with her silent father, trying to cheer his troubled spirit. She nursed the little ones in many childish complaints.

She had brought up the family with chidings and blows and kisses, dealing out good and ill impartially, striving to bring order out of the chaos of the motherless boys and girls, resentful of the housekeeper who came to the farm and set her cap at her father. The children went gleaning in the cornfields, stooping and searching like little mice for grains of corn. They held the cows' tails at milking-time, one child to each cow, and chased the hens to the henplace. They all went to the village school, a dame's school, a few pence a week, and Charity led the way. She carried her little cotton bag of books, the speller, the reader, the sum book, and her slate with a hole bored by a hot skewer in the rim through which a string passed for pencil and sponge. Charity loved school, it was an escape from everlasting work and the nagging of the housekeeper, and she was reluctant when she had to leave at the age of twelve. Life was earnest in those early years of the nineteenth century, and Charity had real work to do, but she had plenty of fun, in her own private way. She helped Mrs. Booth to make the candles in the candle mould and she strung them up to dry. Like Bluebeard's ladies they hung, white ghosts. The candle moulds were there on the pantry shelf in Virginia's childhood, but candles came from the grocer's, in neat packets, twelve dozen at a time.

Charity filled the kettle at the trough in the field, and bent under the weight as she carried it up the yard to the kitchen. She laid the handkerchiefs on the orchard grass to dry, when Mrs. Booth was washing, and spread the kitchen cloths over the nut bushes and hawthorn, clipped to a round smoothness in readiness.

Up on the mossy wall she climbed with her basket of clothes, to cover the green bushes. She imagined she was draping shawls and dresses on the trees. There was always the wind doing its magic for her to watch, making its wave motion on the water-troughs, rippling the corn, sweeping across the mowing-grass seed heads, with visible motion, brushing the straw round the yard in laughter, ruffling a hen's feathers with impudent raillery. Charity took the wind to her heart as a fellow-worker. It dried the clothes in the orchard, and when she carried the washing back to the house, all clean and sweet-smelling in the basket, she nodded to the wind and felt its tug at her petticoats and hair as if it wanted her to stop out with it.

The walk to school was full of enchantment, for even the trees talked to her. She could hear them through the chatter of the younglings who went with her. "There goes Charity Woodiwiss, the teacher, the missionary, the explorer," they said, and she was each person in turn. She glanced up at the invisible ones in the air, she talked silently to one who walked beside her. This unseen one accompanied her when she drove the cows and washed the milkcans. It flew from room to room light-foot, unseen, part of the house, an immortal who was always there.

Even when Charity was a little child she had known there was something vital and compelling about the house. It had a personality of its own, an awareness of the life going on around it.

This hadn't seemed strange to her, for it was part of her experience; it was as natural as the life of the beasts and the Christians who surrounded her, but she realized with a child's quick intuition that others were not fully aware of it. Perhaps her mother had known, but her father said nothing, and certainly Mrs. Booth saw and heard nothing or away she would have gone. There were no ghosts or queer happenings, or uncanny noises, but there was always that sense of companionship, of an intimate life of growth and slow change, even a sharing of sorrow and joy. She could swear the old house knew and experienced the beauty of a summer's day, or the tears of the sorrowful. The kindliness of the orchard was like a warmth under the apple trees, even in winter; the companionship of cups and saucers, of fire and gates and walls, was her daily experience.

If the knowledge of the house were true, as she was certain it was, then it remembered days past, centuries ago, when the nameless dead who were known to it alone, had moved and breathed and loved in those small close rooms, with the thick walls around them, and the little windows peeping like bright eyes at the garden, the farmyard and the fields. It remembered other children who ran there, who played round the haystacks, who went whooping through the yard, driving cattle, riding horses, catching hens, watching the sheep-shearing with wide eager eyes. Children's life was much the same through the centuries, among the common people. The rich could sit in their sun-parlours and embroider and study, they could ride in carriages and wear fine clothes, but not the poor. Always they ran and danced and played and shouted, they worked and sweated and often they died, but the little house gave them something of itself, it made a signal to them, and so perhaps their songs were shriller, their games more joyous, their grief was borne more bravely with that unseen companionship. The poignancy of death, of youth and innocence was there, and the strength to bear it.

So little Charity Woodiwiss went to school a few years before the young Queen Victoria was on the throne and she liked it. She felt immortal, with the round world held between her small rough hands. The schoolhouse was an ivy-clad cottage in the village, with gabled roof and a good-sized kitchen. There a stern little round-faced woman taught the children who could afford to pay her small fees. They paid their pence and sat on the oak forms.

These benches were against the wall, with a stool and pointed hat for the dunce, and an arm-chair for the teacher. It was a merry little schoolroom, for in winter a big fire of logs burned in the open hearth, and one could gaze at it and make dreams as the flames sent flames like gold-antlered stags up the chimney, and the caves showed their hidden treasures of great wealth. In summer the windows were wide open to the garden of lilies and cottage roses, and sometimes butterflies and bumble bees joined in the lessons, or hens walked in at the door or birds flew down to see what was happening there.

The schoolmistress kept one eye on her potatoes boiling in the iron pot over the fire, and the reward for good work was to be allowed to sit near the blazing logs and perhaps stir the stew with a long iron spoon, or turn the little Dutch oven, but the punishment for bad children was a switch from the cutting twigs of the birch rod which dangled from the hook close to the teacher.

For stupidity there was the dunce's cap and stool. Charity never wore this emblem of inferiority, but she had many a cut from the rod on her outstretched hard little hand, so that blood was drawn.

In the spring the children took bunches of bluebells and water-bobs to the teacher. In summer they gathered roses and bears' ears and ribbon grasses for her. In autumn, when harvest was done, they brought apples and walnuts. Parents sent small gifts of food, the farmer a rabbit, the miller some flour, the innkeeper a barm cake, and in return she showed some favouritism to their children.

At night when Charity came home she called the cows up from the fields, and drove them to their drinking troughs. The children gathered the eggs and washed them for market on the stone sink. They chopped the wood, and helped their father. For Charity the outside work was filled with enchantment because she saw it that way, and she shared her imaginations with the others. It was Charity who named the cows, romantic names from the Bible, Bathsheba and Miriam, Eve and Mrs. Noah. She talked to them in a language they seemed to understand. The hens too were magical birds, each one a friend, and the eggs were fairy gifts. She had long conversations with the sheep, and the old mare. The trees sang to her, the birds knew her, the spring that fed the water troughs was her companion who lived underground. Charity's thick ugly frock was transformed to silk as she talked and the little children listened, wide-eyed and entranced by their eldest sister. She tossed her fair hair in its snood of crocheted cotton, and played hide-and-seek with the little ones. The world of farm life or washing clothes and feeding calves was one life, the other was the world where every tin milkcan had a name, every potato had a voice, every tree a heart and soul, and the house itself was the mother of all. Her affection for all things overflowed, the sentient and the inanimate were filled with life. Stick, stone and water spoke to her, yet she kept this secret, wary of betrayal to Mrs. Booth, shy with her father, free only with the children.

In winter they rode to school on rough sledges, or they trudged with old stockings bound over their heavy boots. These they left in the porch with their coats and hats and bonnets, all tumbled in a damp heap, and there was a great sorting out before they went home. All ages were taught in one class, and sometimes Charity was chosen to help. Then her school money was handed back to her, and she proudly took it home to her father.

"I could do with you to be my assistant, Charity," said Miss Martha one day. "Ask your father if you can stay on at school."

Charity flushed scarlet and curtseyed. "Yes, Miss Martha." She walked on air back to Shepherd's Fields. She saw herself with a house like Miss Martha's, but larger, grander, filled with little children, and every one happy and clean. She would give them pegs to hang their clothes, and soap and even hot water to wash their hands, and a comb for their shaggy hair and barm cakes to eat. She would sing to them and dance to them, and play the piano. She would be Miss Charity, the famous schoolteacher. She had even got as far as making the barn into the schoolhouse and bringing them all to the farm when she reached home.

All her hopes were dashed to the ground. Her father shook his head. He was proud of the honour, but Charity was needed at the farm, and there was no more to be said. She was already a good milker, and her hands were growing. They were cool for butter-making and it was time she began. She must be a farmer's assistant, not a school-teacher's.

Charity made the best of it. She left school and Mrs. Booth left the farmhouse. Charity taught her brothers and sisters small extra scraps of knowledge, using her common sense, and the wisdom and folk lore she picked up from people at fair and market, now that she went abroad with the butter and eggs.

Up in the morning at four in summer, the washing done by six, the farm family fed by seven, the days were long and the hours filled with work which she never thought of as hard but accepted as her part of life. It was her home, the farmhouse had nurtured her, and she served it with devotion. It repaid her for every thought she gave to it. She was bound to it by cords stronger than the bonds of her family. Its personality was stronger than those around her.

Often she helped her father with the milking, and she was glad to escape from the housework and to sit under the patient cows, listening to the gentle chewing and mutterings of the beasts, singing softly to them in reply.

She was growing up, her face was pretty, young men stopped and talked to her, but she had no time to spare. She laughed and shook her head. She cooked for the large household, and washed up the dishes, which were not so many for she only allowed one plate and a knife and fork to each. Pudding had to be eaten on the meat plate which taught the children to wipe their dishes clean and leave no scraps.

When they grew up and married and left the farm she made their wedding clothes, and cooked the feasts for the neighbours, and packed little wooden trunks with linen cloths and aprons and shirts, which she had stitched with tiny stitches and tucked and feather-stitched.

She was over thirty, and the rest of the family had decided she must be an old maid, when she suddenly fell in love, passionately, deeply with a farm labourer who had come to help at Shepherd's Fields. He was different from other men, thought Charity. Timothy Dale was ten years younger than she, placid, yellow-haired, soft spoken, shy before the impetuous mistress of the house. He was a friend of Charity's youngest brother Sam, who asked his father to take him on. Charity did the courting, making excuses to have him near her, driving to market with him, asking his opinion.

She, who had waited so long that the neighbours never even gossiped about her or linked her name with others, now was filled with love. Through him she loved the entire world. Through her love she entered into a harmony with nature that lasted longer than life itself.

She felt she had loved him always, in the fields and rain and sunshine, but she was afraid he wouldn't have her. His good

34

looks, his giant frame, his pleasant manner made him attractive to many women, who were young and pretty in their straw bonnets and muslins on Sundays as they walked the lanes. She did not know that her own unlined face had a sweetness and strength that was sometimes beautiful. She had taken no thought for men although many a one had made a small advance to her, until this tall stooping young man had come to the farm, and now she was filled with foolish longing for him. Instinctively she took more care over her dress, she brushed her shining brown hair till it gleamed like gold, and the small tendrils curled over her brow under the print bonnet she always wore about the farm. She was fresh and clean, always sweet-smelling, for she was fastidious by nature, and her love for the man made her look younger.

It never entered Timothy Dale's head that the mistress liked him especially, and he sat at the dresser with the plough lad and ate his meals at the scrubbed bare oak with the pewter plates and horn drinking cups which had always been for the servant's use. He came from a cottage over the hills, three valleys away, and he went home once a month with his bundle under his arm.

One Sunday morning when he started off down the yard, Charity called to him. She gave him a small errand to do on his journey, a message to take. She stood there, in her Sunday crinoline frock of blue lawn, blue as her dazzling eyes. She talked a minute and there was something in her voice that startled him. Her eyes looked into his, they seemed to speak another language from the words of her tongue. Her fingers were restless, she stretched up and gathered a rose from the house, and pinned it to her breast, suddenly shy. Then he had guessed, and all the way to his home he had pondered it. He liked her, and admired her, but he hadn't thought of marriage with anyone. He had no money and position, he was easy-going and carefree. At night when he returned he brought a bunch of red roses from the cottage garden, a kind that didn't grow at Shepherd's Fields. He laid them on the kitchen table when nobody was there, and Charity found them. She sought him out and thanked him, but he said never a word. He was dumbfounded and he waited, puzzled about it. It was pleasant to have kind words and glances from bright eyes. He was a simple man and he couldn't pluck up his courage to talk to her, so he gave in his notice and went away.

Charity was heart-broken, but she concealed the blow. The

effect of the separation on Timothy Dale was revealing. He realized that he missed her, he missed her merry laugh, her flash of humour, her managing ways, and a certain charm she had which showed itself in her speech. He thought of her night and day, and he sent his mind back to the farm which seemed to hold him. Charity and Shepherd's Fields filled his thoughts when he went ploughing at a distant farm, they destroyed his peace. He was haunted by the old farmhouse and its mistress. He was aghast at his stupidity in leaving a place where he had been so happy, and he found himself comparing his present work to that at Charity's home.

One day he was at the market and he saw Charity there with her great baskets of butter and eggs, and the young lad in attendance. He left the cart and went across to speak with her. Her smile was so inviting, her forgiveness so complete, for she was convinced he cared nothing for her, that he was touched. He was falling in love with her now that she was out of his reach. He went back to work, cursing himself for a fool. On the first opportunity he made an excuse to visit the farm. Matthew Woodiwiss received him with his usual heartiness, although he had been put out by the young man leaving in the midst of hedgecutting and stone-walling. Charity set his tea at the dresser with the young lad, and there he sat tongue-tied and lost but this time his eyes spoke for him. They followed Charity about the room, seeing fresh beauties and new attractions in her slim, tight little figure, and her smiling face. Round him flashed the firelight, the warmth of the kitchen fire, the comfort of that homely room. Across the yard were the beasts he knew by name, the horses that were his friends. There was something special about that place, perhaps it was love he felt, perhaps it was something deeper, the house calling to his heart.

"I'll up and speak," he told himself. "I'll tell her I love her and if she turns me down she won't laugh at me, and if she has me, well, I'll be in heaven."

So on his next visit, for he made an excuse of bringing a sample of corn for seed, he spoke.

"Mistress, Charity, do you think you could put up with me? I've nowt to offer, but I'll work hard for you, and yours as long as I live and love you till the end of my years. If so be you'll have me," he added.

It was his longest speech, and he was embarrassed, for it

wasn't what he had meant to say. He had learned a fine declaration but it was all forgotten and he had spoken from his heart.

Charity nodded her bright head, unable to get out a word.

"D'ye mean it?" he asked, astonished.

"Yes, Timothy," she answered, and in a moment she was clumsily crushed against his heart.

He couldn't believe his good fortune even then, but when he came again to the farm he sat at the master's table. The old man accepted him as he accepted everything Charity did. It was decided they should get married and live at Shepherd's Fields. Sam was going to a farm of his own on more fertile land, and Charity would inherit her portion. Matthew Woodiwiss would sit in the chimney corner, and direct things, but Charity would be the manager. Charity's sister Abigail came across the room and took his hand. His heart turned over, he stooped and kissed her too. It was wonderful to be received in such a household, to sit at the table and share the talk. Not that Timothy spoke, he was a listener to the end of his life, and Charity talked enough for both.

They were married one autumn day after the reaping was done, and before the cattle were shut up for the winter. Charity and Abigail set the rooms ready for the guests, and the little parlour was bubbling with excited whispers and secrets. Memories were made, little intimate scenes were preserved in the golden air that day, to be brought out and displayed many years later for the wonder of invisible ones. The maidenhair for ever bloomed on the windowsill, the bouquets of roses scented the air for a hundred years, and Charity could smell them when she was an old woman.

Charity had a new merino, plum-coloured like the autumn fruit, with velvet flounces, and a tiny bonnet to match. Later on Virginia's mother wore this same bonnet's trimmings on a hat, and Virginia herself had the scraps of velvet to make a bonnet and a muff for Sundays.

The night before, Charity heated water in the great copper boiling-pan and brought indoors the tin pancheon for her bath. She had a sweet-scented soap-ball, and a new piece of flannel. She bathed in front of the kitchen fire, and then she sat on the settle in her nightgown with a shawl on her shoulders, drying her lovely hair. She listened to the clock ticking, and the old house murmuring to her.

"Life is before you, but you belong to me. We are one, you and me. My service comes first. We are one, you and me."

But Charity's mind was singing another song.

"We are one, Timothy darling," and all her thoughts were on her lover.

Their life was happy. Timothy let Charity lead, and she adored him. She had borne him three children when death came suddenly. Timothy was caught in the primitive threshing machine and whirled into the cutter. They brought his mangled body back to the house, but Charity knew before she heard the shouts. All morning she had feared something. She had been sick and ill with a strange apprehension of disaster. She was standing in the kitchen, hesitating over her work, listening to the murmurs and sighs of the house, when the shout came, and then the sad procession wended across the yard from the barn. She stayed with her hand in his, whispering to him, as life ebbed away.

"I'll meet you, dear lad. Wait for me," she said, and he nodded and died.

After her husband was buried Charity worked harder than ever as if trying to wear herself out and hurry her own end. Her grief hurled her into the fields, where she slaved with her own hands as if death were waiting round the corner again and she was hastening to get all the work done first. One night, as she lay exhausted on her lonely bed, she heard the voice of the house.

Before her eyes she saw a procession of farm people who had lived and died in the service of the earth, old men and boys, full-skirted women and little children. They walked through the door out into the yard, carrying sheaves of corn, halters, sickles, lanterns, staves, and they were laughing and beckoning as they went out to work. With them walked her beloved Timothy, and he turned his head to smile. Across the cobbled yard and through the gate they went, down the field and into the distance, and the murmur of their voices was like music with no words. They were part of the house, and she knew she must take up her burden and do her own share before she could join them. As she lay there she faced life anew and happiness came back. After all death was a little matter. There was the grand happiness of living in each moment of time. Life was triumphing over death. That core of happiness would be there for ever. Those others were in the present, Timothy was in her, dissolved into the being of the old house, and sharing each moment of her existence, as she shared that of others, and as those who followed after would share her life. Three little children, all part of her, lay asleep in the low room down the little stairway. Some day they would perhaps find this secret, and their children too. A little shadow with small pointed face and questing hands climbed on the bed, and drifted over it. Then it wavered round the room, touching the china bowl on the medicine cupboard with the Chinese figures painted upon it, rubbing its fingers along the mahogany chair backs, feeling the reality of this world. It shook its brown hair, and held out its short skirts in a moment's dance. Then away it faded, with never a look at Charity half-sitting in the bed. It was not one of her children. It was one unborn, perhaps due long after, but she knew she would recognize that small peaked face if ever she saw it again.

She lay down and accepted life, breathing in rhythm with the house, content with whatever might come.

Her father died peacefully the same year, but Charity did not call her brother back to help. Instead she managed with the young lad and the shepherd. She did a man's work herself, buying stock, judging with the keen eye of her father, tending the beasts and doctoring them, driving to market, sowing and reaping and selling the corn. Abigail helped with the three children and took them to school till they were old enough to go by themselves. There was now a long low school building, with desks and teachers, instead of the casual lessons at the Dame's school. It had none of the friendliness of Miss Martha's cottage, and the children had no desire to stay on when their time came to leave.

Charity's son William helped on the farm and Charity's burden was lightened. The two girls went away to far lands. The house hadn't held them with its bonds. Adventure sent them off, for many girls were fired with the tales they heard and the books they read. Tales of Canada, of Australia, and Africa lay on the dresser at the farm. Kate, Charity's favourite child, went to America, as nursemaid in a family from the nearest town. She went for a year or two, but she never returned. Jane had married a neighbour's son and emigrated with him to Australia. She had been absorbed in her adopted country, with only a passing thought for England, and a laugh at the old farmhouse with its candles and water troughs and old-fashioned ways. She had no children, that was her grief.

Kate too had married, and her letters told of her delight and happiness, but the joy suddenly ceased. Her husband was an American, clever, wild, who had deserted her after a year. She wouldn't come home, but every moment was filled with longing for the farmhouse. Charity never knew what happened in those years of bitterness which Kate concealed. Kate, with her laughter and fun and pretty ways, her dark curls and smiling lips, had died in poverty. Her little daughter Virginia had travelled home to her grandmother, in charge of a doctor and his wife. Charity Dale would never forget the day she met the child at Liverpool and her first sight of the wide-eyed solemn baby scarcely three years old who looked so lost in a hostile world. There she stood in her close-fitting bonnet, shy and frightened, with never a smile to be coaxed to her lips. The doctor had promised the dying woman to bring the child home. That was all. Never a word, only the child as a token of the heart-break of the young mother. The look on the child's face had brought tears to the grandmother's eyes, and a sharp pain. She set about making little Virginia happy with her other grandchildren, and teaching her to smile. It was the small pointed face she had once seen in dream and vision, forgotten for many years and now brought vividly before her.

Virginia Brown became Virginia Dale, and only her Christian name reminded others of her birth in a far country.

Chapter 4

It was October, the month of warm earthly happiness when the land has a respite before the sleep of winter. In October the farm looked its mellowest, as if the crimson and gold colours of the overhanging trees and the rusty lichens were the dress that suited its age the best. Crab apples were yellow on the twisted branches of the little trees in the hedge, briars made crimson archways in the lane and the thorn bushes held out stiff grey arms with bunches of aiges in the sharp fingers. Cob nuts were ripe and the farm children and squirrels made forays upon them. There was a pocketful on the dresser left by young Richard, and nutshells lay in green heaps on the cracking-stones—the rare flat stones of a wall or of the earth. The walnut trees in the cow-lane had dropped their fruit and each day somebody was there, rootling with strong little iron-tipped boots in the decaying leaves, crushing the rotten husks and pouncing on the wet new shell that was a thing of beauty. Twittering flocks of tits and chaffinches flew from bush to hedge, swinging in their airy path, playing their autumn game as if they were glad their family cares were over. A robin came to sing his intimate song on the haw-thorn drying bush, pheasants were cluck-clucking in the woods, and the ploughboy whistled as he walked across Starlings Field.

The sun streamed through Charity's bedroom window and she sat up in bed and looked about her. She put one foot on the floor and then the other, seeking the strip of carpet for warmth, avoiding the bare scrubbed boards. She walked unsteadily across the room and gazed out of the window at the farmyard, very close to her. Nobody was in sight, there were no sounds of voices. Beyond the road and the water-meadow was the shining river, flowing as serenely as ever, as it would continue to flow long after she was dead. She stared at it, filled with the mystery of that water, whose music had been in her mind since she was born. It was untameable like the wind, she felt she could sit a thousand years on its banks and look at the changing wonder of ripple and wave, and never tire of the beauty.

Reluctantly she lifted her eyes higher, and in a moment the river was forgotten in the hills. There they were, blue, indigo, misted in thin sunshine, smiling through their veils of distance, hiding their farms and cottages and villages she loved. The two familiar hills by the farm were green and brown, clearcut like onyx, with a thousand tiny paths of rabbit and sheep and many a wild creature.

Charity dressed herself in secret haste, softly opening drawers in the chest and lifting out her clean clothes from the piles of flannel petticoats scarlet and white, and chemises of calico. She smiled to herself in quiet triumph at her cleverness as she dressed. They didn't know she was up and about. They didn't guess. On her head she put a starched white muslin cap and she tied the bands under her chin. Austere and simple, it framed her oval face so that she might have been a peasant woman in a Flemish picture of the seventeenth century.

Slowly, one step at a time, she walked down the steep stairway which led to the kitchen. She unlatched the noisy door that always shouted a warning, and peered round the corner half mischievously, but there was no one to witness her entrance. The kitchen was filled with a warm peace, with smells of cooking and baking bread, and with the sense that somebody had just gone out. She glanced up and saw that the gunrack was empty.

The door was wide open, and shafts of sunlight streamed in sending long shadows of dresser and chairs over the bare floor, bars of darkness like cages to hold the light. The sun was teasing the jugs and pans to laughter, twinkling on the bowl of water, sending sharp white splinters over the ceiling, as the tap dripped into the bowl. The room seemed to rejoice in the gaiety of late sunshine, it expanded, its walls receded before the old woman's eyes, it was a palace of gold. Gold wire dropped from the clothesline, gold stains dripped from the lustre jug. It was like a jeweller's shop with no stiff-cuffed, black-coated man behind the counter, but everything was free, given away, and Charity was receiving it.

She stood there, with a hand on the blackened post, and listened. She had caught it this time, she thought, and she held her breath to hear what it said. The long-dead were there, laughing together, holding hands in the light, touching the dear familiar things. The gleam wavered and spun webs of gold and fingers were touching them, feet were moving with gliding lilting step over the stone floor. Then as she moved forward there was a sidelong getaway and all had gone. Only the kitchen was smiling its restrained and secret smile. She had been very near that time, she told herself. From the stable came the sound of whistling, and the swish of a besom. Everything was waking suddenly. Hens chuckled in the yard, and the cock flew on the lower barn door and crowed lustily, to be answered by others afar. A flock of pigeons on the cottage roof fluttered with a swish of wings, white angels in the sun.

Charity stood in the doorway a minute, tasting the sweetness of the air. Lazarus could hardly have enjoyed it more. She held out her thin hands as if to grasp the sunshine, and she turned her face to the sky, sniffing the feeling of the weather, the sharp tang of autumn, and the high clouds that might hold ice crystals in their hearts. It was grand to be alive, to have another day, and another, a week, or a month, or years, anything of the good-smelling earth.

Not that she minded death, she told herself, as long as there was sunshine and a drop of rain and a friend. Surely these things were immortal like the soul. Music there would be, the Bible said so, nice tunes. Privately she hoped for "Drink to me only with thine eyes", and a fiddle and an elder-pipe and a piano of some kind, and water flowing close by just like the river across the water-meadow.

Her lips puckered into a smile that irradiated her face. She knew something. She had been told a secret. Who had told her, and why was she so certain? It wasn't a dream. It was a word the old house had whispered to her that night when she lay poised between life and death, swinging in its arms. Death was only another room, an unseen doorway opening off the kitchen, or leading from her bedroom. Life was a gleam of sunlight and a few dark shadows like those barring the floor, with nothing to frighten you if you accepted it in the spirit it was given.

"I must tell little Virginia that," she said aloud, and she picked up a doll that lay on the stones. It was made out of the potato-masher, the smooth wooden head bonneted with a pink handkerchief, the rounded body swathed in a small shawl. Carefully Charity laid it on the settle. Then she went round the kitchen peering with her keen housewife's eyes into pots and kettles, touching with lingering fingers the familiar things that were the shape of her world.

Yes, the stewpots and saucepans were up there. She had known them since she was a little child, for they had rested in a row on the kitchen shelf above the corner sofa, and always she had looked up apprehensively at the projecting dipping handles. More than once a saucepan had tippled off when the children leapt too high in their games, and the brass pans were heavy on an unprotected head. They had been worn as armour in the Easter mumming play, when Saint George fought the Saracen knight.

> *Take a little out of my bottle,*
> *And pour it down thy throttle,*
> *Then rise up, bold Slasher, and fight again,*

Charity had recited, as she held out the bottle of black drink to her brothers acting in the play.

They were all gone, but the saucepans were still in use. There was one saucepan tall and narrow like a nobleman's hat. It was smoked by many a fire, dinted by a hundred falls, but its battered sides were strong and it had never been mended. It had the smells

43

of broths from beef and fowls and mutton, an all-pervading aroma that gave a richness to anything cooked in it. Perhaps ordinary water if boiled within its deep interior might be changed to a brew of magical qualities. It was a grandfather of a pan, and it had many a tale to tell but only Charity heard its voice.

Then there was a little old brass pan, clean as a new pin, and scoured with silver-sand till it was bright as the sun. It was her own special pan, the saucepan for poorly days, the cure-all, the doctor of the family. Milk was boiled in it, cream was "cruddled", drops of custard and arrowroot gruel were made. It had cured many an illness, had that ancient brass pipkin, without the doctor's help.

There were a couple of heavy brass saucepans, inherited from Charity's grandmother, who brought them with her to the farm on her marriage. One had survived the years. It was as strong and beautiful as ever, in use every day, sanded with sand from the hills, polished with a soft cloth. The other had been soldered by the grandfather, sitting in the yard on the mounting-block, with the pan between his knees many a year ago. He was tinker and mender at a time no travelling tinker came that way. The sides were still smooth as glass, and Charity could see her own face distorted and grotesque in the yellow reflecting curves.

She was back again among them, smiling at them, listening to them, and they blinked and winked down at her from their places under the low ceiling. The dishes, the pans, and even the besom she loved, they were filled with kindliness, with their own beauty, and even with an intelligence which she apprehended. They were like that because hands had worked with them. They made life itself; sorrow and happiness, laughter and tears were mingled in their usage.

She stood still listening, lost in dream, and from the walls there seemed to come the hum of voices, the reverberations of long past tales told by others. From the beams came song and whistle and piping, dim sounds out of the centuries, soft and murmurous, but audible to her ears. There was no silence in the little old kitchen now. It was brimming with its own invisible life and song and talk. She could divine the hopes and passions of those others who had lived and loved under the roof that sheltered her, as she too shared their life.

Her ruminations were cut short by the report of a gun close to the house, and the startled flurry of the pigeons' wings. She went to the door and peered across the yard. William grinned at her from the garden and held up a pheasant.

"Hey Mother! Got him! What do you think of this? You've come down for a taste, I reckon."

"Surely I have," cried Charity, laughing and waving her hand excitedly. He came through the wicket gate across the yard, bearing the fat cock pheasant, with its long tail feathers dragging on the ground. He walked slowly, for he was a good-natured, easy-going man like his father. His face was smooth and ruddy, his grey-blue eyes searching and quick, and an odd smile hovered on his lips. He accepted whatever life gave, his uneasy wife and his masterful mother, and he kept the peace between them when words flew fiercely about. He was tall, with broad shoulders, bowed a little with heavy weights and hard work. When he spoke his voice was warm and kindly, and he pursed his red lips as he went about his daily work and let out a stream of soft whistling sweet as a wren's song.

He wore no coat, but a striped blue cotton shirt, and round his trousers were leather straps, over which the stuff hung in harsh folds. His hair was thick and curling, fair like his father's, his expression open and straightforward, and he spoke with simple directness when he troubled to speak at all. He loved his wife, and admired her looks. He was proud of his mother and her managing ways, but his grey-blue eyes twinkled as if he had a secret amusement at the oddities of womenfolk and animals.

"Here he is, caught eating in forbidden ground. You can't say anything about it. Nobody saw me kill he, and if the keeper heard a shot, why, 'twas in our garden where I does as I likes. I saw something move among the bushes, and I crept up and looked over the wall, sly as a weasel. Then I got the gun, I had it ready in the stable for a rat, and I got him."

"He's a beauty, Will," said Charity, feeling the plump breast of the warm bird.

"You'll fancy a bit, won't you Mother?" he asked.

Charity laughed again and put her hand on his arm. Together they went into the kitchen, and Will threw the bird with pride on the table and slipped the remaining cartridge into his pocket.

"Did you get up by yourself, Mother?" he asked.

She nodded, her old eyes bright with mischief. "I wanted to show there's a bit of life left in your old mother."

"You've got more life than any of us, I reckon," said he.

45

Charity went along the passage to the dairy and peered inside.

"Have you seen Virginia, William?" she asked. "It's all very quiet. Where's everybody? Where's Hetty?"

"I expect they've gone out together after the eggs," he replied casually. "I saw them cross the yard some time back."

Footsteps came hurrying down the yard and Hetty Dale came into the room. Her face was flushed, her dark fluffy hair was blown in a cloud over her smouldering eyes. She brushed it back angrily, and one could see the deep violet colour of those eyes. William had never ceased to marvel at their beauty. Now he looked for a hint of friendliness, for he was fairly under her thumb.

Hetty started when she saw old Charity sitting in the corner by the fire. The old woman looked calm and self-possessed, a mistress in her own home, and Hetty resented this.

"Mother! You ought not to come downstairs. What's the use of paying for a doctor and then not taking his advice? How did you manage to dress yourself? And your things weren't aired, either."

"I'm all right, Hetty, thank you. I'm doing fine," said Charity sweetly. "Have you see our Virginia?"

"Jinny? Yes. I've seen her. Look what's she done. This is her work. A dozen eggs smashed and twopence each."

"Oh dear! I am sorry. Well, we must make custards and cakes with what you've saved of them. Where is she?"

"Where she can't do no harm," said Hetty, beetling her fine brows, flouncing into the dairy for the bowl.

"Where is that?" asked Charity.

There was silence as Hetty busied herself with the broken eggs. At last she came back to the kitchen. William stood at the window staring out at the yard, wondering at the little clouds that came up so suddenly when all was fair. He loved them both so much, and he waited to pour out his oil on the trouble.

"Where is the little lass?" asked Charity again with great patience.

"Where? Why, in the far barn."

"In there?" cried Charity, rising. "You mustn't put her there. She's too little. She's easily frightened of things she can't see. She's always been a scared child in the dark."

"Teach her a lesson. You spoil her. Leave her alone a bit," said Hetty, yawning and showing white even teeth. She looked

46

at William's back, and a shadow came over her eyes. She took up the pheasant and ruffled its plumage. The dead bird lay with head outstretched, and closed wings, its lovely feathers still for ever.

"So this is what you were after Will," said she in a low seductive voice. She adored Will, and she hated him to disapprove of her.

Charity went to the door, and into the yard. She walked across to one of the farm buildings, a windowless stone house, grim and strong like a small fort. She stood by the shut door listening for a moment with her ear at the crack. There was never a sound within.

"Virginia, my love?" she whispered. She lifted the latch through the round thumb-hole and threw wide the upper door. She leaned over and drew back the heavy wooden bar that fastened the lower door. Hetty had made everything secure. A small figure stood close to the whitewashed wall, pressed against the rough undressed stone, hands up to her face, body crouched in a tense attitude. The eyes were wide with terror, she stared into the corner as if keeping something at bay. Her face was like a little white flower in the darkness of the barn, the rest of her almost invisible.

"Come here, Virginia. Come out now, child," said Charity going into the darkness of the raftered chamber. A heap of firewood lay in the corner and a pile of sacks sprawled like drunken bodies. There were faint rustles and squeaks of rats. Cobwebs and bats hung from the heavy beams in the dim high roof.

"Come here, Jinny darling," said Charity again, but Virginia didn't move. She seemed petrified with fear, unable to stir from the protection of the wall at her back. She didn't cry or utter a word, nor did she turn to her grandmother. She was watching something in the darkness, yet she saw nothing. Some pale phantom seemed to be hovering above, emanated from the past when some cruel deed was done. Unease was in the air, Charity felt the vibration of fear. She shared the sudden dread of one who had once filled the air with sorrow. It had entered into her, and possessed her.

Charity took the child's hand and drew her out to the sunshine of the yard. She closed the door and bolted it, and led the child away to the croft. Virginia was stiff and restrained, wooden with the ancient fear upon her. A great walnut tree grew in the croft, the largest on the farm, with the little stone closet sheltered under it. Charity began to stir the leaves with her slipper.

"See. There's a walnut and there's one. Pick 'em up, Jinny. There's happen a treasure inside. They do say that once a girl found a blue dress covered with silver stars in a nut that she cracked, and in another nut there was a golden dress with gold stars on it."

The little girl forgot her troubles in her eagerness to gather the nuts and strip off the rotten black husks. She cracked them carefully on the washing-stone by the little clothes-line, and hunted for the magical secrets.

"I'll make you some boats out of them to sail on the water trough," promised Charity. "We'll line one with red velvet and make a tiny doll's cradle. There's no end of things we can make— pincushions, thimble cases, and even a money-box."

Virginia began to laugh. A silvery peal rang through the croft, and the walnut tree echoed it. Happiness had come back again, to seep into the rocks and the tree, to lie there till some future child evoked it again.

"Why did you drop the eggs, Jinny?" asked Charity, clasping the small stained hand in her own and looking down into the suddenly veiled eyes.

" 'Cos I jumped when I heard the gun go bang," said Virginia, trembling a little.

"You mustn't drop things every time a gun is fired, my little Virginia. That would never do. Why, when Grannie was young, she used to fire a gun herself," murmured Charity and her voice was soft and old and infinitely comforting.

"It frighted me," explained Virginia, solemnly. "I don't like bangs close to me, Grannie. I'm sorry about the eggs. They was nice ones and Aunt Hetty let me carry them. There was a banty egg for my tea." Her lip quivered, and the tears at last welled up. She sobbed bitterly and Charity held her to her side. The look of strain was gone, and the tears were healing. Virginia smiled through them, and dragged her hand from her grandmother's clasp.

"Where are you going?" asked Charity.

"To tell the banty hen and the banty cock Jinny's sorry she broke their egg, and she won't do it again," said the child, and she ran through the gate to the flock in the field.

Charity went back to the kitchen. Her forehead was wrinkled in a little frown, her mouth pursed with determination.

48

"Has she been put there before, Hetty?" she asked.

"Sometimes," admitted Hetty. "When she's been troublesome I've shut her up out of the way."

"Never do it again," said Charity sternly and her old blue eyes flashed. "Never while I live shall you shut her in that place."

"It won't harm her. She's nesh," remarked Hetty airily. "She's the most troublesome child I've ever set eyes on. She's been a nuisance ever since she came here."

"That's enough, Hetty. She belongs here. No more." Charity spoke with quiet firmness and Hetty was silent.

"Come Hetty. Don't take it like that. She's only a young 'un, only a little mite," pleaded William, trying to bring concord, for he was a man for peace and quietness. "Her mother was just the same, nervous of gunfire. I remember her running off to the woods when somebody fired near her in sport. Don't scold any more. Let her be."

"Oh yes, take her part," muttered Hetty under her breath, but she had enough awe of Charity to keep her voice low. Charity was mistress as long as she lived. There was antagonism between them, and some admiration, for Hetty was a good cook and a clean housewife, and the old woman gave her thanks and praise. She was the daughter of a retired townsman, a stranger who had come to live in the country, and William had been charmed by her eyes and the sidelong way she glanced a him, and the manner of her speech, foreign to his ears. Quick of temper, sharp-tongued and anxious, her prettiness soon faded when her second child was born. When Virginia came to the house she was deeply resentful. Two children were enough without a third. She had been slighted by the child's mother, Kate, when they were at school together, and she never forgot. Kate had been careless, teasing her for her clipped speech, unaware of the resentment in her breast. Kate had been popular, and Hetty didn't like that, and it was the presence of Hetty in the house that finally decided Kate to go to America. There wasn't room for both. Now Virginia had come. Hetty accepted the new addition to the household with bad grace but she couldn't love the elfin child of her rival.

But Richard took Virginia's small confiding hand in his, and led her about the farm, swinging her up to the back of the mare when she went to be watered, wiping her when she fell from the garden wall into the manure heap, shielding her from his

49

mother's wrath. She padded after him, through the herd of cattle, under the bellies of horses, a solemn child, climbing, creeping, oblivious of menacing horns and sharp hooves. He scolded her when she did wrong, which was often. He was bringing her up in the way she should go. He bullied her, but she didn't mind. Emmie never obeyed him, but Virginia was his slave, fetching and carrying for him, and Richard became her champion. Hetty was angered by this, and she took every opportunity to impress her own will upon the little girl.

Late in the afternoon the children came home from school. Virginia swung on the wide gate that spanned the lane by the farmyard. She had watched the brass fingers of the clock turn slowly round and she knew that when they were in a certain position she must go and meet Richard. She saw the two figures afar by the river, but she was forbidden to go out of the farm land. They passed into the field, and she dropped from the gate and ran down the rough path. Richard came ahead with his school-bag on his back, his torn cap stuffed in his pocket, his eye bunged up and black. Behind him singing loudly, was his sister. Her fair hair was tied with a ribbon, her cheeks were pink and round, her tongue licked in and out, for she knew a row and scolding awaited them.

"Dick! Dick!" called Virginia, racing down the grassy verge with arms outstretched to the wind. She fell and scratched her knees on the stones, but she picked herself up, and ran on. The boy took no notice of her. He walked up the field path, his heavy boots scuffling as he kicked a stone and dribbled it along. The child ran after him, keeping a yard behind, not speaking any more. She threw her arms about in a gesture of joy for here was her beloved Dick, home from school. It didn't matter that he was cold to her. She understood this was not a time for talking. He had been fighting again, and until it was explained and settled with Aunt Hetty Dick would be remote and grown up.

Into the yard they went, a little procession, and into the house, where Hetty pounced and scolded, and Charity took the boy's cap and fetched her workbasket, and the dog leapt up licking his face.

"Get down! Down, will ye?" cried Richard angrily, but secretly he was glad and Virginia knew it.

"Fighting again. Who with this time?" asked Hetty sharply.

"James Gulley," said Dick. "He bloodied my nose and I knocked him down."

"Why?" asked Hetty.

"He said summut, and I told him to eat his words, and then we got hot and jackets off and fists at it. I won though. He lay in the dust and I stood over him. Then the mester came up and he laid about me with his strap."

"What was it all about?"

Dick was silent, but Emmie spoke up.

"Jim Gulley mocked him and said he was a grannyboy and our house was run by petticoats, and did he wear a pinny when he got home?"

Dick flushed scarlet. "It was because you made me put an apron on to keep my Sunday breeks clean, Gran. Jim Gulley saw me, and he's never let me alone since."

"Never mind, lad. You've given him something to remember," said Charity. "We shall wear what we like, aprons and sackcloth, and do as we like, and be beholden to nobody, and take no account of stuck-up folk as has made their money by clerking."

"I don't care," cried Dick. "I'll fight him again."

"And I don't care," echoed Virginia, tossing her little head and gazing admiringly at her cousin.

"You go to the barn and see what's hanging there," said Charity.

Hanging there! Would it be a man? Would he hang by his head or his feet? Virginia choked with horror, but she ran after the others to the barn.

There was the astonishing pheasant, in all the wonder of its plumage, and the children danced round singing:

Here we go round the cushy bird, the cushy bird, the cushy bird,
On a fine and frosty morning,

and exclaiming at the beauty of the feathers, touching the shot-silk plumage of the throat and ruff. It was rarely they had possessed one of the squire's sacred birds.

"'Oh I say! Did my father get him? He's a grand 'un. Bags I the tail feathers."

"And what did little skinny-wig think of it? Was she afeared when the gun went off?" teased Emmie, pulling Virginia's hair. "I bet she was! Shall I put you in the boggart place?"

"Let her be," cried Dick suddenly pushing his sister away, so that she stumbled against the corn bin. "You're always at her.

A quarrel flared up, and Emmie struck back. Hetty appeared in a moment, and separated them.

"Shame on you, Dick. Take that!" she cried, dealing him a box on his ears that sent him reeling.

"Get the firewood chopped, and behave yourself. Get it done before you have tea. And you, Emmie, go to the kitchen and wash your dirty hands. As for you, Jinny, take those rags off the potato masher. I want it and don't go cluttering it up again."

The children scattered, and Charity made room for the little girl on the settle, and watched her undress her wooden doll. She looked closely at the pale face, but Virginia was bright with interest in her task. She whispered softly to the potato masher, explaining to it that it was going to work now. She carried the rags outside, following the sound of wood chopping. In the big barn Dick was chipping with the axe on the block. Virginia sat down on the lowest step and watched him. The branches lay in the corner, and she chose pieces and handed them to her cousin with a sense of pride and comradeship.

"Get me another, Jinny. Now that one over there," said he. He liked her society, and her silence. Her admiration was food and drink to him, and he was flattered by her devotion.

Virginia found a knotted log and held it up.

"Can I have this, for a doll, Dick? Look!" It was in a rough human shape, with a head and two little side branches for arms.

"Why, yes. It's like a man. I'll trim it a bit," said Dick. He tidied away the shoots, and trimmed the head. Then with his pocket knife he cut a slit for mouth, two nostrils and a pair of sunken eyes. It was a wooden image, sombre, baleful.

"There's a dolly for you. It's made of a bit of that apple tree that falled last winter."

"Oh Dick. I do love you," said Virginia, clasping the doll to her heart. She gave him a crooked little smile.

"Have you been bad to-day?" he asked, looking down at her.

"I broke the eggs, and Aunt put me in the boggart hole," sighed Virginia. "I was frightened."

"Pooh! There's nothing to scare you. You've got to be brave or I shan't have you for my cousin. I can't abide cowardy custards."

Virginia regarded him solemnly. "I've got to be a brave girl," said she, slowly. "But not in the boggart hole."

"Yes. You'll have to go there if you're naughty. I did, when I was a little lad, and I warn't feared. I kicked and banged till she let me out."

"But did you know?" asked Virginia, her eyes wide.

"Know what?"

"A man once hanged from the roof," whispered Virginia, going close to him, speaking into his ear. "He hanged till he was dead like the pheasant. He cried out, and then he was still. I heard him."

"Who told you that?" demanded Dick crossly.

"I heard somebody say it once. Somebody talking to Aunt Hetty when I was little."

Dick cursed under his breath.

"Look here, Jinny. Don't believe that rot. See what I'll do. I'll clean it out and make a nice chamber of it, all tidy."

"Yes," she nodded gravely. "He'll like that. He's lonely I expect."

She dressed the little apple log and nursed it, crooning a song to it. Dick went on chopping, whistling, puzzled as he took a glance at her. A queer little toad she was, keeping that old tale to herself, never letting on about it till now.

She smiled up at him again with that wistful crooked smile that he liked.

"Just you tell me and I'll take care of you," said he. He gathered up the sticks in the stick-box and together they went in to tea. All was right in the world.

Chapter 5

Winter work was stopped for the frosts bound the fields with bonds stronger than iron, and snow covered the earth with a smooth white sheet. In a week or two maybe the thaw would come and the ditches would run with water but the frost was doing its own farm work, breaking up the soil. An invisible spirit was the frost, stepping from airy spaces, welding, and splitting the clods of earth, rubbing its icy fingers over the walls and fences, so that the waving horse-hairs caught where the animals had rubbed their sides were like silver ropes hanging there. The frost breathed on the brooks and water courses, and snapped the rocks with its knuckles. Only the frost seemed to be alive, and the old house shrugged its shoulders and huddled down with closed eyes. Birds flapped on noiseless wing from the woods, and the flocks of finches hopped among the fallen grain in the stackyard, or sheltered under the warm sides of the haystacks. Threshing was done, the machine had brought excitement and laughter and hard days to the farm, with a kitchen full of men to be fed, and tales to be told and gossip repeated, but that was over, the clatter of the machine had moved to other villages. Only Charity had been silent, thinking of her husband, for in remembrances of the dead there is intimate sharing. That is why there is something poignant about the snow, one almost sees those shades drifting by in the mists, wreathing in the vapours.

The cattle were shut up for the duration of winter, and their long low houses were warm with their breath. Their warmth and life seemed to affect the other inmates, for the family of beasts and the human beings were living very near each other, all part of one another, with lives and perhaps thoughts interwoven. The farm was their home, the place the horses hurried to when they returned weary from long journeys, the familiar smooth stalls where their noses and necks rubbed, and where rough kindly hands of people touched them, and voices harsh but affectionate spoke to them. Dogs and cattle, calves and children, all were intensely aware of the feeling of stone walls and wooden doors and strong posts, of the air and the spaces around them, the farm that sheltered them and spoke in its own way to them.

Inside the house the kitchen was the cheery centre with its great fire and lamplight. Everybody congregated there, to warm themselves, to gaze at the flames, to draw fresh strength to face the elements. The glow from the fire shone into the yard, and cattle and horses turned their heads to it as they walked past the window to the sheds next door.

There was plenty of discomfort and extra work, for the tap over the sink was frozen so that not a drop of rainwater could be used. Instead buckets of spring water must be brought from the troughs. Charity insisted on carrying her share. She went out with her cloak wrapped around her, and stepped across the yard to the near field where the great stone troughs lay. Her strength seemed to have returned with the coming of winter. She looked like a witch out of a fairy tale, as she drew the scarlet hood over her lawn cap and went off with her buckets. She dipped them into the troughs, after smashing the ice, and let them swing a moment in that pure water. She lifted the heavy weight of them to the encrusted earth. It pulled her nearly double, but she never thought of asking for help. Then she carried the burden back to the kitchen.

Her own life, her childhood, her womanhood, and now her old age was bound up in water. Sipping it from her hand as it came from the earth's depths, carrying it, caring for it, housing it in the troughs, keeping it unpolluted and clean from the cattle who had their own places for drinking, their private stone troughs among the ferns in summer, the icicles in winter, she kept the house supply crystal clear in the great sandstone trough, carved and cut many a hundred years ago from one block of stone.

The water seemed to have magical properties, and Charity was a primitive woman in many ways. Her ancestors had dressed the wells in springtime, with garlands of flowers and votive offerings of ribbons and small ornaments. She, too, dressed her water-spring with ferns and flowers growing near, and fossils decking it, to please someone, the water deity, perhaps, although she would have been shocked in her piety at such a thought.

The spring that came rushing out of the earth, unfrozen and untamed by frost or man, in a clear white arch of transparence was the water that had flowed there for a thousand years. It was the continuity of life for it linked all generations together. Its proximity had been the reason for the first small hovel that was made near it, in old times. When one died another carried on a tradition of service to the land, and the same qualities went through them, an ancient strength, and earth knowledge with flashes of wildness and beauty to leaven it.

The water, Charity thought, had a personality of its own. She was shy to confess it even to herself, but there it was, it glittered, and laughed and reflected the sun by day and the stars by night, it moaned and darkened and struggled against the winter's frosts which bound the troughs, it burst out and roared with anger as the ice tried to stem its force, and then it was free to sing and whistle as it fell.

Water buckets stood on the kitchen floor by the sink with the dipper alongside in winter, ready to fill kettles and boiler. As soon as a can was empty somebody went out to refill it. Even little Virginia took her small milkcan to the spring for water. As natural as breathing was the service demanded by the calls for water.

When Dick and Emmie came home from school they had a

big tea by the kitchen fire. It was always ready, Charity saw to that. Apples roasting and bursting their skins in the oven, meat steaming on their plates, jam eaten with teaspoons and mixed with plentiful supply of thick cream. They sat round the table, under the yellow pool of the lamp, with Hetty in a sharp humour, and Charity with her benign old face smiling upon them, and Virginia all eagerness and eyes, as she listened to the tale of their adventures on the way. Virginia longed for the time when she too would go out in the snow with a muffler round her neck and a school-bag on her back, to slide and run with other children.

The kitchen with its thrilling memories, its movement and life, seized hold of them, and took their own tales to add to its secret life. The yellow bowl lay on the hearthstone with bread rising there, the kettles were boiling and singing, and little jets of steam were pouring out to take the skin from one's hand, as it often did. A kettle lid bobbed and fell like James Watt's famous kettle.

"That's how James Watt thought of the steam engine," said Charity solemnly, as she poured the water on the tea, and Richard stared and considered the wonder of steam.

When William had gone to the station with the evening milk, and the washing up was done, Charity settled by the fireside with the younger children. Dick had outside duties, in stable and barn, and Hetty fetched her sewing machine and got her darning, but the two girls sat with their grandmother who told them tales. Even Hetty paused to listen, and Dick came in from his wood-chopping, his face scarlet with cold, his fingers raw, to crouch by the fire and turn his head to his grandmother seated on her low chair, sewing and talking. Then Dick took out his homework, and spread it on the table, with ostentation, but he kept his ears strained for her words, eager to hear all she said. He pretended he wasn't listening, and when he had finished his lessons he took up his adventure book. Red Indians and scalp hunters were mingled with the tales his grandmother told, and the book slipped from his knee. Charity's voice was sweet and low like dropping honey. It was attuned to the quiet rustle of leaves, to the murmur of the flames, and the sough of the wind in the chimney, for the house was listening too, and speaking through her voice.

Emmie stitched her doll clothes with clever fingers, for she was swift with her needle. Dick turned the pages of his book, or chipped a piece of wood into the fashion of a boat, or made small

56

furniture for Virginia's rough doll. Virginia rocked her log doll in the stick-box and listened with bright-eyed enchantment.

The grandmother cast a spell over everything, so that ordinary and everyday happenings had the glamour and romance of fairy upon them. She could pull a rainbow out of the sky and set it across the Water Meadow, with children running up and down its beams. She could send the lambs skipping under its archway and the swallows flying through its shining strands of blue and green. A crock of gold pieces lay at its feet among the kingcups in the field's marshy places which they all knew very well. A crown hung in the thorn bush in the middle of Greeny Piece, right there, by the lambing hut, thrown away by a fleeing king. A queen rode down the narrow footpath to the river and washed her smock in the water and dried it on that black stone there. A shimmering ball gown lay somewhere in Daisy Field, made of the gossamer webs that netted the hedges on misty mornings. The tales fitted the seasons, but the winter stories were the best, with wolves and bears and goblin sprites, living in icy caves in the hill yonder, dwelling in the bare wild woods, leaving tracks in the snow.

"Once upon a time, my dears. Once upon a time," she murmured, her voice mysterious and warm as a haybarn. There was always an element of truth in her tales, a legend, a saying of old folk, and although Hetty snorted with indignation at some of the fantastic will-o'-the-wisp stories, Charity held her in the spell of witchery, just as the children of other generations had been captured in Charity's youth.

The stars peeped in at the windows, and Hetty closed the shutters, and no longer could Orion watch the lamplit room. The milkcart came back from the distant station, and Dick ran outside to help with the horse. William entered, weary and cold, and they welcomed him and hung up his coat on the oak post by the fire. Emmie and Virginia washed their hands and faces at the sink, and stripped off their frocks. Then away with lighted candle they went through the narrow door to bed. Dick stayed up till nine o'clock for he had to help his father with the simple accounts.

Christmas day came with its small pleasures, unchanged from other years because nobody had any thought of anything different. There was no money to spare for luxury and Christmas fun cost nothing at all. Shepherd's Fields remained as it had always been, poor and unconscious of poverty, rich and aware of its wealth.

The Guisers had been singing in the kitchen, their faces blackened, their teeth shining white as they grinned sheepishly. Instead of the old songs and ballads of Charity's youth, they sang plantation songs, "Poor old Joe", and "Swanee River". Instead of playing the flute and whistle, one of them had a brand new accordion, and another a set of bones. The men sat by the fire on Christmas Eve, in a semicircle, and asked riddles and told topical jokes, old jokes the farm kitchen had heard every year for nobody knew how long, and a few new ones, to add a flavour. The family listened with deep interest, it was their theatre and variety show, but the old house took in every word, and stored it with the dusky scene in its memory. It was indeed a night to remember, that once-a-year festival, when mincepies came hot from the oven, and possets were warmed on the kitchen hob, and poured out for each to sup. The house stored up these impressions, dropped them in a time-layer with the past, and kept them for the future, when at a touch, a hint of fragrance, a whiff of smoke, it could bring them out like a peepshow for the old farm's enjoyment and for the delectation of anybody who could see these shadows.

Mulled ale with nutmeg, hot elderberry wine, gin and water, blackened faces gleaming, eye-balls flashing in firelight, colours and odours for the secret travelling in time of future generations, fantasy for the long-dead, and entertainment for the present.

Holly berries and glittering sharp-toothed leaves hung among the brass and copper vessels; the ancient grandfather saucepan had a bunch of ivy berries round his handle; a mistletoe bunch with mysterious waxen berries dangled from the iron hook on the ceiling, waiting for kisses underneath, alluring but sinister with its dreams of Druid murders, and its pagan memories. Black ivy berries decorated the fish-kettle, and the preserving pan. The berries were dipped in red raddle from the sheep marking, and in flour from the sack on the bench, to disguise them, to make a pretence of a strange unknown fruit.

On the clothes-line which stretched round the ceiling, hung a fleet of Chinese lanterns, like lovely fragile ships sailing up there. On Christmas Eve they were lighted, and for a week they added to the beauty of the room. Each night the lanterns were lifted down by their tiny hooks, their concertina folds were closed, and the candles lighted by Emmie and Virginia. They were opened out again, and slung to the white rope that always hung ready for washing. The little paper lanterns bobbed and glowed with their dim yellow lights sending grotesque and numerous shadows dancing round the room. The pictures on the lanterns were romantic to Virginia and Emmie, who never tired of looking at them. Chinese men with fishing rods, women with babies on their backs, and feet in small wooden sandals, bright red peonies and tall blue irises, plum blossom, great feathered cocks, boys flying kites, they made a panorama of colour with the pale light of the candles showing through. Crinkled balls, and cylinders and bells, they swung in the draughts, guarded by watchful eyes from catching fire. Every year they came out of Charity's drawer to bring a feeling of Eastern mystery. They were the symbol of Light in life. They were the lanterns the Wise Men had carried in the desert. They were the lanterns that had swung in the stable of Bethlehem. They were the lanterns that men had carried to barn and field, seeking the lost sheep, curing the sick, tending the new-born, for a thousand years. Little fragile toys, they gleamed like exotic fruit growing on the clothes-line, lighting the old room. They had amused Charity and her children for many years, and they remained a curiosity and a tradition, which nobody thought of discarding. Surely the house would have been disappointed if the illumination hadn't taken place? Even the pots and pans seemed to click their brass tongues with pleasure when the darkened room was made coloured and romantic by their tiny flickering lights, and the new shadows came to join the old ones. So with a deal of ceremony the Chinese lanterns were lighted on Christmas Eve, and extinguished with snuffers when they burned low. Each night there was the ritual of lighting the lanterns. On Twelfth Night they were packed away in the Christmas drawer along with the silver bells and golden balls of the Kissing Bunch.

Winter days passed at last, and suddenly it was spring. The snowdrops were out under the apple trees. Then the yellow colt's-foot bloomed in the croft where the horses grazed, and a primrose pale as a ghost of last year's flowers, opened its tight bud in the green rosette of leaves by the cowhouse. There was a primrose patch in the little garden concealed there. The real garden lay like a small brown handkerchief at the opposite side of the yard. In summer it was so tightly packed with flowers and vegetables it gave the absurd impression of a band-box packed by Persephone ready for her journey, crammed to bursting lid, for the stone walls hardly held it, and flowers climbed up and fell out in the yard. It was too small for the farm's needs, but nobody at Shepherd's Fields was a gardener. Charity and William had considered taking in a piece of Low Meadow to add to its fruitfulness, but nothing was done, and the same wall of great old stones surrounded it that had been there for time unknown. The wall was cemented with stonecrops, and spleenworts, and multitudinous pink and mauve wildings, with toadflax and robin-run-in-the-hedge, and harebells, making a rock garden in a place where such fine things were unknown. Each of the farm children had a piece of wall for themselves, with the ferns and mosses and flowers to play with, where dolls of matchstick and cattle of pith of rushes dwelt in the deep ferny moss. Even Richard was not too proud to play there, in the miniature mountains and ravines of the walls, where sometimes a rat peered, or a weasel played.

To make up for the lack of garden there were small beds close to the house's walls, silver shoes for the feet of the farm. They were netted from wandering hens, and cows, and guarded by rockery piles. Here grew snapdragon, and red daisies, and lad's love. Everybody had their own private garden patch somewhere among the dark stones and many corners of the farm. Each secluded spot was peered into for spring flowers, for a blue primrose and a cowslip of strangely frilled bells, or a daffodil.

Enamelled celandines grew thickly in the lanes, and Jack-in-the-Pulpit stood high among his spotted leaves and preached his sermon. The old plum trees along the garden wall were snowy with tiny budded flowers, and the bees awakened and flew to discover violets and white rock in the orchard, and all the store of honey which the old house kept in its scented flowery garments.

Crab-apple blossom came out in the hedges where a few trees were left, and soon the cherry trees were like snowballs. Young green leaves opened in a single night, and a chaffinch's nest was built in the lichened crook of the smallest apple tree. Larks flew high over the ploughland, and sang with rapture. Jays screeched and quarrelled, the goldfinches flitted in the rough copse. A magpie perched close to the kitchen door and flirted his tail, staring wickedly through the window at the silent parlour. Cocks crowed and calves blorted. Everything was awake, and the house looked round with enjoyment, seeking all the sights it knew so well, breathing the smells of animals and flowers, of herbs and earth. All sweetness and happiness and grief was there, waiting for someone to taste it, and the house held the store in its heart, sending out thin streamers to bring in more. It held Charity's own valiant spirit, and Hetty's puzzled frustration, and William's patience, it took the currents of fear that ran through little Virginia, who imagined too much, and the new vigour and growth of Richard, and the soft prettiness of Emmie. It wove them together like threads of silver and shadow, and it hung the web up, to wait for somebody to find. Everything was there, in the house's mind, the past, the present and the future to come, but life seemed uneventful to the house's inmates, with little worries and upsets, with quarrels and loves.

Every morning when the beds were made and the calves suckled and pig food made, the old woman and the little Virginia had something they called "lessons". It gave Charity a new feeling of importance, and Hetty was glad to be left to go her own way without any interference. Charity couldn't remember much about her own school days, but her powers of invention filled the gaps in knowledge. It was practical schooling, to prepare for the village school which was too far away for the little girl to walk.

The reading lesson was from the Bible, and the two read in turns, spelling out the words very slowly, learning the story of Adam and Eve, of Moses in the bulrushes. Arithmetic came next and Virginia counted beans and peas, buttons from the button box, saucepans on the stove, and hens in the yard. There was a small abacus, very old, with coloured beads that ran along silver wires, brought out from nobody knew where. It was older than the horn-book that hung on the wall. Then came writing, but Virginia made her letters on Charity's own little slate with the hole bored in the rim. The farmhouse kitchen was the school-room, and Virginia looked around at the walls while her grand-mother taught her. The flat irons, reared in the hole in the wall, were personal like small iron dwarfs, listening to the lessons, or warming themselves on the trivet before they skated over the white linen cloths. The powder horn hung ready for the drawing lesson. The birch rod swung from the ceiling, with twiggy stems alive and cruel, a threat used by Hetty. The slate, the little old books that Charity brought out, all were entangled with reading, writing and sums in Virginia's mind.

The stone-flagged floor was ready for chalk marks, and draw-ing, and games of marbles and tops. The ceiling was hung with bunches of herbs, whose names and scents Charity taught her. From the coloured almanack Virginia learned the days of the week, and the numbers of the months.

On the shelf was a book of songs, and "pieces" which Richard took out to the stable to practise. The tuneless wailing of his fiddle came from the closed doors, and Virginia stood in the yard, listening, not daring to enter uninvited. The horses seemed to enjoy it, as they turned their heads and stared in surprise when Dick roamed unsteadily up and down the scale, or faltered through "Home Sweet Home", and "Annie Laurie". To Virginia it was music of heaven, but the others laughed at the queer sounds. Charity turned the ragged leaves of the book, and taught the little girl the words and tunes of many of the songs.

In the afternoons when it was fine old Charity took Virginia into the fields, ostensibly to carry messages to William, or to see the crops, or to drive a horse to another field, but the occasions were an excuse for looking at birds and flowers and small animals. So the child imbibed a mixed collection of fact and fable, of legend and truth, unscientific and ancient lore mingled with observation and real knowledge and love for the earth.

Chapter 6

When Virginia was six she went to the village school. The three children started off together with their dinner bags, but very soon they separated. Dick ran ahead, Emmie called at the carpenter's cottage for Judy Gray, her bosom friend. Virginia plodded behind alone, her short legs stumbling, her round cheeks scarlet with suppressed excitement at all she saw and heard in the fields and lanes. Every day she was very late, for punctuality meant nothing to her, and time was eternity. She shook the bluebells and stroked the grasses and knelt down to watch the golden-brown beetles hurrying on private important errands, for they at least seemed to be busy on affairs. She stooped over the strong brown ants carrying logs, meeting one another, talking and asking for assistance. She stayed to stare at the beauty of a beech leaf, crimped like Emmie's hair, shimmering with hair of its own, just out of its case, where it had been carefully folded by someone, perhaps by God Himself. There was writing everywhere, mysterious scrawls, as curious and undecipherable as that of grown people, printed on leaves, scribbled on the dust where a silver snail had trailed his coat, blotched on the walls in lichens, written in wavering lines by trickling water which dripped from the low roadside walls, where the springs came through. Cobwebs and scents, whispers of grass blades, sighs from trees, all kept her back. She became a willow branch with silver balls, like raindrops, soft as a cat's fur. She was a wren running like a mouse in the hedges, peering through the twigs. She was an excited robin singing on a bough. "I see you hiding there" said robin and wren to the child. All the way there were friends and acquaintances. The milestones stood like grey men, huddled close to the walls. "Two hundred miles to London, and two miles to Ditty Minor", said one. The next one, hundreds of miles away, said "Two hundred and one miles to London, and one mile to Ditty Minor". Virginia knew that Dick Whittington sat by this milestone, with his bundle and his cat. She sat on the heap of stones by its side, and stroked the grey limestone, running her fingers in the deep incisions, noting the curls of letters and the crookedness of the ancient carving.

Far away the school bell rang, singing down the river. Then there was silence. Virginia awoke from the intercourse with the real world and took to her heels, clumping along in the dust. The first few times when she entered the ivy-covered infant school nothing happened. Then when she continued to be late, she was scolded, and after that she stood on a form with a dunce's cap on her head. Older girls teased her, provoked by her solemnity and the calm direct gaze that seemed to look through them. Somebody snatched her bonnet, and swung it on a tree. Nobody else wore a bonnet. Somebody held her by her pinafore till it tore, and this distressed Virginia more than anything. They larked round her, singing her curious name, mocking her and Emmie took no notice.

"Virginny tore her Pinny," they shouted. She was unhappy, frightened by the threats of being drowned in the river or hung on a tree like her bonnet, but she kept silent before her persecutors, and remained dry-eyed and grave. The bonnet was kicked in the dirt, and she rescued it, dusted it, and put it on. The next day she was later than ever, and again she was a dunce with pointed cap.

Charity had no idea of the changing fashions in head gear. She didn't like Emmie's hats, and she had made a small quilted bonnet to keep Virginia warm in the cold winds of spring. She was unaware of the trouble it caused, and the agony of mind it brought to Virginia. She only saw it as a lovely frame for the dark blue eyes and the golden-brown hair of the little girl.

One day Richard found Virginia in the centre of a group of children. He had avoided her at school, for she was in the small building with the little walled playground, and he was with the big boys in the larger schoolroom. She came home before him, and he knew nothing of her misadventures. She stood with her back to the wall, as she had stood in the dark farm building, her face white, her body taut, her hands clenched on her chest. Somebody was swinging her little bonnet and catching it, others laughed and sang her name. If she had wept they would have relented, but her silence goaded them on.

Richard leapt the wall and dashed among them, whirling his fists and striking wildly. He seized the bonnet and Virginia too, and marched off home, although it was early in the afternoon playtime.

"If any of you touches her again, I'll skin you, I'll scalp you," he shouted fiercely, remembering his Red Indian books. For a moment he could feel their hair in his hands and his knife slicing off their top knots, and twisting them in his belt, with the double snake clasp. Together they ran, and long before they arrived at the home field Virginia was laughing and happy. Richard went into the kitchen and tossed the offending bonnet on the table.

"Grandmother. Jinny oughtn't to wear this thing. It's like blinkers on an old horse. Haven't you got a proper hat for her, same as other girls?"

He was truculent, defiant, and Charity stared while Hetty went into a sudden temper.

"That's no way to speak, Dick. Wipe your shoes, and take off your cap and don't stand there so cheeky. Jinny's got to wear what her Grannie says."

"It's a lovely bonnet, Richard, but you've spoilt it, tousling it about like terrier with a rat. What have you been doing? She must wear it." Charity spoke quietly, for that was her way when Hetty flared.

"No, Grandmother. No. They laugh at her. She mustn't wear it."

64

"Let them laugh Dick. Haven't I told you time and time again to take no notice of laughter?"

She turned to Virginia, standing there by the table, waiting anxiously, her brown hair shining in the firelight, wet with rain, her cheeks flushed with running. She was like a lantern, filled with light, tremulous as the wind blew upon the flame.

"Don't you like it?" asked Charity.

Virginia shook her head; she couldn't explain that she loved the velvet, soft as moss, and she hated to have it laughed at and destroyed.

"Very well. I'll make a hat for you. I understand," said Charity quietly, and she folded up the little bonnet and put it away. That night she fashioned a small hat, and Virginia went to school feeling years older and wiser, aware of her cousin's protection, no longer lost in an unkind world. She was still not happy, but the lessons were easy, and Dick kept an eye upon her and saved her from the teasing. He hurried her to school, and all the little intimate talks with creatures had to be left for Saturdays and holidays.

He took her with him in the fields, and showed her carelessly the thousand secrets hidden there, the nest of the long-tailed tit, the holes of wild bees, and the rocks where a fox was known to live. They collected the gum from the spruces in the wood, pulled it sticky and aromatic from the rough bark of the trees, and stuff- ed it in their handkerchiefs,—golden brown, transparent drops like indiarubber, which stuck their fingers together as they held it. They set their faces close to the trees, staring at the pink flesh of the spruces, under the flakes of bark, and they peeled off the thin skin from the silver birches and wrote their names on the new whiteness. Everything held a secret for them. The green rushes had ivory within them, which could be revealed and woven into baskets and roses. A stone held a spark which flew out when you beat it on another. Feathers and flowers and bits of moss, skeletons of birds and snail-shells, all held some mystery which they tried to fathom as they explored the fields and woods in those early days.

Richard was a young god and she was his humble servant, following where he went, through bramble and briar, torn frock and bleeding hands and knees, and never a complaint. Emmie often went with them, but she drifted away, to gather flowers, and to play with her doll. They made most of their own toys, for there was no money to buy them. They made five-stones from clay, painted bright blue and red. Richard carved boats from slips of wood or they fitted sails to walnut shells and sailed them on the streams. The toys were intimate, they were real and "lucky", with a personality of their own, with character and life, and when they were thrown away and new ones made they drifted back to the earth from which they had come.

At night, when the three travellers came home to the warm kitchen, they could see the light from the open top door in the distance, and they walked the last part of the way with their eyes fixed upon that glow. It meant home to them, and all that the words mean. The old house with all its enchantments was waiting there, as they straggled up the yard, with bags dragging in the dust and hats thrown back from their tired heads.

Hetty might grumble, Uncle William might be morose and troubled, Charity might be anxious about something, but there would be a smile and a word from her. The table would be set for tea, and the kettle singing on the fire. That was something as secure as the house itself, and Virginia took off her things and sat waiting on the settle, while the tea was made.

In the steam from the kettle she saw little James Watt also sat staring at the fire, crouched on the hearthstone before the red flower of the flames, dreaming as he watched it. Hans Andersen too sat on a stool watching the kettle boil, dreaming of the Elder Flower mother who lived in the teapot. The lovely rainbow steam blew out in a funnel from the great copper kettle, it spread fan-wise in the room, and disappeared by the black post of the roof.

"Where has it gone?" asked Virginia, and she held out her hand to catch it one day and was burned. "Sarve you right," said Hetty sharply. Charity wrapped a greased rag round it and comforted her in the sudden sharp pain. Discoveries brought danger and adventure, and the kitchen was full of them. It was the place of tears and laughter, where one was bound and free.

The kitchen, with all its thrilling memories, its movement and life, its dangers and its security, filled the lives of all the family there. The china dogs on the mantelpiece, the great pancheons of dough rising mysteriously under the white cloths in front of the fire, the kettles boiling and jets of steam pouring out to take the skin from one's hand, the great table always filled with food or work, or ironing or butter-making with just a little corner for Dick's lessons, all spoke to those who could hear the words.

The room was packed with glances and sly smiles, with conversation going on underneath all else. In the morning early, over the breakfast of slices of hot toast and dripping, salted and rich, piled on a dish, washed down by tea, and at night when the little Dutch oven hung in front of the fire and delicious smells of toasted cheese lured the mice from the holes and made the rats sit up in the yard to smell, invisible ones seemed to join in the feasts, to hover round the table, dipping a finger in a bowl, tasting tea and thick cream in a saucer, called out of the shadows by Charity's talk, as they listened and joined in.

Sometimes the tall dominoes came from the box, the oblongs of ebony and ivory, for they could be nothing less precious, and they spilled in a heap and turned over on their faces. Everybody sat round, and Virginia was her Grandmother's partner. The long row was formed down the middle of the scrubbed bare table, the only time it was left empty, under the hanging lamp in the yellow pool with shadows around watching, and the game was played. Light and shade, black and white, with fire gleams and shadows playing their own game behind, this was a time of happiness to remember always.

Richard Dale was already looking forward to leaving school and working on the farm. He was going to have wages when he began, two shillings a week pocket money, which was great wealth. He was anxious to start, but his father wanted him to learn all he could first. School books irked him, discipline from women teachers angered him. He was up before the headmaster every day to have his hands caned, but Virginia and Emmie kept it secret lest he should get a belting when he came home as well. He fought, he swore strange oaths, but with all his roughness he had a streak of gentleness which he showed to animals and to Virginia, who was like a small dog to him.

"Let Jinny go down in the cart with us to-day," Richard asked one Saturday morning when William was getting ready for the weekly market. William seldom took the children, for they were a nuisance in the cart, but Dick was useful to help with shopping, to hold the horse and open the gates.

"Tell her to be sharp, then," said William impatiently. "Wrap up well, for there's a biting wind. Emmie'd better come too or there'll be a fuss."

So Virginia and Emmie were muffled in coats and shawls, and packed in the spring-cart. Virginia was wedged between her uncle and cousin Dick at the front. At the back, on a sack of meal, sat Emmie, very comfortable with the square sides of the cart around her. On the floor was a basket of fowls clucking indignantly, as they tried to peep out of the broad lid. There was always some livestock to take to the village, a calf with its body in a sack, and its dark eyes staring about and its tongue licking, a few ducks, a little pig, all company for a journey. Richard pointed out the sights to Virginia as they drove along the lane, and her head turned to right and left as he cried out at a kingfisher over the river, a goldfinch on a kexie, a yellow-hammer running close to them in the hedge. Her dark blue eyes flashed with pleasure, her tilted tender mouth was trembling with joy, and her little head nodded. She talked little, but she was a good listener. She heard far more than her companions ever dreamt. Already she had heard the voice of the house speaking softly, and now she caught the song of the river, and the urgent talk of the trees, rivalling the remarks of the boy at her side.

"Sithee Jinny. A cock pheasant in yonder spinney. Hey, look there! D'ye see him? I wish I had a gun. When can I have a gun of my own, Father?"

"Some rainy day when it's fine and you've earned your keep," said William drily, and he clicked his tongue to the little mare and softly stroked her back with the whip. She needed no lash, only she wanted to know whether he had remembered to bring it. When it was left behind she dawdled shamelessly, and she always tried it on a bit to find out.

"I've 'membered it, Betty," said William, and they all laughed, for it was an old joke. Even Betty pricked up her ears and joined in silently.

Virginia began to sing to herself, as she swayed and bumped between the heavy body of her uncle and the restless corduroys of Richard. She was caught up in a wave of bliss, evoked by the motion of the horse and cart, and the rushes of cold air on her face. The overhanging branches of trees tugged at their hats and swept cold fingers across their cheeks like fine lashes. Dick ducked his head, but Virginia felt the stinging touch, and stretched up her hands to catch those clinging earthly fingers. She leaned back and watched the clouds and the little lanes in the sky where angels walked.

The song went on, and Richard looked curiously at the thin delicate face pressed close to his coat, upturned to the clouds. It was elfin, like that of some fairy child turned out of fairyland,

68

dismissed for lack of beauty, but retaining an exquisite air of another world. He was bewildered before it. There was a hint of beauty nevertheless, which the boy sensed rather than understood. It was different from the regularity of feature of his sister. There was an expression he had surprised on his grandmother's face when the old woman was unaware of his intent gaze, or perhaps she merely pretended not to see him, for Charity was alive to many things. So he took sidelong glances at Virginia, lost in her childish contemplation of the sky. She was a queer little stick, he told himself. She seldom grumbled, although she wasn't treated fairly by his mother, she played as if she had a secret companion, but she would leave all at his bidding.

Suddenly she felt his look and she smiled rapturously at him, with a crooked smile of joy and he nudged her to make her laugh, and then she slipped her warm hand into his dirty one and held it tightly.

"What was you thinking about?" he asked.

"Dick, do the stars make honey?" she asked, very softly.

But Emmie at the back eating an apple, shuffling on her soft cushion of the meal sack, heard. She gave a shriek of laughter and slid a malicious finger through the seat and pinched Virginia. Richard turned quickly and boxed Emmie's little pink ear. A fight flared up in a moment, the hens squawked as Emmie stood on the basket and caught Virginia by the hair with one hand whilst she beat with her fist on Richard's head.

William swore with anger. He seized the whip, and threatened them all. "Now then, you children, I shan't bring you never no more if you can't behave yoursens. You're a disgrace. I wish I'd left the whole bag-lot of you at home. As for you, Richard, keep your hands to yourself, and don't hit a girl."

The three sat subdued, eyes glaring, but they knew he might stop the horse and turn them out to trudge the miles home again. They sat prim and mute for the rest of the journey, and soon their antagonism was forgotten in the excitements of the little stone houses of the village. Old men in various shapes of ancient hats sat on a form sunning themselves, arguing over football and politics, calling "How 'do?" to William. Old women with shawls over their heads went into one another's houses with scarcely a tap at the double doors. The cats were walking serene and aloof down the road, the dogs eyeing them lazily, and a sweet, grand wind was blowing across the market square from the hills.

"No Admittance without Business" read Emmie, pointing to white painted words over the double door that led to a mill, and Virginia spelled out the letters. For ever they were related to that ride with Richard, and the feeling of happiness by his side. She counted the number of a's and i's, and made fancy words from the meaningless notice. Softly she sang them. They were music. They went up the scale in a tune which fluttered clearly around them. The cart waited while William went through the great doors with his basket of hens. Richard left the cart also, after giving stern instructions to the girls, and he went to the saddler's with the bellyband to be sewn. The girls each held a rein, and called "Whoa, whoa" when the horse was for starting off. In the end they both tugged so hard that the horse began to back, and William came running out to save them from bumping into a wall.

They called at the miller's watermill, and then at the sawmill, and the carpenter's shop. They visited the druggist, with his enchanting bottles of coloured red and blue liquids, and William bought liniment for a mare that had strained her shoulder and a bottle of the same stuff for Charity's rheumatism. Old black mare and wrinkled little grandmother shared the same cure-all. They they drove down the narrow lane to the little grocer's shop for a twenty-pound bag of brown sugar and a cask of treacle. There the girls descended, and entered the dark doorway down two steps, to tinkle the bell and tread on the dusty boards, and smell the mixed odours of ham and flour and mice, of pork pies and tarred rope. They watched Mrs. Mole twist the blue paper into a bag for the barm, and they spent their halfpennies on sweets. It was a wonderful experience.

"And this is Virginny, is it? She gets mighty like her mother was," Mrs. Mole told William. "And yet," she added truthfully, "she's not got her mother's good looks. She's kind of peaked, isn't she? I should get a bottle from the druggist for her. Emmie'ld make two of her." She turned to Virginia who was trying not to look peaked. "You must sup your new milk, my dear," said she kindly, "and do as your aunt tells you, and then maybe you'll get to be not so homely."

"She'll do," said William gruffly. "She's not so bad looking."

That was indeed kind of Uncle William, and Virginia's pale face flushed with gratitude.

At Thomas Drake the cobbler's they all stayed while Uncle

William talked and Virginia was fitted with a pair of strong school boots, with iron heels and lace-ups. The stout little man held Virginia's foot in his hand, against his leather apron, while she sat on a low stool.

"How would you like a glass slipper, like Cinderella, my dear?" he asked, and they all laughed at his joke. But there in the case was a lovely sandal of silver going to the Hall. He took it out for them to see and then he put it on Virginia's foot. It fitted exactly.

William and Mr. Drake began to talk about the wondrous amount of wealth the gentry had, and the grand rich way they lived, but Virginia was staring at the shoe. Only in one of Grandmother's fairytales had she heard of such things, and here was one in Mr. Drake's own cottage shop. He told them he had made it for the little girl who was Virginia's age. He put it back in the case, and they went slowly out with the heavy boots tucked under William's arm and climbed into the cart. This time Virginia sat among the packages and bags on the floor and Emmie took her place at the front. The horse trotted very fast to get home to the stable, the cart swayed with the uneven surface of the road, and everyone swung with it. Up and down, to left and right, they leaned and rolled in unison, but Virginia was in a pumpkin chariot going to a ball with white horses drawing her and a footman like the Squire's to open the gate. Glass slippers on her feet and a silver dress. "Cinderella," the cobbler had called her! In the song of the river she heard the shrill fiddles and high flutes and deep drums of the band. The prince came out of the green shadows of the overhanging trees and sometimes he looked like Richard, all dressed in velvet with lace edges, and sometimes he was somebody whom she couldn't see.

She sang a wordless song of joy, her voice wandering softly as she bumped about among the packages. The smell of a bag of meal for the calves was rich to her. Her little feet scrabbled in the dusty cart bottom, among hay seeds and straw. She wanted the journey to go on for ever. Rain clouds like tattered flags waved above. Trees staggered to meet them, bowed and passed on. Cattle stared with knowing eyes over the walls, and she caught their glance, and made a little sign to them. On the front seat the three backs of Richard, Emmie and her uncle were stout and strong, keeping away the wind. She crouched lower in the corn and meal bags, put her head on the basket, and fell asleep.

71

She accepted gladly all that came her way, unquestioning the right and wrong, accepting injustice, beatings and scolding from Hetty, being made a dunce at school, as something unavoidable. Sunshine and rain came her way, she got wet through, her hands and feet chilblained in winter, tired little legs in summer's heat, but there was always something secretly wonderful. The rainbows on the sink when the lamp oil was spilled, the curling potato peelings lying in the bowl, the starry mosses on the garden wall, were all daily miracles.

The next winter Virginia fell ill through the exposure. Wet shoes all day, wet dress unchanged while she sat at her lessons, gave her pneumonia. Charity moved her to her own bedroom and sat up day and night untiringly vigilant to watch her. When she left the room Virginia called her in delirium, and only her wrinkled hands could soothe the child. Dick and Emmie stepped quietly in at the door, bringing gifts of oranges and snowdrops, but Virginia took no notice. She called out in sudden fears, asking to be taken out of the dark hole. All her troubled life was exposed to them. The doctor shook his head, and Charity listened impatiently to his words. There wasn't much chance, he said. Charity carried out his orders, adding her own private incantations and prayers. The old house was not ready for this youngling to come into its shadows. She and the house would fight Death and send Him away for a time. Down through the orchard He would go. Away, far away.

One day Virginia called for Richard. "Richard. Richard," she cried, in a shrill unearthly voice, that turned Charity's heart to water, and made her limbs tremble and shake. The boy stayed with her for hours. Her eyes were shut, and she held tightly to his fingers, but although he had cramp he remained by her side, clutched in that hot grasp. All night he stayed, listening to her irregular breathing, and to other sounds that seemed to come to mingle with it. There were other watchers he was sure, and he dare not release his fingers or speak lest she should call again in that terrible young voice of a child lost in infinity.

Towards morning she slept soundly, her breathing had changed, and he drew his bent painful fingers away. The doctor said she had miraculously passed the crisis, she was on her way to recovery, and Richard had helped to save her.

When she was well enough to return to the room she shared with Emmie, Charity decided to keep her in her own room, in a small bed in the corner. Then began a secret and fascinating life for Virginia. They had their own games and delights, they were company for one another. The old woman came to bed early, and the little girl lay waiting for her. She lay there in her green cot, watching the shadows move across the wall, as Charity undressed. She saw a pair of hands uplifted as Charity said her prayers, and flickering shapes move across. The bedroom was filled with shadows and with the words that Charity read to her. It was a friendly room, and Virginia lost the fears that had haunted her. It put arms around her and comforted the deeply hidden frights, and healed her torn heart.

The tales she heard seemed to echo from the beams, they rang in the chimney, and tinkled in the water-jug, fairytale and Bible mixed together, seven dwarfs and Joseph's brethren, Balaam's Ass and the Marquis of Carabou's Cat, Ruth and Cinderella. Icy winds crept under the door, and the candle flickered and the shadows jigged, but Charity took a rug and threw it over the crack so that the cold was banished. A coal fell from the fire and again there was a flurry of movement, as the shades fled. They were friendly, happy shadows, and Virginia got to love them as if they were brothers and sisters coming out of nowhere to play with her.

It all happened when Virginia went to bed and Charity made the shadows appear. Charity took the matchbox in her bent bony fingers, and Virginia watched breathlessly to see the queer things happen. The matchbox had a picture of a tiger on it, in grand rich colours, a yellow and black tiger very fierce with teeth and snarl coming from a green jungle of spiked leaves. Charity struck the match and the tiger came into the flame. Virginia had heard it roar, and seen it spring as the long wooden match was struck. She waited, and she wasn't disappointed. The tiger flared out and sprang to the candle and bit it. The wild blue flag of a flame flickered with yellow and black tiger stripes, but the white candle in the ancient pewter candlestick was firm as a rock. Down its side trickled a tiny curl of wax. The old woman always snipped it away very quickly with her finger nail. "A winding-sheet," she whispered. Sometimes a little golden-red atomy burned on the wick and Charity removed it. "A letter," said she. "A letter from God," and perhaps she read what it said, Virginia didn't know. Sometimes there was a black demon in the flame, which cut a hole in the tiny cup of wax so that it ran down in a gutter of tears. Then Charity frowned and took it away with a matchstick. "A thief," said she. "A robber in the candle."

So the candle was lighted with ceremony and sorcery, and the brave feeble light shone out to the world, and perhaps sent a message to the Universe. Shadows arose from the invisible air, and leaped up the walls and snickered over the ceiling, bowing to the candle flame. Virginia inclined her head to them. The picture over the mantelpiece shone out as if it were alive. The books on the shelf caught the light on their gold lettering, *Tennyson's Poems*, The Bible, *Pilgrim's Progress*.

That moment, when the candle was lighted and the light ran round the room putting beauty and mystery upon every stick of furniture, was so exciting that Virginia always hid her face and shut her eyes for a moment to keep the pleasure fast. Then she raised shining eyes to her grandmother.

"Lie down, child. Lie down, God bless you," said Charity, when the girl was in bed, prayers said and hair brushed.

"God bless you, Grandmother," replied Virginia and obediently she put her head on the pillow. She shut her eyes and called to the lovely spirits that inhabit the world of dreams. They came to her bidding, Goldy Locks, Red Riding Hood without the Wolf, Swans and Wild Geese, doves and rabbits and nightingales. In a world without end they played and with them was Virginia.

The bedroom that was Charity's was brimming with life, it looked at the child in the bed, and waited for the old woman to come upstairs again. It whispered its tales and murmured and sang, all night long, till day came and the sun looked in at the window.

Virginia grew tall and thin, her face lost its roundness, her eyes were larger, deeper, and for some weeks she was left free to play and wander in the fields, with no duties, and no cares. Time stretched out, the past and the future were one with the present, she forgot everything that had troubled her. She went up the fields from the valley farm, to a crest where she looked down on William in the pasture, and her aunt Hetty in the garden, like toys moving about their work. She sat on a rock, little Virginia, staring across the fields, waiting for the wind to come. It was there, somewhere. It ruffled her hair, it was ever present, but it was also future, behind yonder hill. Soon it would come. She watched the green slopes, and then the deep shadow of the clouds swept down and the wind ruffled the grass of the valley fields to silver. Ah. She had seen the wind! "Dick, I've seen the wind", she would say. Not Grandmother, nor Aunt Hetty, but Dick should be told.

She looked at Richard far away in the Water Meadow, riding on the stone-roller shaft. She wanted him to draw his coat around him, when he felt the silver wind, to pull it close like the ballad, "The Wind and the Sun disputed, one chilly autumnal day". She wanted him to do it. "Dick. Look at me," said she softly, and she stared hard at the boy. Suddenly he turned and waved to her. He had seen her, tiny as she was, crouched in the grass among buttercups and daisies.

She sprang to her feet and called "Cuckoo, cuckoo", frantically, but he couldn't hear. The wind caught her voice and drowned it, and carried it away to the woods, but Dick put his fingers in his lips and sent that shrill whistle of his hurtling to the hidden stars. It caught her heart. She would hear it when she was dead.

"Mizpah," she whispered. "That means, 'The Lord watch between me and thee when we are absent one from another'."

Then she forgot, and she became the wind, and rushed down the fields with outstretched arms for wings. Suddenly she knelt by a gate, and she was a spider running across the grass without bending the blades. She was a blade of grass, a fine green sword, and she was the dewdrop upon it. She knelt with her nose close to the round drop and gazed into it startled to find a real rainbow there. For a long time she stayed, and the shadow of a bird went across the ground, and the wind blew her dress over her head.

Then, back from her airy adventures she ran down the lane to the farm, and sat on the wall overlooking it. Smoke from the chimney was weaving patterns like writing in the blue air, which she tried to decipher as she sat curled on the stones. It was one of the ways the house talked. It sent messages by smoke writing, but only the trees and hills could read the words. Perhaps it wrote, "Aunt Hetty is cross. Anger is flying about," and black smoke belched out like a dagger, or it said, "Content. We are sitting by the fire dozing and all is peace," and a little blue curl came meandering through the tall chimneys up into the trees.

This was the message Virginia read, and she came home, and darted round the door. Grandmother should be alone, and yes, Charity was there, with her puckered face, and Roman nose, and her keen blue eyes.

Oat-cakes were cooking in front of the fire, an iron pot hung over the flames, and the big brown teapot was drawing on the hob. It was a friendly teapot, and Virginia took a quick look at it, to see if it remembered her. Charity was mixing flour and milk and currants, shaping them into little cakes and setting them on the girdlestone to bake.

"Where have ye been, chuckabiddy?" asked the old woman.

Virginia put her lips to Charity's face and touched her soft wrinkled cheek. She seized the worn thin hand and found the wedding ring and the keeper. She let her fingers move gently round each tiny letter inset among the gold.

"It's a magical word, isn't it?" she asked.

"Mizpah? No, it's a Bible word," said Charity.

"Grandmother. I've seen the wind."

"Have you, my dear?" Charity never mocked or disputed anything serious like this. It was quite sufficient that Virginia had seen what she herself had known, that the invisible can be made visible. Charity too was listening to the wind's voice, for it was telling everybody its news. It was no ordinary wind, blowing from God knows where, but a West wind, coming over the hills through the crack between them. It had come from the sea, Charity told the child, for England is an island; it had blown great ships and tossed them like leaves. It had reared up the waves in white horses, and thrown them on pebbly shores, and the noise of that shore was in the wind sometimes as it roared across the yard.

It brought other things with it, the smell of moors and heather, of little old villages and dark church towers, and the sound of bells and voices. Like water it was, rushing through space without destroying it, and it came to the old farmhouse, whipping the trees by the garden walls, singing through the squarecut holes in the sides of the barns, and it gathered up the aroma of the farm. Everywhere it went it collected something, and left a fragrance and memory, and now it was charged with its experiences and essences and it went on. It was on its way to the towns, the industrial towns where the milk churns went and the butter. The folk in the mean streets would smell it, and say, "There's a smell of spring in the air." For the wind carried pocketfuls of scent from primrose leaves and moss and woods, from gardens and farmyard and river. It would, maybe, run up a street and down a street just for fun, and then on it would go, right out to sea again.

So Charity talked to the little girl, but the house was speaking of other things. Wind and moonlight and stars, these are the unchangeable strength behind everything, it said. Land and hills, these too seemed as immutable as the sun and stars. No wonder the house laughed to itself as it listened to the wind, and gazed up into the sky.

Chapter 7

The long village street climbed unevenly and crookedly uphill till the little stone cottages gave up the struggle and left the fields to continue alone. Doors were open, and rosy firelight streamed down the strong stone steps, each a solid block of dressed sandstone, to the cobbled path and the road. Inside each cottage there was a glimpse of a chest of drawers with photographs and ornaments upon it, set for the passer-by to admire, but the interior of the living-room was protected from curious eyes by a wooden partition which stretched behind the door and held a little glass peephole for those sitting in the corner by the fire. On the doorsteps sat children with little bare bottoms on the cold stone. Boys played whip and top on the sloping road, lashing the tops uphill to counteract the downward spinning motion. The girls played fivestones, and chinked their blue and white cubes as they tossed them and swept the stone step with a hand. These stone steps made admirable playing grounds, and theatre seats for the game of life in the country road. Across some doorsills were wooden boards, fitted in slots, and over them peeped little tots of babies, who were too young to be allowed to sit on the cold stones, but already they were eager to go out and join in the games.

Up and down this road went Virginia, swinging her bag, looking with quick shy eyes through the doors at firelight and chests, and tables set for meals, never cleared away, for people were coming and going and the teapot brewed on the oven ready.

There she was in summer running to school along the lanes, stopping to pick a flower, to grasp a berry, then panting past the cottages when she heard the school bell. There she was on winter mornings, her grey muff swinging on its grey cords as she clattered along in her heavy boots. She was part of the pattern of the village street, stone houses and hard-working people,—the pendulum of the clock swinging behind the bull's-eye glass in the kitchen, the changing moon swinging to the rhythm of the tides, and her own small life swinging to and fro with the earth's motion. Charity watched her, and felt the same rhythm of earth, but her own amplitude was lessening, the mechanism was dying down. Charity went about the house with her little black shawl on her bent shoulders, her worn hands with scarlet knitted mittens over the frost-nipped wrists and stiff fingers, indoors and outdoors, in the dairy to look at the milk, to the water troughs for a cup of icy sweet water, or a pailful for the boiler. Her strength was amazing, she could go on when many a young woman would have faltered, but there was a slowing down of all things, and she was aware of it.

The house too went through a changing rhythm with the seasons, breathing in fresh life in spring and summer, glowing in the autumn and cowering in muffled white cloths in the winter months.

The house looked out across the river to the hills, speaking to them, listening to their talk, and the leaves of the hanging boughs shook a dancing pattern on the walls, and made a sigh and a whisper of a tale repeating what the wind had said.

Every morning Virginia went to school along this village road, hurrying as she heard Billy Jorkins pulling the school bell rope, making the ting-tong of the iron-tongued bell ring down the valley and over the hill. Her rough little boots beat a march as she tramped along the road. Clip, clop, they made a tune that sang to the music of the bell. The clamorous bell called her name, Jin-ny, Jin-ny, as if it were for her alone, and she raced into the school yard, and peered into the boys' doorway to watch Billy Jorkins drag the rope as if it were a church bell, and to see the bell toss and turn in its stone tower on the roof. Virginia longed to be a bell-ringer, but it was a boy's prerogative.

"Hello, Jinny," mocked Billy Jorkins, swinging on the rope.

"Let me have a pull," begged Virginia.

He hesitated, and regarded her eager morning face with a satyr's grin. His pointed ears and bright eyes gave him a goat-like appearance as he shook his ragged hair and tugged harder at the bell to show his importance.

"Aye, come along and be sharp," he cried, suddenly relenting. "You've got to be sharp, and whatever you do, don't let go, or

78

th' mester will know a girl's ringing, and won't he tan ye!"

Virginia took the rope and pulled it. The bell sent its voice down the hill over the trees to the water. She turned her face upward to watch it answering her tugs.

"Keep on! Dinna stop!" shouted Billy Jorkins.

A spirit of mischief seized the boy. He leaned forward and kissed her cheek with his wet red lips. He clasped her in his arms and kissed her mouth. Virginia slapped his face, but she went on ringing. Tears were in her eyes, and he snatched the rope away. Off she walked, wiping her mouth on her pinafore. She hurried to the water-tap in the playground, and washed her face, rubbing to remove the hateful touch. Boys were cruel wicked creatures, smelling of dirt and corduroys, she hated them all except Dick. Dick would have lathered him, but now she had to fend for herself.

In class Virginia put up her hand. "Please teacher, can I have a drink?" she asked. She was desperately thirsty, her mouth was dry as a bone, and there in the corner was the water-bucket which the water-monitors had filled early in the day. On the side hung the mug with a curved handle. Nobody was allowed to go to the tap for a drink during lessons, or water would be wasted.

Miss Blow had given permission, and Virginia tripped out with dancing step, eager to sip it. She dipped the enamel mug in the bucket, and swirled it round. She drank with eyes peeping over the rim, and drops of water falling upon her hot arms.

As soon as she got to her place Billy Jorkins put up his hand. "Please Miss, can I have a drink?" he asked, and he lurched out to the bucket and filled the mug. Billy Jorkins was a nuisance to her, like wasps and weasels and wild bulls. Then she found a new friend, who took her part.

She was eating her solitary dinner in the school yard, when Ronald Youlgrave walked across the square of grass. He was the son of a farmer over the valley, behind the great oak wood. He went to school along the bridle path across the hill while Virginia took the valley road, so they never met. He was older, too, and in a higher class, Dick had been one of his friends. He lived too far away to go home for dinner, but his father paid sixpence a day for the boy to have a hot meal. That lordly sum set him apart from the rest. He was remarkable too because his hair was flaming red, and he wore a blue jersey when other boys wore coats and waistcoats. Virginia had seen him driving with his elder brother, and riding a pony in the market-place. He was one of the important people, and Virginia regarded him from afar with wonder.

He came across the playground to Virginia as she bit with sharp white teeth into her beef sandwich .He walked with a slow swagger, dribbling a stone as if life depended on its progress, his red head bent, his lips curved into a whistle.

"Hello, Virginia Dale," said he carelessly. He brought a new top from his pocket, and wound the lash of a whip round it.

"Hello, Ronald Youlgrave," replied Virginia, and she took another bite and removed the scrap of gristle. Each sandwich had to be opened and Aunt Hetty's gristle taken out.

The boy whipped the top skilfully, and it spun on the smooth ground near Virginia's feet. He lashed it and it took a little leap and whirled like a dancer. Virginia pushed the rest of her sandwich away in her bag and watched with deep interest. A spinning top was beautiful, it had a quality of its own. It could be endowed with life, with speech and motion. As long as she lived she knew she would love the sight of the whirling little spindle, with its secret life, moving so quickly that the eye was deceived.

"Look! It's asleep," she cried admiringly, as the top spun in one place with such rapidity it seemed motionless. Then it awoke and darted away.

"Do you want a try?" asked the boy, suddenly.

Virginia nodded. This was a great honour, and she must prove herself worthy, but a top's motion always frustrated her. The farmyard was too stony, and Dick was impatient with her efforts. She took the bright green whip with its new bootlace lash, and struck at the top which was still whirling in rapturous motion, as if it were possessed of a spirit. It had leapt like a horse at the touch of the whip, but now it swayed, it rolled drunkenly and rolled over.

"Oh dear, I've deaded it," moaned Virginia.

"Silly. Not like that. See-thee. I'll show you," said the boy, proudly. He taught her how to spin the top with the initial flick of the wrist, and how to catch it at the right moment. He stuck coloured papers on the surface and showed how they combined and changed. The dinner hour passed in companionship, but when the first child came round the corner, Ronald whipped the top away and instinctively they parted, the girl to her skipping rope, the boy with his top to the lower playground, with never a word.

The next day he came, this time with a book under his arm. It was *Coral Island*. Virginia turned the pages and saw magical scenes.

"I'm going to live on a coral island," proclaimed the boy. "I shall be a trader. I'm not going to stop on our farm."

"Nor me," said Virginia. "I'm going to be a missionary."

"Not on my island. I don't want any missions. I'll tell you what I shall do. I shall stay at home for a bit and earn some money and then I'll be off. You'll see, Virginia Dale." He spoke fiercely, and Virginia looked admiringly at the adventurer.

He brought more books about islands and travel, and Virginia shared them with Richard, and even with Charity. All their talk was on those far lands, and Charity, who hadn't gone farther than Liverpool in her life, now journeyed in spirit to desert islands. Each night Virginia took one of Ronnie's books and sat by the fireside in a rush-bottomed chair, her fingers in her ears. She was unconscious of the chatter around her, as she read of Indians with tomahawks and the early American settlers, of blue islands, of foreign legions, and Russian steppes. The fire beat upon her bent head, the lights and golds of her thick tresses were fastened by a black ribbon, and now and then she raised her face, and threw back her hair. In the kitchen they were discussing the latest gossip from the village, a sale that was billed, when a farm would change hands. Some of the stock would be dispersed, and Hetty wanted a few things for the house. They spoke of a wedding, and read aloud with comments the list of wedding presents, and their own among them. That was a fine thing but Virginia never heard a word. Emmie, who was learning dressmaking from a clever sewing woman, had helped to stitch some of the clothes. Richard, who was earning his two shillings a week from his father, sat there, in his own dreams. The heroes always ran away from their offices where they were clerks. Richard, who had never sat at an office stool, who knew nothing of book-keeping and little of figures, seriously contemplated running away to sea. He took his watch to the pawnshop one day when he was at the market town, but the pawnbroker looked so suspiciously at him and offered so little, young Richard backed out. Money was the hindrance, but his two shillings a week was religiously kept for the crisis. He hid his savings in the hole in the attic wall as his ancestor had done when he was buying the house.

One day Virginia sat in the schoolroom writing with extreme

care in her copy book, keeping her pen on each word till it was completed. The round script lay there with its curling capitals and its morals and proverbs. She had reached the letter P. Propaganda. Prognosticate. Pride goes before a Fall. They were fine long copy-book words which were used by the great people in the world. The longer the words, the deeper her pride in writing them, and she leaned her head on one side, stuck out her small red tongue and glided the Waverley pen over the paper with immense satisfaction.

The copy book was her own possession, paid for, and soon to be carried home for her grandmother's admiration. School books were free, but they were used by generations of children, who turned back the pages, and dog-eared the corners, and left their communal smell of soiled hands and dusty clothes soaking in them. Copy books were private, virginal, and lovely, and their odour was of printer's ink and good thick paper. They were kept in a special drawer.

The monitor came round with the tin can to fill up the ink wells. He poured a thin black stream into each white little cup and wiped it round the edge with a duster. Billy Jorkins was the ink monitor, and grand and important he looked with his black-stained fingers and darkly smudged cheeks. Virginia glanced up at his black eyes and red mouth, and then as he grinned at her, she bent to her copy book in confusion. He was like an executioner, stained with ink instead of blood. When he came to Virginia's ink well he deliberately overfilled it, and a black snake of ink ran down the fair page of the copy book. In a second it was spoiled. Virginia stared with fascinated horror at the coiling stream, while Billy murmured "Sorry" and went on.

Virginia was speechless. In a flash the world had changed, the skies were raining misery upon her. It was in her heart, she could feel the sorrow spilling there, but even then she was aware of the beauty of the awful disaster. She could see a tiny reflection of the school window, complete with window frame and mullions, in the ink, and she saw the rotundity of the drops, queerly lifted above the paper, like mercury balls. That was indeed a marvel. She stooped and stared at the pool of ink, lost in the surprise of its secret revelation of what it could do.

"Oh dear! How careless of you, Billy Jorkins! Virginia, don't sit there, staring! Oh dear! What a mess! You must bring twopence for a new copy book to-morrow," said Miss Matty, removing the inky book, and fetching another from the desk.

Virginia turned the empty pages. She had to begin at the first page. Adversity. Avarice. Avoirdupois. All is not gold that glitters. The tiny window reflection in the pool of ink remained in her mind. She saw it as she wrote the words in the new book.

"Twopence for a new copy book. Twopence for a new copy book." Her pinafore drenched in ink, and twopence lost and all her work spoiled, yet there was something precious discovered, the secret hidden in the blot. Everything had its mystery, a withheld perhaps sinister beauty which was waiting for those who had the key to unlock, and suddenly, radiantly, the small mirror had been revealed to her. She remembered talk she had overheard in the kitchen, when Grandmother Charity's friend, Mrs. Drake, had come to tea. Mrs. Drake had powers, and she could see the future in a glass ball, or in a drop of ink. She could read events in a teacup, and she had foretold some event, which had come to pass. Virginia hadn't understood the talk, but the words remained in her mind. In a drop of ink a vision may be seen.

Lessons were ended, copy books were cleared away, reading books were piled in ragged companies on a shelf, slates were stacked in the corner, bad little slates for the younger children, and good unscratched slates for the older boys and girls, prayers were said, a hymn was sung, and the children poured out of school like a brook dashing through a gullet, rushing, chattering, swinging like a spate of struggling water. They pushed one another as they ran through the playground gates into the village. Down the narrow street went some, up the road went others, down field paths, and over the river. At the village trough Virginia stopped for a drink. There was an iron cup on a chain, and water from this rude vessel had a queer human taste. It was civilization, for there was a tap in the wall, and water gushed from it and fell down into the mossy trough where horses drank. Ronald Youlgrave came up and drank after Virginia, but he refused the cup. He dipped his face under the tap and laughed as the drops fell from his eyelashes.

"I'm going your way, Virginia Dale," said he.

He didn't offer to carry Virginia's schoolbag, for that would have been a challenge to others to chalk remarks on posts and gates. He didn't even walk by her side. He raced ahead, and climbed a wall, and balanced as he went along the uneven summit. At the

gate he leapt down, and turned a somersault for bravado. Polite-
ness constrained him, and he held the gate open till Virginia
skipped through. Her usual progress was skipping, not with a
rope, for that would have been impossible along the stony path-
way under the wild hedgerows untrimmed and overhanging, but
with the dancing step which country children call skipping. It is
a progress that is breath-taking, and prevents speech.

The boy stopped to swing on the gate before he latched it,
and she skipped ahead. Then he dashed to the brook they had
to cross. He flung himself down on his stomach with his head
under the water, and held his breath while she counted the
seconds. His freckled face was scarlet, his red hair dripping, and
he walked by her side for a minute. Virginia wondered at the
ways of boys; this breath-holding was a mystery. It was a preparation for the future, a hardening he tried on himself, a test of
wildness and endurance. She darted away and swung her dinner-
bag round her head in a circle of joy, and after her he ran.

Together they made a pattern of youth, weaving into and
through one another's path like the aimless but ordered flight of
the swifts, their cries shrill as the birds', only their wings invisible.
Inky pinafore and torn collar were forgotten in sheer exhilaration. The cold air of the hills went to their heart's core, it blew
through their small skeletons and whistled through their white
skulls. For a few minutes out of eternity they tasted the abundance of living, unconsciously rivalling the animals who forget
the past and are unknowing of the future. Like two long-legged
awkward foals they dodged and ran, leaping as the impulse took
them, saying nothing at all, because they were free of speech.
Above them was the blue sky, with clouds wandering home from
school, weaving and changing every moment as the wind caught
and tore them. The earth had seen many such riotous pageants
of children, and animals and clouds. Paths like green ribbons
wound along the fields, twisting about the hillsides, where sheep
and farm folk walked, only visible by their slightly different shade
of green. White roads in the valleys were clear and important,
bordered by walls and hedges, but the field paths were like ghosts,
where the long dead and the living country children ran. Trees
stood sentinel by the massive boulders on the hills and pastures.
The ancient stones had given shelter to seedling trees which now
in time grew tall and made a shade for the rocks in their turn.
Like one of the old stones was the farmhouse in the valley,

sheltered by its trees, which had grown up under its walls and now hung their branches in love over its roofs. The two children stood by the gate and looked at the farmland, the girl with possessive love, the boy with question and curiosity. Then, "I must go now," said he, and he galloped off down the woodland track.

In the playground the next day, dancing on the flat stones was a ring of girls, whose short skirts and white pinafores fluttered like feathers in the wind. Their hair floated behind them, drawn out and tossed, shaggy locks of some, well-brushed, sleek tresses of others, curls and ringlets and little short-haired girls like boys. Their voices came shrill and unearthly sweet as they leapt round, and their feet skipped in time to the song they sang.

> *I wrote a letter to my love,*
> *And on the way I dropped it.*
> *One of you has picked it up,*
> *And put it in your pocket,*

they sang.

The dance stopped, the girls still swayed on tiptoes as Virginia ran round the outside of the circle, flicking her little handkerchief, which had already cleaned her slate and polished her boots, on each shoulder as she passed. Every girl turned her head to see if she were the chosen one, for they wanted to be her love.

"It isn't you. It isn't you. It isn't you," she chanted touching the sleeves of her friends with light flick of the handkerchief, her eyes bright, her cheeks on fire. Then her voice changed, she tossed the handkerchief to fair-haired Nancy Drake, the cobbler's granddaughter, and cried, "It's you", and away they ran in opposite directions till they reached the gap in the ring. The cries rose to the hills, like shrill bells ringing, the children skipped and flew with the joy of life running through their veins. There was nothing better on earth than to dance in the playground unconscious of everything outside that circle of magic. The robin sang its hardest in the holly bush at the school gate. In the lower playground the boys played football and shouted, they wrestled and played leapfrog, they fought like animals. They were less than nothing to the bevy of girls skipping in their ring, and a letter written to their love was a dream.

The little brass bell tinkled, and they formed themselves in two straggling lines like ragged ribbons, one brightly coloured, one dark with corduroys and tweeds. The boys entered the iron-studded door and tossed their football in the corner. The girls walked through their narrow cloakroom, panting and laughing, pushing their wild hair into their ribbons and combs, tying up their shoelaces.

Lessons began again, but the children had brought in with them a part of the country, a scrap of beauty, a bird's song, a flurry of wind and kiss of rain, and a snatch of an ancient game. Nothing was quite the same to their eyes. Ink was darker, goblin-black, paper was snow-white, slates were magical slices of stone upon which children had written for a thousand years, lesson books had an intimate touch of sorcery, and the dog's-eared pages wagged knowingly. The hills outside were beckoning the children, trees nodded through the long window panes, they waved and leered, struggling to say something to them, the robin sang so shrilly that his voice drowned the teacher's high clacking tongue.

It was the reading lesson, and heads were bent over the brown-backed books. The three top classes were put together for reading, squeezed close on the forms, sharing books, and the teacher was Miss Blow herself, fierce and stern.

Virginia's little willowy body was pressed close to other hot bodies, her hands held the soft-backed reading book with other hands grasping the pages, her feet were side by side on the dusty floor, touching other little leather boots that scrabbled like mice in the dust, only her mind was absent, chasing shadows over the hills, singing, "Stand and face your lover", dancing on thin feet that never touched earth but floated a yard or so above the grass. The line between reality and imagination had gone, and she had slipped over the border to another world. Dimly she heard some-body stumbling over words in the reading book. Usually she listened with impatience, longing to supply the words which eluded the others, but to-day the sound receded and faded in the robin's song. She was walking, nay running on a cold hillside with someone, showing him the secret hiding-places among the rocks, speaking in a silent tongue which had no words. They came to a green door in the tall bracken, and he held aside the tangle of honeysuckle for her to enter. She felt the sudden hush as all living things watched her. Birds sang urgently, "Beware. Beware". The calves raised their heads and waited with wild eyes and slobbering lips, the doves peered at her from the high trees.

She was going in. Maybe she wouldn't come back for a hundred years. She was going, going. She saw the door dark with lichen, she touched the stone of which it was made, rutted and pitted with rain, cold to her fingers. It swung on noiseless hinges, out of the face of the hill. She put a strong little boot on the sill, and she saw her bootlace was untied. Would it matter? She looked up into the face of her companion. "Stand and face your lover," said he, but he drifted away like smoke. She met the eyes of Miss Blow, and felt the sharp nudges of her companions.

"Well, Virginia Dale. What do you think you are doing? Where are we up to? You don't know. You weren't attending as usual. Go out for the cane."

Miss Blow was furiously angry. She was tired and exasperated, the wind had got into a hollow tooth, and the nerve was nagging.

Virginia stood up, confused and lost. She hadn't come back properly. She stood, wavering, puzzled, not offering to leave the class, or understanding. There was a commotion at the back and a boy sprang to his feet.

"Please Miss Blow. It isn't fair. She didna hear you."

The class swivelled round to stare at Ronald Youlgrave. They were filled with malicious glee. It was a welcome diversion, a tale to tell, and their own turns at reading might be missed.

"Didn't hear me? She's under my nose. You go too, Youlgrave. Tell Mr. Samson I sent you for impertinence."

Miss Blow rapped the desk with her knuckles, and the two children struggled from the packed rows, Virginia bewildered, Ronald bold and careless.

"Spit on your hand, Jinny," he muttered, his mouth askew. "It won't hurt. She's an old bitch, she is."

Virginia put her hand to her mouth and furtively licked the palm. She pushed aside the curtain that divided the room and went to the headmaster who sat at his desk. He glanced up at the two children, the shy little girl, the red-headed truculent boy.

"What are you here for?" he asked, although he knew quite well, for he could hear every word from the other side of the curtain.

"I'm for imperence," said Ronnie. "But she's done nothing."

"I wasn't listening," said Virginia.

"Hold out your hand. I'm surprised at you, Virginia Dale." He gave her a blow with the cane. "Now the other." He struck hard, and Virginia drew back flinching. It was hateful to be

87

beaten, and she went back to her place with head lifted high and tears blinked away. They should not see that she was hurt. She smiled with trembling lip as she met the curious eyes all turned to see how she had taken it. Behind the curtain they could hear the swish of the cane. Boys always got harsher treatment than girls. Then Ronald appeared with a deep frown and flung himself to his place.

In the playground after school, Virginia showed her weals to inquiring friends, and she held her hand under the water tap to ease it. Dick endured the cane every day when he was at school, and he never flinched, she thought. Now she knew the pain he had, and she was drawn to him in sympathy. Then Ronald Youlgrave came to her, and walked along the lane after she had left the village.

"Thank you for what you did," said Virginia.

"Oh, it was no use. I thought she'd let you off, the old fossil," he grunted, but he was pleased, and he picked up a stone and sent it skimming over the river.

"Let me look at your hand," said Virginia.

"Oh it's nothing. He's often hit me harder than that," laughed the boy. "I don't care a damn. I'm leaving soon." He wiped his hand and held it out, half ashamed. She stooped over it, gulping back a queer sensation that caught her throat. Three deep weals lay on the swollen palm, and there were drops of dark blood.

"I'm sorry," said she softly. That curled hard hand in front of her seemed to bring a message to her. The happiness and grief and endurance of humanity were there, on the small dirty palm. She fumbled in her schoolbag for something, and when she couldn't find it she turned the contents on to the grass by the roadside. There they lay, her treasures, a penknife, a bit of butterscotch wrapped in silver paper, a whistle Richard had made for her, and a crust of bread. She returned them, all except the penknife. It was her most precious possession. She held it out to him.

"Oh no," said he, but she insisted, and he took it. She felt her heart contract with sudden emotion which it would never do to show. She stooped and chose a stone carefully, and took aim. Richard had taught her to throw like a boy and she knew exactly what to do. She bent sideways, and flicked the flat pebble with quick motion. It flew over the water, bouncing on the waves and dropped among the reeds. He looked surprised and he welcomed her on a level with himself. Virginia felt very happy, as they

88

threw stones in turn, counting the bounces, the boy's beating hers by a narrow margin each time. She tossed back her shining hair, and breathed deeply the heavy rich smell of burdock and nettle, of wild rhubarb and mud on the river's bank. It was a moment of remembrance in her life, a picture painted on her mind till the end should come. Ripple of waves, flight of dipping swallows, glint of sun on the green-tipped water, and the flat mica-flecked stones left by the roadman in a convenient heap, the harsh odour of the boy's corduroy coat, and the bright smile of his face.

Ever moving, always changing, life went on, but this moment remained crystallized for her, caught and chained like a jewel to hang in her heart's secret chamber. The pain and ignominy of the day were forgotten, but this stayed.

All summer she was happy, running her way to school with a new rope with blue handles and bells that Uncle Will had bought for her tucked under her arm, singing, "Buttercups and Daisies and all you pretty flowers", as she leaped to and fro over the slowly swaying rope held by two leaders, or "Salt, mustard, vinegar, pepper", as she skipped the rapid measure in lightning speed. She was growing fast, she was changing too. Then somebody drew a chalk heart with her initials and those of the young boy. It was a thing of shame, and she withdrew to herself. At the end of the year Ronnie left school, and she seldom saw him. Perhaps he kept her treasured penknife, she didn't know, but she hoped he used it and remembered. Billy Jorkins had gone too, and Virginia was free from his mocking tongue and the sly looks he gave her.

Chapter 8

The old house was full of sounds and aliveness, and the best time of all was when school was over, on Saturdays or holidays, and those with ears to hear could listen.

"Take care of the house, Jinny. Mind the fire and watch the kettle and get the tea ready for your uncle and Dick," warned Aunt Hetty, as she slipped a shawl on her shoulders and went out to visit a friend across the fields. Grandmother Charity pottered in the dairy, and Virginia minded the house, and the house minded Virginia.

When they had gone, the men to the work, Aunt Hetty to the next farm, and Charity upstairs, and all was quiet except for a mouse in the corner, and the hens scrabbling in the yard, then the house came awake, to creak and crack, to rumble and laugh. There were subdued chatterings and whisperings in kitchen and dairy, and in the narrow passage by the parlour. Shadows peered from cupboards and came out to the kitchen, silvery beams danced up and down the stairs lighting up the duskiness. Virginia listened, and nodded to the shadowy ones who came to sing and whisper to one another from out of the past.

There was a rustle like a skirt, and a clatter in the dairy, but the girl did not venture to look through the door. Perhaps it was a mouse running among the dishes, or maybe a ghost was there, staring at the milk bowls to see if the cream were setting, supping with faded lips at the yellow wrinkled cream, dipping a thin bone of a finger into the skimmer and leaving a track there. Someone who once lived there, had returned to see that all was right. Leave her alone, don't disturb her, she was happy tasting once more those earthly delights, which had been hers! The skirts swished again, hands were outstretched, and another joined her. Later, when all were in bed, and the kitchen was left with the fire low and the firelight rising and falling in darting questioning flames, when the tap dripped with warning note, and the clock ticked companionably, welcomingly, the delicate ghost would come down the stone passage, tripping lightfoot to meet those others waiting for her, her husband in that great armchair in the corner, her children dancing round the table playing blind man's buff, or, suddenly older, crouching by the fire, to talk of this and that.

How glad they will be to find a warm room, and a cushioned settle, and homely smells, thought Virginia! How happy to return and share their loved house, to finger the iron-hard oak pillar, to find their names carved there, to hang their ghostly hats on the pegs, to discover creases in the cushions and flowers in the mug on the table! All night they would sit there, and talk, and enjoy the feeling of home,—wanderers returned, to sew and spin, to defeat time and live in eternity doing the things they loved. The old house knew all about them, it shared their life, and gave them kindness and happiness.

The next day, when the shutters were unfastened, even as the door at the foot of the crooked stairway was unlatched, and William entered, they went. When the early sun flashed across the trees, and the yard was bathed in milky mists of morning, they had fled. The iron tongue of the latch clicked to warn them. The stair cried out. The door with its wooden bolt and ancient leather thongs, creaked and called, "Away, shades, away", and the faint delicate shadows shuffled off in their pattens and hobnailed boots, away into the walls, out to the barns and haychambers, to leave the house free for the living. Only when it was very quiet did they come back in the daytime. The house was never lonely with all these visitors talking of past days.

The smallest sounds came to Virginia's ears. She seemed sensitive to the earth's movements, so that she was like one of the small animals that creep in the undergrowth, ears cocked for intelligence, eyes bright as she peered about. She was like one of the birds that fly in the wind's domain, knowing the sighs of the airy vapours where it lives, seeing the invisible lanes in the sky. She was aware of the leaves pulling on their stalks, dragging from the tree before they fall. She heard the faint rattle of the small seeds on the green mosses carpeting the walls, and the rustle of the filmy threads. Perhaps she heard the words of the trees themselves, and the moan of the fibres deep in the earth as they clung to the rocks and twined themselves in the crannies.

She learned that the farm world, which was the whole wide world to her, was dependent on the weather; that the house, built on the rocks with foundations deep and strong, looked to the sky for meat and drink, that it was one with the earth, and she too was part of that same earth, dust of its dust. The silence of night, the presence of the stars, the tall elms which stood drinking in the cold air, all drew the girl to the heart of the world. She lay in bed, no longer now in Charity's room, listening to the evocations of the house.

She learned to welcome the sound of rain pouring with the rattle of shot on the overhanging trees, stabbing like an army of silver spears at the fields. Rain clouds were tattered flags, torn by the wind's hands, tossed by that giant, who had been visible when he fled down the cornfields. She loved the hiss of water overflowing from the great wooden rain-barrels, swishing against the windows, and pouring from the stone roof gutters, down the round open mouth of the worn little beasts carved up there by the long-dead mason who had enjoyed himself while he built that part of the house. The parched fields would sup the water up like thirsty cattle, their brown mouths agape for all they could get, their sides panting with pleasure as the rain ran down their millions of throats. The dry pastures with cracked surfaces into which Virginia's small fingers had poked in sorrow when Uncle William had shown them to her and explained about them, would have these dark wounds healed with the welcome spate of rain.

The spring would be renewed in its health, the water would come tumbling afresh down the little leaden spouts to the troughs, the streams would hurry across the meadow to the river. There would be an abundance of rainwater for the house, no need to carry any except drinking water from the spring. Aunt Hetty would have plenty of water for washing the great baskets of clothes, for cleaning and swilling the stone floors of the dairy and kitchen and pantry. The cattle troughs were full, the horse trough brimmed over and ran to a pool on the ground, and all the stone troughs hidden in the fields, by the gates, in hollows and dimples of the stony pastures would be reborn to singing life for the birds and animals of the wild wood.

Rain and wind, sunshine and frost, were realities, vividly present as if the ancient Boreas himself with blowing puffing cheeks had swept down to the farmhouse, or the sun god had stretched out his long fingers of light to point to a lily in the garden, or the frost king had stepped from the arctic circle where he lived to lock the streams in winter and bind the pools with hairy icicles. The farmhouse deep in its hollow between the hills was shielded from the worst winds, but the fields spread out around the house were exposed to gales which swept up them with the fury of demons. Then the old house seemed to thrust its head low and stand like rock, defying the waves of wind that beat upon it. The coming of a storm, the creaking of the weather-cock on the little two-storied farm building, was the signal for a hurried battering down of hatches, closing of portholes in the stone ship. Doors were fastened in the farm buildings, shutters closed over open spaces where there was no glass, cattle driven from under the trees, where there was the danger of lightning. Thunder rolled in the hills, and reverberated with a long continuous roar, and lightning flashed with golden forks like trees over the darkling sky. Hetty covered up the looking-glasses, and crouched in a dark corner, but the old grandmother walked from room to room, muttering to the house, talking to unseen ones, excited and restless. For the house was wide awake when electric forces were strong in the air, the vast layers of past emotions were tapped by the storm, and Charity, with her mind attuned to them, could enter into the past sweetness and happiness and grief.

Virginia sat by her aunt and Emmie, holding tight to the hands held out to her. The door into the yard was left open, no matter how fierce the rain, and the downpour beat to the floor, and ran in little runnels to the cracks between the stone flags. A thunderbolt or a lightning flash could go out that way if it entered the house, they said, so the door was left ajar for the wild guest. Virginia stared at the purple sky, and waited for the grand sight, for that visitant from heaven, a gold ball of forked lightning that would dart down the wide chimney, leap through the kettle sitting there like a broody hen, perhaps melting it on the way, and roll across the stone floor out through the doorway. She waited in vain for the lovely dangerous visitor to dart on gold wings from the sky, but there were compensations in the lurid colours of the land revealed by storm.

At other times, when rain was an unwelcome and dreaded intruder she lay awake at night, listening unhappily to the destructive downpour that laid the corn flat, that beat down the mowing grass and spoiled the cut hay. She was filled with despair to think of the scented hay rotting on the ground, becoming sodden and lifeless so that it couldn't be gathered, and the cattle wouldn't have enough to eat in winter. No man could control that great sky which had such power. She prayed to God, closing her eyes, folding her hands together as she had been taught, insisting with all her puny power that the rain should cease.

"I get sick of trying," groaned William as he stared at his broken crops and spoilt corn. "I sweat and struggle and strain and it's all spiled."

"Nay, don't be down, William. We've weathered far worser nor this," said Charity.

Then the house seemed to speak to them all, to tell them that to-morrow will come, that life goes on, and that it would remain faithful to the end. They must be steadfast, and keep the chain unbroken.

But the winds were accepted as travellers arriving from far lands with baggage and messages and hope. On their backs the winds carried their sacks, puffed out into great clouds. The north wind which swept from the high ridge struck at the house's back. The house shrugged its massive shoulders and pressed close to the earth, where it was warm. The walls at the back were strong, there were only slit windows, and the cold wind passed by. Then came the south wind, blowing to the parlour and kitchen, and all the front of the little farm, filling the sheets and pillowcases hung in the orchard with warm breezes and sweet scents The house smiled softly and blinked its eyes when the south wind blew in its face, and wakened the roses and brought the swallows back, with their news of other lands. The wind changed, it backed, and the sun set in the wind's eye. Then down came the rain. The moon, too, was watched by all for the weather changes, and when she lay among the clouds on her back, it was a sure sign of rain, said Charity. The old moon lay in the new moon's arms, and Virginia, staring up from the kitchen door, saw an old woman like her grandmother up there, reclining in the golden lap of a young lovely girl. But out there, in the woods, under the sparkling skies other things were happening. Unseen ones were walking there, invisible guests were sharing the trees' shelter, not shaking the branches as they went among them, going about their private business. The house was watching them, hearing their rustling steps, waiting for them to invade and to seek their old shelter.

Early one morning Virginia was awakened to the deep silence of snow, to the strange exhilaration in the air, which swept to the house's walls, and the muffled sighs that came from the window as the flakes dropped there. She crawled to the foot of her bed and pulled the curtain. Snow was piled against the glass, and a thick pall lay over the garden and orchard. Across the yard a light flickered under the cowhouse door, and a gleam came from the wooden shutter that spanned the cobwebbed window of the beasts' place. It was the sign that her uncle and Dick were milking. Then the door opened and Dick walked to the next cowhouse where the Jersey cow was kept. He carried a lantern which sent long yellow streamers across the dazzling blue snow. He seemed like a figure from the past, hooded and tall, with crooked shadow.

She tapped at her window. "Dick. Dick," she called softly so that Emmie wouldn't wake, but he didn't hear. She crept back under the bedclothes, and covered her head except the tip of her nose, drawing her knees to her chin in ecstasy. Dick had promised

94

to take her out on his new sledge when snow came. Then sleep dropped on her eyelids, almost at once, and she was lost in dreams.

Just as suddenly she awoke again, with joy running through her veins like racing blood. She put on some clothes, and with her dress on her arm, her slippers in hand, she crept to the passage. She stayed listening in the darkness. She could hear her grandmother in the kitchen, and from her aunt's room came thumps and thuds, as drawers were opened and shut.

"Poor old Grandmother. She's always down first," thought Virginia, as she went softly down the stairs. Her heart was filled with compassion for the old woman whose hair was white as the winter snow.

Charity was on her knees sanding the hearthstone. A crackling fire newly lighted burned in the grate, and a candle flickered on the table. Over the fire hung the kettle on the ratchet, and the flames licked greedily with red tongues at the sides. They were eager to warm the ice-cold water, to taste the snow melting.

"Grandmother! Hello! Is there ice on the troughs? Is there thick ice?" demanded Virginia, pushing her head round the door and leaping into the room from the bottom stairs. She ran swiftly to kiss her grandmother, and then went to the window. The shutters were already fastened back. Uncle William saw to that and the filling of kettles when he came down for milking.

"Now then, Jinny. You're early to-day. Yes, there's ice, Dick says he had to smash it when he got the water. You get yourself dressed and don't let your uncle see you like that."

"I'm going sledging and sliding," whispered Virginia to the world in general. "It's my holiday."

Charity raised herself and dipped her cloth in the tin of powdered sand. She rubbed the wet hearth and smoothed it with her hand till it was a warm mellow richness, the colour of gold. It was an everyday ritual, this adorning of the hearthstone, making a bright earthy decoration at the altar of the flames. It might have been a primitive act of adoration with old Charity as the kneeling priestess. Virginia saw only the age-old rite, which women had performed for generations, so that the broad stone was smooth as silk with the touch of many hands.

Virginia leaned across the sink and scratched the ferny fronds of the winter's garden, grown in the night. Then, sighing with wonder at the mystery of those crystal flowers, she turned away.

"What makes the frost garden, Grandmother?" she asked.

"It's life's secret," said Charity. "It's one of the things to pleasure us, like candle flame, and running water. It's the happiness of the world, shining through, and to some folk it's nothing at all, but to me and you, it means something."

Virginia nodded. Frost crystals, starry moss, thin threads of ice on the muddy pools where the horse had left his imprint, these were happiness, better than most things because they were private and secret.

She drew a ladecan of hot water from the boiler by the fire, and washed herself. She tossed the strong-smelling rainwater over her thin arms and dabbled her fingers in the soapy suds, while she stared outside at the beauty of the yard, through the aperture she had made. It fairly took her breath away. The loveliness was beyond that of earth. A moon hung in the sky, an intimate kind of a moon, and the snow was not white but blue! Hans Andersen blue! It was the colour of the ice in the fairy book she had discovered in the kitchen drawer. That was a queer thing! Nobody knew where that book had come from. Aunt Hetty certainly was unaware of the presence of such rubbishy trash. Even Charity shook her head when Virginia had asked about it. Uncle William never spoke. He listened silently to the chatter and chuckled to himself. He had picked it up at a sale, found it in the drawer of a chest, and with his customary caution he kept his find to himself till an opportunity arose to slide it under his wife's aprons. Emmie read it from cover to cover. Charity dipped into it and smiled at the old-fashioned woodcuts. Then Virginia got it and avidly read the tales, learning them by heart. She lived for a time in that world, peopled with princesses and singing swans and ugly ducklings, of ghosts and matchgirls. She sat in the corner under the horse-collar and traces, lost in a land that was strangely enough part of the farm life. The Ugly Duckling was outside in the yard with the hens. The elder tree grew by the pigsty, the tinder-box was on the kitchen shelf, the flying trunk was the old wooden brass-studded trunk in the little chamber up the outside steps. Now the snow queen was driving along the highroad across the valley, and she was Gerda, and sometimes Richard was Kay, and sometimes Ronald Youlgrave was there.

The snow was piled on the broad flat bench at the door and deep circles showed where the milkcans had rested all night. It drifted on the flight of stone steps leading to the upper room. The slopes of the hills across the river caught the light of the rising sun, but the farm was in the valley, hidden away. Little rounded woods dividing the fields were wreathed in snowy flowered hats. The barns and stables, the walls and gates seemed endowed with mystery as if they belonged to that other world which was sometimes visible, and sometimes far away. But the old house was awake, and gazing over the steep little valley. It was secure and comfortable in its warm white dress, and little white bonnet like Charity's housecap, and it was laughing at the rising sun and having a word with the departing pale moon.

Virginia rinsed her face and dashed some cold water from the can on the floor over her eyes. It was her grandmother's injunction. The old woman attributed her good sight to this practice. To the girl it was a formula to help her to see the invisible. Now even the tiniest feather of dust shone with a new glory, the stones glanced with quick eyes, the chairs nodded, the candle flame shook its gold hair.

Pots and pans, kettles and logs of wood, all reflected the atmosphere of quietness and bliss. They seemed to rock gently in their places, on fire and shelf and floor, in time to the ticking of the clock and the minute crackles of the flames. They whispered and told their thoughts, and each one had its own peculiar personality to the girl who listened to them.

She reached on tiptoes to the shelf, and took from behind a mug an ancient toothbrush, bequeathed to her by Emmie. She scrubbed her little white teeth with an ill-tasting mixture of salt and soot that filled the mug. It was another command of her grandmother's. Salt for strength, and soot either because the chimney sweep had white teeth, or because black induced white by the law of opposites. Virginia hadn't yet found out the reason. The toothpowder cost nothing, and this was its greatest advantage in a household where every penny was saved.

Then, water dropping from her face and thin chest, she went with dancing step across the kitchen to the family towel behind the door and rubbed herself till her cheeks were like apples. Already Hetty had come downstairs, setting all awry, scolding and upsetting the peace, but she couldn't spoil the loveliness of snow.

"Now, Jinny! You've come downstairs not dressed again! Shame on you!" she cried, as she bustled about and set the table, banging the cups and slicing the bread with angry fingers.

Virginia slipped her frock over her head, and hid herself in its thick folds for a blissful moment like an ostrich. It was a hateful dress, an old one of Emmie's. She detested it because it kept something of Emmie in its touch, but it was strong and thick, and it would never wear out, they said.

"Be sharp. Make some toast, and then go upstairs and call Emmie. She ought to be down now. Look sharp, child."

So the morning began, and Virginia ran here and there at her aunt's bidding, but outside the snow beckoned and called, secretly touching her sleeve as she opened a window, even coming indoors to lure her away when Uncle William threw wide the door and came in for breakfast.

The smell of frying bacon, the hiss of the fire, the steam as the kettle boiled, and the great iron pot for the pig food was hung over the flames, the voices of the men, stamping of feet and barking of dogs filled the kitchen. The shadows of snow and frost went back to the woods. Dick came in, and threw off his cap, and Emmie ran downstairs.

"Good morning all of ye," said Charity. "Snow and frost and all, praise the Lord."

Queer snow figures seemed to peep through the window and call at the half-door.

"Now Mother. Don't ye be talking like that," Hetty frowned. "It's not proper. Trouble enough without you thanking the Lord for it."

"Hetty. Let me have my bit of fun," said Charity, smiling at her daughter-in-law.

William hung his soft hat on the post, and warmed his hands by the fire.

"Breakfast welly ready? We'm starved," said he.

"Are we going sledging?" whispered Virginia, pushing close to Dick. He didn't answer, but he gave her a knowing look and a twist of his mouth. He pulled her hair as he passed and she smiled back at him. Nobody could hurry Richard, or make him speak. Meals were silent. There was only speech when somebody asked for more.

Hetty sat at the head of the table, pouring from the great brown teapot, serving the bacon from the pan on the fire, refilling the teapot with boiling water from the kettle there. There was an enormous mound of toast, heaped against the sugar bowl and basins. They ate slowly, thoughtfully, each immersed in his own mind, planning the day. Now one held up a rind of bacon to the waiting dogs, or another soaked a hard crust in his tea, or poured the steaming liquid into a saucer and supped it noisily. The cloth was clean, the cups were bright and polished, and hands were washed before anyone came to table. It was something right and proper, not an occasion for hilarity. Job Glead, the shepherd, sat at the dresser, drinking his tea from a blue basin, wiping his shaggy little beard on his hand, munching his toast. He looked straight ahead of him, taking no notice of the family across the floor. When he had finished he arose, pushed back his stool and waited a moment, with his cap in his hand.

"I'll be coming in five minutes, Job. You go down to the fold. I'll meet you there," said William, and the old man nodded and shuffled out.

The meal was ended. Charity said Grace, and they went about their work. Emmie and Virginia washed up, Hetty disappeared upstairs, Charity went into the dairy. Richard loitered a moment. "I'll get the sledge later on, before milking to-night," said he, "if you two say nothing."

"Oh, we'll keep quiet," promised Emmie.

"You can help with turnip-chopping if you've a mind, Jinny," said Richard graciously, and she trotted after him down the yard to the barn. She tossed the mangolds into the chopper as he turned the handle, and caught the sweet morsels in the wisket.

"Can I go milking with you to-night?" she asked, and he nodded. A whole fortnight of helping on the farm, and playing in the fields and buildings stretched before her, like an eternity of bliss, and the coming of the snow was something added even to this, as if God had arranged it all for her.

But in the kitchen, after the rapturous early morning, the air was heavy and warm. On the fire steamed a pot with a piece of bacon, and Hetty blew the ash under the wood and settled the iron pot more firmly. Smoke came into the room, and swept round the hearth in grey curls like a witch's hair. There was a smell of washing and clothing, and bodily sweat, and a dog's pelt. Emmie was conscious of these, she sniffed and snorted angrily, but Virginia was deep in another land of magic, and the ill odours had no effect upon her.

Hetty wrapped a coarse brown apron round her waist and went out to shovel the snow from the doorway.

"Get the floor done, Jinny," she called. "And don't go

99

trapsing out after Richard. You stay here and help me to rid the things. Snow brings enough bother withouten you adding to it."

In the afternoon they went sledging down the steep slope of the field above the farm, swooping down the hillside almost through the little squinting window into the kitchen, but all too soon it was milking time, and Richard was called away. It was four o'clock, and watering had to be done. Virginia went to the cows, wandering about in the yard, taking the air, supping the water. She took up the switch and guided them, allowing two to drink at once, and keeping others away till it came their turn. Slowly the cows went to the icy water, stepping over the stone sills, sleepy eyed after the duskiness of the cowsheds. It was their short recreation, and they sniffed at the snow, and shivered a little, before they went back to their own stalls.

Richard went across the yard to get his pair of yokes, and Virginia finished the chaining by herself, hooking the heavy chains round the animals' necks, as they waited. Instead of returning to the cowplace, Richard went into the little houseplace. Then back he came, glancing up at the windows.

"Come here a minute when you've done after milking. I'll show you something. Keep it quiet. Don't say a word. I've something to show you," said he. Virginia nodded and glanced swiftly at her cousin. There was an air of secrecy and excitement about him, and her own face immediately reflected his eagerness. All day she had known there was something astir. Richard had been out to meet the postman. Away down the road he had gone, that morning, driving with the milkcart early to catch the man on the way. Even when they were sledging Richard had been too quiet, as if he were keeping something inside his heart. She darted into the cowhouse and chained the last cows ready for the milkers. She had to stand on the edge of the mangers to reach their necks, and as she put her arms around them she felt their warm breath and their pulsing hearts. It always gave her a queer sensation, that unknown strange life of animals, lived so close to her own, separated only by a wall, cattle drinking from the trough near the sweet drinking water, eating the grass of the fields she loved, creatures very close to her own life.

William came in, with his stool and bucket.

"Can I milk to-night?" she begged. "Can I?" He hesitated a moment, and looked down at her. She was too little but it was good to break them in young. Emmie didn't care for farmwork, she took after her mother, but Jinny was his sort.

"If you'll be a good gal," said he.

She took a small milkcan and the sturdy oak stool that hung on the wall. She had only lately learned to milk, and she had charge of two easy cows who gave their milk freely. She was proud to be one of the milkers, for Uncle William was adamant with those who came casually to try their hand. They spoilt the cows, he said, for cattle held their milk back from the harsh clumsy fingers of any strangers who pulled as if they were ringing bells.

"Stroke them," he cried. "Go gently with them, and stroke it out. Go easy and don't startle them."

Virginia's hands were scarcely big enough, although she had the art of drawing the milk freely. She hung the lantern on the wall and sat close to the cow, warm in the shelter of its side, just as her mother and grandmother had done. Soon there was no sound but the tinkle of the streams of milk in the cans and the deep homely breathing and comfortable munching of the cattle around her.

Her own heart beat pleasurably with the warmth and comfort of the cowhouse, and the thoughts of Richard's surprise, and the evening with a book by the fire. It took very little to give her pleasure, for everything was new and fresh each day. Even a stone, a cobweb glittering with dew, the act of catching water, the spurt of new milk from the cow's teat, the row of icicles hanging from the eaves, had already brought a century of happiness, compressed in a day, and there were other joys to come if she kept her mind ready for them.

When the milking was done, and the cans had been carried to the house-dairy, the doors were shut to keep out the winter wind, and all was left snug for the night. Richard went to the little old houseplace, the ancient part of the farm, and she hurried after him. Always, as soon as she put her foot over the threshold of this small house, she felt a thrill of expectancy for strangely mingled smells of apples and milk and soapsuds came to her, and many an old smell of musk and roses lingered there. It was a place of ghosts and memories, of footsteps and voices, so that all her senses were alert, as she listened and stepped softly, and held her plaid frock tightly against her legs.

Richard climbed the step-ladder to the upper chamber and she followed through the trap door into that little attic room that she loved.

From under the unused fixture bed, he brought out a box, and she held the candle, shaking and dropping the tallow with excitement.

"What do you think of this?" he asked. Together they bent over the object Richard unwrapped.

"What is it?" she whispered.

"A magic lantern. I got it half price. A good 'un."

"Oh, Dick. Like that one we saw at the Church Meeting? That's what I've wanted to see all my life," she cried, her eyes shining like stars, and the candle swaling so that Dick had to snatch it from her.

Together they set up the lantern and examined the black japanned parts. They turned up the little wick in the lamp and filled the receptacle with oil from the barrel in the chamber down the stairs. They could hear people walking across the yard, but they had shut the door and not a chink of light showed. Then Richard struck a match and they watched the little yellow flame waver. A good rich smell of burning metal filled the room, and smoke curled up.

"It's a real good 'un," said Richard again, as he placed the lamp on the floor, and fitted the lamp glass, and lantern complete. "It's first class."

"Where did you get the money from?" asked Virginia.

"Those savings," he confessed, carelessly.

"Oh Dick! So you're not going to run away to sea?"

He didn't answer. He took up the cardboard box and held up a slip of glass to the light.

"See? There's a whole collection of slides with it, places in foreign parts, and sets of animals, and some comics."

Dazzled they looked at them. The crudely painted little circles were like glimpses into fairyland to the girl. Six magical pictures were on each strip. There were scenes from Italy, from Japan, pictures of elephants and a tiger hunt, of a storm at sea, of London.

"Twelve sets of pictures included," said Richard, proudly reading the titles, and holding them in front of the candle flame. "In the lantern they look real you know. We'll have a show of them. Nobody round here has a magic lantern."

"Oh where? Where can we have it? In the kitchen?" asked Virginia.

"Yes, we'll put a sheet across the wall. I'll give my mother and dad a surprise, and gran will open her eyes! Then maybe we can do another show in the barn and ask the neighbours in to see it."

Virginia leapt up with excitement, and the swing of her pinafore blew out the light.

"See what you've done, careless," cried Dick crossly. "You're too impatient, Jinny. You should keep calm like me." He struck a match but they could hear William shouting for them.

"Hide it away. Pack it up carefully," said Dick and he ran down the ladder and left her in the tiny room. The little lantern was hot to her fingers, the smell of it was rapturous, and the pictures seemed to be there in the air. She thought she heard laughter of others who had peeped over her shoulder. She put the slides into the grooves, and slipped the lantern back in the box. Then she crept carefully downstairs, step by step, backwards, feeling her way in some trepidation for rats and shadows and dim laughter. She felt honoured and grateful for the secret. Her face was flushed with excitement as she stumbled through the snow to the house door. She had been in another world, of fairy-tale come true.

The little attic room she had left behind would treasure the secret. Even now, as she turned and looked back she felt sure that others were taking the lantern from its box and peering at the slides. Dim figures of children were playing up there, with small inquisitive fingers touching the glass plates, questioning one another. They wanted no candle to see, they had the light of the snow and the stars to aid them.

After tea there was the washing up to be done. Hetty was in a bad temper, snow always angered her, and Virginia's escape to the cowhouses and milking was an affront. William was silent, he retired into himself, and let Hetty blather. Dick had gone off to the station with the evening's milk, and Virginia hugged the secret to herself.

She went to the sink with Hetty's scoldings sounding in her ears. Ungrateful girl! Hiding away when there was work to be done! She wanted to stop her ears with her fingers, but that would have meant a blow. Hetty's hands sometimes itched to strike her.

She began to wash up. There was comfort and kindness in the common things she had known intimately all her life, and Hetty's words had no power over her when she touched them. She fetched a ladecan of hot water from the boiler tap over the hearthstone, taking care not to spill a drop on the sanded hearth, which Charity's hands had smoothed that morning which seemed a hundred years ago. The smell of the water, aromatic of the woods and leaves, with even a few leaves lying in it from last year, carried her off to those enchanting woods whence the water had come. Steam rose from the long-handled can and weaved above her head like the genie in the ragged fairy book. She could see a goblin face bearded and grotesque laughing at her. The candle on the leaden windowsill shook in the draught and its reflection in the glass wagged too. The two flames bowed and curtseyed to the invisible wind that eddied under the door and through the outside shutter. The window with its background of shutter reflected the whole room, and the two candles, reflection and reality, sent gleams of light upon the lead sill and the china dishes and cups, so that the pots smiled and nodded through the encircling wreaths of steam.

Virginia washed each cup carefully, and each thing spoke to her in its own fascinating manner. The brown-bellied teapot was a fat old woman, an ancient woman, almost it might have been a great-grandmother of a gipsy; the cups were charming young ladies going to church to be baptized under the rainwater tap; the saucers were young men engaged to the aforesaid young ladies, and the spoons, ah, they were lots of children chattering and tinkling and wagging their little silver tongues. Plates were middle-aged folk, in different clothes, for the plates were odd, some painted with flowers, some with gold edges, some with lustre leaves on their petticoats, and they were talking of domestic troubles and pains and aches in their bodies. Pains, yes, every crack was a hurtful pain, and every chip was a small wound. Virginia washed up very slowly lest she should hurt any of the small, lively, helpless, dependable family of pots and pans and dishes. She whispered below her breath to them, she wiped them lovingly, and admired their gold bands and blue flowers and ships and clouds and all the ornamentation that found itself on one and another.

And all the time the gay little candle mopped and mowed and the rainwater tap tinkled on the stone sink, and the water splashed round the tin bowl, and Hetty talked and grumbled, but no word of it reached Virginia's enchanted ears. For upstairs in the little attic in the oldest part of the house, was a magic lantern, and Dick had shown it to her first.

Chapter 9

They went to the barn the next morning to consider the possibilities of that great old chamber. The rough walls were hung with scythes and ancient pieces of harness, mildewed, grey with age. Flails and riddles and rusty gear swung on the pegs, things that might come in useful some day, and indeed they were often pressed into service. Under the back wall were the great cornbins, enormous wooden receptacles with lids so heavy Virginia could not lift them.

"They would make the best seats, if we had the little steps for people to climb up," said she, stroking the dusty whitened sides and sniffing the smell. Ah, the smell of corn and meal was ravishing to her heart! Unconsciously she sniffed it up and stored it for ever.

"We'd have the sheet across the barn end, over there," said Dick. They looked up at the cobwebbed rafters, upholding the high roof. There was no way of concealing that dark expanse of beams and birds'-nests and dim mystery of bit-bats and owls.

"We could carry all the chairs inside here, and the forms we let out for the school treats, and the planks across the tree stumps for some if we hadn't enow," added Richard, seeing the barn as a small theatre, like the one he had visited with his father in the market town.

"And we'll make programmes," said Virginia, leaping on the chopping block. "All different with texts painted on them."

"Silly kid. We don't want that," Richard spoke scornfully, but Virginia refused to be snubbed.

"Won't the old barn love it!" she cried, holding out her arms to embrace the building.

"The barn?" he echoed so loudly that the barn also gave a faint echo from its stone walls.

"It won't have seen such a sight before," said Virginia. "It's never seen a magic lantern show."

"It's seen many a sight, I'll bet, Virginia. Gran says they used to have meetings here. Cruel sights too I reckon. Why once on a time a man was killed in this barn. There was a fight or something."

"Oh Dick!" she cried, shivering and drawing close to him. "Oh Dick. You said no once when I asked you."

"It wasn't in your little end barn, but in here, so I spoke the truth. Besides it was many a year ago. Over a hundred, nay two hundred years ago. They had prayers for he, lest the ghost should harnt the place, and so it was all right and proper."

"Ghost, did you say?" faltered Virginia, turning pale.

"It's all right. He was buried in churchyard, and all tidied up. You're a big girl, and you shouldn't ever be scared of old stories. Suppose you lived where a battle had been fought! Why, everywhere there's some tale if we but knew it."

"If we but knew it," she murmured.

They walked slowly across the barn and regarded the flight of steps that led to a haychamber over the stable next door. The steps were of blocks of stone, worn to a deep hollow by the feet that had gone up and down carrying hay, and so smooth that the children had spent many hours flopping down them on their bottoms.

"We could set up the magic lantern on these stairs," said Richard. "Then we get the right height for the cloth on that far wall. We could cover up the scythes and flails, and make it more homelike. And there would have to be a fire in the fireplace yonder, where we cook the pig potatoes. And we should all have to sit in the dark, you know."

"In the dark? In here?" asked Virginia, her eyes wide with sudden fright.

"Of course. Don't tell me you're frightened, Jinny Dale, after all I've done for you."

"No. I'm not. I don't care a snap," Virginia hastened to assure him, but she wished he hadn't told her the tale till later.

They had a trial performance in the kitchen. William and Hetty were as pleased and excited as children. Charity nodded her head and recalled the harvest homes and revival meetings they had once held in the great barn. They had all been to the village to see Holman Hunt's "The Light of the World" and other sacred pictures shown in the church when a travelling lantern came that way.

A screen was placed in front of the fire, and the lamp was extinguished and everybody stumbled over chairs and buckets in the darkness.

"This way! Fix it up like this," cried William, seizing Charity's

106

linen sheet, and they strung it to the hooks where the Christmas hams hung for curing. The magic lantern was fixed on a stool, placed on the table, and raised higher by the volume of Shakespeare. The little lamp was lighted, and the now familiar smell of burning lacquer filled the room. The two girls fell into the sheet, and the stool perilously rocked. Dick seized them both and boxed their ears.

"Sit still, won't you?" he shouted. "You'll go and break my lantern. Sit you both on the settle and don't move away or I'll lam you."

"He's hit me," choked Emmie, furiously angry. "Mother. Our Dick's hit me."

Virginia nursed her ear in astonishment and pain. It wasn't like Dick to strike people. Subdued they stood in the confused rattle of chairs and milkcans, Hetty scolding and Charity soothing, all talking at once. When the circle of light came on the screen and a picture of Vesuvius upside down appeared in bright colours, and the little thin spire of smoke from the lantern wavered against the low ceiling, they forgot their indignation and chattered like magpies.

"You come and hand me the slides, Jinny, and don't forget to hold them upside down," called Dick, and the girl edged her way to him and climbed on the table.

"I'm sorry," he whispered, and her heart was warm and happy again.

Every scene was greeted with clappings and cries of excitement by the little packed audience. There was the thick smell of hot metal, and paraffin, and smoke. Black curls wavered spirally over the ceiling, a circle of light stayed there, and a pencil of flame leaped from behind the firescreen as even the chimneypiece tried to see what was happening.

Charity and William decided that it was safe to have it in the barn, for it hadn't exploded, and it was too wonderful to keep to themselves. It was nearly as good as the fine lantern at the church meeting.

"We ought to charge something," said Richard. "Let's have it in aid of something or other."

"In aid of ourselves," laughed Hetty grimly. "We want helping."

"Nay. A foreign mission," said Charity firmly. "We'll open with a hymn, with 'Greenland's Icy Mountains', and after the show we'll have a collection, and let them give what they like, a few pence."

"They are real good pictures. They're better than those I saw at the Band of Hope," said Hetty. "I'll buy you an extra set of slides, Dick, out of my butter money."

"It's a brave sight," added Charity, "to see all these fine views of foreign parts, and the sea in a storm and that shipwreck, and rescue. I've enjoyed myself as much as going to the theayter, where I only went once and comed out in ten minutes."

They all laughed, for Charity's visit to the theatre was a tale often told, her indignation and scandal at the things she saw and heard. She was old-fashioned, they said, and the little old bowed figure drew her shawl more tightly across her bosom and the blue eyes sparkled in the flashing glimpses from the shaded fire.

Virginia's heart beat high with pleasure. Her crooked little smile of joy stayed on her face, she was at a pinnacle of bliss. The room was eager and expectant for the painted show, it silently joined in the laughter. Everything was looking and peering at that coloured wavering circle of light, the dresser plates leaned forward, and laughed with their wide flat faces, the clock ticked with a different sound, it almost forgot to tick sometimes, and hesitated, lingering between the seconds, spinning them out to a small eternity. Shadows came hustling from the walls, called forth by the lantern light, and staying to see the new invention of another century. They whispered in friendship, they touched the grandmother's hand and laughed into her ear, and they slipped their fingers over Virginia's as she held the slides, and gently tugged at Dick's rough hair.

"You saved up and bought it," William kept repeating, and Dick nodded proudly. He didn't mention the high hopes of foreign travel he had given up.

Then Charity lighted a candle at the fire, the screens were removed, and the little hot lantern was wiped and put away in safety with the slides on the pantry bench. Outside the snow came dancing down in great flakes, eddying one way, then caught by a breath of wind and swaying to the barns. The cattle moved softly in the cowhouses, lifting a foot, and settling themselves comfortably in their stalls. The warmth and happiness of the house seemed to spread to them, carried along the roof, passed through the stones to their bodies. William went out with a lantern to see that all was safe for the night. He was pleasurably excited, and smiling to himself, as he flashed his light on the shut doors, and went into the stable for a moment. The smell of snow always had a queer intoxicating effect upon him, although he hated the discomfort and difficulties that came with it. That night it seemed as if the house spoke to him too. He was possessed with love for those walls and buildings, out there in the snow, the trees shaggy with frost crystals, the cobbles soft as velvet under his feet. He had an intimation of eternity from the serene look of the house as it stared down at him, knowing him, and accepting him.

Upstairs there was a dancing light on a window blind, and two shadows passed. The girls were laughing and planning the lantern show, friends again, as they plaited their hair, forgetful of their quarrels. Their candle flickered against the window and then the curtain was drawn across. Other lights appeared, as Charity went upstairs to bed, and old Job went to his chamber. William picked up his lantern and went back to the house.

He mentioned the lantern show to his neighbours when he saw them in the village. Hetty went to the shop with her basket and dropped a few invitations on the way. Emmie asked her friends to come, girls who were working in shops, or post office. Dick invited a few boys, of his own age. They swept the barn and cleared the floor, and brushed the rough-hewn stone walls with a besom. It was a vast airy chamber, and when they had decked the walls with branches of holly and draped festoons of ivy from the wooden pegs, and round the embrasures with their candles ready, it made a fine hall. Charity smiled to herself, remembering it was the barn where she had once decided to keep a school, where she was to be the all-wise, all-beautiful Miss Woodiwiss.

William brought wooden hoops, put aside from old casks, for many a year, and Hetty and Emmie made fringes of coloured paper, twined round the narrow rims, fluttering red and yellow streamers. These were nailed on the walls, with lanterns hung inside them. They brought the wooden benches from the back kitchen, that original Shepherd's cottage, stored there for the church meetings and treats. Each was made from a trimmed log of oak, with four short legs splaying outward, and seats smooth with generations of sitters, and carved with initials and dates. There were no backs, nor would anybody miss such a luxury. Six or eight people could sit on a form and there would be no sag in its stout strong body.

They filled sacks with sheep's-wool, and put them for the children at the front. There were a few chairs for the aged and anyone of importance who might appear. The largest linen sheet, hand-woven by Charity's mother, was stretched against the wall, hiding the ancient tools that they didn't trouble to take down. Opposite, on the flight of stone stairs they put the magic lantern. Candles were stuck on the walls, on the rough protruding stones which made natural ledges, and a fire was lighted in the hearth.

In the semi-darkness when the doors were shut the room looked like a cave, with tiny points of light hanging on the walls like glow-worms, perched there for some gnomes' entertainment. No need to dowse those lights, they would not interfere. The rafters were in darkness, but high up there wings fluttered un-easily, and movements and rustles were heard, and murmurs and thin delicate song. The barn came alive and remembered other days.

In the farm kitchen the women were busy with the refresh-ments. Cakes and pasties and home-made wines, mincepies and iced buns and great quartern loaves of fruit bread. The missionary meeting was becoming a party.

"We'll put the missionary box at the door, and pass it round," suggested Charity. "We shall get quite a lot maybe when the men put their hands in their pockets."

The neighbours began to arrive soon after milking time, and they sat round the farm kitchen and in the parlour till there was scarcely room to move. Carts came up the yard and men and women got stiffly down and shook themselves and stamped their feet. Children ran across the yard, in their thick clumsy boots and peeped through the doors at cows and horses and calves. They were ushered into the barn, after they had had their hot tea and cakes, for already the stars were out.

They sang "From Greenland's Icy Mountains" and then they spread out their skirts, and sat on the bare forms. The word of the hymn soared in the barn, and awakened the old songs that slumbered there, so that there was a continuous vibration, and beat of music in the air, which continued long after the audience had settled itself on the oak forms and the sacks of sheeps'-wool. The essence of the past was squeezed out among them. Many a song was there, plaintive and gay, coming out of the layers of time, dropping softly from the roof beams, swelling up from the stones, voices long forgotten sang their country songs, cadences came drifting there for those who had ears for their melodies. The sheep-shearing songs, the harvest songs, the hymns of old women working with their hands in the shadows, and ballads of love sung by the aching forgotten ones.

Out of the far distant past came a treble voice of silver, singing "Greensleeves was all my joy", and a rough hearty ghost voice, singing "The Farmer's Boy", and the ballad of the Derby Ram. Thin whistling piping voices, shrill as the wind in the attic sang, "Green Gravel, Green Gravel the Grass is so Green", and one voice was like that of Charity herself when she was a child with her brothers and sisters in this same barn.

The music intermingled with a soft sighing like the sobbing of the wind, every tune was there, but the airs were tangled like the webs of faded silks in the parlour drawer where Charity kept her embroideries. Like a rainbow skein they hung there, this music of the past. Sometimes a whistle flung its notes higher than the others, perhaps a human whistle, perhaps the wind's own voice calling, "Whistle and I'll come to you my lad." A fiddle brought out a warmer note, a flute played a trill. Charity heard them, and Virginia listened and picked out scraps from the coloured tangle, carrying away fragments of tunes in her mind, but the audience was only vaguely conscious of wind music, wailing through the roof beams, swaling the candles.

Dick put the slides through the lantern, and Virginia and Emmie helped him, and this time there were no mistakes. Everything went well, with the little brightly coloured pictures shining like life on the white sheet. Draughts swayed the sheet, and billowed it as the wind cried round the barn. The circle of light wavered, and the lantern flickered, but the men and women expected such things. It was a treat to them, a farm party such as they hadn't had for many a year, and they clapped each new scene as if Richard had invented the magic lantern himself. They accepted everything with gratitude. The presence of dust and meal, the smell of clothes and humanity and paraffin, the rustles of mice, the snow puddles brought in by wet boots, the cold draughts, were not noticed. They knew nothing of fine entertainment, they enjoyed the simplest amusements, and the excitement of coming out at night on a snowy road, and staring at their neighbours' kitchen, and parlour, at Charity's home, and the barn all decked out so grandly. It was something to remember, and they enjoyed every moment. High in the roof there were rustles and murmurs. The barn was enjoying itself once more, for living chattering company was there and another experience was written in the barn's history which future generations could draw upon if they loved the sky and the earth and were aware of the unity between themselves and it. Then, in that future time, Charity and Hetty, Virginia and Richard, William and all the company of friends and neighbours, farmers, shopkeepers, labourers, ordinary people, would be the forgotten ones, but they would live and share their lives.

Charity sat in a corner, on her small low-backed chair. On her knees she held the collection box. She wore her Sunday dress, and her white cap as usual, but a thick shawl draped her shoulders. She watched the faces of the people lighted up by the lantern, and nodded and smiled when she caught anybody's glance, but there seemed to be many more folk than she knew sitting there. There was a crowd, squeezing among the guests, moving sometimes, dim people, hardly discernible, in smocks and leather coats, and rough sacks over their shoulders, and strange boots on their feet. Their faces were laughing, their eyes wrinkled up with mirth; they were brown-faced, weather-beaten folk like her own people, but unknown to her. Everywhere they crowded, jostling on the steps around the lantern, although Richard took no notice of them, moving like mists through the villagers, yet never disturbing the sitting people. Charity caught her breath. She put out a hand to stay one of them, but her fingers grasped nothing.

"Who is it?" she asked softly, but the shadow didn't reply. It was an old woman who stood close to her, staring across the room, and Charity's eyes followed the gaze. For an instant the magic lantern pictures faded, the bright crude colours drifted like smoke, the circle of white light was non-existent, but the sheet was there. On it were black shadows, animals and grotesque people. It was a shadow show those folk of long ago were watching in the barn. Charity saw the dense black shadows come and go, a swan, a donkey with long ears, a witch woman, a nun, all nodding and moving and producing laughter in the audience. The shadow-maker stood there, by the screen, with his arms stretched out, and his hands making the pictures. The country folk of another century were enjoying the fun, clapping their hands, and wagging their heads in silent laughter. Then the vision faded, the circle of light shone out with its bright lantern

112

pictures, and there was Richard putting in a fresh slide and making his little speech.

"This, Ladies and Gentlemen, is one of the Pyramids of Egypt. No, it's the Leaning Tower of Pisa. Notice it isn't straight, but it doesn't fall down, because it was built that way." Then he muttered, "Emmie. You've given me the wrong one. Where's the Pyramid one?"

"Nay, it looks as if it had had a drop," remarked old Job, and others joined in with laughter and jokes about the poor Leaning Tower. The laughter seemed to crackle round the barn, like sticks breaking, it soared round and flew up to the great beams, and again Charity heard the laughter of the people at the Shadow Show, and saw them once more.

"The barn is enjoying itself to-night," remarked William. "It's fair echoing up there."

"Yes," said Charity. "It's seeing a lot we can't all remember," and little Virginia came close from the woolsack and whispered, "I saw some shadow pictures on the screen, Gran."

"Yes. The barn is remembering other days, I'll be bound," said Charity again, and she drew the girl down to sit near her.

"Where can I sit?" asked Virginia, looking at the dark floor.

"Why, sit on your thumb," whispered Charity, and she patted her lap. "Come here, my chucky. Have you enjoyed yourself?"

"Yes, Gran. I saw many things, all at once, beside the lantern show."

"Well. Well. It's a big old place, and there's people moving about and shadows coming on the screen and a lot of things. Sit still by me, Jinny, and we'll watch together."

The vision changed, more people came thronging into the barn, women with white neckerchiefs and white aprons, as had the others, but their faces were solemn, their heads were covered, their full pleated dresses were thicker even than Charity's own. Their menfolk came in from the fields, carrying bill-hook, and sickle, and rope and long-stailed fork. They knelt down on the floor of the haystrewn barn and prayed. Their heads were bowed to the earth. Then they arose and stood facing the end of the barn, where the sheet hung. There on a cornbin stood a preacher, with black gown and little white bands at his neck, and long curling hair. His words came musically through the air. "In my Father's House are many mansions." His bright eyes stared straight into Charity's, he was speaking to her, he saw her in the future crouched on her low chair, a shadow among the realities of his own time. Then they faded away, they drifted back into their own dimensions, and Dick was standing on the steps with his magic lantern, and Emmie holding up the slides, but Virginia was watching her, she too had seen into the past.

With an effort Charity came back to the present. Somebody had spoken to her, and she could hardly answer. She couldn't drag herself away from the shadowy world.

The magic-lantern show was finished, people were rising, the stable lantern and the old horn lantern were brought out from their corners, and the forms were pushed back. Charity stood with her little missionary box held out by the door.

"It's been a grand show, Mrs. Dale."

"Yes. In my Father's House are many mansions. We shall see lantern shows maybe up there when we go," said Charity.

"Nay, Mrs. Dale. I doubt it. It will be more solemn than that," said Mrs. Drake. "But you never ought to sit out here in this draughty old barn at your age."

"I feel a bit dazed-like, watching the lantern pictures," explained Charity. "If you will excuse me I shall go to bed, and it's time Virginia was in bed too. Good night all. I hope you have enjoyed yourselves."

"Good night. Good night," they called, and Charity went across the yard, leaning on Virginia's slight shoulder.

"I'm getting old, Jinny," said she. "I forget things. I don't know present from past sometimes, but you are young. You must remember this night. You've seen how it is with those the house accepts as its own. It lets you share its life, but it wants something in exchange. It wants devotion and deep love, stronger love than human love. It wants something eternal from you. Never be ashamed of your home, Jinny. Always treat it well, for it has pride, and grandeur hidden in it."

Virginia stared up at the house. She didn't understand, but she felt the warm hand of her grandmother, and she saw the beloved house waiting there, in the snow, with all its doors, firelight coming from the kitchen, a glimmer from the parlour and all the twinkling lights in the barn where people were already lighting their lanterns, ready to go home.

Yes, everybody who had lived there had given something to the house, and the little lantern show with its gaiety and colour had gone into the store of its heart. They passed the dark doorway of the small original farmhouse, and went towards the kitchen, where the firelight flooded the yard.

Chapter 10

War against the Boers was going on. Shadows moved about the house, and Charity lay awake at nights, trying to bring peace to the world. There had been wars before that only the house remembered. It knew of the Napoleonic war when Charity's father had been on guard at the bonfire on the hill, and one of his brothers had enlisted and been killed. There was deep sorrow at the farm then. It remembered the Civil wars, and persecutions and griefs for centuries, and it only wanted peace and love and kindliness. Downstairs the clock ticked on, and the house listened. The milking had to be done, and life went on as usual.

Charity remembered the Crimean War, and she spoke of it as if it had been the other day. A newspaper print of Florence Nightingale in the hospital at Scutari with a lamp in her hand hung in the parlour. It was framed in a narrow black frame, very quiet and sombre. The house felt very close to the Crimean War, as if it had had a part in it. It spoke too of the Spanish War, and the defeat of the Armada, as if it had been last week. That was partly because the Queen of Scotland had spent many years imprisoned in the neighbourhood, and pedlars and sheepshearers and raddle-men and tinkers had brought news of the queen to the farm, and the womenfolk had ridden across the hills to try to get a peek at her Majesty's beautiful face. The house had been stirred by tales of escape and treason, and Anthony Babington's trial. It had wept for the young man, whom it knew very well, and his brothers and his newly-wed wife. There had been tales told for many a year in the kitchen, of these neighbours who were part of the life of house and countryside. That had been a tragical time, and the house remembered, and Charity could tell many of the tales which had been handed down to her. There was the Forty-Five, too, the Jacobite rebellion, when once more hearts had been stirred and rumours spread as the soldiers marched along the high road across the hills with Prince Charlie at their head. At the farm they were not Jacobites, they had waited anxiously, along with many others, and seen the ill-fated army retreat. So the house recalled other wars, and told tales of the past, but faint shadows came out and spoke of wars to come which would make all these happenings pale as moonlight.

One day Ronnie Youlgrave walked up to the farm to say good-bye. He was only a boy, but he had given the wrong age. He was going to find the adventure he had read about. He was careless and excited, talking all the time of riding and shooting. He sat in the kitchen, and they all crowded round admiringly. Hetty opened a bottle of cowslip wine, and poured out glasses for them to wish him luck.

William listened to his talk and Richard envied him his chance. Virginia stared at him, he seemed a stranger, a man suddenly in a flash. She never spoke, and he hardly glanced at her as he told his plans. She was sick at heart, but proud of him. Then he rose. He spoke casually, making jokes. She was only a girl of no importance.

"I must be off, Mrs. Dale and Mrs. William. I must say good-bye. See you when I've made my fortune," said he, holding out his hand. He shook hands round the room, and when it was Virginia's turn he chucked her under the chin, as if she were a child.

"Good-bye, Jinny. Take care of yourself."

"Good-bye, Ronnie," she replied, half choking with sorrow and frustration. He would never know how much she liked him. She stood there in her flowered cotton frock, very young and solemn. Then she sidled away and dashed up to her bedroom. He was walking down the yard, through the gate and along the field path. She dashed after him, her long legs flying, her dress above her knees.

"Ronnie. Here, take this," she panted. He looked at her crooked little red mouth, and her dark blue eyes. He took the flat pincushion with safety pins and needles stuck into it. It was the size of a crown piece, and in the centre was the letter R in fine Turkey red cotton.

"Did you make it for me?" he asked surprised.

She nodded. He suddenly dived forward and kissed her lips. Then whistling he went off. She never saw him again. She stooped to remove the dandelion entangled in her bootlace.

When she stood up the sky was darker. Slowly she went back up the drive. She had lost someone, and life was different. He was her first love, and he had never known. Only that moment was she aware of it. Soon she would be leaving school and she had many unsatisfied desires. Richard and Emmie had rejoiced when they left, but Virginia longed for books and more learning, for beauty and music and something else, she knew not what it was. Truth, beauty, the meaning of the world. There was a gap in the clouds, silver white edges and turquoise blue inside like a locket. She gazed up at it, and lifted herself there, and she seemed to feel the aspirations of all those who had once lived there. She had felt happy when Ronnie was near, even when she didn't see him for weeks, and now she was alone. Dick was reserved and silent with her. He seemed to have lost the gaiety of youth and to be weighed down by the cares of the farm and land.

"We sweat and struggle and strive," said he, "and for what? Nothing happens. The farm takes it all. It takes everything, and we never have a penny to spare."

"We share it," said Charity, quickly taking the house's part. "Shepherd's Fields doesn't keep and not give back. It gives us plenty. We get a living, and we can just manage. Perhaps next year it'll be better."

There had been trouble at the farm that year, loss of stock, and the bankruptcy of a neighbour who owed William money. In November William went to the hiring fair in the little market town at the top of the hill beyond the village. He walked through the market square and talked to the farm men with their straws in their caps, or with their whips, each denoting his trade. It was one of the last places to have the hiring fair, and people came from many villages to look over the strolling men, to bid for them and make their offers to the likely ones of good wages. William was after a new cowman, for the old helper, Job, had gone to hospital with a poisoned finger that had turned badly. He would maybe lose his arm. It was a sorry business and William felt depressed and his usually cheery smile deserted him. He wished Richard had come with him. The farm men were fewer, owing to the war, they were snapped up at once, and William went against his judgment. He came back with a new man, ungainly and ill-favoured. Sam Wheeler was a strange fellow, very ugly, with backward glancing eyes, and twitching fingers.

He wanted only a small wage, and he was a glutton for work. His strength was prodigious, William could see that at a glance, and he was not one of those talkative chaps, indeed he was too quiet. He could hardly articulate his words.

"Where did you get that man from?" asked Grandmother Charity. "Why did you hire him? There's something odd about him."

"I don't like his looks," said Hetty with distaste.

"Nonsense. Because a man's ill-favoured, you would send him away. I've had trouble enough. This one wanted but a low wage, and he's steady. He doesn't drink nor smoke. He's got a good character from his last place too."

"Then why did he leave?" asked Hetty.

"Some trouble or other at home. They wanted him to stop but he wouldna. He can plough and reap and mow and milk. What more do you want?"

Charity wasn't satisfied, but she rebuked herself for unjust suspicions. She watched the man from her corner, and saw nothing amiss. Hetty treated him well, and piled food on his plate. He seemed to be grateful and decent enough, only sometimes there was a strange look in his eyes. Then he neither heard nor moved, he was transfixed in some queer mood.

William dare not tell them that Sam Wheeler's brother had been hanged for murder. The tale of the murder was well known. Everybody had seen pictures of the cottage and buildings. Sam Wheeler had had nothing to do with it, but he changed his name and address and left his home village. It was by the merest chance William had discovered the truth. He was unperturbed, for he was sorry for the man who hadn't done any harm, and he wouldn't turn him away on account of another's guilt. Charity would have kept him, but Hetty would have screamed and scolded with fright, so William kept the secret. He hoped the man would settle down and forget his unhappiness.

Sam Wheeler was a good milker, he went quietly and methodically from one cow to another. He had the sure touch of a natural farmhand. The horses would let him do anything, the sheep were undisturbed when he walked among them. His step was lithe and soft as a cat's, as he strode along, with his eyes glancing about. There was nothing wrong with Sam except that he was simple in his ways, unable to talk clearly. His table manners were uncouth, but nobody need watch him when he ate his meals at the sidetable by the door.

"He's only a bit wanting," explained William, and they all accepted the fact as quite natural. It was well known that now and then a softie was born in a large family, one of those fools who have no bright wits to guide them. It happened to the rich as well as the poor, and the simple one was the best loved. Virginia had a tender heart for softies. Young Boy Sallet who went to the village school was a bit daft. He couldn't do his sums or read from books. He stumbled in his talk, stuttered when folk spoke suddenly to him. He was a gentle creature, birds and beasts trusted him, and Virginia often walked along the lane at Boy Sallet's side, doing the talking for both, while the lad gazed with silent wonder and adoration at her. Sam Wheeler's ugliness repelled the girl and she avoided him, but after a time he became part of the farm. He fitted in with a certain crooked aspect of it. He was like a queer distorted shadow coming from the barns, with buckets held slantwise, and towsled head on one side. He picked up the calf when it was sickly and carried it to a warm corner. He carried great sacks of meal up the steps to the chamber without troubling to use the grain-elevator. The loads of hay he bore on his back were enormous, so that he looked like a walking stack. William was filled with wonder at the man's power of endurance, but Charity was faintly uneasy. She watched him from her chimney corner. He never seemed aware of her or of anyone else. He lived a life alone, struggling against queer impulses, fighting back the black cloud which came over his brain. When he was with the animals he was safe. They soothed him and turned away the evil thing which haunted him. Gradually he was accepted, the house seemed to be aware of him, it was surely helping him, and he knew it. His black fogs of darkness and death became less frequent, his eyes lost their dull panic, an intelligence came into them, a sanity. But he was always a little strange, losing himself as he listened.

"What art listening to?" asked Charity suddenly one day.

"Them voices," said he.

"What do they say?" asked Charity and her own tones were soft and gentle as she watched him.

"Dunnot be afeared," said Sam Wheeler.

"Well, Sam. Dunnut ye," said Charity smiling, and the first grim wavering smile came upon his wide ugly mouth making him akin to some man out of the Middle Ages, a lost wanderer from another time. He stood in the shadow of the stable door, uncouth and crooked as the stone figure carved high on the front of the wall. There was a queer resemblance between them, Charity noticed it for the first time,—the tiny ill-balanced grotesque, carved centuries ago by some country mason, and this ill-favoured man. Perhaps the little stone figure was a cowman or a labourer renowned for his ugliness too. So Sam lurched about the yard, working always, never wanting to rest, unable to read or write, clumsy but capable with his hands, his wits wandering in another world than this.

The kitchen door always stood wide open to the yard and midden and the white lilies. The smell of manure and of lilies came into the hot room, mingled as each strove to outdo the other. The square of sky was deep blue, and the sound of the river across the field came like an intimate warbling song, telling of summer and of days to come, of days far ahead, a hundred years, two hundred, of days long past. Virginia tossed her cold soapy hand-water from the washing bowl through the doorway upon the lily roots. The glistening white flowers seemed to thrive on it. Manure from the stable, soapsuds from washing, fed the lilies and they grew into celestial flowers blooming in heaven's fields. Across the yard ran a little silvery streamlet, running away from the water troughs, hurrying across the stones to the fields, where it paddled along the gentle slope to join the brook and then to enter the river. Charity carried her dishwater there, Hetty strained her vegetables over it, and away it ran. In a minute all was clear again, fresh white water from out of the earth.

It was here that Sam often stood, staring at the little crystal stream, turning to look at the lilies, and once even venturing to touch them with his great brown-as-earth finger. Virginia had seen him, and she nodded to him in a friendly way. He regarded her as if he had realized her presence for the first time. He turned from the lilies to the girl, as she stood in the doorway in her white frock freshly laundered and starched to go to church. He stared and pointed to her and the flowers and said something unintelligible. Then he backed away to the shadows.

"What is it, Sam?" asked Virginia kindly.

"Don't 'ee be afeared, Miss," mumbled Sam in a harsh whisper, squinting sideways.

"I'm not," laughed Virginia, a little nervously. "What is there to be afraid of?"

"There's a smell of rain," said Sam, veering like the weathercock, and lurching away. She stood there waiting for Emmie to go to church with her. She lifted her face and stared at the blessed blue of the sky. Up there the rain was hidden away, silver streaks across the blue and animals and Sam knew of it. How did he know of her own secret fears? She stooped and picked up a little cornered stone and the touch of it gave her courage. Only by keeping close to the earth could she keep her courage shining bright. She had as many fears as Sam, she knew.

A sharp little wind blew across. It would keep the rain up there, it would toss it in the upper air for the pleasure of it, as she tossed a ball. Then it would be loosed on the fields, and the earth would sup it greedily. Cows were moving in the tree-shadows in the fields over the hedge, slowly meandering down to the river's edge. Always there was that sound of water—from the undying spring that flowed unceasingly into the troughs with a high silvery note, that was the violin in the water's orchestra, from the brook whispering noisily in the field, from the brawling, talking, multitudinous waters of the river in its broken rocky bed. The sun caught the flecked waves of it, the sun flashed from the fronds of the bracken on the opposite hill, it dropped upon the white lilies, and upon the manure heap in equal beauty. The old house caught the flash, and sent an answer back through space, a gesture of recognition, and Virginia, standing there, saw it.

She was now a little head monitor. She got to school first in the morning, and unlocked the door of the schoolhouse. As she turned the key she always leaned back to say good-bye and good morning to the landscape behind her. Blue were the hills, mysterious in their early mists, blue green were the cold fields, and brown the pastures and ploughland, but snow white was the little dusty road creeping away out of sight higher and higher to the hills. The trees were pointing to sky, hands upheld, and they gave her a token every day, something different to hold. Every day she went back in time, by some subtle influence given off by God knows what, for she couldn't evoke it, it came of itself. A smell of dust, the look of a stone, the glance of a common chair waiting patiently, the touch of sunshine or rain, the swing of a branch, and out of time came a moment of time-lessness like a kiss on her lips. So she waited at the doorway by the big rusty iron studded boys' door, and looked around. She let her eyes slide over the world and rest on the little housetops of the village, and then soar to the crack in two hills. In between lay Shepherd's Fields, where her heart was, so she turned and said good-bye and good morning to it as she entered the dusky schoolroom.

"Pray God send us a drop of rain. Just a drop," she would whisper as she stepped down the three stairs into the room and began to polish the master's desk, and put his cane in position. She wasn't afraid of it now. She threw away dead flowers and rinsed the jampots in the bucket at the door. She dusted and straightened, and threw wide the windows.

A little boy came in, sidling with his cap in his hand, just as Ronnie Youlgrave had once looked. He grinned and began to ring the school bell. Two more boys put their heads round the corner and she summoned them. She liked the boys best, they were dirtier, but merrier, their hot little grimy paws held hers, and she felt serenely happy with their company.

"Fill the water bucket for drinking," she commanded and they quickly obeyed, proud to be chosen by their favourite monitor. They filled it from the tap in the playground wall, and carried it to the corner of the room. A mug was on the windowsill ready for the thirsty ones and Virginia took a drink first.

Then the bell rang, ting tong, and children came into the playground, thirty or forty of them in all. The schoolmaster came from his little house, and the day's work was ready. Virginia taught well, with realization of the needs of children, knowing the different homes from which the children came, poverty or riches, for it was poverty to have broken boots, and riches to have a servant girl at home even if she lived with the family.

Grandmother Charity spoke with grave decision one night. Her words were slow and grave, measured like a tune.

"That child, Virginia, must have more schooling. She's worth it. She's my Kate's child. Kate didn't have much chance, but Virginia shall do better. She shall learn wondrous things."

William looked up from the account book where he sat struggling with milk prices and long columns of dozen gallons owing to him by the milkman. Nearly thirty pounds the dealer owed, and he never offered to pay. The burden of this was troubling him.

"Where's the money to come from?" he asked. "Verey's going bankrupt it's my belief. I shall have to put the lawyer on him to get my money, and then I doubt if he'll pay."

There was silence, the old woman sat mumbling softly to

herself. She was very old, she was perhaps losing her wits, thought Hetty glancing up sharply, pursing her lips and returning to her sewing. It had been a bad harvest, so dry the hay made only one stack and they would have to buy; and then to talk of extra schooling!

At the door a blackbird was singing to them; its evening song came fluting through the room, and beyond they could hear the murmur of the river. It was so quiet they all listened, as if others were speaking, to this age-old music of bird and water. The shutters were unclosed, and the light of a trembling planet came through the greenish glass, twinkling and moving, as if it were looking for its companion the lost moon.

Hetty spoke, and her words shattered that silence of stars and bird. "Why should we pay for Virginia's schooling any more than Dick's or Emmie's?" she asked. "They are your grand-children too."

"Yes. All of them are my grandchildren, but she's different," muttered Charity.

"How different?" asked Hetty sharply, and William sighed and took up his scrub of pencil and made marks on the blotting paper. There they were, at it again, and both were right.

"Nobody's different. Don't talk like that, Mother," he said quietly. "You know quite well it costs money to send children for education and the village school was good enough for us."

For answer the old woman rose and slowly left the room.

"She's offended," said Hetty. "She's going to bed."

They could hear her thumping softly across the bedroom floor. In a few minutes the stairs creaked, the iron latch rattled and she returned with a stocking held tightly in her gnarled hand. She dropped it on the table and the coins inside chinked gaily. Hetty glanced at her husband and he stared open-mouthed. Gold pieces rolled out, sovereigns clean and bright.

"Where did you get these?" he demanded.

"That's my affair, William." Charity's little stubborn jaw snapped like a trap. "But I don't mind telling you they are my savings, years of stinting and doing without. Will they pay for Virginia's schooling?"

William counted the gold. Fifty pounds lay there. "I should think they will. You've been close, Mother, hiding this from me. I could have done with this many a time. It would have got me out of many a tight corner."

But Virginia refused to go away to school. Fifty pounds was a fortune. Nobody ever spent so much money. The house was in need of many things. They all talked it over for this hidden money of Charity's was like a fine fortune coming from the sky. Part of it must go to buy hay, they said, and then Virginia should have her schooling.

"A year at the fine school in the market town would just set her up, and set us all up," said Charity. "She'll be able to help the farm more by going to school for a while and leaving this teaching she's doing."

"Oh Jinny, do go," cried Dick. "Rather you nor me. You get the learning and you can teach us all of nights. It'll save us a mort of trouble."

"Four pounds a term, twelve pounds a year, and your railway fare and extra clothes and keep," said Hetty. "That's what it will be."

"No, I shan't go," said Virginia slowly.

They were discussing and arguing every day, when news came of night classes. That settled it, in their minds.

The talk of the new education came in a roundabout way to the farm, through the corn-dealer, passed on to the miller, confirmed by the miller's agent, whose sister went to a dressmaking class there. When the young man came for orders for linseed cake and meal he was always invited to sit in the kitchen. There he told all the news of many a village before he got his business done. It eased the tongue and gave him more orders, for it was a friendly way of doing business.

He put his hat between his knees, and talked to William and Dick came in to ask questions.

His sister went to the classes, which were held in the empty grammar school at night when the children had gone. There were carpenter's benches for boys, and a good fireplace and cookery for girls. There were French lessons, speaking that foreign tongue, and drawing in a room with plaster casts of Romans and such. There was science too, with glass retorts and an electric machine that made sparks. Anybody might go if they promised to take the examinations at the end. Even Nancy Drake, the cobbler's grand-daughter, was going.

Virginia listened, eager and excited with all she heard of this knowledge that was much better than school. She had a deep longing for knowledge of certain things, a desire strengthened by the smattering of information she had picked up here and there, from the schoolmaster and from her grandmother. Old Mr. Drake the village cobbler was full of knowledge. He said the world was evolved, it wasn't created in a day or two. He was sending his daughter to find out about this. Virginia too wanted to know about the earth, not about cooking and dressmaking. The wind came from the hills and blew over the shining waves of corn, and its visibility was something to wonder at. Then there was Echo, and Shadow, and sunlight and moonshine, and how it bleached the linen and how thunder turned milk sour. So it was decided that Virginia should go to the night classes to find out some of these things.

Chapter 11

Autumn came, with its rich heady smells of walnut leaves decaying on the paths, of moss damp by the troughs, of golden bracken bending to the earth ready for its death. It was the time of colour and sadness, of regrets for the old and longings for the young, of preparation for winter and home-keeping. But winter seemed far away on that bright day when Virginia started her new education at the night school. Earth showed her bravest colours, a last flaunting beauty, before the winds destroyed so much. The fields glittered with sparkling drops, the woods were clothed in splendour. High on the hilltops the mountain ashes were loaded with orange clusters, each berry sent out its own light to add to the conflagration in the woods. The beech trees were ruddy gold, the silver-birches were filigree of delicate gold, the blackberry trailers made crimson arches through which the rabbits and field-mice ran to their holes.

The old farmhouse seemed to take on the same autumnal beauty. Its grey-green roof was blotched with fresh patches of moss and stonecrop. Its timbers were silver. The fine-leaved elms that overtopped the roof of barns and stable dropped their coins in launders and through the open windows to the bare floors. These trees were the gilded ornament of the house, fine old gold that framed the little windows and pushed their long branches against the attic in the little old house-place, like a jeweller's handwork. The azure sky, ineffably pure in that limpid air, gleamed through the thin leaves like water, so that the golden elm leaves seemed to have a tinge of blue in them. Away to the hills a deeper blue, violet and sapphire hung like a cloud, but even in the valley close to the house doors the same blue seemed to linger in the windows with their old crinkled unevenly annealed glass, in the stone eaves and gable ends, in the shadowed barns and steps.

The swifts had gone, the robin sang his autumn song close to the house end, and late work was beginning. Dick and William were in the fields ploughing and the new man, Sam Wheeler, went about the fields, minding the sheep, foddering, cutting turnips, making hurdles, always working in a fierce withdrawn silence.

So Virginia rode to the station in the milkcart with the evening milk with Uncle William, standing up among the four churns bumping and rattling among them, steadying herself as the cart lurched over the rough stones and dipped into hollows. Bruised and gay she kissed her uncle at the station and leapt down over the wheel.

"Be a good lass, and learn all you can," said William with unchanging jocularity. "God bless you."

"Good-bye. God bless you," returned Virginia lightly, and she tossed her misty hair and shook her skirts free from dust and walked serenely on the platform, with secret pride in the railway, the station, the guard, as if they were a pattern into which she now fitted. She was filled with elation over the classes, over the journey by the riverside, in a train with red velvet cushions, and travellers who were going on equally romantic errands if one but knew.

It had been difficult to chose among the alluring subjects, science, art, English literature, and French, but science won. A class of half a dozen girls sat in the deserted school, taking notes on the earth and the sky and all that lies between. They compared their notes on the way home and discussed the homework set by the sandy-haired master. Two girls left the train at the next village and Virginia and Nancy Drake, the granddaughter of the atheist cobbler, and Milly Slater, sister of the young man who came for orders, were the only ones left in an almost empty train. They scampered across the wooden bridge laughing at the clatter of their echoing feet, chaffing the solitary porter who was waiting

126

for these last passengers before he locked up for the night. They ran out into the darkness of the unlighted road as the train slowly puffed and rumbled away. They heard the door of the station house bang, and the porter whistle as he locked up the booking office and blew out the lamps. They kissed each other good night and parted, for Nancy and Milly lived up the village hill and Virginia had to go down the valley road.

The lane was in the shadow of trees, but the real lights of the night were visible to country folk, stars and moon, white-faced flowers, moths flitting on silver wings, snowy cattle, glittering river, and these made a company for Virginia on her way home. She swung along the country road with swift light foot, her heart uplifted with the beauty of night when the earth is most alive with meaning and subtle approach, when trees and water can convey something to a listener. Her mind was busy over the wonders of the Universe which had been opened to her by the dry little scientist who talked on and on without any recognition of the sentience of his listeners. They were common village girls, and he was teaching for his living, so he spread out his wares, unconscious that at least one pupil was tasting and feasting, too shy to ask questions but drinking all in with a great thirst.

Dick offered to meet her on the lonely road, but she refused to have him. He was tired after the long day's work, he was morose, and queer-tempered, grown up and disillusioned. It was jealousy holding him in tight grip, torturing him to bitterness. Virginia was moving away from him, and he couldn't bear it. She didn't want his company, striding along the dark lane with a lantern spoiling the night's blackness for her, when she was filled with bliss unutterable. He thought she was in love with somebody, perhaps a boy at the night-class, perhaps with Ronnie far away. Love, yes, she was in love, but it was with life itself. Her assignations were with no human beings. The first star came out, in the great dome of blue. She felt a sudden tug at her heart as she found it. It made the sign of recognition and she responded. She seemed to leave her own body and fly up there to meet it. Something greater than love flashed between them. She was part of it winged, immortal. She walked swiftly along the road, with her mind rushing ahead of her, speeding upward and onward to eternity. Away in the distance among the trees by the river she could see a light burning like a smaller star. There was the farm and her own room waiting for her. It was there, secret, inviolable. Nobody would ever know.

As soon as she went up the yard her thoughts flew to her room. She ate her supper, answered questions about what she had learned, told them strange theories which sounded fantastic in the farm kitchen among the pots and pans, but all the time she was wondering what her room had to say. Then she ran out of doors, and up the ladder to the trap door and the chamber in the loft. It had kept something for her, her dreams and thoughts were waiting there. They were in the vibrant air, in the dancing shadows as the candle swaled. Each day she had more to add to the store which the room held. Sometimes there was a little glowing fire in the grate to warm her. The light flickered over the beams and upon the trap door, shut against invaders. These whitewashed walls of great thickness and ancient days held her thoughts and those of others who had lived there. The memories of other days were mingled in the atmosphere. The room was compact of them, brimming with them, and the walls receded as if the volume of dreams pushed them back with its pressure and its intensity of emotion.

Grandmother Charity had given her the outside room for her own. It was like having a private house, and Virginia who had always shared either with Emmie or with her grandmother, was proud of the promotion, delighted with the solitude of that little upper chamber over the ancient tiny kitchen of the farmhouse, the original shepherd's cottage.

"Why do you want to go out there? It's sheer contrary of you," grumbled Hetty. "It's cold in winter and hot in summer, and no staircase, and old as the hills, and not a fitty place for a nice girl to sleep in. Why not be sensible and take that little room next to Emmie's and I'll take the clothes-press out of it and the odds and ends stored there and make it proper for you."

But Virginia persisted in her choice of the outside room that was the apple-chamber. It had always been her favourite spot, her hiding place and look-out, and her secret playroom.

The window of this upper chamber of the oldest part of the farmhouse looked out over a wide stretch of country with hills in the background, blue and dim with mystery, hallowed by memory and dream. There she had gazed as soon as she was big enough to climb the ladder to the apple-room, and clamber up to the tiny square of glass. In the foreground was the sight of horses coming from the fields for watering, ridden sideways by Uncle Will and Dick, with their brasses swaying and jingling and their bells and chains ringing. As soon as she saw them she went crawling backward down the ladder and out to them, to demand a ride to the troughs. From this vantage post she could get the first glimpse and catch them before Emmie ousted her. From this window she watched the lambs racing in a bevy of youth along the narrow grassy tracks, leaping from a fallen tree trunk, and dancing on little knobbly legs. From here she saw the cows coming from the far pasture, with Dick calling them at the gate, and off she trundled to help him. The little loft had been the source of most of her childhood pleasure, for there was always something to watch, some unending supply of magic and wonder to be caught from that tiny slip of glass let into the thick side of the house.

She had escaped from Hetty's fingers, from toil and scolding and angry words, by climbing softly and determinedly up the ladder and crouching hidden in the apple-chamber. So when the choice of a room was offered to her, she took it for her own.

Down below in the room that had once been the kitchen of the tiny original farmhouse, were the tin pancheons and the mangle, with its great cubic iron weights and heavy wooden rollers, the squealing protesting mangle which cried out in pain when Hetty and Charity put the heaps of sheets and towels through it. The mangle had its own tempers and vagaries. It creaked and groaned like a dying man, its voice rose in a crescendo of screams glorious to hear, waking the echoes in the barns alongside. Then, when it had reached the highest pitch of excited protest, it dropped and with a clatter of weights fell to the ground. There was always an expectant and exciting anticipation as Dick turned the handle with Hetty at the opposite side and Virginia held up the wet garments from the clothes-baskets. It was an enormous machine, dating from the time of the invention of the steam engine and containing some of the primitive devices of that period. It was inimical too, fingers could be trapped in it, toes could be crushed with the weights.

The bedroom above echoed with the queer human cries of the great old mangle, but these sounds were part of the house, and Virginia loved them.

Then there was its friend and companion, the merry little tool called the Dolly. That was a gay little person, like a wooden girl with head and shoulders and two outstretched arms, a thin body, and five little legs upon which Dolly could walk on occasion. There was also a washing machine, called Peggy, with a wonderful splasher and a handle which only a man could turn. It was a modern invention when Charity was young. Peggy and Dolly and the mangle ruled the place.

There were age-old worm-eaten oak benches, stored there against the wall, which had once been farm workers' seats. They were dragged out when a Sunday school treat came to the farm field with its crowd of laughing youngsters, or when the Mothers' Union came with its charabanc load of stout mothers to take tea in the hay. They were taken out to the yard, washed clean, and put ready for old and young to rest upon them, to admire the view and sit and talk before they went home to the distant villages.

The fireplace was wide and the chimney open to the sky. Mice scuttered on tiny feet over the stone floor, and hens strayed in to roost in the chimney corner.

The bedroom was reached by a ladder as if the people of long ago had made themselves safe from thieves up there at night, and nobody in the centuries had bothered to make a wooden staircase. The broad squat ladder stretched up to the trap door, and light entered with it. The tiny window was latticed, and hinged with delicately wrought iron. It swung open to the boughs of a tree. The rough oak floor was crooked and bowed, bare of carpet and scrubbed clean every year. At the end of the room was a small fireplace, rusty and dark, but a good fire would burn there. The green painted bed was built into the floor, part of the room, immovable, solid as a rock. Nobody knew how old it was, there no decoration, no carving, except the intertwined love-hearts of sweethearts long dead, who had lain there, the room never forgetting.

There was a layer of wooden bars across the frame, and upon them a straw mattress, which crackled noisily when one touched it. It was hard and prickly, but men had slept the sleep of youth upon it. The curved beams stretched across the ceiling, whitewashed like the walls, and they too were cut and marked with rude letters, initials and hearts.

The little bedroom had been prepared for her. Virginia scrubbed the floorboards and turned out a hoard of spiders and their kin. The green wooden bedstead was piled with a feather bed newly filled with disinfected feathers collected for the purpose from the great bath in the barn. Fragrant sheets clean from the orchard drying, and woolly blankets were laid across. Hetty's great virtue was cleanliness and everything shone to a holy whiteness from soap and brush bristles. In one corner of the room stood a little wooden washstand, also painted green, bought at a sale. A lavender sprigged bowl was fitted into its hollow, and the cracked jug was placed on the floor underneath it. What matter that a piece was out of the spout, and the soap dish had no lid. Virginia had never possessed a washstand before, she had always washed at the kitchen sink before the family, baring her arms and flat little breasts unconscious of their soft beauty, unaware that everybody in the world didn't wash at a great stone slab, and lave themselves on part of the earth's foundations. Stone to wash in, stone to sit upon, and stone for drinking water bowls, for shelves and larder, stones for playthings, for little houses of make-believe, in the woods, for look-out castles. Stone was an everyday familiar thing to her, and its hardness seemed to give her a grip on life. The Rock of Ages was stone, and the ancient crosses in the churchyard.

She looked admiringly at the small crooked three-cornered washstand, and felt that now she was a real lady. A piece of scented soap, reserved for months, since somebody had brought it from a fair, lay ready on it, and the jug was filled with ice-cold water from the troughs. She cupped her hand and dipped it in the jug, and drank, then she washed her fingers daintily in the smallest possible amount of water, and dried them on the little fringed towel.

There was no place on the sloping walls for a looking-glass, and the little square of mirror in its mahogany frame was propped on the window hole, so that it reflected the green of the waving trees instead of Virginia's lively face. On the bed was the patch-work quilt made of bits and pieces of her grandmother's and great aunt's clothes. There was a rush-bottomed chair, and a few wooden pegs on the wall for wardrobe, where she hung her Sunday dress and coat. From a peg at the end of the oak beam swung a lantern with a pointed top and a bit of candle inside. It made the little room like a cabin in the trees.

There was a tiny cupboard in the wall, close to the bed head. The little oblong door was heavy and thick, for it had guarded the treasures of the old farmhouse long and long ago, when folk were poor as mice. Perhaps only a few shillings had been hoarded within, close to the shepherd's head as he lay with his wife and children in that small high chamber. Virginia kept her poetry book and diary there, locked away.

The walls were lime-washed afresh each year. If only there had been a wallpaper with roses and sweet peas, such as Virginia had seen in the schoolmaster's house, but such a luxurious thought never entered Charity's old head. Wallpaper was for downstair rooms, not for attics, and certainly not for a little old apple-chamber where nobody had slept since goodness knows when.

It was a beautiful room, Virginia thought. On the floor was an oblong rag rug, made on winter nights by Charity herself, with Virginia holding up the strips to her as she pegged them in, crimson in the centre and grey as the background, from an old grey suit of William's. There was a rocking-chair, with a cane seat and back, and tied to it a padded cushion. They had only just managed to get this through the trap door. On the wall was a rough oak shelf, covered with cut white paper, and on it Virginia placed her treasures, a hand-painted vase, a doll's teaset, a shell box. The beauty of this room came from no ornament or tapestry made by hands, but from the light of heaven. On the whitewashed walls the ever-changing meshes of light fell through the elm branches, making a pattern of shadowed leaves and tracery elusive and mocking as a bird's call. No curtain fluttered at the window, no blind obscured the sun, no shutter was closed across the square. The window was open to the tree top, to the boughs of the elms, to a nest in the rose tree, to the soughing and murmuring of the flat ever-swinging branches with their myriad tiny exquisite leaves.

The sunlight poured through and sent shadows and tracery upon the white walls, so that the dreamer could lie and watch a pageant of intricate weaving light, a maze of patterned shades, a quivering picture of ever-changing design. The girl put a bowl of water on the deep sill, to catch the sunbeams and flash them in facets over the white ceiling. Dreaming, she sat watching it, fascinated by the curves and cusps of cutting light beams, the blades of fine gold. In autumn when the leaves were thinning, the pale drifts floated to the room and lay on the water. In winter when the boughs were naked, there was a glimpse of the river between the branches, of snow-flecked banks and tossing water white against the dark rocks.

It was a treasure of a room, her own beloved part of the house, and when she climbed the ladder, and let down the trap door, she felt safe as Robinson Crusoe in his tree-house.

The attic always welcomed her. It seemed to rejoice that it was inhabited again. It talked to her, and to itself, whispering, showing its moving panorama of light, telling tales of magic and enchantment, of love and fortitude. "Faithful" and "Steadfast"— the words came softly out of the past, woven into the texture of grey stones, into the thickness of the ancient building. It was a place for all time, and outside, close to the small window, the woods were singing their tunes, unseen ones were walking there, invisible guests were invading the spaces wishing to share their knowledge with those who were aware of their presence. They beckoned with green fingers, they called, and Virginia leaned from her narrow casement, and shook her head, acknowledging their presence, refusing to join them, filled with happiness because she knew of them.

So the autumn passed and the little wings of Mercury grew on her feet. She lived in two worlds, the everyday life of the farm, and another that had half opened its doors to her. Her eyes were straining after the invisible world, her senses alert to the unseen. She was moved and excited by some trifle, a finger of moonlight on the garden wall, a pear tree pointing to the sky, the violet gleam of earth turned up by the plough-share, the print of a bird's foot by the spring. There was magic in all things and joy in the smallest happenings. She ran off in pursuit of some elusive glance, a flurry of wind, a rainbow, a bird's flight, but no, it was something else there in the air beckoning her. It couched in the trees, it swept over the pastures, it danced and leapt and she never caught it. It was the promise of life, immortality drifting about those stone walls, seeping from the house. The promises, the visions could never be captured, save for brief moments in music, in sunset, in a flash of understanding with some patient dumb beast, or flower or tree. Her heart ached with happiness and grief for no reason, except for the fleeting steps of time.

She read poems in the little school books, and caught at the words as if they were songs. She clasped her marbled notebook and wrote down odd facts about light and sound, and the age of the earth, and she marvelled at the amount of knowledge going begging. The dusty classroom was transformed. Her bright hair gleamed in the gaslight as she bent to her work, her eyes were wide with the wonder of it all, even of the flickering gas-jet and the classroom desks. A transmutation took place in her mind, turning the dull lecture of the tired and bored teacher into something gilded and jewelled.

She walked fearlessly along the lonely footpath to the farm, speeding between the dark hedges with only a startled rabbit or owl for company, but the stars were overhead, often invisible, and the heart of the warm earth beat under her feet. Events she had taken for granted now had a new significance for her. Darkness and light, morning and evening, snow and sunshine, each was a living part of herself. Light was a sword flashing out, coming from the sun with a fixed speed, incredible as it seemed, travelling through vast spaces, making shadows, affecting the invisible and visible. Light was a juggler, playing with glittering drops in water and air, dazzling the human eyes, cutting dark figures in shadow, like the paper men she made with Dick and Emmie on winter nights when she was a small child.

Then there was darkness. What was the terrifying deep where all light was absent, the blackness that filled certain places with horror? Not the velvet darkness of nights, when the stars were present whether one saw them or not, when the trees moved and the earth talked, but something else, a nightmare dark which had existed before God separated it from light. She pushed away the haunting thought, for the air was pulsating with colour, and movement, of dusk and starlight and shifting clouds and swaying murmuring familiar trees.

Kind darkness was a living person, wrapping the house in a soft blue robe like Virginia's own winter cloak, listening to the chatter in the kitchen, breathing as it moved around, watching with its thousand eyes. It rustled its old gown, and shook its leafy fingers, and moaned and sighed and laughed again, like an old woman who remembers her youth.

On dark nights Virginia carried a little lantern which she kept in the porter's lamp room. The slender beams lighted up the lane, and she walked secure in her own freedom from mankind, going over in her mind all she had heard and seen, of electric forces and magnets, the glimpses into other rooms of students bending over their drawing boards, of boys in white aprons with plane and hammer, and young women cooking, and dress-making.

When the moon was high in the heavens, Virginia was filled with a strange exaltation. She became moon-struck, for the world of field and wood was changed to something unreal. The road was silver, the fields frozen pearl, and the river caught the beams and reflected them. Then she walked very slowly, listening and looking, time-travelling.

The mood of the house changed with the weather, also. When the sun beat down in the hollow and flooded the yard the house grew larger. It stretched itself like a cat to feel the warmth, and it absorbed the heat into its body, secreting the warmth ready for winter days, when people would come in from the storms and cry, "Ah, it's grand indoors. It's real comforting to get inside," and the little birds and animals would come close to its walls for shelter.

Moonlight coming up from behind the hill, and casting its beams over the old house changed it to an enchanted castle, a place of fairytale, secret, holding ghosts and goblins in its walls. Snow poured down upon it, made a transformation scene for the most splendid pantomime, with a turret here, a battlement there, each formed from a bush or rounded tree. The little clipped bushes, the bird-bush in the garden hedge, all were changed to grotesque and lovely goblins.

Rain could make the house a place of poverty, streaked with rust and damp, when rivulets of manure and dark pools ran over the cobbles, and the draggled cocks crowed to remind every man that Saint Peter was denying our Lord at that very moment.

By moonlight, the dark windows of cowplaces and barns were eerie, faces seemed to look out from them, white faces pressed against the glass.

"Which is worse? A face looking out of a window when you know there's nobody there, or a face looking in when you think there's nobody about?" asked Virginia one night.

"A face looking in," said Richard. "You can't get away from it. You can be free of a face looking out."

Richard took a deep interest in Virginia's homework, and tried to share her books. She was quicker than he, and he stumbled along, not understanding, half angry as she tried to explain. She was too impatient, too lost in dream for him, and he took himself away in a huff. They were drifting apart, and Virginia didn't seem to care. He looked wistfully at her, and retired hurt and unhappy, while she was filled with bliss.

At the end of the year's work the examinations were held, and the girls received certificates. Charity held the blue and silver cardboard, and read it many times. It meant something very important, and she treasured it in her bedroom. Virginia begged for another year, and they agreed. Nancy Drake also persuaded her father to let her go again, only little Milly Slater stayed at home, for she had failed. Education was not for her she decided.

Chapter 12

One night of full moon when Virginia came home, stepping softly along the white road and the green lane, one night when all the fields were silver, something happened to break the spell of education. She heard a faint crackle in the high bank of trees which bounded the lane. It was a night of intense stillness, the witchlight of the moon had put a spell on the fields, to keep them supernaturally quiet, and the tiny sound brought the girl out of her dreams with a jerk. She thought something was watching her with eyes inimical, she tried to pierce the darkness of the glade, but there was no motion or sound. Nothing came out of those pointed shadows, and she walked on, thinking it was a night animal disturbed by her passage. It wasn't far from the farm, she could see the light at the window for a moment between the hills. There was a steep climb up a field path and a stile to reach before she reached the hollow where her home lay. The sudden panic of unreasoning fear aroused by the noise had gone, but a slight unease remained. She walked boldly forward, up the stony path which went alongside the home meadow, separated from it by a wall. The field dropped to the river, a shining stream flashing as its waves caught the moonlight. Out from the shadows she came with relief, and she paused to still her beating heart, and to lean over the wall to view the beauty and tranquillity of the scene that always stirred her. She was now in her own land, her grandmother's land, and every stick and stone was precious and well known. They belonged to her, and she felt a pride of possession as she stared across the dear fields. They lay in dream, silver-grey, with no hurtful thing among them. Here no enemy could come, for safety and home and firelight were in the distance, behind the trees that had swum into vision. Shepherd's Fields with its company was waiting for her. The teasing of Emmie, the kindliness of Uncle Will, the upward glance of Richard that meant so much, the deep love of Charity were there, like flowers growing. Some places were cruel. There was the hostility of a tree in the wood, where perhaps an evil deed had been done, a place where something remained of evil, there was the tumbledown house where a harlot once lived, and the small barn which had always frightened her. She thought of these, and dismissed them from her mind, as shadows evoked by moonlight.

The moon coloured the land with strange remoteness, and moon-shadows lay like filigree trees on the grass at the feet of the real trees. A great solitary oak which she loved had its own indigo tree with lacy boughs spread out on the ground at its feet.

"Never step on a moon-shadow," the poor fool Sam had told her, finger raised and head nodding, and she thought of the queer tales she had heard of beings dancing on the hillside and dryads coming from ancient trees, and witches riding under the moon, all the old tales she had picked up from country folk, stories which persisted alongside the new learning of science. She turned again to the moon full in the sky, where the mountains and craters were distinctly visible. It was suddenly baleful, staring down with ice-cold malignancy, powerful and cruel. The whole valley was illuminated by that reflected light and the fields on the opposite side of the river were crystal clear with dark walls and silver squares like a chessboard.

That light was so intense it might materialize the dead and bring the ghosts from the churchyard to gibber and shake, in some nightmare terror. It was not the kindly moonshine that was her companion, a lantern along the way. It was not the sweet moon that was a candle in her bedroom. These thoughts were born from that faint crackle in the trees, she realized, and she stared in their shadows. A flock of William's sheep moved slowly in the hollow, cropping as they went in serene peace like a picture in the Scripture book. Their white wool was of unearthly beauty, their heads were bent to the earth, and they moved in gentle unison, as they ate. They were companionable and friendly in a safe land, far from the hostility of that moon. Virginia was comforted watching them, as they trod with slow patient little feet, and licked up the sweet grasses. She felt their own pleasure, in the cold touch of grass on their lips and the soft cushions of earth under their hoofs. She pressed her hands on the rough stone wall, enthralled by the night. The only sound was the continuous murmur and ripple of the river. Not a branch stirred, not an owl hooted, the world seemed to be frozen to a lovely death like a scene in "Sleeping Beauty". Even the sheep seemed to stand and dream, with their heads cropping low. She stood immobile, lost in that dream world she had evoked.

Suddenly there was a change, as if the sleeping earth had been awakened by some nightmare age-old happening which was repeating itself. There was no sound, even the river was silent, listening, watching, in that second of consciousness taken out of eternity, and made into an eternity. The sheep down the steep slope of the field stopped grazing and turned their heads all in one direction. Every long white face was pointed to the bank of trees. The flock stood expectant, filled with fear, and Virginia too felt the deep apprehension. She too was a little animal, waiting for something to happen, and the fear of the sheep communicated itself to her straining eyes.

Sheep and girl stared at the dark trunks of the small group of trees. Perhaps there was a mad dog, a sheep-killer such as runs by night and slays many ewes, she thought. There had been such a dog one winter and the farmers had sat up for nights with their guns, for it was cunning and terrible as a devil in the way it worked, hunting so silently that the sheep were rarely disturbed until it was upon them with wide jaws to slay and drink their blood.

Something moved across the lacy shadows, a dark shade went across, and a large black animal came out, walking queerly, lobsided in its clumsy movements. Virginia stared fascinated, secure behind the wall, while the sheep stood transfixed with curiosity.

"It's a great black ram come after them from somebody's flock," the girl reassured herself, but the sheep were seized with wild panic.

With one movement, they swung round and fled leaving the animal to lope in its ungainly manner after them. It went slowly, hesitatingly, long-legged and black and sinister. Its shape was truly terrifying. The sheep were clearly puzzled, for they stopped and stared again at the intruder. Then they ran a short distance bleating in piteous confusion and dread. Virginia expected the beast to follow and destroy them.

A wolf! The absurd thought flashed through her mind, unreasoning fear caught her, as the terror of the sheep came to her and possessed her, so that she too was a defenceless animal exposed to danger and horrible death. The animal was unlike anything she had known. It was a nightmare beast as it ambled about in the hollow, long-legged and misshapen. She could not move from her place by the wall, she stood fascinated as she watched it, waiting for it to pursue the quivering sheep. But it also waited, its long shadow fell before it, over the grass, the moon gave it a goblin shape, and it raised its forelegs, and ran with queer antics, rearing and pawing with long thin forelegs raised. It was gesticulating, bowing and smirking to the moon. It was stealing the moonshine for its own wicked ends.

A werewolf! In a flash of memory came a Russian tale she had read, of a great supernatural wolf. At that moment she could believe in anything. It was evil, animal and human too, and she stared fascinated with growing horror. Then the creature seemed to be aware of her standing on the hillside in the wall's shadow. It had seen her, for it left the flock and started up the field towards her. She turned and walked swiftly up the path, she was well ahead and there was a stout wall between. A wall was a safe protection from a bull or savage horse, and she felt thankful for its presence. The animal came on with its ungainly horrible walk like an ape, and its long shadow added to its grotesque form. Virginia determined not to run, lest it should race up the slope. It must not know her fear. Her heart was beating like a hammer in her throat, her mouth was dry. She would soon be at the corner, where she could run without being seen.

Even as she glanced at the enemy she saw it was cutting across the field, making for a spot in front of her, where a gate crossed her way. She would lose time opening the gate, and the stile brought her close to the wall. It was the one vulnerable place, and the beast with uncanny knowledge had divined it. At the same instant it rose upright on its hind legs, tall in the moonlight.

The sheep standing huddled on the slope now took to their heels and galloped out of sight, bleating and crying. With their disappearance the world was empty of comfort. Naked fear stalked the earth. Virginia stood frozen with horror. The un-earthly thing now gave up all pretence and ran with swift strides up the hill, its arms dangling loosely, its head bent. It was a human being. Virginia lost her power to hurry, her strength had gone. She walked on, looking at the wood of beech trees, staring at them, as if they were the last glimpse of life. The lights of the farm were hidden, she was shut away. She sent a desperate cry to God, to Charity sitting by the fire unconscious of her child's doom, to the house itself, invisible but surely aware of her danger. The cruel, the terrible hidden primeval things were about her. If she could only see the house, she would get courage, but she was out of sight, it might not know.

She was certain it was the end, there was no escape from that menacing figure, swinging up the slope to the corner where field and lane joined. She was desperate, but her strength held sufficiently for her to scramble through the tall upright stones of the stile as a long arm stretched over the wall to catch her. She was a second in advance, she pressed back to avoid the touch and she was just out of reach. Her mouth was dry as ashes, she could not cry out, and in the silence she heard the panting, and saw a face, half in shadow, silvered to a strange cruelty, the eyes glittering malignantly, the fingers on the wall like white talons. Where were the dead to save her? Why did they linger in their own land and leave her to face such horror alone?

She staggered on, a yard or two ahead, gained as the man climbed the steep wall, higher at his side than at hers. There was no escape, because she couldn't run. Her long slender limbs had betrayed her. Death was behind, not the kind death who carries people in his arms, but something else.

Then a miracle happened. Footsteps came running along the field, stones rattled and loosened under a heavy tread, a voice shouted to her from the distance, and a lantern gleamed. A lantern when the moon was full, a human being when a devil was abroad. Strength returned, she answered the call in a quavering voice, and she ran, hallooing, and laughing. Fear had gone, she was safe. Even if she were struck down she would be found and rescued. Oh, come, come quickly, went her thoughts, and the lantern flashed in the distance.

There was Sam Wheeler, like a winged angel to fight the devils of hell. Already the footsteps behind her had stopped, the dark shadow leapt the wall and disappeared down the slope to the river.

"Anything amiss?" cried Sam, flashing his lantern on the wall. She stood shivering, choking back the sobs of fear and joy.

"Oh Sam, Sam," she stammered at last, as he continued to stare at the wall. "What made you come?"

"I dunno know. Who scared ye?"

"Nothing. Let's go home," whispered Virginia, and she hurried along the path. "What made you come to meet me?" she asked again.

"I dunno know," said he abruptly. "I just heard something telling me to come. Danger, it said. Just like that, so off I came straight from the stable, as fast as I could run with the lantern in my hand. I left the mare uncobbled, and the door wide open, and she'll get a cold if I don't hurry back, and Master'll be right angry."

"I'm glad you came," said Virginia. "I was——" She couldn't speak of her encounter. She could never tell anyone in the world.

"Was you afeared of summut?" he asked, looking at her with his bright eyes, awakened from their sleepiness and oddly aware of her thoughts.

"Yes. I was rather frightened, Sam. Sometimes you get scared in the moonlight," she faltered, as she walked by his side, under the wood's shade. The uncouth man was like an angel. He had flown down from heaven, nailed boots and corduroys and all. Smell of cows and horses, and sweaty feet, all were perfume to her senses. Her strength had returned, she nearly flew along the lane, by his side. She knew how Lazarus had felt lifted from the dead.

He grinned acquiescingly, and shook his head.

"Yes, moon does scare you sometimes," he agreed. "But I was told to come. They told me. I heard them."

"Who was it Sam?" she whispered after a long pause, when their boots had rattled comfortably on the rough stones, and the warm gates had touched their hands, and the trees had murmured in comfort and companionship, the witnesses of her anguish. They would never tell, but they would speak to one another of what they had seen. That moment of intense fear, by its intensity, would be present in a time layer. A hundred years later another girl would slip her arm in her lover's as she passed that way, by moonlight, she would shiver as if with an ague, and he would kiss her lips and draw her close to him. "What is it dear?" he would ask. "Nothing. I just felt a goose walk over my grave," and shadows would run out of the trees and away.

"Who was it sent you?" murmured Virginia again.

"A voice. House's talk maybe. I heard it clear. It told me to go and meet you quick."

They went into the Home Field, past the tree with the swing, up to the white gate, past the row of farm buildings to the house. Virginia's eyes were fixed upon it as she walked. She was drawing strength and resolution from its walls. Its permanence and vitality filled the air, so that every breath she took was made of its strength. She must not tell her fears, it seemed to say. Keep them and fight them yourself. It welcomed her, its own child, it put arms around her, and she wished to be a spirit like the wind, who could clasp the house and kiss it in return. It was warming and joyful in its welcome. The branches of the elms shook with no wind in them, for the trees had told one another, moving their leaves, and sending a message by their own secret way.

"I'll never forget, Sam. I'll never forget," said she, stopping a moment at the gate. She held out her hand and clasped the rough warty hand of the man beside her. He shuffled, and apologized and muttered, "They told me to come."

Then together they went into the yard.

The kitchen door was ajar, and a reflected glow came out on the cobbles. Dick and William were in the yard. The dog sprang out from his kennel, barking and then wagging his tail in the moonlight as they stumbled up the yard.

"There you are, Sam! Why did you leave the mare loose like that, and stable door open? She came to the kitchen door, clattering with her hooves, knocking the cans over, startling us all. We didn't know what was the matter. Where have you been?"

William was severe, startled to see the fellow with Virginia.

"You left the gates open too, and foal might have been kicked by the young 'oss. Whatever was you thinking about?"

Virginia ran to her uncle and threw her arms round his neck, half choking with relief to see his good angry face.

William thought the man had been molesting her. Dick swore and went up to Sam.

"Now then! What have you been up to, frightening her?" he demanded threateningly.

"No, no," cried Virginia. "Sam came to meet me. I was a bit lonely coming up the hill, by the river, and I was very glad he came. It's all right, Uncle."

"He needn't have gone off like that with nobody sending him, and leaving all doors open and that cow in the sick cowhouse, and mare loose. We never sent him."

"It's all right, Uncle," said Virginia again, recovering her wits, and making a great effort of concealment. She calmed herself and went into the house. How beautiful it was! Hetty was angry, Emmie was curious, and Charity looked at her with questioning

142

puzzled gaze. They knew she was concealing something, but she stuck to her story. She had been walking home, and Sam had come to meet her.

The man came in to his supper, and sat at the dresser with his bowl of milk.

"You'd no call to go and meet Miss Jinny," said Hetty. "It isn't your place Sam. Dick will go, if she wants anybody."

"Don't scold him," whispered Virginia. "I was glad."

"What made you go where you wasn't wanted?" asked Hetty again, and she slapped his plate of bread and cheese down by the milk.

Sam looked at her sharp eyes and shook his head. His face was averted, he refused to speak.

Then Old Charity spoke from her corner where she had been watching. "What happened Sam?" she asked, and her low persuasive tones made him look up.

"I heard summat talking, it said 'Go and meet Virginia'," said he, simply.

Hetty flounced to her chair. "Well, don't you be hearing voices again," she snapped. "Houses don't talk such nonsense."

Charity shook her head. "It was maybe the voice of the house he heard."

"Nay, I'm sorry I left the mare loose in the stable, with that foal and all. I went off all in a swither and sweat. I didn't stop for nowt. I runned all the way lest I should be too late." mumbled Sam suddenly articulate.

"Too late for what?" asked Dick.

"I don't know. Too late. They said I had to go now."

"Don't talk to him," grumbled Hetty. "He's soft."

Sam's eyes glittered. "I was minded of summat I'm trying to forget," said he. "My brother was—was——"

"All right, Sam," interposed William. "I know about him. Don't say any more." William silenced the family.

"Defend us from all the perils and dangers of this night," prayed Charity that night, folding her worn hands and kneeling on the stone floor. Ah! Perils and dangers were always about them, and angels were defending them if they only knew, thought Virginia, peering through her fingers as she knelt in the family circle. Charity always said her prayers downstairs, with the kitchen listening, and then her extra prayers upstairs later.

"Would you like to sleep in the house to-night, Jinny?" she

asked as they rose from their knees. "You seem a bit over-wrought, a bit worked up. You've been studying too hard."

"No thank you, Grandmother," said Virginia softly. "I have done rather a lot of work. I don't think I'm going back to the night class. I've learnt enough."

She took her hot brick from the oven, wrapped it in a bit of old blanket and tucked it under her arm.

"Not going back? Not taking the exam?" they demanded.

"No. I've finished my schooling." She smiled round at their astonished faces. "Good night and God bless you," said she, and she kissed them, and went away with her little lantern to her outside room. It was waiting for her, it rejoiced she was safe in its arms again. It seemed to be filled with dusky sweet laughter, and the dim bodiless shadows ran here and there, talking to her, singing their own wordless songs which mingled with the wind and the soughing of the trees at the narrow window.

"I might never have come home again," said she aloud, nodding to the little room. "Then what would you have done?"

The little room laughed. Why should you be afraid? What is fear? The house doesn't know fear. You are always part of us.

She undressed and lay in bed, wrapped in the warmth of the hot brick and the snowy blankets. She sent her mind out travelling, to the farmyard below, to the stables where the mare now stood in her stall, to the dog in his kennel, and the cattle shut in their building, with the warmth of their breath and the smell of good hay. Then her thoughts flew outward, skimming the lane, not dwelling there, but going on over the fields to the village, to blacksmith and post office and the cobbler's yard, and the silent night that held them, to the roofs under the moonlight, and the shuttered windows, and the quiet church with its many graves, those narrow houses in the earth itself. The city of silence. Away flew her mind, high in the air, over the seas to the desert islands she and Ronnie had shared, then quickly like a bird returning to its nest it flew back to the little attic room and the house she loved, and she slept.

But she did not forget. She had always had the frightening power of the imaginative, who people the cracks and marks in the walls with uncanny shapes, who see faces in the stones and shapes in the mists. The images crowding her brain were projected into space. The old secret fears that had haunted her childhood days came back in strength, and only the house kept them at bay. She hid her terrors, and faced them, concealing them from others and fighting them by herself with the house's help. A shape of bed-clothes tumbled in a heap became a reality of horror. Discarded garments bulged with ghostly shapes. A scarecrow gave her a panic fear. Only old Charity guessed her fears, and she said nothing. She used her influence to help the girl in her fight against them.

If the light disappeared, if the shutters were closed and the lamplight hidden, and firelight cut off, a dreadful panic swept over her. It was as if the light of the world were extinguished and only outer darkness remained. She saw herself, a lost spirit, flee-ing for ever in the vast spaces of the universe, abandoned in the immensity of a black abyss of nothingness where even the stars had gone out and only the nightmare of infinity remained. Such fear possessed her, holding her down, that it was a lifetime of agony compressed into the time to draw a single breath. Death and Eternity were one.

Then she rushed indoors, flinging wide the door as if a pack of wolves were after her. She dashed into the kitchen seeking warmth and brightness and speech, light and humanity, leaving the empty spaces outside. She wanted to clasp a warm hand, to touch the familiar Windsor chairs, and the smooth oak table, to hear her grandmother's cheerful cracked voice, or Hetty's scold-ing tones, anything to make her forget the vision of the lost and lonely one she had been.

Sometimes she went to the stable and stood close to the mare, or ran into the cowhouses and listened to the calm breathing of the cattle.

"I know what's the matter with you, Miss Jinny," said Sam one day when she came in, white and shivering, and stood close to the flanks of the cows waiting to be milked. "You've seen Fear same as me."

She gave a little laugh, and tossed back her hair. "No. I'm rather cold. I came to help with milking," she stammered.

"Nay, you can't deceive me," he said. "I've been through it and I've mastered it. This place will cure you if you'll let it."

The others were not so understanding.

"Jinny," cried Hetty sharply. "What do you mean by coming in like that, never stopping to rub your feet on the mat and bang-ing the door to shake the houseplace?"

"There's a boggart after her," scoffed Emmie. "I've seen her looking scared."

"Yes. A boggart," laughed Virginia, her cheeks flaming, her mind so happy to be there in safety that she felt she could kiss them all.

"What's the matter with you, Jinny dear?" asked Charity one day when they were alone, and the girl told her.

"It's because I think you might all be dead and I left the last person on earth," said she, and Charity didn't laugh.

Lovely things and terrible, the world seemed full of them, but gradually the shadows of fear went from her as the peace and understanding of the old house possessed her and held her to its heart.

Chapter 13

The house was talking to itself one day. The low sibilant murmurs of blackened oak beams, of timbers and furniture mingled together. Thinking of queer happenings the house went back to Tudor times, and the old yew tree which stood at the end of the yard, shadowing the closet, leaned forward to listen, as the house talked and nodded its head. Next it was telling how the farmer at a steading across the valley had sold his wife for a golden guinea, an ancient tale it had heard long ago, but everybody liked to listen for the story was fresh in the house's mind. It remembered every word of the gossip of that day. It remembered the lewd jokes and sorrow and laughter of the people who sat round its fire. So now it brought the tale fresh from its vast store of memory and repeated it to the unseen listeners.

The parlour spoke out, the crooked staircase to the kitchen crackled, the west bedroom shook its head. Chests of drawers, club-footed tables, creaky chairs all talked to one another, but they stopped their tongues when the house spoke. They are the witnesses of events, they know what has happened, and they just stay there listening all day to secrets and quarrels and kindly speech. They carry old tales from their own past, and relate them again when all is quiet, but when the house speaks they are silent.

Charity sat by the fireside, plucking a fowl into a great heap of brown and gold feathers. Her apron was round her and the fowl on her knee as she worked. It was very quiet, she could hear the murmurs, but not a word of that strange conversation came to her ears.

Surely the kitchen had seen many scores of fowls plucked in its time, for the feathers, cured and cleaned, filled many a mattress. Pillows and bolsters and feathers bed were part of the dowries of the girls and they went to farmhouses and cottages in the neighbouring villages. Charity strained forward, with her little face puckered, as she listened and entered that other layer of time.

Then she caught a few words of housewives and farm boys and the laughter of children. Quarts of cream and dozens of eggs and nips of brandy were mentioned as one told a favourite receipt to another. Farm boys whispered how they sucked the eggs, a dozen at a time, when the wife wasn't looking. A cradle rocked, Charity could hear it, and the spinning wheel hummed. Then all these sounds faded, as the house itself talked.

"House talking of summat," she sighed. "It foretells summat afresh. It's wide awake, and it only talks when summat is going to happen. I'm old. I could talk too."

"Do you remember that day when I falled from the apple-tree and cut my head open, and was carried in?" she demanded aloud. "Do you remember when the pony walked through the door into the kitchen, and how we laughed? We gave her some sugar and wheedled her out before she got upstairs. Do you remember the day that gypsy came and read our hands, and told me I should live to a good age? Do you remember my Timothy's smile, and my father whipping us when we'd been up to tricks?"

The house listened respectfully, but it went on with its own far more exciting tales. Nobody knew the times of stress it had borne, long before Charity's birth, the sorrow deep as the ocean, the grief of women, that had wrung its heart. It had steadfastness of its own. Its character had been influenced by all that had happened there. It was aware of all. Everyone who lived there had given something to it. Every song, every prayer, every cry was registered in its walls. It gave and it received. It had suffered with a man whose young wife had died two hundred years ago, and left him with a brood of little children to manage in loneliness. It had rejoiced when he found another wife who shared his burdens and gave him comfort. None of these things heard Charity, but lulled by the vibration of its talk, she fell asleep.

In the great barn Sam too was listening to the voices, but he heard a word that the house said. He stood very still with the besom in his hand, forgetting to sweep up the slattered hay, forgetting to fill the mangers, to chop the turnips, to attend to the horses and cattle. He forgot all as he stood there, caught up in past and future. Ah yes, there would be warmth drawn from the sun and stored in the valley and brought to the barn, said the house. The house remembered old days of rush lights, and moonlight and dips of mutton fat made in the little farm kitchen under Virginia's bedroom. Even Charity remembered that, for she had helped to mould them. Now the farm was moving forward to future days, to electricity brought by straddling giants.

It spoke of something else. Fire. It warned everyone who could hear. Fire from the sky, it said. Dark winged birds and fire.

"Fire from the sky?" whispered Sam, and he kept the secret and talked to himself as he went about his work. "Fire from the sky."

But old Charity heard that sinister warning. She raised her head and tapped the floor with her stick, demanding attention.

Hetty came in, and waited impatiently. "What's the matter, Mother? You've been asleep, see the feathers all blowing about and door open."

"Fire from the sky," said Charity, dazed.

"There is no fire, except on the hearthstone and you've welly let it out, Mother," snorted Hetty, seizing the poker, and throwing on more coal.

"That's what it said. Fire from the sky," repeated Charity.

"I've no patience with you, Mother. Talking so soft. You've been dreaming of the Bible, Elijah, calling down fire."

"No, Hetty," said Charity firmly. "I heard the words. The house is warning us against fire from the sky."

Hetty turned away and stamped across the yard to William.

"You mother's talking about fire from the sky, some warning. What does she mean?"

"Lightning. She remembers something that happened once, the end cowplace struck, and her mind wanders. I'll go and pacify her, poor old thing."

He swung his heavy frame across the garden, walking slowly, hands behind his back, staring up at the sky, at the weathercock, and the clouds and the vast inverted bowl of heaven.

"Sam. What ar't doing?" he shouted as he passed the open door of the barn, and Sam awoke from his dream and began to sweep. Everybody seemed bewitched at times, thought William moodily.

He bent his head as he entered the kitchen doorway from long practice, for the lintel was low and the bunch of herbs tickled his hat.

"What is it, Mother?" he asked, leaning over the crouched figure with solicitude. He put his hand on the thin shoulder and looked into the piercing blue eyes.

Charity nodded. She seemed tired. It was hardly worth speaking. Nobody ever understood her nowadays. She was getting worn out.

"You're thinking of that day the little cowhouse was struck when I was a nipper," said William. "Well, I tell 'ee what I'll do. I'll put a lightning conductor up there on the roof. I'll do it properly, and it'll protect the house and all."

She smiled vaguely at him and nodded. "Like the Church?" she asked.

"Aye. We'll have a grand lightning conductor up on the chimbley of the apple-chamber, and it'll catch the forks of 'lectricity and lead 'em safely to the ground. I've thought of having one but somehow I've never had time to fix it. I'll do it to satisfy you."

Charity nodded, she wasn't sure about it but it sounded a good plan. Still she was uneasy. Even when the spiked conductor was attached to the twisted chimney she regarded it with concern. It didn't seem safe, it was an open umbrella attracting the storms.

Sam too was changed nowadays. He never seemed to be aware of anybody, he was for ever listening, standing in dream. William would have got rid of him, but he was sorry for the man. At last, persuaded by Hetty he gave him notice to leave in November when the hiring fair was held.

"I'll give you a good character," added William. "I'll get Dick to write it out in black and white."

"Aye," mumbled Sam. "But I dunno want to go, master. I want to stay here. I'm happy here. I knows the house and all of you. It takes me a long while to know folk. I dunno want to go elsewheres. I'll stay for my keep alone."

William discussed it with the family. Charity wanted to keep him. "He's good at heart, and we must abide by him," said she.

"He's going daft," cried Hetty. "It's not safe. I can't sleep at nights. You don't know what might happen. I found out about that murder his brother did. I thinks of it at night. Mrs. Badger told me. 'Do you know who's servant at your place?' she asked. 'Brother of a murderer,' said she. Of course I denied it, but it's true."

"It doesn't keep you awake," scoffed William. "I can hear you snoring before I've said my prayers."

"Never mind. I wake up later when you're snoring yourself," said Hetty fiercely. "You must get rid of him. Besides, Ben Clay wants to come and we can't keep both in vittles."

William compromised by finding the man a good place at a neighbouring farm, where his secret was unknown. In November Sam left, with deep regret and many a backward look.

"I'll get back some day," said he. "I can't keep away. I've known a bit of peace here, in stackyard and stable and cowhouses. I knows 'em all."

He couldn't settle at Greenleas Farm, it was stark and bare and cold. He couldn't remember his manners and he forgot to remove his cap in the kitchen, and everyone was against him. The food was poor, and he was very lonely. His wits were going, he was haunted and lost without the invisible company he had found at Shepherd's Fields. He might have cried "Poor Tom's a-cold", for he was shut out from the warmth and comfort of the world.

One night Sam Wheeler walked up the lanes and across the hills to the farm and stood outside the sleeping house. It waked up and watched him. With stealthy tread he went to the stackyard, opening the little wicket gate to the enclosure with its long wooden poles barring it from cattle. He let his hands move over those smooth old poles, and he touched the iron sockets of the uprights. The stacks stood like rich houses, glowing in the moonlight. Their golden straw was powdered with snow. They looked secret and warm. Icicles were in the wind's breath, death in its fingers. When the frost touched the little bird crouching under the ivy tod the feathers ruffled, and shook, the tiny heart quivered. Sam knew all about it. It tucked its head closer, made itself into a ball under its brown cloak, but its strength was not enough. The tiny curving feet of the little creature loosened their grasp, and with never a sound it fell. Sam picked it up and held it in his hands. Cows in the byres moved forward in the wooden stalls, and crouched lower in the straw. Sam would have joined them but the doors were locked and the keys lay on the dresser end. Horses, patient and steadfast, pushed their noses in the mangers, and rubbed themselves against the warm comforting wood, smooth as satin, black with age and friction. A bitter wind shook the branches of the trees, and rattled them together like bones. It thumped the shutters of the house, and the house shrugged its shoulders and kept its back turned, but it was watching Sam.

The trees were shaggy with frost crystals like collie dogs. Sam Wheeler ran his finger tip over the rough crisp silver strings, where the horse hairs had gathered the crystals. He was filled with wonder and awe. He walked across to the grindlestone and turned the handle, and the great stone slowly revolved. It needed two men to turn it, and Sam saw a shadowy figure swinging his naked arm on the opposite side of the round white stone. It was surely Old Death himself, come to help Sam. The wheel of stone revolved, swung between the two upright pillars of sandstone, and the dim Aged One turned his handle so swiftly the wheel whizzed round, and sparks flew from a scythe he held, and a hiss and a cry went up.

Sweating with fright, Sam dropped his handle, and the wheel went on for a minute alone, but there was nobody there. Sighs and whispers came from the farm. Everything was speaking of the cold. The stacks rustled, and a rat ran out, gazed at Sam with beady eye, and fled. The moon hung above, in a halo of rainbow, and Sam looked up at it and watched the moon shadows on the fine snow. Moonlight! He was different when there was a full moon. He had power. He heard voices at full moon, the voices of the house, talking. He had saved Virginia from the Man in the Moon. Like a grotesque moon-shadow himself, he waited, knowing nothing, waiting for something he knew not. Then, when a moonray fell on the stacks, lighting it to molten silver, he knew.

It was light and warmth he wanted, to see the house by, more and more light, warmth and gladness for the farm.

He drew out a box of matches and piece of paper, struck match after match and pushed them in the stack.

The yellow flames licked at the hay, swift as a thirsty beast, and Sam Wheeler pushed dried grass into the fire and laughed as the darkness in his mind was brightened by the flame. Light, candlelight, moonlight, stackfire light. The house would like a good fire round it, he thought, glancing back at the dark shadows blue on the snow of the long low buildings. The stack was beginning to burn. He warmed his hands at the small blaze, muttering aloud.

"Fire from the sky," whispered Sam crazily. He was filled with happiness.

"Look! Beware!" cried the dairy window that looked out to the stackyard, to the rest of the house.

"Something's amiss," said the little cheese room over the dairy where the cheeses lay in rounds on the stone floor. "There's danger about to-night."

"We must stop it," cried the house. All spoke, the clock in the kitchen, the dresser, the chairs. The wind whistled down the chimneys crying, "Fire! Fire!" The house was wide awake, its stones were watching with a thousand eyes. They put forth their strength to resist the danger. Charity too was awake, and troubled. The house was uneasy, she knew. There was the sound of many small voices, whispers and rustles and a thin crackle.

Curtains of shut windows blew out as a sudden wind caught them. The old staircase creaked as if ghosts were running up and down stairs. There was an audible humming and murmur everywhere.

"Awake! Awake! Awake!" cried the voices.

All mortal men were abed, but there was surely somebody abroad that night. Dogs were silent, not a beast lowed, but the voices grew more insistent. Charity rose from her bed and went out on the landing, and threw wide the window. The fields were silver, and the barns and stables were in violet shadows. Then the acrid smell of burning came to her and she heard a new sound, a crackle of flame, and the most dreaded thing in a farmer's life came into being. Fire!

"Will! Dick! Fire! Fire! Stack's on fire!" she shouted, hammering at the doors.

They ran downstairs, dragging on their clothes, and calling to one another in panic. Everybody rushed out in the moonlight.

"Get buckets. Get water from the troughs. Where's the ladder? Wake Ben. All on you must get to it."

They carried water to the rising flames, they formed a chain from the troughs, but the spring water didn't run fast enough to keep them supplied. Nothing they could do seemed to make any difference. The flames shot higher, and the largest stack was well ablaze, sending a sheet of flame to the sky. A neighbour appeared, roused by the glow, and then another galloped up on his horse, and away he went for the village fire-engine.

From out of a doorway came Sam Wheeler, his face wild, tears running down his cheeks. He worked with superhuman force, trying to mend where he had broken, to put out the fires he had started. His madness was as terrifying as the fire itself as he leapt upon the flames and beat them and strangled them with his great hands.

"Back! Back!" he shouted to the fire, pushing it away and neither William nor Dick could dissuade him.

"I made it, and I mun put it out," he roared and whimpered and sobbed in his frenzy.

"Save the house," they cried. "Throw water on the buildings. Soak the other stacks. Douse them well."

They worked with blackened faces, and scorched hands, beating at the hay, pouring water. The flames like gold hair flew upward from the big stack. They could not save it. There was a ripping tearing sound in the sky, the screaming cry of hay being torn asunder. The house cried aloud too, its high thin cry was clear above the crackling of flames. Then the wind changed, as if by a miracle, and the flames were blown away towards the field. The little hand engine came rumbling up, but it was not much use. The stack burned itself out, and lay a dark ruin, but the house was untouched, and the stock of hay in the barn was saved, with the cattle and horses.

Sam Wheeler lay dying in the corner of the stackyard by the wall, his hands and body badly burned. He opened his eyes as they carried him to the house and whispered between broken lips.

"Aye, master, I did it. I set 'em afire. I come back to see the place, I lighted stack to see better. Sam was cold. Is the house safe?"

"Yes. It's safe, Sam," sighed William. "Don't 'ee fret thyself."

"I'm sorry master."

"You get well and you can come back."

Sam smiled with his crooked, charred face.

"Thank 'ee," he whispered and he died.

The house moaned softly for him. He had understood and tried to serve her, but he had nearly destroyed her. Now he was going to that land of shadows whence he had come, crooked and strange, a shadow himself bearing life for a time.

Chapter 14

Spring had come with the suddenness of a shower of green rain. One day there were naked boughs, and twigs like a filigree of grey lace, and the next day the hedges were misted with tiny rosettes of leaves, and the hawthorn buds were beads on the tangled harsh old trees. Hawthorns were geometry trees, said Richard, and he showed Virginia the right-angled branches, and the straight lines of boughs. Soft warm showers and a burst of hot sun had brought forth the miracle of creation. It was almost unbelievable that the earth could move its old limbs so quickly and bring out such hidden treasures from under its dark brown shawl. The spotted curling sheaths of cuckoo pint, the airy wind flowers, the clusters of primroses suddenly flew out of the earth, the cowslip buds raised their palest green knobs from the stiff loam of the pasture, and over all the rich scent of the larches drifted, sweeter and more aromatic than any smell for the farm's pleasure.

Spring is a time of concealment of secrets and revelation for those who have eyes. Virginia peeped into nests. Warm and inviting were those little homes for the people whose language we do not know, whose lives go alongside our own, with love and fortitude and self-sacrifice. She unrolled a leaf, and discovered a spider, intent on something too small for her to spy. She peered into the trunk of the sycamore, through the round hole in its crackled trunk, for there might be a ring stolen by a starling, or a scrap of parchment with hieroglyphics written by a wood mouse. Indoors as well as outside there was spring in the air. Inside one of the leather-covered boxes, in the farmhouse, uncovered by the spring cleaning there might be a book of magic. Herbal books, and sermons she found, but no treasure of past enchantments. She cracked a nut always with the feeling of expectancy, looking for a ball dress of cobweb. She opened the inlaid workbox with the tiny interlaced key, hoping to find treasures of gold headed needles, and coloured spools of silk, and the patchwork pincushion, which never disappointed her. How was it that each time she looked at them, they were fresh and new, and gave her continual delight? The secret that lay under a stone, the hidden quality of flower petal, the loveliness of a butterfly, each was so exciting that every second of time was like a hundred years. Immortality surely couldn't contain more in all its eternal years, than one day of spring, when each moment was packed with bliss, and the joys and accumulated essences of others long dead swept through her mind.

The old house was fresh as one of the spring flowers. Winter smells were transmuted by the new wind. Cheese, and milk, mildew smells and mould, ancient odours of long stored garments, and faded dresses and stiff silk wedding gowns, all were stirred up by the winds of spring.

In the orchard the rough-skinned cherry trees tossed their snowballs, and the silver birch trees poured their waterfalls of golden green in the wood over the garden wall. The solemn trees waited, proud and withdrawn, walnuts, yews, old oaks and beeches, and elms. They watched the profligate, common flaunting of colour, but they bided their time, like the old aristocrats they were. They too held a secret, which Virginia had tried in vain to discover. Their life was hidden, their secret was strength of earth, and the wind doing its magic. They kept their secret, and suddenly they revealed it as they accepted her. She knew she was admitted to a dimension where human sorrows do not exist, but something fuller is there, for eternity. That was the real meaning of immortality.

The earth was alive, and she was part of its flesh and bone, aware and brimming with the feeling of unity with it that spring. It had revealed itself to her, as to her grandmother. The everyday wonderment at simple things made each day a new birth. She stored them in her heart, packing unconsciously a trunk of memories to take on her long, long journey through eternity.

There were special times when the air was stilled, as if listening, and everything became radiantly clear, the veins of leaves, the texture of a wing feather, the hairs on a petal, and even a vibration of air brought something to her senses. Then she was aware of the house, she felt a wave of knowledge going over her, the earth had granted her a favour, the certainty that her love was returned. Then she knew the thoughts of those who had lived there, she felt their presence, and although she saw nothing of them, she had entered into their lives and shared their happiness and their sorrow. Yes, on certain days, when she was in tune with some emanation of the house, she heard the dreams and longings and shared the bliss of those forgotten simple folk.

Charity was left alone in the house one day. Virginia had gone off to the market town early in the morning with the two big flat baskets packed with butter and fowls. The enormous lids were slipped over the handles, and the white cloths poked out like ears from the space which lies directly under the flattish handles. Dick had harnessed the little mare, and given her an extra grooming. Virginia, fresh as a flower, with her last year's hat and a new ribbon upon it, took the reins and drove off.

"Good-bye, God bless you," she called, and she waved to her grandmother through the kitchen window.

"Good-bye, Grannie. Take care of yourself. God bless you," she called again. It would never do to take a journey without a blessing.

"God bless you, Jinny. Get a good price for your fowls," said Charity, in her wavering voice. Dick opened the gate and held it while Virginia drove through.

"Drive straight! You grazed the gate stumps," he shouted crossly, but his eyes followed her till she was half-way down the field road. Then he drove off with his father in the spring cart in the opposite direction to see some cattle put out to grass.

Hetty did the suckling and feeding, but the day was so fair, she was tempted to leave the rest of the work and go.

"I'm going to the village this morning. Now be good, Mother. Stay by the fire in chimney corner, and take care of yourself. Don't you put a foot out of doors. There's nothing to see to. It's a lovely day, but there's a treacherous wind. Stay here and mind the house. I shan't be long."

"I'll mind the house, Hetty," nodded Charity. "We two've been left alone together before, you know."

Hetty pecked the old woman's cheek, and reached her basket from the peg on the oaken pillar. It was a feminine basket, with dainty straw-work round the edge like lace, and Hetty felt like a lady as she dangled it on her finger. She went away with quick hurrying step, picking her way across the manure heaps in the yard, and then turning through the stile to the short cut. She was glad to be free of the house for awhile, and there were friends to meet and gossip to hear, and ribbons and hats to look at in the small milliner's shop.

As soon as Hetty had turned the corner, Charity, who had been watching from the window, disobeyed her commands. Like a naughty child she looked round and clapped her hands with glee.

She reached her bonnet and shawl from the hook behind the door, put her pattens over her shoes, and got herself ready for a private jaunt. She looked round the kitchen to see that the fire was safe, and the cat asleep, and the canary's door shut. She pattered along the passage to the dairy and took a glance round, and latched the door. She opened the parlour door and stood for a minute looking at her reflection in the gilded old glass. It was misty, for it hadn't been dusted for some time, and the room was heavy with ancient scents, lavender, and mildew and sweet old stuffiness, from furniture and geraniums and bottled sunshine. She threw open the window and a butterfly flew out, to taste the first breath of spring. She turned to the mirror again, and now she could see herself. She wasn't surprised at what she saw. There stood a lovely young girl, with a full white dress edged with pale blue, and a little white straw bonnet with blue ribbon bands. The young face gazed back at hers, the sparkling eyes twinkled, and the rosebud mouth smiled. There was a smell of violets. Charity took her handkerchief from her pocket under her skirt, and wiped the beads of moisture from her forehead. When she looked again the radiant young face had gone and there was an old woman whom she scarcely recognized.

She went slowly away, not going back to the kitchen but unlocking and unbolting the front door, as if she were quality. She wasn't going far, because nobody ever left the house all to itself. That was unthinkable. Houses want company, they hate to be quite alone. She was just going to take a little walk to welcome the spring.

She steadied herself by the door post, surprised to find that her legs were not so obedient to her wishes as they used to be, and she had to walk slowly across the cobbles, feeling her way with her stick, holding on to a wall and a stump for safety. She was old, old, but inside her there was something very young, like the spring itself, bursting out into leaf and flower, responding to the sun. She felt it stirring, this new spirit, and she felt strong again, renewed by it. There was the mossy old wall with its tiny ferns and lichens and mosses, with bud and star, across the yard, and she walked towards it, stepping through the little silver stream which ran from the troughs. She grasped the stones tightly, staring across at the river, and the high road in the hills with its carts and cars and walkers, a dray now and then, a coach twice a day. There was more traffic than formerly, and it was a source of interest to watch and guess, but she soon tired of the midget vehicles swirling along in the distance. She touched the wall, and ruffled the yellow stonecrops, the "Welcome-home-husband-though-never-so-drunk". The smell of stables and cowhouses came to her and the warm sweet breath of calves. With it drifted the scents of the wood, trees, primroses, elder leaves, and the walnut bark. Her senses were very acute in those last hours on earth. She raised her head and snuffed rapturously, as if she wished to take that smell down into the grave with her. The earth was clean and good and soon she would be part of it. There was nothing to fear, and much to welcome.

"But I still love life," she argued softly. "I don't want to end yet. I want to see Flower's foal born, and the chickens come out of the eggs, and I want to smell the laylock again, and the medder-sweet from riverside, and haymaking, and to touch the eggs in throstles' nesses."

Then she gave a little chuckle, and spoke up as if she were addressing God Himself.

"I don't ever seem ready, do I Lord? But I'll come without a grumble when You really want me, even if it's this very day as ever is."

She turned her back to the wall and regarded the house, seeing it with the freshly-washed eyes of those about to die. Her sight was better than ever it was. There was the room where she was born, her own bedroom, and William's and Hetty's next to it, and Emmie's that had once been Sister Abigail's, and then had been Kate's. There was the little chamber where Virginia slept, above the mangle and the washing baskets and forms. Windows were wide open, and curtains flapped eagerly, as if they were hands waving to her. Hetty was a good sort. Yes, she had not always got on with her daughter-in-law, resenting Hetty's hardness, but Hetty had her points, and one was fresh air and cleanliness. She couldn't have borne with a woman who was a dirty slut like James Fuller's wife, never having a proper washday, even sending sheets and towels to the laundry to tear and mess about.

It was a lovely house, she thought, plain as a homely woman, but beautiful in its way. The shadows in the stones were like hidden bunches of violets, which one could almost smell. Yes, she could smell violets again. Mothlike shadows flitted out of the house shadows and the smell of violets was everywhere, drowning all the other smells. She leaned over the wall, and saw them, where they had not bloomed before. She looked up at the sun, and held up her wrinkled hands for his warmth. He didn't care that she was old, he remembered her when she was young and pretty, and his love stayed with her. He had seen her work in the fields, binding the golden sheaves of corn, stooping low to the earth. He had seen young Davy Morton make a wreath of corncockle for her hair, and kiss her red lips secretly behind the stooks. Now her skin had taken on the colour of ripe corn, her eyes were bluer than the flax flower, her hair was white as the clouds. The beat of her heart was the same to the sun as the beat of the earth, and when she died the two would be one. The old house and herself looked up at the sun, and he laughed down at them. Spring time and harvest, sowing and reaping, were part of them both, and the sun brought both to perfection. She would die, and then she would walk the green fields of heaven, but she would walk her own fields too, step along Daisy Croft and Meadow Lea, with the best of them. The house too would be in heaven, it was there now, quivering with light, scarcely of this world. In the future the cycle of life would continue, the child would be conceived, and born, it would be warmed by the same sun and the house would enfold it and give it grace and courage. Like the wheat in the cornfield it would ripen and grow, and the last harvest would take it, the great reaper would cut it and store it, and life would go on.

She saw the house dimly as if a veil hung from the sky, softening the deep sun shadows. People moved behind the veil, all held by their kinship to the house. People moved there, in barn and cowhouse and yard, those who had lived there and loved the farmhouse. She felt her kinship with them warm in her heart. She was drawn by overpowering love for them.

She grasped her stick and ventured farther, down the yard to the field gate. She lingered for a time here, watching the young stirks with their thick coats, playfully nudging and pushing each other. How seldom animals quarrelled! How seldom they fought or tore at each other! One came through the bushes, with dark inquiring gentle eyes, and another met it by chance entering at another gap. Immediately, with no hesitation, the first one backed away and made way for the other. She pondered their secret talk, their knowledge of man and their liking for soft speech and music for awhile. Then she pressed her hands on the gate, remembering when it was new, many a year before, made by the carpenter, chosen by herself to take the place of the ancient moss-covered narrow gate that had stood there for a century. She had been proud of that gate, and she was still proud of it, but nobody knew its history except herself. Long ago the carpenter died—Jim —— Jim ——, she forgot his name. Even his little shop had gone, and a new man was in his place.

Then she went through and closed it carefully behind her. A calf came butting up to her, and she gave it a tap with her stick, renewing her old vigour. "Now be off with you. I'm too old to be bothered with you."

She walked with slow deliberate step down the drive, head bent to the wind, shawl drawn tightly around her sturdy old body. Half-way to the river was the oak tree, where the swing hung. Every farmhouse round about had a favourite oak or walnut tree, with swing or seat. The Sunday school treat was held in this field, centring round the good-natured oak where the mothers sat. Then the boughs echoed with children's voices, as boys and girls scrambled for the swing, and helpers pushed them high in the branches. Two or three at a time could sit on the capacious wooden seat, between the iron chains. For over a hundred years the tree had been used for Temperance meetings, and revivals and parties. They said that once upon a time Charles Wesley himself had preached under its boughs. It held a hymn tune of his in its branches. The tree was getting old, like Charity, although its span of life was long. She must have a talk with it, to renew her strength at the source of its own vigorous life. She had longed for this, but they wouldn't let her go out alone. Now her chance had come, and she glanced at the oak tree and the path that lay between. Slowly, deliberately she walked, planting her feet carefully, aware of the grass beneath them, her own land, her father's. Arrived at the oak she stood for a time gazing up at it. The great branches stretched out in a canopy of brown, with tufts of green and gold, all awaking. The trunk was bossed with horny pads of bark, which formed footholds for those who climbed in it. It was a magnificent tree and she laid the palms of her hands upon it and stood there. Through her fingers ran the sap of life from the tree. Through her palms went the warmth and vigour of that growth. She was deeply aware of the pulse running up from the earth, filling the great tree, streaming through the bark, to her own body. She was the tree. She leaned closer with her ear to the trunk, listening for the beating of its heart.

She knew the past, through an awareness of life running through all things, flowing into her being. Her apprehension of other centuries was due to her knowledge of her own time. It came in visions not hearsay, although she had heard enough from the lips of old labourers and shepherds to realize the integrity of her vision. There was her land, her farmland, her England, whose strength came from those past ages. Deep in the earth went the roots, spread out among the rocks, twined in the soil like the tendrils of the oak tree, the tiny brown rootlets that hold the tree upright in the fiercest storms. She had often sat under this tree on summer evenings with Timothy her husband, long dead. Close together they sat, unspeaking, each one filled with slow-moving thoughts, listening to throstles and blackcap, eyes watching with quick intentness the movement of birds and beast, mind content. Perhaps Timothy would whistle under his breath, or hum the tune of a familiar hymn, "Abide with Me", or "The Old Hundredth", but no word would he utter to break the peacefulness. A labourer perhaps walked along the field path, with his rush basket on his back, his step a long slouch, and their eyes turned to watch him till he was out of sight. Their thoughts were the same. Abel Smith had finished his soughing, he was off home to his kitchen for tea. John Thomas was looking for rabbits. He would come back when it was dusk. Yes, their thoughts had run alongside but they didn't speak.

The corn in the field, the bird on the tree, were part of herself and she sat waiting for the reaper to come. Yet she would remain, to dwell by the dying fire, to touch the face of children unborn, to sing to child, to whisper to the lonely. Tales would come out of the air, thoughts would flash into minds, sweetness would descend on tired bodies, and a touch on aching hearts, and it would be herself, Charity, who would be there, part of the house, the disembodied spirit of the farm, speeding on winged feet to the cornfields, sharing the sun's golden work, standing in the ruddy grain, falling with the steely rain upon the hilly lands, hiding among the haycocks, walking in the crystal snow, wrapping it round the house's gables, shielding the wild white wind from its walls. No being forlorn, but one brighter than the sun himself she would be, no ghost of dim memory, but a vital being with power and bliss.

She saw other things besides green grass and brown earth. The land was peopled with those who had once lived there, friends of her youth, even by the men of other generations of whom she had only heard stories from her own father and mother. Invisible ones walked the roads, sat at doorways, their feet traversed the field paths, they rode in old-fashioned carts, they drove in the post-chaise. They were alive, generations of the past came to her, alive as she summoned them, as they came to the house itself.

She recalled that Strong-i'-'th'-arm's plough had turned up that field yonder, which now was left a derelict bracken-covered hillside. She knew whose hands had builded that barn standing in the shade of beech trees, on the horizon, hidden from the eyes of casual lookers. She had had tea up there with the children of that lost farm long ago, and played in the new barn. She remembered who had planted that group of firs on the hill crest, a landmark of pride to all, and who had made the walnut drive and who had bought and planted the lilac at the tiny cottage gate down the valley.

She knew which tree was the cuckoo's favourite, and in which grove the nightingale came. Even the railway was peopled with ghosts of workmen, digging out the foundations of embankment, making a bridge, and girdling the river with steel.

Life was vast, cruel, curved like the dome of heaven above, spun out to infinity, with myriads of humanity padding down the years, losing themselves, falling into space. She put her hands out to the tree and held it tightly. Only by thinking of small things could one keep fear at bay, only by holding on to daily happenings, and small pleasures, the secret beauties of the earth and sky, which unfolded every day afresh for man's delight. Always she had felt the passage of Time, the strong beat of his wings, pushing her through the days and years and now hurling her into the unknown. She had seen him, not as a man with a scythe, like her husband, Timothy, or like her son William, and all the men she had known but as Somebody, running through the heavens, blowing the stars out of the sky, drawing the sun from east to west, changing, shifting, and she dragging back for one more look, clutching the dear familiar things which broke under her grasp, even as she held them—the wooden doll, the young calf, the lambs, all had been swept from her. Then her mother had gone, and her husband, and young Kate had flown away in Time's arms. That was all over. Now she had one more week, and one more day. Perhaps this was the last day. He might be there, blowing his trumpet, for her. She had snatched one more day from eternity. The last day of all, and she wasn't ill either. That was a triumph. She was ready now. It was leaving life she had minded so much, but she remembered what the house had told her. Death was only going to another room, through an invisible door, and they were all waiting for her. She wasn't ill. But she had boasted too soon for the old pain came flowing in a wave through her, beating her down, her eyes were veiled, she could see nothing. She held tightly to the tree trunk, it was breaking her out here, and she must beat it away and return to the house. It wouldn't do to die out in the field. The house wanted her there. The field was meant for love and joy, for courting and kisses, for laughter and song. She must get back to the house. The tree was looking down on her with compassion, sending new strength to her, easing that strange pain. She had had it before, but not like to-day. She wanted to creep back like a wounded beast and hide herself in the house. She measured the distance with her eyes, the pain had lessened, but it would return. Where was Hetty, why didn't she come back? William was gone to the cattle market with Dick; he would be away till night. Ben was in the far field, ploughing, she could see him. Virginia,—the girl was at Upper Weever. Nobody to help her, and she helpless by the oak tree, dying maybe, if this was death, this wave of black sickness. She leaned back and shut her eyes and waited. After what seemed a century, she heard a faint sound and she slowly opened her tired eyes. There stood Flower the great mare, rubbing her soft sides against the tree.

Charity called her name. "Flower, Flower. Come here, lass. Come here." The mare walked deliberately round the trunk and pushed her soft nose to Charity's caressing fingers. "Wilt thou help me to get home?" she asked. "Wilt thou help me, lass?"

The mare whinnied with pleasure and Charity's hand wandered up and down the long face, touching the flicking ears and scratching the starred forehead.

Charity dragged herself up, holding the black mane, and stood for a minute leaning on the mare. The great heavy beast seemed to understand for she waited patiently, while Charity recovered herself and put her arm on the glossy neck.

"Now take me home, Flower lass," said she coaxingly, and the mare obediently walked across the field to the gate of the farmyard, with Charity leaning on her. Slowly they went, very slowly, and the warmth of the animal's blood came through to the old woman, and its strength helped her. Now and then she stopped, and the mare waited, and then together they went on that last journey, home.

The field was netted with gold shadows, the air was molten gold, spilling across the yard, flooding the garden, spilling in the water troughs. Charity looked aside, longing for a drink, wondering whether her strength would hold out.

'It would be a caution if I felled in the troughs and got drownded there," she found herself chuckling as she thought of it. "I munna drown. I don't want a wet death, and the water wouldn't be so nice afterwards. But I'll dare. I'll make a bid and get a last sup of spring water."

As if the mare understood her muttered words, Flower swerved aside at the gate and went to the troughs. Charity slipped her arm away and stood wavering a little drunkenly by the running crystal water.

"Let's both have our drink," said she to the mare. Flower lowered her great head and drank deeply from the horse trough, and Charity lifted the wire netting and dipped her hand into the clear ice-cold spring as it gurgled out of the clustered stone of the channel into the trough. Like a transparent glass rope it twisted and fell, ever singing and whispering in high shrill sweet notes, and Charity drank it.

"I'd come back from heaven to taste this here water," said she to the mare. "Don't ye forget, this time here with me. I'll come back here and sup it for there can't be water like it up there."

The mare waited, the drops falling from her lips, and Charity rose and replaced the wire netting.

"Now come along lass. I've had my last wish, and I'm ready for home, for home."

They went across the yard to the open door of the house.

"Thank ye, Flower. Thank ye," said Charity and she gave the mare a last pat and kissed her muzzle. Tears were coming, and that wouldn't do. She wasn't thinking of anybody now, she had forgotten them all. She was alone in the world, she and old Flower. There was nobody else alive at all. They were all waiting for her to go through that door, somewhere. She walked unsteadily across the kitchen, to go to her bedroom, but the door of the crooked stairs was too far away. It seemed to be retreating as if it didn't want her to get to it. It was miles away, and the pain was coming again.

"I beat it. I got here fust," said Charity aloud to the room. "I got here, and I'd better stay here. The door was out of this room, the door I have to go through to get to those others."

She sat down in her little low chair, in the corner. The kettle hissed quietly on the hob, and the clock ticked loudly, talking, saying something. Over and over again it spoke, waking up she room, telling it to look at Charity. Charity could hear it, but the couldn't speak or move. Her thin hands were cupped over her heart. Her blue eyes were wide open, fixed on nothing, she was waiting, listening. Then at last she heard it. The old house itself was talking to her. She heard the beat of its great heart, and the sigh and murmur of its voice.

"Are you ready, Charity?" it asked. "It's time."

"I'm ready," she said, but her words made no sound, her lips didn't move. She was smiling, for she saw all those others, standing at the door, flooding into the room like a swarm of dark bees, laughing and shaking their broad shoulders, holding out hands to her, clasping her. They took her by the hands and raised her up, and she was light as a feather and free as air. They all went laughing and talking out of the door and the house was talking too.

But Charity sat so still that a hen came into the kitchen and cocked an eye at her, and then began to peck the crumbs under the table. The hen became bolder and walked with tripping step under the table and through the legs of the chairs. The kettle hissed and sang on the hob, the clock ticked loudly, imploring somebody to come. Shadows moved over the room, and the sunlight flickered from the stone sink to the dresser and wavered across the floor till a beam fell upon Charity's cheek. Still she didn't move, and there Hetty found her when she came back from the village.

Chapter 15

After Charity's death the house seemed to shrink and draw inwards to itself. It refused to speak to others. There was a questing air about the rooms, as if they waited for the familiar footsteps and missed the light tap tap of the old woman's stick. The inhabitants missed it too, and sometimes when the wind knocked on the shutter, or a leaf fluttered on the floor, they were startled and looked up as if expecting to see Charity. William was dull and morose, lost in his thoughts, confused in his mind for he had leaned upon his mother for advice more than he realized. She had known so much, she had been steady as a rock, and she had a prevision of events, an intuition inbred from past generations. She knew what to do when a crop failed, or disease came striking suddenly. He had somehow thought she would live to be a hundred. But her endurance and joy lived on, waiting to be caught up by another. The air was full of her vitality if they had only known.

William listened with an absent air as Hetty talked to the neighbours who came to pay their calls of sympathy.

"Her was white as a new-washed sheet and clear as wax," said Hetty to this one and that. "Her said to me many a time, 'When I'm dead and gone, Hetty, there's my best linen nightgown with fine stitching on it, and my snowy best cap with the Buckinghamshire lace, and a pair of white stockings folded ready for me in the bottom drawer of the chest. And don't spend money on a grand coffin.' That's what she said, but we gave her a coffin of oak with silver fittings and a good funeral with port wine."

"And you found her sitting dead in the house when you came in?" they asked reprovingly as if they thought Hetty should never have gone out. She resented their remarks, and explained to each one. "I'd nubbut gone to the village for a breath of air. I'd been cooped up here all winter and on the first warm day when I happened to go out this came on us. I told her not to go out, but she wouldn't be bid. I told her, but she was ever strong-willed for her own way. She was wearing her bonnet and shawl when we found her, and the front door was open."

"She'd been to the oak tree," interrupted Emmie, eager to have a word in the tale. "We knew because Ben saw her sitting there. He was ploughing in the far field. We'd lately put it under plough. Gran wanted it to be ploughed. He saw her sitting there. When he got to the end of the furrow he saw her going back to the house with the mare. Of course he thought it was all right. People who are ill don't lead horses."

"And when you got home you found her?" asked the neighbour again. "What had she been doing with the mare?"

"That we shall never know unless old Flower speaks. Flower

166

was loose in the yard, standing at the kitchen door, when I got back. That gave me a turn," said Hetty. "She wouldn't move. She stood there with her head down, as if she knew all about her."

"I think Flower helped Grandmother to walk back from the oak tree," interrupted Virginia, who had been sitting silently in her black dress by her uncle's side.

They all turned and stared at her, at her white face, and dark violet eyes, ringed with shadows.

"Maybe you're right," said William. "It's an idea. Your grandmother was always fond of horses, more than common fond. They had both gone to the troughs, we saw the prints of mare's shoes and her pattens. Flower wouldn't drink a drop that night when we took her to the watering."

So they pieced together the pattern and sometimes they could almost hear Charity laugh and clap her hands as they talked. "That's right. You've hit it," said she. "That's what I did."

Money was tighter than ever, and the little bit left by Charity was divided up and made only twenty pounds apiece. Richard worked hard along with his father, and Ben was the only help. Prices were falling rapidly, milk brought in not enough to pay tithes and taxes. There was a run of bad luck, wet weather for harvesting, and a couple of cows had been lost. Richard had gone against his father's good sense and bought cattle in the open market instead of from good farms. He had been done over them, and learned a lesson too late. They advertised and took in summer visitors who helped to pay the growing bills. Virginia cooked and washed, and cleaned for the families who invaded the farmhouse, strangers who asked inquisitive questions, who were often arrogant and hard to please with their demands for hot water and varied meals. Hetty enjoyed herself, it was life for her to meet them, but William withdrew in bitterness, receiving the money grudgingly. It was for the farm, he told himself. He wouldn't bear with them if it wasn't for Shepherd's Fields. They tried to economize in a thousand ways. Fighting the falling prices was like something intangible, beating air. Hard work killed nobody and he could work with the best, but this was different, the drift of men to the towns, the losses on cattle, the low price of milk and farm produce.

"Can I talk to you, Uncle Will?" asked Virginia, waylaying him one day in the yard out of sight of the kitchen. "I want to earn some money same as other girls do."

"Well stay here and work hard and you'll be earning, my dear," said William, looking at her with kind eyes, seeing her old dress and worn shoes, and the pallor of her cheeks. "Do you want to go away and leave us?"

"No. No, never," she cried, "but I can't please Aunt Hetty whatever I do."

"Never you mind, my lass. You be a good girl and do as she tells you. We all have our faults."

But Virginia studied the newspapers for advertisements, she wrote answers in neat handwriting in her little bedroom at night, when the boughs of the elm tapped on the window and the moon peeped in and laughed at her efforts. Nobody wanted her, for she had no accomplishments. She thought of going back to the village school to beg for work, but Richard and William would not hear of it. There was plenty for Virginia to do, and she was only too glad to get out to the farm and stay among the animals, in the peace of haybarns and cowsheds, but constantly Hetty called her indoors to clean and cook. She was serving two masters, but there was always consolation and happiness waiting for her in unassailable things. A rose nodded from the house wall, and sang "Keep your heart up", a bird called the same shrill encouragement, a torn cloud in the sky signalled to her. Nobody could touch these.

There was one place where comfort and salve for wounds could be found, and there she went. The little attic bedroom was her refuge, as it had always been. The pungent smell of apples and rue which had filled it for so many years that the odour remained in spite of repeated scourings, was part of the comfort. It was sweet and clean, and indivisible from it. The smell was deep in the beams, saturated in the walls. It was a care-free room with a life of its own in a different dimension. It seemed to say, "What-does-it-matter?" and she answered, "Nothing at all", and again the room sang, "What-does-it-matter?" like a bird's call in the tree outside and she replied, half-laughing, "Nothing at all." Then her troubles were easier. She escaped to a world where human cares are not known, to a world that has existed before man and before the gods, the first world of all.

"What does it matter if you are downhearted and frightened? Forget. Forget," it sang.

"I'll forget right away," said Virginia.

"I've seen many a downhearted one rise again. I've been here for hundreds of years, and I know. Nothing matters in the long run. You must dree your weird."

"Nothing matters. I'll dree my weird," she echoed, and she went back to the kitchen and Hetty's scoldings.

Sometimes she felt she hated everybody and everything. Her mind was troubled, flames of anger swept over her, scorching her young heart. Then she ran to the barn, hot-foot to escape from them all. Nobody understood her. She was miserable. Even as she entered the great chamber she felt a change come over her. Perhaps it was the shadow of that high-roofed building that cooled her inflamed mind. Perhaps it was the silence after Hetty's harsh voice, but she thought it was something different.

She stood there among the wooden corn bins and stone benches, great slabs of primitive sandstone, rough-hewn as folk had made them long ago, she waited under those dark time-blackened beams of the great roof, and the serenity of the place flowed through her, a peacefulness of other days, as if time had been sieved of its uproars and disturbances and only the essential essences of life had been left. That was it, something was present, permeating the ether, something indestructible, the faith and the endurance of other lives was still there. Troubles and worries and miseries had gone like dross before the refiners' fire, and only the important parts were left, the eternal verities. It was present, that sublimation of life, in the stones themselves, marked in the hollows of the flights of steps which led to the upper chambers alongside the barn. She was aware of a spiritual world, a counterpart of the visible. Nowhere was this feeling so strong as in the ancient barn, and in the little attic room over the old kitchen-place. In the kitchen there was something else, a life vital and real as the present day, a daily life which still went on from generation to generation. She shivered with joy and apprehension at it. The knowledge seemed too great to bear alone. The life of the past, the consciousness that it still existed, that nothing was destroyed, that it was eternal.

She walked out into the sunshine and stared up at the house. It nodded its head to her, its windows blinked. The lichened roof held a mystery of immortality which was of eternity. Evil to come and strength to meet it, and her own mind adding to the sum total of its courage. Every room, every chamber of the house was invaded by this strength. Humble folk, bearers of simple names, common folk of England had lived there. Their lives flowed into the ocean of eternity, unimportant and nobody, they were there and she was one of them.

The grief and sadness lessened, the days streamed by in a coloured chain, with black beads and bright ones, with sunny days turning to colder ones, leaves falling, snow swirling from the sky, and bitter weather gripping the land. Every day was filled with work at Shepherd's Fields. Virginia was up early, helping to milk before she cooked the breakfast. She went to the cowhouses with a lantern, and settled on the stool under a warm silky body, in the shadowy stall. She could think there, and she found a leisure she lacked when Hetty was hurrying her about the house. It was then she received strength from Charity, a fountain of help for the day, and the old woman might have been standing on the little raised stone platform behind the cows, talking to her as she milked. Sun bonnet on head, Charity seemed to be there, a tiny humped fragile figure, blue eyes sparkling, small mouth puckered into a smile.

One day in the kitchen she looked up suddenly and across the room she saw old Charity's wrinkled and smiling face, shifting in and out of the shadows like a beam of light. Her voice was sweet and slow, her skin was ivory clear, with a thousand wrinkles softening it.

"You mustn't be ashamed about your home, mind ye," said she. "Be proud of it. It'll know if you think ill of it. You'll maybe meet girls as is richer in this world's goods, and finer spoken and more delicate in their ways, but don't forget. This old house isn't fine or delicate. It's better than that. It's strong and brave and you've got to be like it. Now mind ye."

And Virginia never forgot.

Virginia picked up little messages which Charity had left behind in the warm cow-steamed air of barn and byre. The old woman had spent most of her life in those surroundings, and her thoughts and admonitions remained for the future. In death it is easier to share, a barrier is broken, and thoughts can get through, their own thoughts, evoked by scents, and music.

"Never you fret about life, chuckabiddy. Never you pine. There's plenty of good round the corner. It's there, waiting for you, and Shepherd's Fields will always give you itself. The good will outbalance the bad. The world would tip over if it didn't."

The lantern light streamed from the whitewashed walls, sending deep shadows over the strong oak stalls and the cattle chained to their smooth posts. There was a warmth and strength in the companionship of animals that communicated itself to the girl. Her fingers worked rhythmically, she sang softly, and the cows moved their soft ears, listening. Shadows and cattle heard her, and the walls of the building absorbed the moment. They echoed with song and story, once told and never lost.

There were layers and layers of experiences, of joys and sorrows in those old barns and outbuildings, waiting to be tapped, absorbed against the day when one who was attuned to them would recapture them. Virginia was finding them there. Human experiences and love, sweetness and bitterness, for hundreds of years were there, and she was adding her own contribution in one more layer to that essence of Time. It must be a good layer that she gave, she thought, to help those others in the far future who would want courage and help from the past. So each gives to the future a small crumb which is all important.

She sang grand old hymn tunes, and plantation songs she had heard the Christy minstrels sing, and tunes she had heard at the Wakes. Her clear young voice came ringing from the bedrooms as she swept the floors, from the cowhouse as she milked, from the stable as she fettled the mares. It wasn't good singing, but it banished gloom. The house was listening, smiling to itself, storing the songs in its stones. Aunt Hetty was better tempered. As for Richard, Virginia loved him deeply. He wasn't of much account but he was like the grass growing, or the spring flowing, part of the naturalness of the earth.

She was sustained by an inward exhilaration which swept over her, nearly drowning her in a flood of happiness. She was immortal, she would always be young, fortune and fate couldn't desert her, because she had found the secret of living. The more bitter and sharp Hetty's tongue, the deeper Virginia escaped into the earth, absorbing currents of the past which flowed into her, living in serving the common objects of life, taking pride in the inarticulate which depended for their well-being upon her services. Pots and pans, stone and iron, all were hidden sources of bliss.

"When Richard is settled and all, with a woman to care for him, your uncle and me'll retire. We shall go away from here," said Hetty.

Emmie was already being courted by a young man who was

acceptable to Hetty, but Richard took no notice of straying eyes.

It gave Virginia's heart a turn; she looked across the misty fields to the slopes of the woods with startled eyes, newly awakened. Time was rushing on. It was bringing changes. She might be immortal, but it was going to divide her from the things she loved. Not only from the human kind, but from the things themselves, dips and rises in fields, stone walls, dews and frosts on the kexies, streams in the earth, and blades of grass. There wasn't so much time in life as she had thought, if she were separated from Richard. For her it had stretched to infinity, filled like the horn of plenty with stars and sunsets and dawns, with youth and that inward bliss that assailed her and made her drunk with joy, but it was going past, and she couldn't stop it. She looked round at the house as if to question it, and it seemed to nod its old head, and glance sideways at her.

"Yes, a woman to care for him and to love him," said she quietly. "The house too will be glad of somebody to love it."

The dear familiarity of the place made her catch her breath. "I'm not afraid, but I can't leave you," she whispered to it.

The service it demanded was unending.

Virginia went out with bucket and scrubbing brush to scrub the flagstones of the path. Down on her hands and knees she knelt, her coarse sackcloth apron wound round her slender figure, her hands red and rough with cold. She scrubbed till never a trace of green was left, and then threw buckets of fresh spring water from the troughs over the flat smooth stones. In her iron-rimmed pattens, lifted above the water, she clinked and tapped like a bell, until the stones were clean as if they had been newly hewn out of the quarry. They were hollowed by many feet and the curves had to be dried and wiped.

"I canna abide green moss on a paving-stone," Charity had said once in Virginia's hearing.

"Why, Grandmother?" asked little Virginia.

"Because there's a grand beauty in stone," said Charity.

"You'd like to go down to the churchyard and scrub the tombs, Mother," suggested William drily.

"Yes, I would, and I've done it too. I went there when I was a little one, along with my own mother, and we cleaned up a lot of gravestones, friends and neighbours, my mother said they were, and she told me the dead folk were saying, 'Thank ye.' We spelled out the writing, and had quite a laugh over some of the epitaphs, but we said a prayer for each one under sod. Good clean stone is something to be proud of. I hopes somebody'll scrub my tombstone and not let the moss eat into it."

"And I've never done it," thought Virginia with compunction. The sun shone on the water-buckets, and reflections darted and quivered from the surface, cutting the air with light. House and paving-stones were part of each other, and the house was pleased by the service. Hollowed stones wore by generations of feet, scrubbed by many hands, by old, hard fingers and by young strong ones, responded.

"One would think you were struck on swilling," cried Hetty, as the girl tossed the brightly flashing water down the paths and ran after it with her brush.

"I am," retorted Virginia, pertly. "It's a race, to see who gets there first, me or the water."

It was true, there was happiness to be found everywhere, if one only looked, and people left you alone to find it. Life was in the drops of water, hurtling through the air, and it was the same life that filled her own body.

"There's the dairy wants doing then," said Hetty, sourly. "You get to that, and leave outside."

It was heavy work, but Virginia went obediently indoors, leaving that glittering rainbow yard to its game of light and shadows. She opened the dairy door quietly, rattling the latch at the thumb hole for a moment to tell them she was coming. It was a chamber of voices, a place where the echoes of other days lingered perhaps more than in any room. She could hear those dim whispering voices of mothers and daughters who came to skim the milk in thick yellow wrinkles with copper skimmer, to sort the eggs, and to count the pounds of butter into the great flat butter baskets that stood ready. It was so quiet in the dairy, shut away with its thick walls, built into the rocky bank, cold as ice even on hot days, that she always hesitated in the doorway lest she should disturb their talk. Round the wall were the broad stone benches, carrying their large yellow pancheons set for cream, and on the shelf were little white cheeses that Hetty had made. There was a strong sweetish smell, of milk mingled with the harsher smell of sandstone and the lime of the walls.

Virginia carried everything out of doors. Then she swept and scrubbed the benches and stone flagged floor, and outlined each stone and each bench with a yellow band of sandstone bright as a buttercup.

"Why are you doing this? Why are you troubling?" she asked herself.

"Because the house expects it," she thought, answering her own question. The house had its own proper pride of well-being, it liked to be well-treated. It had its grace and beauty to be preserved.

She was sent to the yard to clean the churns, for Hetty wanted Ben to drive her in the trap. Ben was glad to get out, and Virginia did his work while he was away. That was hard work, too heavy for her thin arms and slender body, but it had been done often by Charity, and Virginia vowed under her breath she wouldn't be beat! The milk churns were old-fashioned, very heavy, made to last for a hundred years, cupped and lidded and bolted with brass and decorated with brass nameplates. Boiling water must be used and nothing else would do. She carried the kettles of steaming water from the kitchen stove, and tilted them into the milky depths. Then she stooped, almost hidden from sight, her arms and head in the deep churn. She scrubbed it, and tilted it on its iron rim, swirling the steamy water round, panting and struggling with the weight. Inside and outside she washed it, and polished the brass plates with sand and vinegar.

"Charity Dale. Farmer. Shepherd's Fields" was incised there in the flowing letters of early Victorian days, and underneath was an older strip of brass with "Matthew Woodiwiss, Farmer", upon it.

Like five old grey men the churns stood, drying in the yard. They were travellers who went to a far away town, voyagers who had secret adventures. They wore ancient metal hats, and topknots of brass. When Virginia saw them packed in the milk van in the slow train, alongside the more shapely modern churns which had none of the stamina of these antique people, she was sure they told stories to one another. What tales they told each day, as they went away, bouncing along the stony roads in the milkcarts to the station, clean and bright and full of milk and plenty of cream! How proud they were, of their brasses and chains and latchets, like a farm horse! What secrets they whispered when they returned empty, dirty, unwashed, smelling foul, bruised and bumped, but never dinted! The feebler churns from other farms had hollows and scars, but not the strong old churns from Shepherd's Fields. Like warriors they came home, to be scalded and washed and sweetened, and rested for a time.

They told tales of the milk-sellers, with their little carts and spanking horses, of the hurry and bustle and noise, of stealthy cats, green-eyed, thin and wicked, of brave old horses pulling at loads of wet coal, of servant girls singing, of hawkers bawling, and little children dancing on thin feet to the music of a barrel-organ. Virginia had never heard a barrel-organ, but the milk churns told her about it, as they jingled their chains and rattled their lids.

The milk dealers emptied the milk with a special nod of recognition to these famous old churns. Inside the lids, within the metal-cupped lower lid, were letters hidden, touching notes reminding them of money owed, bunches of flowers, cowslips, white violets and roses, and little presents for the milkman's children. They were sent by Charity, and Hetty kept up the old custom. Virginia packed these gifts, adding a few extra country oddments of her own. She thought of this as she scalded the churns, and rolled them to their windy corner, to air.

Every fortnight there came washday, and the farmhouse was a turmoil of steam and boiling water. Hetty was in her element when she was washing. She was like a witch over her cauldron as she leaned over the boiler and took off the lid and sniffed at the steam. A good smell had steam, she seemed to think. She opened the fire door and poked the glowing embers with an extremely long iron poker. She rammed in more sticks and shut the door with a clang that echoed like doom.

"Hansel and Grethel are shut in the oven," thought Virginia, who wanted to escape but dare not. She carried buckets of water from the rain barrels and poured them in the copper. Sparks flew, and water splashed in great wet daisies dark upon the stone floor.

The tiny washing house which had been the brewing house in former times, was cosy with the glow and warmth on a cold day, but like a region of hell in summer. Virginia plunged her arms in the soap suds of the great tin pancheon, and Hetty with rolled up sleeves dipped her own red arms into another pancheon. The bubble and hiss of water made a sound like music, and there was a rainbow playing in the steam when the sun shone through the open door. Outside the lilac bloomed, the cock crowed, the swallows dipped, but the washing went on. Hetty took the boiler lid off and plunged in a bundle, as if it were a human body, and pushed it out of sight with a pole.

"You go on alone, Jinny. I've got to get the next boiling ready. Get a move on, my girl. Don't be afraid of work."

"I'm not, Aunt Hetty," gasped Virginia, raising her scarlet little face from the steam. The moisture played round her head, curling her hair in wet tendrils. She rinsed and tossed the clothes to fresh water, and the work went on, starching, mangling at the ancient mangle under her attic bedroom, listening to the squeals as the mangle was turned. Higher and shriller cried the mangle, and then with a thud the heavy square weight fell and the rollers were released.

Virginia was exhausted, but she said nothing. Grandmother Charity would not have allowed her to do this.

"I shall have to call Dick to turn it," muttered Hetty. "He hates it, says it isn't farm work. Ben ought to be here. That fellow Sam turned it with no trouble, he was so strong, poor creature. Weak in 'th head goes with that strength. You're a poor tool, Jinny."

So they struggled on, and the birds sang in the trees overhead and the mangle roared out its protesting cries of anguish like some inhuman child. There were always many sheets for some town folk had been to the farm, but now the house was empty and quiet from them, and the invisible inhabitants were free to roam.

"Take them to the orchard, Jinny," commanded Hetty, piling up the basket. "Can you carry it by yourself?"

"I think so, Aunt Hetty," Virginia surveyed the great double basket. She stooped down and lifted it with both arms outstretched. She staggered in the wind that met her as she went across the yard to the orchard gate. Her arms were strained with the wide span of the basket, which was so big Falstaff himself might have hidden in it. Clothes must not be dried by the fire even in wild weather. The kitchen must be kept comfortable for the men coming in from work, not filled with wet sheets. That had been the rule for all the years, so Virginia had no thought for the labour as she traversed the path to the windy orchard, where the line stretched between some distant aged apple trees.

Her hair was blown out in brown streamers, the pins were lost, her cheeks were scarlet, her old print dress fluttered behind and caught the thorny bushes as she walked, and twined round the gatepost. When all the clothes were pegged out, she stood watching them, waiting to see if they were safely tethered, loitering in a precious moment of freedom to gaze over the hills to the ever-changing sky. The blue striped shirts fluttered among the glittering mirrors of leaves, the wind was blowing from the water, bringing cold smells of heriff and dock, tossing the garments in twitching fingers, playing some private game of its own device. The sheets were lifted high, bellying and tossing, to buffet her with wet slaps. She retreated, watching them, half apprehensive of their strange antics. They were suddenly endowed with a life of their own, as if the wind had breathed a spirit of creation into them. Suppose it was life they had, these ghouls, and they went off by themselves, ghosts wandering in the woods, flinging their arms around anyone they met, strangling them in baleful coils, carrying them wrapped in wrinkled winding sheets to their deaths! She thought of a tale she had read. "A face of crumpled linen." Wet clothes were inimical, and she backed away from their influence.

It was then she saw a slanting figure striding along in the wind, someone whom she didn't recognize. She stood waiting, holding the empty basket in both hands, the red colour running bright under her skin, her eyes shining with the fight with wet clothes, and the latent fears of her imaginations. The calf dealer was expected, but this was surely no dealer in cattle. This young man, smooth-cheeked, brown-eyed, had an air of distinction about him, and Virginia hesitated. He came to the orchard gate, and raised his cap.

"Have you lost your way?" asked Virginia sternly, adding "Sir", as an afterthought. He looked like a relation of the squire's, so smoothly shaven were his brown cheeks. But it was impossible to be dignified with one's print dress kilted to one's knees, and bare legs. The young man looked at her in puzzled admiration. She was quite pretty in her rags.

"Cinderella?" he asked mockingly, "I've brought your slipper."

It was Virginia's turn to stare, as he held out a brown paper parcel with a slipper falling from it.

"A thing of patches," said he. "A bit worn, isn't it?"

"It's mine," stammered Virginia, dropping the basket. She dried her hands on her apron and took the old slipper. "It's my slipper. Mr. Drake mended it, and he said he'd send it up by somebody coming our way, but he shouldn't have bothered you, mister—mister," protested Virginia.

"True. The cobbler said it would save somebody a journey when I asked the way to Shepherd's Fields. He seemed to expect me to bring it, so I said I should be delighted."

"Thank you very much," Virginia said.

Virginia walked up the path with him, and left him in the yard. She wondered what he wanted at the farm. Perhaps somebody after the rough shooting, or perhaps an artist who wanted to paint the house, or even a talker. There were all kinds of strange people about, coming from the great world, exploring the country, discovering its beauty, explaining to the country folk that they didn't appreciate the loveliness around them.

"There's a gentleman at the door wanting you, Aunt Hetty," she called through to the kitchen, where Hetty who had seen the young man coming up the path, was hastily tidying her hair, and donning a clean white apron.

Virginia disappeared to the little chamber, and ran up the stairs, past all the wet clothes lying below, to her room. She removed her heavy boots and put on the patched slippers. Then she washed herself and brushed her hair.

"Why am I doing this?" she asked herself, but she could only answer, "Because I look such a sight."

She peered cautiously through the kitchen door but only Emmie was there. Aunt Hetty had taken the young man to the parlour, a sure sign of favour. Their voices came from the closed room. Then footsteps went upstairs, thuds and thumps as they walked across the floors, the flip flop of Hetty's list slippers, and the masculine tread of the other. Ordinary men didn't wear boots upstairs, and it was an unusual and astonishing sound.

Virginia scuttled out of sight and went to her favourite hiding-place, the water troughs in their bowers of ferns. It was the spot where she felt safe, and for some reason she was disturbed by this intrusion. She knelt down and looked at herself in the water. The reflection gave back her flushed cheeks and dark rose skin, her freckled nose and her thick curls, smoothed and pinned up. Cinderella! He had called her Cinderella. Men whom she had met at market and in the village were not interested in fairy tales. Only the cobbler had once given her that name in joke. It was her first compliment, and she wasn't even sure of that. She was bedraggled, and he had given her a slut's name. All the same, her heart fluttered with excitement.

Voices came from the house and she crouched lower.

"Then I may come next Monday?" asked the young man, and Aunt Hetty answered in her smoothest politest voice, "Yes, we shall be all ready for you. What name is it, sir?"

"Winter. Maurice Winter," replied the young man, and he said good-day and went off, turning to look up at the windows for a moment.

"What did he want? Who is he?" asked the two girls appearing like a pair of Jacks-in-the-box, popping their heads up, one from the kitchen, the other from the troughs.

"He's an engineer on that new reservoir in the hills at Hog's Tor. He wants to lodge here while the work is on. It will be quite six months he says and he's willing to pay thirty shillings a week."

"That's grand. That will be a help," cried Emmie, but Virginia didn't speak. She felt as if she were entering a queer unreal fairy-tale.

"It's a real godsend to us," Will exclaimed when he heard. "The regular money will help me out."

"Which room is he going to have?" asked Virginia.

"Dairy bedroom he asked for. I wanted him to have the best room, but he said he liked your grandmother's room and could he have it. Nobody's slept there since, but I had to say yes."

So Old Charity's room was spring-cleaned and prepared. The feather mattress was taken to the grass and beaten, and then puffed out before the parlour fire for a whole week. The strong smell of warmed feathers pervaded the house, and tiny white feathers flew out to the garden. Virginia scrubbed the bedroom floor and the sweet herbal scent of the walls was that of her grandmother.

She washed the bedroom ornaments, and set them out on the mantelpiece, the pair of Staffordshire jugs, the Bristol glass baskets, and the little cross in the middle. She wiped the pictures, a text, a copy of a winged angel somebody had brought Charity from Italy, and a faded photograph of a shire mare. Virginia thought they were all equally beautiful. She was proud that the young engineer would see them.

Freshly starched blue-flowered curtains were hung at the windows, old material that had been there for years, darned but still pretty. Richard and Will carried the great feather bed which was too heavy for womankind to lift, and piled it on the four-poster bedstead, over the wooden slats. Like an enormous broody hen it squatted, on the frame under the canopy.

"He'll sleep soft in that. He won't want to get up in the morning when he lies in this yer bed," said they punching and pounding it to make it lie down.

When Maurice Winter arrived he was agreeably surprised at his rooms, for both parlour and bedroom were polished and bright. The ornaments and texts he would remove later and put in a drawer, but otherwise he accepted everything as natural for people who lived in the country and knew no better.

"This is my daughter Emmie," said Hetty, introducing the girls. "And this is my niece Virginia. Wake up, Jinny."

He shook hands absentmindedly, as if he had forgotten the first meeting. Virginia stiffened, and answered awkwardly. She had to wait on him, there was no escape. She set the table and carried in his evening meal. Then she lighted the candles and drew the curtains.

"Would you like the lamp, or do you prefer candles?" she asked timidly. "Lamps give most light but candles are nicer."

"I'll have both," said he abruptly. "I have some drawings to work at. The light here isn't very good."

"It's the best we have," replied Virginia, disappointed. "Please ring if you want anything else."

"He says he wants lamp as well as candles," she informed the kitchen later, when she removed the dishes.

"He's eaten all up, chops and every bit of pudding."

"We mustn't stint him. Give him plenty of good food and make him comfortable," said Will. "And if he wants the lamp, then we'll have candles in kitchen."

"I'd rather help with milking than wait on him," said Virginia. "You do it Emmie." She was troubled, startled by his way of looking at her.

So from that first evening, Virginia kept out of his way. Emmie changed to her clean frock, and slipped on a white apron to carry in dinner at night, but Virginia was out helping with the milk when he returned. Maurice Winter didn't seem to notice who came in or out. He was absentminded, forgetful where women were concerned. His great chance, after years of dull office routine, had come and he had been sent by his firm to superintend the making of the new reservoir in the hills. The contractors were slippery people, and Winter and his ancient clerk of works were kept busy circumventing their tricks.

Every night when his meal was finished and the cloth removed from the Pembroke table that Hetty had placed in the middle of the room, he put the lamp ready and spread out his drawings on the drawing board. At bedtime, when Hetty came in to bring his candle and give the usual warnings about fire and putting out the lamp safely, he didn't hear her. She waited, and coughed, and he would look up astonished, as if he didn't know where he was.

"Will you be careful sir, with fire and lamp? And here's your candle ready for bed. Shall I call you at the same time tomorrow?"

"Poor soul!" said she in the kitchen. "He's like as if he wasn't all there. He looks at me as if he'd never seen me afore, and I'm sure he doesn't hear what I say. I'm mortal feared he'll set the house afire, he's so forgetful of everything."

"It's parlous hard work, is head work," said William slowly, and they all agreed. "It wants brains to make water works same as those at Hog's Tor. Catch the water, and keep it from running away is a big affair. Same as making a mighty water-trough, but they've got to put a pipe-line down through the villages and beyond. None of that water will go to the villages, I reckon. They never bother about us, it's all for the towns far away. There's a gang of men, strangers all, up there, making concrete, laying great pipes ready."

The young engineer sat up long after they had gone to bed. Then he put out the lamp, for he had some of his wits about him in spite of Hetty's fears, and he took his square brass candlestick up the stairs to Charity's room.

There was a great jug of cold spring water standing in the basin, and a flat tin bath reared up in the corner ready for his morning bath. The bed was turned down, and the curtains drawn back, for he didn't like to be shut in a fourposter he had told them. He always felt a deep satisfaction when he entered the room. All the worries of the day fell away, the petty discords were forgotten, even the calculations which had occupied him and puzzled him downstairs slipped into their proper places and resolved themselves with mathematical exactitude, so that he saw the correct figures writ on air.

He lay in the great feather bed, uncomfortably tossing, thinking of his childhood days, with a harsh father and a romantic mother. The two had clashed within him. The father had sent him to be an engineer, the mother had endowed him with love for all the things that don't count in the world. He was imaginative and unpractical, a dreamer, struggling to be a practical man. Life was one long struggle between the two warring parts within him. He had thrown overboard his mother's religion, but he couldn't accept his father's atheism. When he was in this old bedroom with its text on the wall, and its perfume of ancient goodness, he remembered forgotten things. He went back to days when he had listened to his mother's hesitating and faltering explanations of his ardent questions. She had died when he was twelve, and his father had married again. Maurice had left home at sixteen to live in lodgings and work at the engineering firm's office.

This was his first outside work, and he was proud of it. He was glad to be away from the dull routine of office work, where he had been a draughtsman for some years. Now his chance had come, and the Wander Valley water works was in his charge.

To him water had been a clear liquid of no interest whatever, that came out of a tap. Now he knew something wholly different. The year out of doors in wild hilly country had changed his ideas. He knew water as a living vital thing, a dominant spirit which could never be caught and tamed, even when it was trapped in a reservoir.

The engineer in charge had fallen sick, and Maurice Winter had taken his place. He came out to the little hill village, near the excavation. Autumn days had brought many difficulties, and winter brought snow and hard weather such as he had never experienced. The work was trying, his lodgings were uncomfortable, and the cooking was atrocious.

"Why don't you move farther out?" the contractor's engineer said one day, when Maurice made a joking remark about his landlady's cooking.

Maurice had kept the idea in mind, and explored the villages for some miles. It was wild windy moorland, but a motor-cycle would give him freedom. He looked at the land as if he owned it. It was the drainage area for the reservoir he was building. He was making something of importance. He had power over the little streams, to capture them and set them to work.

He had followed the streams, away to the valley, and wandered on, till he came to the river. Across the water, half hidden in the trees he could see the chimneys of an old house. He stood very still, with the sunlight running up and down his body, warming him as he had not been warmed for a long time. It was there he decided he would go, if the chance came. "Shepherd's Fields" it was called, they told him, an ordinary farmhouse with ordinary folk, but homely and kind and clean.

Each day he went off on his motor-cycle, with his sandwiches packed in his pocket and his papers strapped behind. Away down the drive, past the cows feeding in the meadow, past the young calves and the frisky colt shying with fear. Richard stood at the gate holding it open, envious of the speed of the machine. Ben came from the stable when he heard the chug-chug of the engine. Will always watched him off, and Virginia peeped from a window. He was an object of interest to them all, not only because he was their guest, but because he was doing something worth while, a piece of real work, like making soughs to drain the land, or building walls. All work which used the natural earth has a kinship, and to tame and train the streams and rivers was akin to leading the little earth springs into the water troughs. To build a reservoir was like making a pond in the fields.

So they watched him ride away in the morning, in rain and fine weather, and they welcomed him home at night, when he rode up the long drive, tired and dusty, dirty and worried. To the young engineer it was becoming a real home, the farm life was entering his blood, he who had known nothing of country life was drawn into it and refreshed and strengthened. The wild hill country of the reservoir, where the curlew and raven flew, and the softer country of the farmland, had taken and conquered him. He hoped he would never again be shut in the firm's town office after this. He must have outside work, away from the bickering quarrels of precedence.

Sometimes he talked to William, and asked questions about the farm, but he saw little of Richard and the girls. He was scarcely aware of their presence. Emmie said he was too proud for them, Virginia thought he was a clever man who wouldn't be bothered with plain countryfolk.

He drew back the curtains from the windows, and threw wide the casement over the yard. Hetty Dale was afraid of night air and she always shut the window. Below him was the line of farm buildings, with sounds of horses cropping in the fields, and cows moving in cowhouse or by the hedge. In the distance he could see the white foam of the river and farm gates guarding each field. It was an island of green, with peace at its heart. There was his old friend, Night, and he leaned out on the rough stone sill, staring about him. Night, with her velvet skin and blue cloak and her sparkling eyes, was there.

Over the hills was the reservoir, his work, where water would lie catching Night to its heart. It must succeed, that work. The room seemed to tell him so.

He dreamed as he lay in the great feather bed where once Charity had found her dreams. He planned bridge-building over wide rivers, tunnelling under mountains, road-making in foreign lands, and bringing water to thirsty towns. India, Burma, South Africa, all called him. Nothing seemed impossible, no height, no depth was too great for his powers as he lay and listened to the night.

There was another reservoir, one of strength, about him feeding him, and although he knew nothing of the history of the old house, he felt its courage flow through his body like water, its love fill his heart like wine. Life is a mechanical process, he had been taught. Christianity is outworn, they said, but this house told another story.

Chapter 16

One autumn morning Maurice Winter got up much later than usual. He had been on the works all night, supervising connections with a local pipe-line. Maurice and the clerk of works slept in turn. It was a luxury to have breakfast at nine o'clock, and he dawdled over it, eating the porridge made from William's oats, pouring on thick cream from the dairy, and following with crisp farm bacon, fat and highly cured by Charity's own recipe handed down to Hetty. It was different from the bacon of the towns, he hadn't liked it at first, but now he thought it was delicious. Again he thanked his lucky stars that he had ridden down the roads to the valley and spied this unknown little farm hiding in its woods like a fawn.

After breakfast he strolled outside, and idly watched the hens pecking in the yard, and the calves butting each other with their immature horns. There was radiant sunshine, the kind that comes sometimes in November, more ethereal than the light of summer. The sky was china-blue, ice-cold, and the sunshine delicate as yellow pollen. This light lay on the walls, already powdered with gold lichens, it gilded the trees, and gave the old farmhouse the appearance of unreality. It was dream-like, it was an old coloured print in a picture book, flat and unshadowed, and brimmed with a living beauty, sending out a light of its own. It was self-luminous, surely, and Maurice Winter was snared in the web of the moment, and struck dumb with wonder. He had caught the house in an unguarded time.

He had never seen anything like this expression of beauty in house and landscape. He stared about him as if his eyes had been washed in May dew in Tudor days, and he saw the world freshly created, for the house itself had opened its eyes at that moment, and he was aware of it.

It too was looking around, at the sky, the fields, the haystacks. It was wide awake. Every stone gave out its inner light and meaning. Currents of thought and happiness came from it, running out like gold threads, weaving in the air to form that luminosity. The house was filled with earthy goodness. The hay harvest had been heavy, the corn was stacked ready for the threshing-machine, the fields were well-walled, the yard was swept clean, there was an air of well-being, for another corner had been turned and luck had come back for a time. The farm-house was very much alive at that moment.

From a doorway came Virginia, her hair uncovered, the curls gilded by the same pale light, so that she too seemed unreal, her blue dress was turned up to keep it clean, and her old-fashioned apron was tied round her waist.

She did not see Maurice standing flat against the wall, quiet and lost as a shadow, for she was looking possessively at the rose tree on the house-front, eyeing the late autumn roses, the long buds and the full blooms. She chose the ones she wanted, and stretched up to gather them. They were out of reach, on a part of the wall that was windowless, over the barn. She stood on tiptoes, and pulled a loose branch so that the dusky roses tilted down. She let the rose tickle her nose, and she stayed for a whole minute, which was perhaps a year stolen out of time, breathing the fragrance, losing herself in the identity of the flower. She became the rose, and grew there, and time dropped away. It was a moment of life, when her whole being flowed into that span of time outside eternity. Like a fountain her love for the earth welled up and flowed around her, spilling on the ground like gold. So days and months fled by, as each was lost in the eternal, the girl in the essence of the rose, the man in the girl, who looked like a transparent figure in porcelain.

Then she gathered the rose, and back sprang the long loose flower-laden streamer, and the house breathed again and drew up the spray to its roof, for the rose tree was part of itself. Maurice walked across the narrow grass and stood by her side.

"May I have that, Virginia?" he asked very quietly in a voice which sounded almost harsh, and before she could say yes or no, he took the rose and kissed her tender lips. They stood looking at each other in surprise, Virginia with her dark blue eyes wide, her lips parted in a crooked frightened smile, the young man wondering what had possessed him. He put the rose in his button-hole, and waited, regarding her, waiting for her to move. She was beautiful he thought, with sudden realization. She didn't speak. She knew that this was what she had wanted ever since he had come to the farm. She was not surprised, it was somehow inevitable. Neither spoke, they stood very still, looking at each other, caught in an enchantment that wrapped them in an invisible cloak.

The farmhouse gazed down upon them, and smiled at a repeated tale. The same rose tree, and different lovers. It remembered. So had Charity been kissed long ago, yet only the other day, as time is measured out of time, but she had pushed away the young man with her stout little arm, and clouted him for his impudence. Other rose trees had grown on that ancient wall, forerunners of this tall straggling bush, and other women in earlier centuries had held up their faces to the kisses of their men. Legend said that two lovers had met there once, the girl from the farm and a rich young Elizabethan, who had married his dear in spite of family resistance. They had planted a tree in token of their love, and it was the ancestor of this windy-petalled scented rose tree, red as blood. They had gone away to live in happiness in a far part of the country and she had taken with her a little parchment with her father's and grandfather's names upon it.

Charity had told their happy story to Virginia and Emmie when they were little children, as her mother had told her, and so the tale was passed from one to another, with an added detail here, an embellishment there, for it was the greatest romance the farm had known, and there wasn't a hint of sadness in it.

On this translucent day Virginia forgot the tale. It was only afterwards she remembered her grandmother's words. So the house laughed softly remembering the kiss, remembering the past.

Maurice went abruptly back to the house, and Virginia finished gathering the roses. She brought a stool from the wash-house and balanced on the top. The blooms were going to the church-yard. Charity always liked roses, and she would welcome them. She might even be standing near on tiptoes with her black bonnet tilted, and her little wrinkled hands uplifted crying out, "A bonny smell! Pick me two-three, Virginia, to keep me company for it's a bit lonely where I am." Then a wind blew over carrying a smell of apples and wood-smoke and leaves, and Charity's voice drifted away.

The motor-cycle chug-chugged down the yard, and the house watched the engineer ride away with a rose in his coat.

Virginia went up to her bedroom and shook the feather bed as it had never been shaken before. Her heart was in a turmoil. She whispered her secret to the walls.

"He kissed me," said she, looking round and the little rippling echoes came from the beamed roof, and tiny kisses fluttered from the walls. "He kissed me," laughed the room.

Then her heart sank. "He'll forget all about it by to-night. He won't even remember which I am," she told herself, and she was plunged into a despair so deep that the sun seemed to go out of the sky.

But Maurice Winter didn't forget although he tried to put the girl from his mind. He didn't see her for several days, but she was there, aware of him, avoiding him. Each night he sat late making his report, listening for her voice. Sometimes she passed the door, but she didn't enter. He was angry with himself, furious and undecided. It was damnable to like her, to feel restless when there was so much urgent work to be done. It was outside his calculations. The house had done it, cast a spell upon him, lured him on. The sun looked into the parlour, and smiled at Maurice, who stared to see it. It ran its finger-tips over the old gilt mirror with the garlands, and across the polished mahogany chairs. It said good morning to the tall white wall cupboards and the door of one cupboard flew gently open to expose Charity's lustre jug with the circle of flowers round its waist, and the wedding tea service. Queer! Maurice rose and closed the door and fastened the latch.

The sun smiled at the furniture, and brought ancient fragrance out of it. The old things smiled back and Maurice caught their look. They pointed invisible fingers at Maurice and said a thing or two.

"Little Virginia! He's falling in love," they jeered, and they laughed and shook their sides, but Maurice frowned and threw down his books.

"I can't settle here. I'll leave," he groaned. He was melancholy and wretched. He sought Virginia out, determined to put an end to his misery. What was a kiss, anyhow? He didn't love her, or want her, he detested her, and he'd tell her so.

He looked high and low for her, the farmhouse was a fine place for hide-and-seek, and she slipped through the shadows of half-open doors, and out at the back. She was avoiding him too. The top half of the calf-place was open, and he strode across and peered into the darkness. Virginia was there, shadowed, stooping to the animals.

"Come in, Mister Winter. Do. Open bottom door. Pull the wooden bolt inside. That's it. Come and see our champion calves," she invited, and her voice was the low and caressing voice she used for animals, she included him with her own grand little calves, licking her hands.

There was a heavy smell of animals and dung and straw, a strong healthy smell, and Maurice sniffed dubiously, as he drew back the great wooden bar which might have barricaded a fortress door, and entered the calf-place. He went close to the wooden pens which held the animals. There were three little rooms, each containing two calves, red and white, like young deer. Their eyes were large and gentle, the skin on their necks was ruckled in silken folds, they staggered about on splay legs, and butted and slobbered, staring at Maurice with solemn eyes, as if asking who he was.

"Let 'em suck thy fingers, Mister Winter," said Virginia. "Don't do it that road! Like this." She was a child among her little herd, she relapsed into her country talk, and Maurice could find no opening for his rehearsed words. She had slipped away from him. He put his hand carefully over the strong oak door of the first pen, and the calf sucked his fingers, raising its curly head and drawing them masterfully, guzzling in ecstasy.

"It likes you because you're quiet and not blustering," Virginia informed him, nodding her head with approval, careless of him. She looked very young standing there with her milk bucket in her hand, and her face turned to the half light of the open door. She wore her milking bonnet loosely over her hair, and her sleeves were rolled up over the elbows from her brown smooth arms. Maurice stared at her arms, so close to his, they seemed to be of the texture of an egg shell, with a faint transparency in them. There was a deep rose colour in her cheeks, which came as he entered, but she was unembarrassed by his presence, for she was at home. All her fears had gone, she was filled with confidence that he would some day come to like her.

The watchful eyes of the young man were upon her, but she was unconscious of his scrutiny, careless of her effect upon him. He was appraising her, taking in the beauty of her face, aware of it for the first time, realizing the strength and delicacy of her bones, the sweep of her brow, the laughter hidden in her lips. In the twilight of the calf chamber, she seemed to shine with an inner light, and her slender brown arms were held out like those of a statue he had seen, so that he longed to touch them, but he was kept off by something.

"They're grand little calves. I've rared 'em myself, all myself," said she. "They'll be good milkers some day, but I expect Uncle Will'll sell two or three. It near breaks my heart, to see 'em go. I can never get used to the parting, not as long as I live. I always lie awake o' nights, mourning and greeting like their mothers when they're gone."

"Virginia. Will you meet me to-night? At Four Lanes End? I want to talk to you. Will you?" he asked at last.

"Why, of course," she replied, shyly glancing at him. "After milking, I can't get before."

"All right. Somewhere about five o'clock," he nodded curtly and went out.

He was at the Four Lanes End early, but he had to wait till dusk before Virginia came spinning along on her bicycle. She was happy and excited, and not a little nervous, as she sprang down.

"I'm so sorry I'm late," said she, "but our white heifer, Snowy, kicked the bucket of milk over. She's not used to being milked, she's only lately had her calf. Oh, there was a fuss! Aunt Hetty wasn't half cross with me. I couldn't help laughing, though it's a loss of good milk."

Maurice didn't speak and she continued explaining. "I'm very sorry I'm late, Mister Winter."

"Virginia," said he slowly, and Virginia's heart sank as he walked along the lane by her side. His face was utterly gloomy, his eyes were clouded with anxiety, and he didn't look at her.

"What is it?" she asked quickly. "Is anything wrong? Has the retaining wall broken? Is it the work?"

"The work?" he echoed, staring at her and stopping.

"Yes. Uncle Will said you told him it wasn't going well, at least, not very easily," she stammered, embarrassed by his hard stare. She had offended him, she thought. Oh, why had she interfered with his affairs?

"You know nothing about it," he muttered, and he turned away as if it were a grievous thing that troubled him. "Virginia. I think I love you," he said.

Virginia was shaken and astonished. It was very different from lovemaking in books. She had no reply ready.

"I think I love you," said Maurice again, as if it were the most direful happening. "Do you like me at all?"

"Yes. No. Yes, I like you," stammered Virginia.

He put his arms around her and kissed her, but there was an awkwardness now, unlike the first kiss he had given her. He seemed to be resisting love.

"I've been unhappy all week, not knowing my mind. Now I know. I don't care what you think or say. I'll make you love me."

"I don't want to marry anybody," thought Virginia. "I don't. I want to be free. I won't love anybody. I love Shepherd's Fields most of all. I won't leave it."

So her thoughts raced on in panic, but all the time something was happening to her. Her heart was singing another tune. She couldn't stop it.

"Virginia." Maurice drew her to a gate and climbed upon it. "Sit down and let us talk."

Virginia perched by his side, uneasily aware that it was Farmer Brown's gate, and old Brown would tell everyone he had seen Virginia courting there. Maurice was speaking, and she glanced warily behind as he put his arm around her.

"I want to marry you soon, Virginia. I've only got a hundred and fifty pounds a year. I expect you thought I had more, with my motor-cycle and all. I've saved nothing. It takes all to pay for board and lodgings, but I shall get two hundred when this job is finished. Will you marry me on the chance?"

"I haven't time to think," she protested. "A hundred and fifty pounds sounds a lot to me."

"Will you marry me, Virginia?" he asked. "Marry me very soon. I don't want to wait for you. This job is nearly done, and then let's get married."

"Oh dear," sighed Virginia to herself. "What a tarnation hurry."

"You are too quick-thinking for me," said she aloud, and she gave a little laugh. "A countryman would take five years to say what you've said in five minutes."

"Five years? We shall be married and have a family in that time I hope, Virginia darling."

But Virginia shivered. The world seemed to darken as he spoke. Death was looking down at them from the sky, his face white and terrible in the clouds. She trembled and hid her face, and he put his arms around her.

"Darling. Surely you want children?" he asked.

"Yes, oh yes. It was something else. A goose walking over my grave," she whispered.

"Virginia. You haven't said yet that you love me."

"I think—I—do. Yes, I do," and he kissed her again.

They walked down the lane wheeling her bicycle, mercifully escaping from Farmer Brown's eyes, and crossed the home fields, Maurice talking eagerly, Virginia shaken and quiet, filled with intense and sudden bewilderment.

"Don't tell them yet," said she when they came in sight of the farm. "Keep it secret. You go in as usual, don't tell them yet."

Love had blossomed in her heart at that moment of insight. It was a love that tried to shield him, to protect him as well as to share with him, everything except this knowledge that had come to her.

They had all guessed her secret. Uncle William and Hetty seemed to know all about it, it wasn't a surprise at all. Maurice was welcomed by all except Dick who was morose and silent. He was drawn into the house's companionship.

There was a singing going on in Virginia's mind, never stopping, tune after tune, careless and free like a bird. There was a new light shed from the sky to the earth. Although she knew the fields and woods so well, she felt she had known nothing of them until now. Now she was led into their secret heart. Now she saw with eyes bathed in a dew from heaven, so that flower petals were magnified to show their beauties, little green paths hitherto invisible in the grasses came into sight, branches of trees formed a pattern telling her something. She didn't walk, for her step was too light. She floated out of her body, over the mossy banks, reaching up to the utmost boughs of the tall trees, down to the depths of the rocks where the springs went on their underground journeys. She could do miracles, out there in the sunlit air.

She tried to show Maurice these visions, as he walked by her side. They went on excursions together, and Virginia showed him the places she loved. Once they went to the glorious Elizabethan Hall, set in its great gardens, with its heavy doors and great kitchens, its courtyard and ballroom, where dreams come to life. Again they went to a little manor house, where cows grazed on the lawns, and apples were stored in rooms where once a queen had stayed. Sometimes they visited the market town, where the carts were ranged round the square, and the vegetables and baskets of fruit were placed on the pavement edge, Virginia's own produce among them. Then they drove in the cart with Richard or William, and Maurice looked round him at a world he had never imagined, it was so different from his own.

They spoke of all their hopes and aspirations, they told their silent thoughts, their unknown unconscious minds were revealed. Every moment they were together was fused into deeper love, and Virginia forgot everything in her new rapture.

The days rushed by and the time of the wedding came. Virginia's preparations were of the simplest. There was no money for anything grand, and she had only a new muslin dress made in the village. Maurice had no idea how poor she was until he saw her little hamper unpacked on the wedding night.

She had packed it with all her worldly possessions. It was a Japanese basket, long and narrow, and she laid her clothes within, piling them up for the lid would cover them. By her side lay the loose straw lid and the pair of straps. She crouched on the floor of her little room with her garments and layers of newspaper. It was difficult to decide about her treasures, her beloved possessions, valuable only to herself. There was a box she privately called her jewel box, because it was lined with rough red satin. The lid was covered with rows of pointed shells which she thought most beautiful. Inside was a blue glass necklace, a string of coral beads, a silver heart, a jet bracelet belonging to Charity, and a thin silver bangle. She wrapped the box in a handkerchief to keep it safe, and then in a vest. Out it had to come again to take a sixpence with a hole in it, which Dick had given her in her childhood.

"Dick! Ah! Dick, I shall miss you," she thought with sudden pain.

A prayer book came next and three books, *Shakespeare*, Wilkie Collins' *A Woman in White*, and *Shelley's Poems*. There were few books at Shepherd's Fields. She had to take something to show Maurice she wasn't entirely ignorant. A bit of Blue John spar came next, a rough piece of stone which she had picked up on the quarry heap. It was deep blue as a violet, with tiny facets which gleamed when she held it up. If somebody with a lathe for polishing stones could have it, it would make a brooch. So she had thought for years, and hopefully she put it in the case. Down in the corner of the hamper she pushed a lucky marble, an alley-taw that had been a talisman against wild beasts and robbers. A pearl-handled penknife went in, and a small magnifying glass. She switched it from its case and looked intently at a spider and a cobweb. Then in among her handkerchiefs it went, buried in the silk sachet with the bottle of lavender water. Finally she added a reading-glass which had magnificent properties. It would burn a hole in a piece of paper if necessary. She placed her new blue dressing-gown over all, and strapped on the lid. Her packing for all her future was done. She was leaving house and home, cows and horses, fields and barns, and going off on a new life.

"Well Virginia. All set for the wedding?" asked Hetty.

"Yes, Aunt Hetty. I've remembered everything," she replied.

"Everything," echoed the kitchen walls, and Virginia heard it.

She went round to say her good-byes to the places she knew so well. She went alone, Maurice knew nothing of these pullings at her heart. She could never tell anyone of her secret life. She stood in the barn and listened to the voices of the past. They took no notice of her, they were used to marriage and death and birth. Disappointed she turned away, but the house knew. It was re-membering her, and saying good-bye to her. She wept as she stood by the wall, watching it.

The morning sun came shining through the little high attic bedroom up the ladder over the mangle and washing pancheons. It wakened her. It was her wedding day. Soft whispers came through the air. "Courage and Love," they said. It was the house talking to her or perhaps only talking to itself, she was not sure.

G 193

She smiled back at the crooked whitewashed walls and nodded to the fluttering little shadows which danced over the walls, from the leaves outside. "Courage and Love," she whispered back.

She could hear the door of the stable opened, and Dick shouting in the yard, and the milkcans rattling. Downstairs in the little kitchen below her room somebody was looking for an empty churn, and in the big kitchen farther along Aunt Hetty was making porridge for the wedding morning.

"Grandmother Charity. Grandmother Charity. Are you there?" whispered Virginia. "Are you coming to see me married?"

She listened intently and all the familiar farm noises faded away, so that she could hear her own heart like a beating drum. Was there a rustle, and a flicker in the transparency of the air? Was there another beat beside that of her own heart? She shut her eyes, and she imagined a soft kiss was pressed upon her lips. It might have been a blessing from the house itself, or a kiss from Charity. She thought of the thin withered face, with skin softer than a rose petal, of the hands worn to a bone, hollowed and frail, strong and feeble. She saw the bright blue eyes smiling at hers out of a mist of time. Then the face faded away, and she tried to bring Maurice to her. It was his day. Yet she couldn't think of him, she couldn't bring his face to her mind. Jacket and round tweed hat, strong-smelling Harris tweed came to her but his face eluded her. Instead there came the face of Dick. Her heart ached suddenly. Life was very queer, and love wasn't at all like the love in books.

"Virginia. Virginia. Are you awake?" called Hetty, coming up the ladder and pushing at the trap door.

"I've brought a sup of tea. Why you sleep in this old place beats me. Fancy spending your last night in this old room." Hetty panted and puffed, and pushed her head through the open doorway. Then she reached up her arm with the teacup. "I can't get through, at my time of life. You must take it yourself. Nobody else will sleep here when you're gone," and away she went down the ladder again and then out to the yard, bearing a clothes-basket with her.

Yes, it was the last time Virginia would sleep in the little attic room, she remembered, for she couldn't invite Maurice to share the crooked loft with its smell of apples and hay. They were going to the sea for their brief honeymoon; Virginia had never seen the sea. Then they would move into lodgings near Maurice's new work in Wales. It was a very small job, but it was important and a step upward. From there Maurice would look for a post in another land, and she would go with him. It was of no use to buy furniture and settle down.

She bathed herself in the tin pancheon of water, and splashed cold spring water from the bowl over her body to harden it. Then she dressed in the white muslin dress with a blue sash and ribbons. Hetty and Emmie helped her to get ready. They drove away in the pony trap to the church in the village. Maurice was waiting there, shy and uncomfortable among so many villagers who were strangers to him.

The wedding breakfast was kept at the farmhouse, and then Virginia tore herself away from the place she loved so deeply, and set out on a new life.

Chapter 17

The harvest had been gathered in at Shepherd's Fields, before Virginia came home. There had been the usual harvest supper in the big barn, with the barrel of beer tilted to its last drop, and a round of beef and dumplings and a great pudding boiled in the copper for the men, and Virginia had missed it. Will wasn't so well, he could no longer work as in former days, but Richard had taken over the control of the farm. Emmie was engaged to be married to the schoolmaster's son. They were all pleased, for it was a good match for her, and she was happy.

A letter came once a month from Virginia to her uncle, but Richard had long conversational letters which he never read aloud to the family. In them his cousin talked of the ordinary things that meant so much to her, the colour of the sky, a white-washed farm where she had had tea, a watchman's brazier and hurricane lamps by the roadside, a tinker with his pots and pans, and everything reminded her of home. The lodgings where she and Maurice lived were bare of comfort, and shoddy with cheap, ill-made furniture, but they only paid twelve shillings a week. The landlady had given them a little iron bedstead with newspaper under the thin mattress and cotton blankets, but they kept themselves warm and laughed at the economies.

Every day she thought of the farm, and she knew without asking what they were doing. She could see them in her mind,— Hetty churning, slapping the butter into shapes, making the little cheeses, Emmie washing up and cooking and sewing for some lady, her Uncle driving to the market, or ploughing, Dick taking the milk to the station, leading, harrowing, everything was there. She asked about the trees individually, the fields as if they were people, the barns and walls. She never got any answers to her questions. Richard put her letters in his private pocket book and read them till they were worn out, but he never replied. Uncle Will wasn't handy with his pen, and he didn't write. Emmie occasionally sent a picture postcard, and Hetty sometimes sat down and wrote a letter with nothing in it.

It was a long expensive journey, but Virginia begged Maurice to take her home for Christmas. She hadn't been well, and the country food would do her good; he considered the cost and agreed to get away for a few days.

"She's feeling lonely," said Dick, when they all read the excited letter giving the news. "I can tell. She never ought to have gone so far away. She's been nowhere before."

"How can you talk like that?" cried Hetty. "She fell in love with Maurice, and he's a rare nice man for her."

"Maybe. All the same that's what I think. I reckon I know our Jinny better nor anybody here."

"It's her life, not yours, my lad, so keep your tongue quiet," interrupted Will with sudden roughness. He missed the girl more than he could say. "She's coming for Christmas, and we must make it special for her."

"Oh, it's always Virginia. She's your favourite," cried Emmie, tossing her head. "I hope you'll make grand preparation for me when I come home."

"No need. You'll look after yourself," retorted Dick.

Virginia was living an unfamiliar life, lost without the farm, restricted in occupations, but compensated by her love. There was nothing to do in lodgings, except to buy the food and suggest meals to the unwilling landlady. Money had a different value from that she had put on it in old days. Milk, butter, eggs, fruit, bacon, cheese, bread, and all the rich farm products which she had accepted as part of the earth's largesse, had to be paid for. Half a pound of this and that, a few stale eggs, a loaf of shop bread, instead of the riches the farm had given to its children.

Maurice went off to his work at seven in the morning, and didn't return till late, when he brought back sheafs of notes. The days were long and lonely to the country-bred girl, a foreigner in the Welsh town. Maurice was absorbed in the work that took all his energy and thoughts.

"Oh darling! Have I forgotten you?" he would say, suddenly aware of her quiet presence beside him. "Forgive me. I'm a mechanical fellow! I do love you, and you mustn't mind."

Then Virginia was happy again, and they walked through the villages to the fields, with flocks of redwings come from the North, peewits calling as they did at home, and even a green woodpecker to delight her eyes.

"Tell me about country things," said Maurice. "I want to know all about you and what you think about, and what I've missed."

So she chattered gaily, trying to lift the weariness of work which settled so often on his spirits, but only too soon she would see that he wasn't listening. Sometimes she could persuade him to forget the little reservoir and the difficulties there, and to speak of far countries where he was going when he got the chance.

"I shall do great work out there, Virginia. Build dams, and make bridges and tunnels. You'll be happy there, won't you? We'll have lots of children and good times together."

So he talked and lived in his dreams, and Virginia in her heart knew it could never be.

At night he lay by her side, speaking sweetly to her, but sometimes a black spirit seemed to possess him, and he thrust her away, exclaiming bitterly, "Oh, you come between me and my work. I mustn't think of you. I mustn't touch you even," and she lay weeping softly to herself by the wall.

Yet there was consolation and delight in the solitude of Virginia's days. The colours of the Welsh hills were ever changing, deep blue mountains which she longed to climb, a golden colour on the rocky coast. Bryony sparkled in red necklaces hung along the hedges and even towards winter the honeysuckle bloomed and pink carnations grew in cottage gardens. The lanes wound between high hedges where flowers stayed securely hidden against the gales. Trees slanted from the sea, bent in shapes of goblin and wandering ghost, ancient little wildings, full of

197

vitality and witchcraft, talking to her of occult strange deeds. Each day Virginia carried a basket of sandwiches to her husband in the hills, meeting him half-way to his work, and they ate the food together sheltered in his rough coat on the stone heaps. He was always enraptured to see her, and kissed her hands and her mouth with hungry kisses, yet there was always a division between them, as if matter and spirit were warring in Maurice's heart.

Virginia was counting the days till Christmas, and at last the holiday came. Excited as two children they packed a bag and caught the Welsh train. They stood in the crowded corridor laughing at each other, whispering a joke, enjoying the throngs as they swayed among them. The day passed, and the thin icy moon was in the sky when they made their last change and got into the slow train with the folk returning from the Christmas market. Virginia knew the people, and she spoke to one and another, introducing her husband shyly, hearing their gossip. The grumbling old train with the same old guard with his button-hole of mistletoe crept into the station, and the two travellers stiffly descended. How cold it was in that wind-swept place with never a house in sight except the station-master's cottage! The North Pole was reached, but the air was champagne, and the stars were gold icicles. The little moon was riding high in the windy sky, and the snow fields had a singular charm. It was two-dimensional, of a cold purity that could only be faery. All their tiredness disappeared as the freshness swept through them.

Maurice grabbed her arm and held it tightly as if he feared she would fly enchanted away, for she danced down the platform in the dim light of the paraffin lamp to seek the cart. Out in the yard they ran, and there by the horse stood Richard. Virginia flung her arms round him and kissed his cold cheeks. There was a horsey smell about him which she knew very well. He hadn't shaved, his rough skin brushed her lips, the odour of the farm caught her heart, and hurt it.

"Oh Dick! Are you glad to see me?" she gasped, in a flutter of skirts and a flick of her muff. "Are you?"

"How are you both?" asked Richard stiffly. "I hope you're middling."

"Dick! I'm here," cried Virginia again, pulling his arm.

"I see you. I'm main glad to see both of you. Where's your bag? Is this all? Give it me."

He flung it in the back of the cart and held the mare's head while they climbed the step and over the high front to the seat. There were rugs in plenty, and Richard tucked them around her and squeezed himself on the box seat at her side.

"Ah! I've been longing for this moment for a hundred years," she sighed under her breath, and she gave a tremulous laugh. Tears were not far away, she could not trust herself to speak. The two men were silent, as the cart drove into the long valley. Maurice felt that she was escaping from him; Richard was holding the little mare in from shying, but he was warm with the proximity of her body, pressed close to him. He had got her again, and she wasn't changed.

There was a sprinkling of snow on the land, but it didn't dull the metallic click of the mare's hoofs. She trotted at a fine pace, now and then breaking into a gallop as she saw something ghostly reflected in an ice pool. The girl leaned back between the two men, gazing at the sky, seeking old friends up there. In Wales they hadn't been the same, they had been a remote nightly miracle.

There was her own star, in that great dome of blue, with its fringe of woodland. She felt a sudden tug at her heart. It beckoned her like a lover and tears filled her eyes. It made a sign of recognition and she responded. She left her own body and flew up to meet it. Something greater than earthly love flashed between them. Something of eternity joined them together. She was out of time and space, lost in memory of others beside herself, looking down at the astonishing world where her body jolted along between the men she loved, where the river flowed under dipping trees and hills rose to touch the sky.

Maurice's arm tightened round her while the cart swayed violently and lurched as a wheel passed over a stone heap. Richard turned his head and spoke to her. The moment was gone, but she knew, she knew something. It was the star that had accompanied her home from night school, and taken care of her. Never would it leave her, but only here could she meet it on intimate terms, here under the high blue fields of heaven. It lifted her up eternally far, and removed her from the earth she loved so passionately to a region where sorrow couldn't exist. Lights winked and glittered as if the sky had wakened to a new day, with comings and goings of heavenly hosts, with beatings of invisible wings as angels flew across to visit one another up there. Life had moved from the earth to the sky. Up there among those blue spaces were happenings and adventures and laughter.

Then down she came to earth, and a good old earth it was, with Shepherd's Fields waiting round the corner.

"What do the stars make? Do they make honey," she whispered, but Richard had forgotten her old question, and nobody replied.

The overhanging trees tugged at their hats and touched their faces with stinging fingers. They drove up the long road, through the field to the gate. The dog barked violently, there were rumbles and shouts as doors flashed open, dairy door, house door, barn door, even the front door in her honour as a married woman. Snow was falling, the stars were hidden, but the earthly stars shone out more brightly than the heavenly ones. The snow, feathers from the snow-woman's heavenly geese, as Charity had told her, fluttered down, and the house put up invisible hands to catch them and bound them in a bonnet on its head and capped them on the barns and draped them on the walls. Hats of birds' feathers they were; the house was busy decorating itself when the cart pulled up.

Little Virginia coming back, a married woman! Is she happy? Is she happy? Let her stay here, said the house, but Virginia heard nothing. She was running fast over the snow from the gate to the house door, racing to the square of gold firelight. Dogs and people ran to welcome her. Uncle Will grasped her in his strong arms and gave her a kiss full on her lips. Aunt Hetty pecked her cheeks, and Emmie clung to her with unusual warmth. The kitchen glowed with a great fire, and for a moment Virginia was startled by the strong rich smell which merged from the room, the smell of flitches of bacon on the walls, of herb hunches, and milkcans, of horses and leather and old forgotten things.

"It smells like home," said she, wrinkling her little nose in appreciation. Maurice stood behind her, bewildered by the noise, repelled by that strong odour of farm life.

"Come along, Maurice. You'll be starved to death," cried Will, drawing him forward and shutting the door.

They took lighted candles upstairs to Charity's bedroom. Hetty had made a fire to air the damp bed. There was indeed a faint scent of mildew which Virginia found enchanting. She stood in the middle of the floor, with the firelight flickering on the old furniture, and Charity's patchwork quilt many-coloured on the bed.

"Oh Maurice. Nobody in the whole world is as happy as I am," said she, and he took her in his arms and bent her head back with kisses on her throat.

"This is what I've wanted," said he softly. "This room and you. This is our honeymoon, Virginia. Forget your sadnesses and love me again."

He held her at arm's-length and looked closely at her. "You're different," said he. "You are a child, Virginia."

"Yes, I'm back," she laughed, and to herself she added, "I'm eager to explore my own secret places. I want to hear and see— and escape."

They washed off the dirt of the journey in the warm water Emmie surprisingly brought them, and went downstairs to the supper of chickens and roast potatoes in brown jackets and beastinny pasties, baked golden in the great tin that had been used for a century. They drew their chairs up in the family circle before the fire. The kitchen was decorated with holly and mistletoe, bayleaves and ivy, as it had been since time unknown, the holly bush hanging so low from the hook in the ceiling it prickled the heads of men and women who were strangers, but all others dodged instinctively as they passed the spot. This habit of dodging lasted all the year and one could see the familiar householders bending as they passed under the hook when nothing hung there. So Virginia bowed her slender neck as if in homage, but Maurice received the prickly bunch in his face. His muttered curses made Virginia look at him with apprehension, but the others only laughed.

"It's reminding you to kiss your sweetheart, Maurice," said they.

Bacon hung on the walls, hams were smoking in the chimney corner, and Will proudly told of the pigs killed and the orders he had fulfilled already. There were smells of greenery and burning logs, of meats and possets. Snow was falling fast, said Dick, coming in from the yard, and Virginia shivered with delight. Perhaps it would make such deep drifts she need never go away. She and Maurice would be encircled in old Charity's room like the lovers in the fairytale. A hundred years she would sleep and the snow wreaths would blossom into white roses. Sleeping Beauty! Sleeping Beauty!

There was the magical Christmas feeling in that old house. Angels were abroad, and miracles could happen every day. Fir trees might blossom with toys and Chinese lanterns in the wood at the end of the garden. Reindeer with branching horns and tinkling bells on their harness might scamper past in the night. Virginia wondered whether Maurice could feel these things. She stole a look at him. He was staring round the kitchen, rather bewildered, and in his hand he held a pointed old wineglass. They all sipped the wine, and praised it, although it wasn't very good, but William had proudly bought it.

The old kitchen, low-ceilinged, heavy-beamed, was very much aware of the life within it. Along with Virginia, it listened and absorbed the talk. It was overflowing with memories of past days, evocations which it shared with any who looked for them, of harvest dinners, and Christmas feasts for centuries, of guisering and mumming, and singing, and religion, of prayers and laughter, of weeping and kissing. It had known lovemaking, passionate and fierce, such as Virginia had never known, marriage and grief. It had seen the new-born child held to the fire and bathed on the broad hearthstone, and it had seen the dead brought through the door in their coffins, or carried in from the fields. Death and life it knew them all, and here was life, laughter and gaiety for a time, and the room smiled, and the house shook its broad shoulders and joined in the hilarity, of tale and jest. Its walls held song and carol, the music was vibrating there, ready for those who could hear to pick up the song and continue. Virginia hummed under her breath, she could hear it. She was knowing past things. She too heard the far voices. The present slipped away, the laughter of Will and Maurice faded even as she sat there, and she heard other laughs, and saw for a brief moment those others, farm men and labourers, women and little children, with dogs at their feet and hats tilted back, and smocks and petticoats spread out, and she saw other hands dark and stained with work, outstretched to fires long returned to the sun, and faces intent and eager, gilded with firelight, and eyes bright with love and comradeship, and some dimmed with tears. She looked up and Richard was gazing at her. His lips were moving, he was whistling softly the same tune that rang from the past. He knew also, he shared her secret. She smiled across at him, in complete happiness.

"Come Virginia. You've been far enough away to have some tales to tell," said Emmie, nudging her elbow. "You've been sat there, mum as a mummet. What's it like in those foreign Welsh parts?" So they talked till it was bedtime, and the clock was drawn up, and the candles lighted. Upstairs they trooped, into their rooms.

"Oh Grandmother Charity! Bless us all to-night," prayed Virginia at the end of her prayers, as she knelt by the bed. Maurice didn't say prayers, but he didn't mock her or try to dissuade her, and she sent her innocent petitions winging to God.

The old house sent its benisons upon them and blessed them as they lay in close embrace. The flickering firelight danced upon the ceiling, shadows came and went over the walls, old faces seemed to peer at their young faces, and perhaps Charity herself smiled there. Outside the frosty stars were sparkling with blue and green like heavenly crackers over the newly fallen snow. The air stinging and sweet came beating on the windows, but it couldn't penetrate the thick curtains to the room where the lovers lay.

On Christmas morning Virginia went to church in the village with Emmie, and Maurice joined them for the first time for many years. He was a gay companion, as he held the arms of the two girls and ran down the slippery fields with them crying aloud to him to stop. He sang in a deep rich voice which surprised Virginia, who had never heard him sing. He listened critically to the sermon, and looked round the church with an eye of approval for the decorations. Never had he remembered such a Christmas, and the carols and hymns were part of the new pleasure he found in Virginia. He joined in the service loudly, but suddenly his voice was silent. He couldn't bring himself to say, "The resurrection of the body and the Life Everlasting", even for his young wife's sake.

He seemed to be in another time and age, as he shared the simple festivities. The house had put on a festive garment, with the holly and ivy indoors and the snow caps on its roofs. It smiled broadly and held its head high and laughed aloud. Singers and laughter and merriment were part of its life and it loved to share the feelings of those around it. For the house was a living entity, growing old in time, bearing its own spark of flame from the eternal. The hills and fields and rocks and rushing river were all part of this aliveness, this radiant life invisible. The knowledge of it was a secret Virginia must never divulge. Charity had known it, and the knowledge had been passed on to Virginia. Richard had sensed it, and so had Uncle Will. Another must bear this wonderful secret, and that one must be the child of her body.

They walked for miles among woods of holly and oak to visit outlying farms and Virginia's old friends. Maurice seemed to be in another world and earlier time, for even the clothes they wore at the farm in winter were old-fashioned garments brought from the great chests. There was Ben, rheumatic and bent, draped in a sack shapeless as a bag of corn, walking the fields regardless of blizzard and snow, as folk had walked for a hundred years. There was Hetty, in a lined hood and cloak which many a one had worn before her. Even pretty Emmie was clothed in a shawl tied in a knot behind her. Virginia discarded her own thin wool coat, and rummaged in her grandmother's chest. She appeared in Charity's brown wool cloak lined with plaid, scarlet and yellow. She pulled the gathered hood over her hair, donned a pair of heavy boots, and faced the weather.

The old farmhouse too was prepared for winter. It had summoned its powers of resistance and was ready to face the gales. Its roofs and gables, its jutting eaves and low barns with coping stones and thatch were white with pure snow. It seemed to crouch low to hold the weight. It spread out its arms and hunched its shoulders and strengthened its knees to bear the new burden of the white covering. The low wall where the milkcans were reared, the garden hedge, and the wall of the farmyard were a snowy rampart round a fairy castle, and even the muck heap was transformed to a hillock of purity. Snow-apple trees leaned from the orchard, little round bushes of lavender and rosemary were cushions for the house's pleasure. Snow garlands hung round its neck, and snow flowers were in its hands. The weathercock, the grindle-stone, the pinnacles on the roof ends were decked with crystals. The little carved grotesque figure grinned down to the yard under his cloak of snow. The house was wide awake for Christmas. It was listening for the age-old carols, it was singing softly to itself in its own warm heart.

"Life! Life! Life everlasting," it sang.

Virginia seemed possessed by a wild spirit. The quiet, repressed wife had gone, she neither obeyed nor listened to her husband, she was fey and reckless. It was his turn to beg her to listen, as she flashed away on swift feet leaving him behind. He talked, and her mind was far away, she heard no word for she was listening to others speaking. She went out in the darkness, her head held high to the stars, her brown hair loose and streaming behind like a flag in the moonlight. She was intoxicated with all she saw and knew, and no man living had any power over her to catch and hold her again. In one short week a whole lifetime was compressed, and Maurice was bewildered and startled by her vitality and insubordination.

"They're all right," said Will to Hetty. "They'll fit in some day. They're opposites, and they'll shake down, like you and me."

Hetty made a grimace, and shook her head. "We've not shook down yet, Will. No signs of anything yet," added she, grimly.

"Plenty of time for that," said Will.

Time had receded once more for Virginia. Life was vast, curved like the dome of heaven, spun out to eternity, and she was immortal again.

They went through the fields where the frost made the most trivial gossamer webs an adornment for a queen, and transformed the merest weed into a jewel. The holly leaves edges were rimed with minute glittering crystals, each leaf outlined as with a paintbrush dipped in silver, the dark glossy centre untouched. Every dead kex, every blade of grass was transformed, and the indeterminate confused shapes defined. "So it is with my life," thought Virginia. "All was confusion and frustration, I have been trying to be somebody else, and now I know. Wait and accept and don't run counter to life. It's here, and I'm nothing if I can't see it."

The ragged unkempt field where she and Richard had played at Indians, behind the rocks and boulders, was covered with curving arcs of grasses like the great slate of a mathematician. Millions of arcs were intersecting and bending in geometrical precision. The tall heads of the giant hemlock, called Kexies by country folk, were wheels of silver with radiating spokes of thistledown softness. It was a revelation even to her eyes, and she tried to show it to Maurice.

The cows were shut up for the winter, and Virginia took Maurice to see them, greeting each personally, making the acquaintance of each newcomer, hearing its name and history. To her they were human beings, sharers of her life, and more interesting than most of the people she had met for some time. Everywhere, in stable where the horses turned their heads and whinnied, in kennel and barn there were friends to greet. Each day was a lifetime to Virginia. She went through a whole series of experiences, and glanced at the clock to see that only a minute had sped. There was something queer about it, the house was using its powers to defeat time and give of its fullness of life. She was a child again, absorbing impressions, enjoying each scent and leaf and stone as if it were the first seen in the world and she were Eve. Flashes back in time came from the touch of the wooden handles of fork and besom, from the movement of a candle flame, the smouldering tip of a spell as somebody lighted the candle, the surface of the stone sink. She went to the cowhouses to milk, she drove the horse to the village, and turned the chopper and mixed the sharps. She wore an old skirt very short, and a tam-o'-shanter, which Maurice said was becoming to her. She looked in the glass, and saw, not herself, but the radiant joyful excited little girl with a hole in her stocking and torn pinafore, jigging up and down as she waited for Richard to give her a ride on the mare's back. Underneath was the same little girl, unchanged.

At night they joined the family circle telling and hearing tales of goblins and ghosts, of boggarts and bad folk and Virginia gave quick glances over her shoulder at swaying coats on the oak post, and shadows in the corners. Legend and country tale were repeated for Maurice's benefit, losing nothing in the telling.

They roasted chestnuts and drank mulled ale from the mugs on the stove, and they watched the yellow flames springing from the logs, crackling and spluttering in the chimney. The Christmas wood was part of an old wine cask Charity had bought for a water butt long ago, and it was impregnated with salts and wine. It blazed fiercely, telling its own tale of days at sea and years in Spain, and it sent out sparks like Catherine wheels and crackers, as if the Inquisition were remembered by it.

"Good Luck to you all. Good Luck to the House. God Bless the New Year, and the farm and all who live within it, and all who belongs to it, for ever and ever, Amen," said Will, standing up holding high his blue striped mug, and all stood up with him.

The last night they all sat as usual in the low-ceilinged kitchen, in chairs drawn up to the fire. Again the room was vibrant with memories. It echoed with other laughter, and moaned with other grief. Couples, boys and girls, were whispering shyly on the settle, blushing and making love under the searching eyes of their elders. Virginia could hear their soft voices, their rustles and giggles but their figures eluded her. She knew they were there, joining in the happiness. The house carried all these things in its heart, it retained everything that had ever happened in its own long life, treasured in its immortal soul.

Maurice was uncomfortably aware of something going on. He didn't join in the talk, he sat remote, a stranger in this intimate company, bound only to one of them, and even those bonds were frail, he thought, for he would never know the girl he had married. He was melancholy and bored with the fantastic tales the country folk believed. He looked at his wife, sitting next to him, forgetful of him, absorbed in the tales her Uncle and Richard were telling. Her flower-like throat was snowy against an old-fashioned ruby velvet dress she had taken from the chest and worn to please him. It was Charity's girlhood dress, her Sunday frock for several years, made of good rich velvet that would never wear out. They had laughed as she strutted and bowed to him in the bedchamber when she tried it on. Now she sat gazing at Richard, her blue eyes brilliant with joy and excitement, her curved lips apart as if she was about to speak, her face flushed like a deep red rose.

"My luv is like a red, red rose," he hummed under his breath, hearing nothing of the talk, watching as a ghost this household which accepted him but could not understand him. She was elusive, strange, exquisite in her own surroundings, unlike the lonely girl whom he had tried to draw into his own way of living. He would never possess her, never know her heart.

It was then that Virginia saw old Charity once more, Charity, with her worn smiling face, Charity joining the circle, sitting there among them, giving a warmth and kindliness that they all felt. Virginia put out a hand, and then withdrew it with a little shock, as she touched nothing, but the old woman remained among them, hearing all that was said. Then Charity went over to Maurice, and stood by him for a short time, she put her hand on his shoulder, and he shivered. She beckoned with her forefinger, and then she went away, but Maurice sat there, unknowing.

"I can't bear to leave this old room where we've been so happy," said he at night, as he stood by the bedroom fire. "I don't know what it is, it's quite an irrational feeling, but there's some comfort and courage for hard times here. I felt it all along, even when I didn't know you. Do you feel it, or are you so used to everything that you don't notice, Virginia?"

He watched her reflection in the glass, her eyes suddenly closed, and she held up clasped hands.

"Oh God," she whispered. "Give us a little longer."

"Virginia," he cried sharply. "Are you ill?"

She started, and swung round. "No. I'm quite well. Yes," she stammered. "Yes. I've always felt it in this room. It's Grandmother Charity's influence or it's the house itself. It's a real live force, like your engineering works, Maurice. As real as those forces you say hold buildings and dams together."

"What do you mean?" he asked.

"I don't know. It's my fancy."

She lay once more in his encircling arm, but her eyes were wide open. She couldn't sleep, the firelight blazed up suddenly and Maurice moved restlessly and murmured her name in his dreams. She raised herself and watched his face, the clean bones and the fine brown skin, and the good shape of him. Ah, how much she loved him, and he had become part of the house now. She lay down and the shadows bobbed about her. There they were coming out of childhood to give her pleasure and pain. Seven dwarfs, and the twelve brethren of Joseph, Balaam's Ass and Cinderella. Cinderella! That was his name for her, it had drawn her to him with a shadowy cord he knew nothing of. A log fell from the fire and the house murmured softly. She could hear it breathe. It was awake and it knew all things.

"Give me courage for what's round the corner," she whispered, and she held tightly to her husband's body.

Chapter 18

In late spring Virginia knew she was going to have a child. The baby must have a home and not spend its early days in lodgings, they decided, and Maurice found a small whitewashed cottage in a village. It would be cheaper to live in a little house whose rent was only five shillings a week, and there was a rough garden stocked with vegetables. They bought furniture at a sale and moved in. There Virginia lived in a tranquillity that astonished and sometimes annoyed Maurice. She was happy and gay, careless of the ugly kitchen with its magenta wallpaper and smoky fire, heedless of the draughts and broken floors and sagging ceilings. Hope bloomed under her fingers and the cottage overflowed with promises for the future. Doors banged, latches hung down, drunken shouts and cries came from the next cottage, but Virginia accepted everything with gratitude.

Maurice was anxious. The work was drawing to a close, the engineers had hinted that owing to the uncertainty of the world situation they could not promise anything to follow. There would be no income while he searched for a job. Virginia refused to fear, she couldn't understand what it would be to have no money.

"But I've never had any, and I can manage," she explained, unruffled. "The boy—for he must be a boy—will go to Shepherd's Fields, and I'll work for my living. It won't cost you a penny. Uncle Will would keep you, till you find work."

The boy would be the first grandson, she was thinking, and he ought to live at the farm. They might even have the little old part of the farm, with the bedroom up the ladder, and the ancient rusty washhouse kitchen below as their own house. She made fairytale plans, her mind flying through space back to the beloved home, her feet dancing across the meadows for flowers to deck the old place, fetching a broom to sweep it out, a whitewash brush to lime it, turning out the old mangle and the churns, dragging a rocking chair and a rug up the ladder to make it comfortable for Maurice. But Maurice stared with amazement at his wife.

"You know quite well I can't go there with no money," said he angrily, and Virginia's face dropped as she watched his expression. He hadn't understood, he did not know what she knew.

"I've to get another job when this ends, either in this country or Burma. There is work in West Africa, but I could not take you there. You don't seem to know the value of security, Virginia. I must make more money. Besides, there's education to consider."

Virginia smiled ruefully. It was true, money meant little to her, and education cost nothing. It was all the same to her, as long as she had Maurice and the baby and the shelter of Shepherd's Fields. Of course, she thought with a pang of recognition, that was at the root of life. She felt safe and secure because the old house was there, across the hills and vales and woods, in England, a part of her, belonging to her in life and death. It called her and she answered it. Through space and time she would go to it. She was fast bound to it for ever. Without it she would be shut out from heaven, she would wander a lost ghost through an infinity of darkness, seeking it.

So she sat in the little patch of garden among the cabbages and blowsy roses, and made the baby's clothes, with infinite patience, sewing the grey Welsh flannel with pricked fingers, leaving drops of blood on the seams. She had always hated sewing, but this was different, and she tried to keep her stitches small as her grandmother's. There was a power of strength in flannel that had the natural oil in it, Charity once told Hetty in her hearing, and now she had bought the drab grey material instead of the snowy flannel she preferred.

She sang to the unborn child, and whispered encouraging words to it to cheer it in the darkness where it slept. She worked in the garden, and made a border. She brought home flowers from the fields, strangers she had never seen in the colder lands of the farm. There were tall blue columbines growing wild in Beggan lane, yellow flags springing from the wet grass, and bee orchis and a slender white orchis in the meadows. At night she made a feast for Maurice, and showed her flowers, and related the queer tales of magic and medicines she had heard, and although Maurice never listened, she didn't care now. The baby in her womb heard the tales, and perhaps he smiled a slow smile as he slept. She planned everything, with wild imaginings, elephant rides in Burma, bridge building in India, but always she came back to one place, as the old house called her and tugged at her heart.

One hot day, at the end of July, she sat with her sewing in the shade of the apple tree, listening to the bees and the quacking ducks, and the voices of her neighbours talking in the strange foreign Welsh language over their wire fence. Her dress was loose at the breast for she felt sick with the heat. She longed for a drink of spring water, cold as ice, from a water trough she knew. She went indoors and drank from the tap, but her thirst was unsatisfied, and she walked slowly back to her low chair. Maurice came home earlier than usual. He kissed her absently, and went to the kitchen to wash. She looked after him, admiring his long stride, the poise of his head, filled with love for him. If only he would come into the garden and sit by her side for a few minutes instead of going straight to the little study, which they called the cottage parlour. To her surprise he came out and flung himself on the grass. He took her hand and began to play with it, turning it over and looking closely at the lines and scratches and the roughness of the fingers.

"Hard-working hand," he said banteringly. "I wish it needn't do so much. I wish I could make more money for you."

"Darling. I don't want any money," she said, pressing her fingers to his lips, and he held them there and kissed them.

"Virginia. Virginia. I want to talk to you," he continued, and he dropped her hand and stared at the blades of grass. Strange how large they looked, as if he held a magnifying glass to them. He could see the veins, the hairs, he could see the green sap rising within them, and the roots going into the earth.

"Virginia. War is coming, and I shall join up. I'm sending in my resignation to-day. Better to send it in than to be dismissed. Besides, I want to be in whatever's coming."

"War? What do you mean? How do you know?" she gasped, and her heart began to beat in a queer fluttering way, as if a bird were in her breast trying to escape. It must keep still, it must not quiver and shake its wings, she told it, and she kept her fist hard on her throat holding it back. It was panic that was there, the blind panic that had risen when the werewolf had walked up the fields. It was the panic she had known when Hetty had shut her in the dark barn. She had thought it was dead, and it was raising its head again. It would harm the baby. It mustn't hurt the tiny unborn one. Maurice was speaking in slow measured tones, in a voice without expression, telling her something, but she didn't hear what he said. She had to stop the panic that was overwhelming her.

Summoning all her power of concentration she sent her mind, her spirit, something of her own, to Shepherd's Fields. She saw herself go in at the door, not the kitchen door that stood wide open, or the dairy door, but the thick rough door of the little ancient building. She went past the empty churns, and the smell of stale milk came to her, past the heavy mangle and the clothes-baskets piled with soiled clothes, and she put her hand on the wooden bench, touching the deep cuts and grooves, letting her fingers stay there for a time. She saw the China roses on the bush at the door and the moss on the steps. Nobody had scrubbed it away, but it was sweet and homely to see it. She might have stayed there a lifetime, staring at those mosses, but she knew there was something else. She stepped lightly across the stone floor, and climbed the ladder, holding tightly to the sides, avoiding the iron band where the ladder had been mended, for it always struck cold to her fingers. Up she went, into the little bedchamber, her own room, the core of life. There was the faint smell of mildew, and the powerful smell of apples from the autumn store, which never left the room. The window was stiffly closed, and a butterfly was beating its wings there. She threw the window wide open, and stood there, looking out on the fields and woods, the corn turning gold in the heat of the sun. Near, in the little strip of grassy croft, visible when she dipped her head under the bough of the elm, she could see the purple blossoms of the wild geraniums, unmown, in that wild spot. She could smell the trees, the roses at the door, the queer scents of the room. Nobody moved, they might all have been dead. She wasn't in their world. The house was quiet as a dream, and there she stood alone, out of time, a ghost, watching and waiting, and the panic fear went, and her heart was lightened. The strength of the house entered her. The stones upon which her hands rested as she leaned at the window, were rough and strong to her touch, hard and unyielding, everlasting. She pressed her hands to them till they hurt, drawing comfort from the stone. The air was filled with whispering and murmuring, and the house spoke to her, comforted her, and she heard old Charity's voice.

"You must abide by God's will."

She sat in the chair in the garden, and she had the sensation that many years had gone by. She looked at her hands, and they were deeply indented by the pressure of the rough windowsill. Maurice was talking to her.

"Did you hear what I said, Virginia? You never answer. Have you been listening? Don't you care?" he asked.

"Oh, my darling. Of course I care," she stammered. "Look at my hands. Look at the marks."

"What does it matter? You've been pressing them too damned hard upon something. Do be sensible, and listen to my plans for your future."

"We can face any future. I was there," she thought.

They went indoors and Virginia prepared supper. The sun shone through the open doorway upon the bright earthenware they had bought at a local market. The table was gay as a butterfly's wings with the mug of wild flowers. It seemed a dream, and the dream was a reality to Virginia as she poured out the coffee and made the omelette on the oil stove by the sink. After she had washed up they went out together, and Maurice talked more cheerfully than he had talked for months. They were filled with laughter, speaking of the fun they would have when he returned from a short and improbable war. The baby would sleep in a little canvas cot, she had seen the very thing in an advertisement, and Maurice would carry it about.

The doctor who looked after the folk in the scattered villages was a rough sort of man who drank more than he ought, but she was strong. There hadn't been a doctor at all when she was born, she informed Maurice proudly, as if it had been her own cleverness in climbing so gallantly into the cold world. He had been summoned, but she was already there when he arrived.

"Kate? Where are you?" she whispered. "Kate and Charity? Are you there? Do you remember me?"

The panic was surely slain outright. The evening was golden. They went up the lane to the fields, and Virginia looked for something to bring them luck. Maurice was leading the way, to the river, and she wished he had chosen another path. She could never get used to that river in Wales. The first time they had taken the field path among the sheets of purple orchis, they had shouted with joy at the sight. On they went, through the flowers, listening to the distant sound of running water.

"A river again!" Virginia had cried, hastening towards the groves of willows. "A river, a lovely river to bathe in, and walk beside. A river like our own river at home," she thought.

Then she had stopped aghast at the amazing sight. The river was coal black, its waters defiling the boughs of the dipping trees, and evil mud on its banks. It was dark as death, evil and cruel. The smell was rotten. Even in hell there couldn't be such a bad desperate river.

"Didn't you know?" asked Maurice, as she held back with horror. "It comes from the coalfields, black with the dust of the mining villages."

Poor river, running with its spoiled waters through some of the fairest fields, racing away to drown itself in the ocean.

Maurice didn't mind it, he took her arm and led her across its waters by the narrow footbridge, but she shivered as she looked down. In its dark waters she imagined she could see foul and ugly shapes leering at her. It frightened her again. Away on the hillside was a white castle, like a fairy palace, standing in pillared woods, and she turned her head to gaze at it.

"We'll go there some day," promised Maurice. "I'll get a side-car for my motor-cycle, and we'll go and explore. I've to go to

Pembroke to-morrow, to meet the chief, I'm going out near that place."

Quite near the dark water were five silver birch trees, that waved their tremulous branches like green waterfalls. They didn't care either, they told of other things, they spoke of the moss at their feet and the clouds sweeping over them, and the thin moon that came to silver their trunks. Brave trees, growing in that place, seeing the desecration, breathing the rank air, and transforming it to beauty. They gave her the thoughts she had had in her own wood, in her childhood, and softly she began to speak. She told him a fairytale her grandmother had told her, of a girl who was changed to a silver birch tree to escape from an evil genie. These five trees were surely young girls who ran crying from the river.

·The air was full of rustlings and sighings as if every leaf were sentient, speaking of the dark river, telling that it was once beautiful as it started its journey in the mountain. The dew was falling, the light faded, and the trunks of the trees seemed to be disembodied spirits waiting there. Slowly they went home, over the bridge in the darkness, back to the village. They lighted a candle and went up the narrow steep stair to the room whose ceiling sloped to their heads. It was their home, and the memory of their days would surely remain for others who would live there, poor labourers, carters, who might feel some touch of happiness come unexpectedly from those crooked walls. So they added to the store that already saturated the walls, the cries of lonely children, of beaten wives, of tears and laughter.

Maurice was late returning from his journey. He had said she must expect him in the evening, and he might be kept to meet the committee. She sat in the little parlour, with the lamp burning and the blinds undrawn so that she could see out into the garden. The drunken groom who lived next door had been shouting, and now his voice was quiet, as he slept. Moths flew about the room and hit the globe of the lamp, and a dumbledore threw itself against the window. There is never silence, except in those fraction of seconds, when a glimpse of invisible things is afforded. Then the flies cease fluttering their tiny wings and the moths stay on the wing unmoving, while the curtain concealing the past and future is lifted.

Virginia sat sewing by the window, her ears strained to catch the pounding of the motor-cycle engine, and the click of the gate.

It was after twelve, and she felt sleepy. She shut her eyes and in a moment she slept. Then she awoke, icy cold, disturbed by something. She heard a faint sound, and she swung round to see a blood-stained figure by the window, the white face pressed close to the glass, the eyes gleaming strangely in the moonlight. She stifled a scream and drew back in horror.

"Virginia. Don't be frightened. It's me," said Maurice, and his voice had a queer dull whisper that scarcely came to her ears. She could hardly recognize him under the bandages.

She ran to the door and unlocked it with trembling hands.

"Maurice. What's happened?" she cried.

"I had an accident. Nothing much. Skidded and came against a lamppost. A woman bandaged me, nothing much," he staggered into the room.

"Maurice. Maurice."

"Give me a drink of brandy. I daren't stop on the way, I wanted to get home first. I thought I should never manage the last bit on these roads."

He dropped on the couch and lay there, silent with the blood oozing from his clothes.

Virginia undressed him and covered him with blankets.

That was a night of agony, and the next morning Maurice was taken to hospital. He was unconscious. Virginia stayed with him, holding his hand, whispering to him, but he never spoke. He died two days later.

"You've been with him to the end, and that's what many would be thankful for," said the Sister. "He might have died by the roadside. He got home to you."

"Yes, he got home," echoed Virginia dully.

She hated the cottage, she was filled with horror when she returned to the silence. She could see the blood-stained face pressed to the window, and hear somebody calling her.

"Maurice, my dear love?" she whispered. "Where are you now?" No tears fell, she was stunned with misery too deep for weeping. She hadn't even written to Richard and her aunt, there hadn't been time, she was in a bad dream that must come to an end. Alone, lost, and alone.

The little crooked house gave her no comfort. She was filled with longing for Shepherd's Fields. She sat listening, her senses alert and quivering as she waited.

There was a tree knocking at the window with its tiny knuckled twigs. No, you can't come inside, she thought. It tapped and snickered with groping hands, and stared through the panes at her as she lay white as the sheets around her on the bed. It tapped again, and she crept from bed and pushed the window catch from the clutching streamer. Glass was there, and it was all she had to keep it out, but suppose it came in? Suppose it entered the room, and Maurice wasn't there to protect her? What would it do? She knew very well. It would carry her off and clasp her to its withered heart, and she would die and disappear in its embrace. So she shut the window and turned the green fingers away, and dragged the blind down, but the skinny wooden hand continued to knock all night and the air moaned through the warped boards.

The next morning she went out to the little village shop and post office, to the stout little kindly woman with her dark hair in a bird's nest on her worried head.

"How are you taking it, Mrs. Winter? I'm very sorry for your grief," said she.

"My grief. Yes, my grief," said Virginia softly.

"You'd best send for your relations," said the woman.

"I've just remembered them," said Virginia, "but I'd rather be alone. You can bear things alone."

She returned without sending the telegram to Hetty. Instead she wrote to say she was coming home, and Maurice was dead.

"But what is death?" she asked. "The fields are free of it, the land doesn't know it. He has gone through the door, that is all."

The funeral was over, the sticks of furniture sent off to a dealer, the trunks packed. She said good-bye to the empty cottage with its blank leering windows, and its garden suddenly grown desolate. There was a sinister air about it, she felt that nothing would induce her to put a foot inside the door. What strange and misshapen things might come out to run and leap in the crooked little rooms, once the house was left! She had conquered it while she lived there, but in the end it had won. Others would take the house, and bring their joys and prayers and sufferings to it, and influence it and help it to make its store of finer things, but she had finished. The straggling rose tree waggled a green finger and struck a derisive blow at the uncurtained window.

The wife of the drunken groom pressed a bunch of flowers in her hands.

"God bless you, Mrs. Winter," said she. "I shall miss you. It's been nice having you next door, knowing you were there, hearing you singing. Good luck to you."

In the distance she could see the clump of green willows shading the black river, concealing their muddy garments, and standing bravely out under the sky. Beyond them were the white trunks of the five silver birches, like angels waiting to fly, and on the horizon the fairy castle in its terraces and tree trunks beautiful as a dream.

"I'm not afraid either," she told herself. "I'm not afraid of walking onward in my loneliness towards that castle, when there's such a brave world about me."

Richard and Hetty had come to the station to meet her. They stood on the cold, wind-swept platform, and she leaned out, unfastening the door as the train went slowly to rest. Behind them, through the open gate of the yard she could see the cart waiting and the patient horse, with head bent sleeping. It was a welcoming sight, and she embraced her aunt and Richard, receiving the little hard peck that was always Aunt Hetty's greeting, and the restrained kiss that was Richard's. He was unchanged, the same diffident, but understanding friend.

The horse turned its head and snuffled at her sleeve, and she threw her arms round its neck and kissed it too, hiding her emotion as it recognized her voice.

"Careful with that luggage," cried Hetty as the porter threw the hamper and the trunks into the back.

"Nowt to break I hopes?" he asked cheerfully.

"Maybe there is," snapped Hetty, but Virginia leaned over the side and gave him twopence, which surprised him so much he touched his cap. The cart lurched and swayed, the horse slithered with its hind legs on a slippery piece of ground, and they drove away.

There was a new moon in the sky, the elms dipped their boughs to it, Virginia saw them. She inclined her head too in homage to the moon.

"I wish——" she whispered. "I wish——" but she had no wish. "Life is sweet," she said under her breath, and Richard heard her. He said nothing at all, except, "It's a bad business, Jinny. God help you."

Hetty talked fast all the way, it was her method of bringing cheerfulness into a sad occasion. Virginia was bewildered, but there was no need to answer. The nearness of Richard's rough coat, and the strong-smelling serge, with odours of horses and linseed cake was so familiar it was as if a part of the house had come down the lane to take care of her. Shepherd's Fields had sent a whiff of itself to comfort her spirit.

"I've just come by train the opposite road," said Hetty. "Such a journey as never was, and folk thronging the station. I've been to get a bit of black. Aren't you going to wear all black, Jinny? I've got a black felt, as winter's coming on, and a black material for a dress. Well, I'm fair tired out, and I'm sure you're done up."

"Yes," murmured Virginia.

Richard glanced at the white face beside him, and Virginia looked up at him, into his eyes with a look of understanding. Words were unnecessary between them, she realized with a pang half joy, half bitterness. Their thoughts were running like two streams, deep and swift, clear water. She turned her head aside and stared ahead. They were coming to Shepherd's Fields, and each was eager for the first glimpse. That was how the farmhouse affected its lovers. Each looked out with longing and desire for the house.

Hetty watched the smoke curling from the chimney and thought of the cup of tea and perhaps a spot of rum in it by the kitchen fire. Black stuff gave one the shivers, and she was cold and weary. Richard was watching the cows turned out after milking, loitering by the gate. Virginia was looking at the house, for its first sign of recognition of her. It was more beautiful than ever, in its own humble way, when they drove up the long field and saw it in a radiance of setting sun. New moon and setting sun were a secret miracle which delighted it. The sun became it, it wore the gold rays like a pointed crown, but the shadows suited its loveliness even better. Shadows conceal and heighten effects, and the house wore them as a blue cloak. In a few minutes they had rounded the bend and approached the gate. Even as they drove there the twilight deepened in that sudden way it has of dropping a veil in a moment, but the house had spoken and Virginia had heard.

Her eyes travelled over the old roofs, and she felt a fierce possessive pain of love for the green moss at the corner where the stone buttress sprung, for the rough-hewn stones each speaking of the masons and quarrymen of another age, and the heavy dirty old doors of barns and cartsheds and cowhouses. She saw the tangled web of wild flowers, late harebells springing from the cracks, shaking their azure transparent glasses, yellow stonecrop, lichens starring the walls, their childhood gardens displayed on the stone walls everywhere. Moth-like shadows, mother-of-pearl stream, shreds of cloud, all spoke to her, signalled to her to have courage.

"I've come back, broken, but with a treasure," she whispered below her breath, as Richard sprang down and opened the farm gate. Uncle William was in the yard, with a warm welcoming look on his face. He looked very worn, bowed down, but his cheeks were ruddy still. Emmie was there, and her husband, but all these seemed to fade like shadows for the house stretched out invisible arms to her. It touched her face, her lips, it kissed her with the cold sweet kiss of mountain air. She talked to the others, she listened to them, she ate and drank and washed herself at the stone sink, and wiped on a rough towel, she drank water from the trough, and warmed her hands by the fire, but all the time she was holding secret converse with the house. It listened. She did all the talking in a silent way inside her, and it hearkened and comforted her.

"She's mazed with tiredness, poor soul, after all she's gone through," said Will. "Let her go upstairs."

"Aye, there's a fire for her," said Hetty. "I thought it would pleasure her." She went upstairs and dropped into the chair by the fire. How kind they were, all of them, and she had never realized it! She sat there, filled with thankfulness to the house and all who lived within. Maurice had tasted the sweetness of it, he had slept in the room, and taken its consolation, she was glad of that.

Downstairs they were talking of her. She was thin and pale as a ghost, and different, they said. She was surely half-starved. She would go into a decline like Kate her mother. The shock had been too much for her. She was like somebody not there.

Richard wanted to go up and speak to her. Better not, they said. Leave her alone till she comes down. Besides, his boots were muddy from the fields.

"I can take them off," said he.

He slipped them off as he spoke, and went up in stockinged feet. He tapped softly at the door. She had heard the muffled tread, the creak of the stair. She raised a warning finger to the room, and back to the shadows crept all those who had come out. Back went the invisible ones.

"Come in," she cried in a wavering voice. The latch was lifted, the old-fashioned bobbin dropped and clicked on the door.

"Lift up the latch and walk in," she cried, in the sing-song voice of childhood, but there was a break in her voice.

"Take a chair, sit down there."

"Good morning sir," echoed the invisible ones taking up the rhyme of their own childhood, but nobody heard.

Richard came down the little stairway and held out his arms to her.

"Jinny. Jinny!"

"Oh Richard." She gave a sob as his arms caressed her and his hand stroked her cheek, with clumsy solicitude.

He sat by her side, she crouched on the floor, leaning against him, her face hidden while she told him all that had happened. He spoke quietly, asking no questions, soothing her sorrow. Her tears were flowing freely, the flood of grief was loosed to him.

At last he left her, and went down to the kitchen, put on his boots and reached his hat from the peg to go out to the stable.

"How is her? Is her all right?" asked Will.

"Yes. She's glad to get home. I think she wants to be left a bit to-night. She's upset, of course."

"It will do her good to cry. I don't like 'em as is dry-eyed in grief," said Hetty.

"She says she isn't hungry, but you get a fresh egg for her supper and boil it light, and tempt her with it."

When Virginia had changed her dress and ventured down, her heart was still from its frantic beating. She had recovered from the turmoil of invading thoughts and regrets. The house was already helping her with its steady stream of strength. She sat at the kitchen fire and warmed her thin hands and talked about the journey and the folk in the train, and she put her faded bunch of flowers in water. She looked round at the kitchen pots and pans, shining bright on the walls, and she made the toast and piled it on the end of the fireplace. It was lonely without Grandmother sitting in the armchair. Somehow she had forgotten she was dead. She half expected to see the door at the foot of the stairs open and the old woman pop her head round before she came in, smiling in the old way. She listened for the warm old voice, and the creak of the chair as Charity settled herself afresh.

The shutters were fastened, the doors bolted for the night.

"We'll show you the new separator we've got, and the milk

cooler," said Hetty. "We don't use the troughs for cooling now. Only for drinking water and housework. We've got one or two new-fashioned things quite up to date. We're moving with the times."

"We have to pump the water through the cooler, of course. There's a lot of washing up with a separator," added Emmie.

"You can't have labour-saving without work," said Hetty. "You save on the swings and lose on the roundabouts, it seems to me."

"Where did the money come from?" asked Virginia, roused from her dreams and solitude.

"We got them with your grandmother's money," said Hetty, waiting for the words to sink into Virginia's consciousness.

"Grandmother's money?" she asked, puzzled.

"Yes. We didn't tell you afore. We found her stocking with two hundred pounds in it, hidden away, and you'll never guess where!"

Virginia stared and waited, as Hetty told the great news.

"Why up in the little apple-chamber, where you used to sleep! There you were, close to it, and you never knew. Nor did any of us! I found it this spring when I was cleaning out the little room."

"But where was it?" asked Virginia. "I knew that room so well. I knew every cranny of it."

"You know that little cupboard in the wall, where you kept your books? Grandmother Charity used to say that folk long ago kept their money there, and I always wondered why, for anybody could open it and help themselves. Well, now I know. I turned out some papers of yours, childish scribbles, and homework, and I whitewashed it afresh, along with the room. I must have touched a spring, for I noticed a crack at the back. I pulled and tugged, and the board slid away and there was a space behind. Inside, in an old teapot, was two hundred pounds!"

Virginia nodded, afraid to speak.

"We told nobody, of course. It doesn't do to tell such things, or the law might step in and grab some. So we kept mum as a mummet."

"There was a bit of paper inside, in your grandmother's handwriting," said William, "leaving half to you and half to Pichard. So we divided it between you."

"And there was nothing for me," cried Emmie. "It wasn't fair, but I don't care."

"Poor Grandmother! She did have a joke with her money, never letting on and leaving us twenty pounds apiece in her will," laughed Dicky.

"And Richard bought these grand things for the farm with his share?" asked Virginia.

"Yes. He spent it on Shepherd's Fields. Yours is in the bank, waiting for you. Nobody's touched it."

"A hundred pounds and there'll be a bit of interest, for it's been there for six months now. What'll you do with it?"

"It's too precious to spend," said Virginia in sudden tears. "Every penny worked for, every shilling saved and put aside. I couldn't spend it. I shall keep it for something very important in the future. Or I'll give it to Uncle Will. He's not had anything."

"Nay, you won't then," said Will. "Keep it for the young 'un as is coming. Mother would be glad of that. Just what she would like."

Virginia lay in bed in Charity's room. Strange she had recovered sanity and strength that night, a night which was like an eternity. She lay there, sleeping in so deep a sleep that they left her the next day undisturbed. Not till the next afternoon did she awake. She slowly returned to consciousness as if she had been travelling in unknown lands of the spirit.

The sun shone through Charity's window upon her, and she lay drenched in light, floating in the golden motes of dusty air, swinging in the ladders that connected sun and earth. She was suspended there, aery as a dream, neither in this world nor out of it. She dressed slowly and went downstairs. Hetty was hard at work, the farm kitchen was full of pans and baskets, and good-smelling cooking. Bread rising by the fire, pasties and cakes popping in and out of the oven. A wide-mouthed, yellow pancheon was on the table, and Hetty was punching and pommelling the dough. She put the pancheon down in front of the fire, on the sandstone hearth and covered it with a clean cloth. A grand smell arose from it. She lifted a corner and pressed the dough so that dimples appeared where her fingers had touched. Slowly they faded away, and Virginia looked down at the well-known work smiling to herself.

There were pasties, great currant pasties quite two feet long ready for the oven, and dinner plates with open tarts crossed with twists of pastry, apple tarts, treacle tarts, and many another. The hot griddle was on the stove, ready for making a stack of oatcakes. Yes, it was Friday of course, baking day.

"Come along Jinny. It'll do you good to set to. There's nothing like work for a woman to forget her troubles. It'll help you later on, and make an easy labour."

"Yes, I know, Aunt Hetty," said Virginia meekly. "I'm strong enough. I can do anything you want."

"That's right, my girl. We want no finicking ways here. I'm afraid you're softened by living in lodgings, and that cottage you had was small enough to be turned inside out in a morning, I'll be bound."

"Yes," said Virginia softly. The cottage? Was it real? Was it a dream? The face at the window? Who was it?

"Your uncle isn't up to his best now. He's poorly. It's you young ones as must carry on. Richard's courting Nancy Drake and they'll be fixed up soon. Can you manage to help with milking?"

"Yes, of course," said Virginia.

"Your grandmother said she used to milk right up to the day of childbirth. I'm not a milker, not brought up to it, and Emmie doesn't like it, but you can do it."

"Yes, I can do it," said Virginia gravely.

Outside in the yard she could see her uncle, leading the horses to watering. Snorts and grunts and thudding clicking hooves rang out, and proud heads tossed and little bells tinkled. It was a world she knew, with beasts and men, slow-moving and serene. A robin was peering at her from the bush, where the clothes were bleaching, he was singing a quick round of song in a great hurry of welcome, as he darted down with smooth head bobbing. Behind the walls were the haystacks, golden brown, one intact, the other sliced like a cake, with the knife stuck in the side ready for another piece to be cut. She stared, fascinated as always, by the clean straight cut, which she could never manage to do, and the near ledge of hay, where the shortest favourite ladder, her own ladder she had called it, rested.

The big gate, the orchard, with clothes-line and beehives, the croft with the walnut tree all excited her and brought happiness to her, but most of all the house itself gave her pleasure. She threaded her way through the company of ducks and hens to the door of the ancient little dwelling house. The top half was open, fastened back to the wall by its fine iron latchet, the bottom half closed and bolted with a wooden bar. She slipped her arm over and drew it back. The same old smell of wood and iron, and stone and milk came to her, and she went up the ladder to the trap door.

"Are you there, Grandmother Charity? Do you see me?" she whispered. There was no answer but a deep sigh stirred the air, and she was aware of the invisible, as if a flowering tree had filled the room with perfume. She touched the wall, and it seemed warm and living to her hands. It sent a kindred warmth through her body. She put her lips to it, and kissed it, and stayed there, listening to the room.

"Don't ye hear it? It's the house. It's the heart of the house beating."

The words echoed through her mind, Charity's words had remained suspended in time. "Courage and Faith. Keep on. Keep on."

The little old house was alive and fresh. It was enjoying itself, and Virginia had the feeling that she had stepped into a communion of gay old spirits, laughing and rejoicing, and chattering together.

Chapter 19

So Virginia had slipped back again to her lowly position at the farm, serving it with her body, communing with it, loving it fiercely, resenting the hard words that Hetty cast on it. Marriage had softened Emmie, and the two cousins were closer together than they had ever been, but Hetty was bitter as gall. She could never forgive the house for its constant need of devotion. She hadn't love enough to throw any on an old house always demanding more.

In the winter the baby was born, and it was a hard birth. Hetty never remembered such days of anxiety, when the doctor grumbled and stayed the night, and the midwife refused to obey him. Virginia had done too much, he said, and she was paying for it. Too much straining at churns and washing when she ought to have rested. She lay white as a ghost. They thought she was dying, but life was too strong for her.

The dark-haired, blue-eyed baby lay in her arms, staring at her, and she roused herself to feed him, and then dropped back almost lifeless.

William came upstairs to her, his slow heavy tread sounded like doom as he tried to tiptoe into the room. He hesitated at the doorway, fumbling with the bobbin latch. Then he entered with a little jug of cream.

"Sup this up, my lass. It'll do you a power of good, and much better nor medicine. It's the Alderney's. Now sup it." He poured it out into a small cup she had used when she was a child. He had remembered it was hers, and she smiled up at him, touched by his care.

"I don't want it, Uncle Will," she whispered.

"Aye, but you munna say that. It'll change you. What would your grandmother have said if she'd seen you so pasty and thin. She never gave way, and here you are pining away at the first trouble, a grievous one, but you must bear it. There's the babby to think on, Virginny. He'll fret if you go on like this, and you'll have no milk for him. Now sup it up."

She obediently drank the sweet cream. It had been Charity's remedy for all kinds of ills. Cream for anaemia, and depression, and overgrowing one's strength, butter for bruises, and a little cobweb to bind up a cut.

Each one brought her something, to give her pleasure. It might be a snowdrop imprisoned in ice, or a robin half frozen to be restored to life by the fireside, or a bantam egg for tea. Gradually she recovered her strength, and came down to the kitchen with the small new life crooked in her arms. The baby slept in the old cradle in the corner of the fire farthest away from saucepans and kettles and dangers of boiling water, or on sunny days he lay out in the new perambulator William had bought for him. She had the child christened Robin, for he was a Christmas child.

The war was going on, and sometimes the planes flew over the farm, when they all ran out and gazed upward. Richard was absorbed and silent, working very hard, keeping accounts as if he were settling for good and all the affairs of the farm, so that his father was puzzled by his odd behaviour.

One day he beckoned to Virginia, and she followed him to the barn. There was something ominous about his walk, and his serious face. He turned round and shut the bottom door, then he leaned against the stone bench.

"Jinny. I'm going to tell you first," said he. Virginia thought he was going to be married secretly, and she waited, with a feeling of distress. "I've had it on my mind for a long time, and now I'm settled."

He stooped and picked up a fallen rake, and placed it against the wall. The touch of that earthy tool gave him confidence, Virginia knew, in whatever he was going to say.

"I'm going to join up like other fellows. I'm going to-morrow."

"Oh Richard. You can't," she cried, her heart standing still. "Why should you go? You're needed here. You can do more good here farming, than fighting."

"It's not that, Virginia. I can't stay out of it and let other men go. Besides, I'm a good shot, and I want to help. Maurice was going to join and he wasn't half as strong as me."

"What will happen to Shepherd's Fields?" she pleaded, and she went close and put her arm through his. He frowned, and pushed her away.

"You can take my place, Jinny. You're getting well now. I should have joined up long ago if it hadn't been for you. I couldn't leave you ill."

"I'm glad you stayed, Richard. I should have died if you had gone away too," she murmured, and she clutched his sleeve and buried her face in it.

"You're not a bad farmer, Jinny. You can strike a bargain, and you know the points of a good beast. You've had plenty of experience, it's only you are timid. You'll get on fine, and you can buy and sell with Father. I shall get leave and I'll look after things a bit, and there's lots of life in Dad. He's master here and will be for many years, like Grandmother was. You do what he says, and you'll be all right. Dad's not an old man yet."

"He looks ill, Richard. This will be a shock for him. He leans on you more than you think. I've noticed it since I came back. He isn't the same. He never has been quite the same since Grandmother died. He's getting on."

"Now Jinny, don't you fret yourself. You'll manage champion."

"Richard. Richard," she said suddenly after a silence. "We shall never leave here, shall we?"

"What makes you ask?" said he.

"I thought—of you, when you get married—shall we all live here, or what shall we do? We can't upset your life," she stammered.

"Married? Who said I was going to be married? If you mean Nancy Drake, you're all mistook. Everyone throws her at me, and I don't want her. As for leaving here, we shan't ever go. Never as long as we live," he promised, stroking her thin little hand, rubbing the fan-like bones with his thick forefinger as if he had newly discovered them.

"And if we die?" she whispered, and she shuddered and stared up at the great beams of the roof. The barn seemed to be waiting for Richard's answer. It was all ears, alert and listening.

"Then we shan't know anything about it," said he.

"We shall. We shall," cried Virginia loudly, and the barn echoed her words. "We shall" it sang in high fluting tones that were tossed from wall to wall.

"We shall. We shall come back, shan't we? Say we shall come back, Richard?" she pleaded.

"Bless the girl. Maybe we shall. At any rate you and me, we'll come back Jinny."

"Oh Richard! You are a comfort. I don't know how I shall go on when you are away."

She began to laugh half hysterically, and he gently shook her shoulders and bustled her outside.

"You get back to that baby of yours, I can hear him caterwauling, and I'll get the mare saddled. Don't say a word about this. I'll break the news to Dad later and Mother can scold as much as she likes, it won't make any difference if I can get Dad on my side."

William accepted it with his usual stoicism. He had had an inkling of his son's thoughts, and it was no surprise to him, but Hetty was different. She raged and fumed, and wept, and everyone was wretched. When Richard returned in uniform she changed her mind and was proud and happy again.

He came on leave later in the spring, and for a time life seemed to have slipped back again. He changed from his private's clothes, and worked on the farm at once. He was in time for ploughing, and they all felt thankful when he took charge. He was very quiet, no tales to tell, but he was happy enough, walking the fields with his father, examining every wall and hedge, leaning over the pigcote wall, spending a long time in the stable. He enjoyed army life, for he was in the Yeomanry, stationed in the West country, where he had never been before. There was a chance of comparing the land and farms, and whenever he got an opportunity he slipped away to chat with labourers, or he was discovered leaning over a gate staring with the deepest interest at the fields instead of minding his business. His companions made jokes about him, and his country ways, but he took it well, for he was always ready to help anyone.

"God! How glad I am to be back in the kitchen, and to feel our old hearthrugs under my feet," he said the first night at home. "Same old holes, same worn patches where the dog lies, same everything here."

"Same walls broken down by the same trespassers, and nobody to mend them. Same gaps in hedges and cattle straying," said William slowly.

"I'll do what I can. It's all going to rack and ruin without me," Richard grinned. "You'll know my worth after this spell. You'll give me higher wages."

They were haymaking the next time he came. The mowing meadows were rich with colours, the bloomy-purple seedheads were nodding on the grasses, plumes of red sorrel, and pincushions of the rufous burnet raised themselves above the highest grasses. White dog daisies lay like shimmering pools here and there in the hollows, and foxgloves stood in serried ranks guarding the borders under the walls. The mowing machine was out, and William Dale drove it. The whirr could be heard a long distance away in the quiet misty morning, and other farmers told each other that Dales at Shepherd's Fields were starting mowing, and they'd better be lively or they'd be beat by the old Gaffer.

Virginia in her print sunbonnet was tedding the grass. It lay in heavy rows, heaped in regular waves, except at the field's corners, where the machine turned. There William had to dismount and remove the heavy grass, which stalled the knife blades. The field seemed to be alive and fully aware of the mowing machine. It shivered even before the horses came near, it shook its pollen, and tossed its filmy plumes, as if trying to escape. Then slowly it fell, sweeping down to the earth as if it were tired to death.

Virginia tedded evenly, she had worked thus since her childhood, and the little tufts of hay flew in the air above her as she picked and tossed and waved, covering the ground with a sheet of the palest green.

"There's somebody coming over yonder," called William. "My eyes isn't as good as they used to be. It looks like—— What do you think, Jinny?"

"It is. It's Richard!" she cried, and she stuck the fork in the ground and ran to meet him.

228

She was sun-warmed, brown, changed to a different woman. Like a harvest queen her colour had become golden. Gold lights in her hair, her cheeks red gold, her hands brown as the earth, she stood before him. She looked shyly at him, then took a little run and flung her arms round his neck.

"Oh Dick! How glad I am to see you. Oh Dick!"

He kissed her, it was a new experience to see Jenny shy with him, but she was different, with an air about her and something else. He looked with astonished eyes at her, quizzing her, teasing her.

"You're getting quite jolly-looking," said he. "Not so homely as you used to be. I always thought you were an ugly, skinny little thing."

"Thank you," said Virginia, quickly. "Am I getting fat now?"

"No, but you're quite bonny. I hardly knowed you," and he poked her with his forefinger and pulled her hair.

"Hello, Dad. I see you're getting on well without me," he called, as William came stumbling over the grass. "A goodish crop we've got? I asked for my leave now, so as I could help. I thought you'd be cutting, and I heard you away at the station. I'd know the sound of our machine anywhere."

"In heaven?" asked Virginia, mischievously.

"In hell," he retorted.

"Are you glad to see me home?" he asked later, and again she moved impulsively to him and he grasped her hands.

Virginia looked down at the hands that held hers. They were shaped for the land, broad, smooth, large, not horny or calloused, but firm and strong, the thumbs upturned, the fingers strong as a giant's, flexible as wire. It was impossible to draw her own hands away. The palms were hollowed like little round bowls, to hold wheat and grain. Yes, they were made for the farm, the fields, the cornland, not for the pen. The finger pads were hard as iron.

He swung her out and in, towards him and away, backward and forward, and there they were swaying together in a childish way, with feet firm and arms outstretched and bodies moving rhythmically as if they were about to set off dancing round the fields. She remembered. It was the way he had swung her when she was little, a see-saw lilt that had always pleased her. He had not forgotten either. It seemed as if old times had returned.

They went to the house, through the white gate, that Charity had chosen from the carpenter long ago, across the yard, to the open kitchen door. Hetty cried out with joy and vexation and happiness and anger at his coming without telling her so that she could have prepared a score of meat pies and jam tarts and iced buns. They would kill a couple of fowls and dress them, and order a ham, for there wasn't a bit left of their own. He had caught her in her old dress, and the kitchen not redded up.

He kissed her mouth to silence, and his happiness seemed to flood the room. He hadn't broken the news that he was going to France the next week. The first evening should be free from anxiety. So that night they sat round the fire, and told their tales, the high prices of things, the difficulties and then Emmie came with her husband and baby. They were all united, and happy once more, and the house listened too and talked of old days, burbling on to itself, whispering and chuckling, then sighing a little, and by the fire sat an old woman knitting, and nobody saw her at all. There sat Charity, knitting a sock for her man, with needles of moonlight and wool of memory, and beyond her sat another, Charity's grandmother, spinning at her wheel, and many another was there. Round the fire they sat, many generations, listening to one who had tales to tell of modern war, and aeroplanes and guns, but they were telling their own tales of far-away battles, Tudor wars, Civil wars, and Waterloo, and people carrying wood from the farm to the heights for the bonfires, and the guard set on the hills, and the flashing sparks as the flames rose in the sky sending messages. The kettle was singing on the hob, and Virginia looked across the room and saw old Charity's face, wrinkled and smiling, shifting in and out of the shadows like a beam of light.

"That's how James Watt thought of the steam engine," said a faraway voice. "Dick, my dear."

Dick looked up, puzzled, as if he heard the echo.

"Will ye lock up for me, Dick, if you know how?" asked William, joking, and Dick lighted the lantern and went out.

"I thought he'd like to do it," William nodded his head slyly at the others. "It makes him feel at home, like. Maybe he's forgot where the keys hang, after his army ways. Maybe."

They laughed and shook their heads.

Richard went to the stable, the lantern flashing over the yard. Virginia could see the light through the little peep-hole window in the kitchen wall, where there was never a shutter. She sat close to the small slit glass, and her heart seemed to be out there with him. He must have known her thoughts, for he raised the lantern a moment and sent a beam through the thick old green glass, straight to her heart, his face turned to hers. They were both thinking of Charity. He stood watching her through the narrow peep-hole. Here was Virginia, her lovely self, changed from a girl to a woman. She was sitting in the kitchen, he was in the stable, not far away, and beyond them were the fields of war. If he flashed his lantern the light would be a signal to her. He stepped over the doorsill of the stable, and raised the lantern and sent a secret message flashing over the wall, over the house side. He could see Virginia in the candlelight, with a faint glow from the fire on her face. He lowered the lantern and stood for a moment watching to see if she responded. It had been an old trick to summon her outside, and he hoped she would remember.

Then he saw someone else. His grandmother seemed to step across the room and stoop over the girl. He dropped the lantern in his fright, and took a step forward. Of course, it was Hetty; he could see her plainly standing by Virginia in the half shade of the candle. He gave a little embarrassed laugh and went back to the stable.

Virginia had known his signal, and she came out to him.

"What is it, Dick?" she whispered as she stepped gingerly across the yard, avoiding the round slabs of cow dung.

"I'm off this time, Jinny. Keep your heart up, and don't forget me," said he lightly.

"Oh Dick! At last," she said.

"Write nice long letters and tell me how you are going on, and tell me about Robin and all."

"Yes. I'll write."

"And you won't forget me?" he asked again.

"No. I'll remember you, Dick." That was all.

"Good lass!"

A week later he had gone.

William had driven one day as usual to the village to fetch the groceries, the bags of cattle food, the mended tools and all the things on the list Virginia had written out for him. He wouldn't give up the drive for anyone; it was his outing and his chance to talk to his friends. He was late returning and Hetty grumbled uneasily:

"I can't think why your uncle's so late," said she.

"Maybe he's met somebody and they're having a good yarn," suggested Virginia.

"Talk! Yarn! Men do nothing but talk." Hetty was troubled by his absence. He hadn't been well, but he had insisted on going for his weekly shave and haircut.

"I'll go and look out for him," said Virginia, and she ran up the stone stairway at the back of the farm and gazed from the top platform.

There was the cart away in the distance, the mare ambling even more slowly than usual. She waited a moment, watching them, but she forgot why she was there. Her thoughts flashed to Richard, at the war. She took from her pocket his last letter. There wasn't a word of the fighting, although she knew he was in the midst of danger. For over a year he had been in France, and only a few letters had come from him.

"How is everybody at home?" he asked. "You'll be picking the apples soon. Don't fall out of the big tree. Have you sold the colt? It ought to fetch a tidy price. How is Dad? Have you got the gate mended?" She glanced quickly through and then paused as she came to the precious words at the end.

"Virginia, if anything should happen to me, remember what I told you, your loving Richard."

Her heart beat quickly as she read the words. She thrust the letter back in her dress and sped down the steps and across the yard.

"Uncle's coming along. He'll be here in a quarter of an hour," and they dished up the dinner ready.

When the cart came clattering into the yard, they saw something was wrong. William was slumped on the seat, his eyes staring blankly before him, his heavy body leaning in an ominous way. The reins were twisted round his hands, lying loosely on the mare's back. The mare had gone to her usual place in front of the kitchen door, and waited patiently for him to alight. Hetty ran out with a scream of fear.

"William! What's amiss? Here Virginia! Your uncle's ill. He's had a stroke or something. Call Ben."

Together they got him from the cart and supported him into the house, half dragging him as he collapsed. He couldn't speak, or use his limbs.

Somehow they got him upstairs to Charity's room. It had the best bed, and they all knew that William would not come down again. Charity had died there, and William must lie in the room where his forebears had ended their lives. It was a blessing he managed to get home they told each other. Nobody but William could have done that. The mare was trusty, she had come without any guidance, and luckily they had met few vehicles on the way. The gates were open, and the mare had walked safely through the middle of the gateways, without so much as grazing the posts, as if she knew something was wrong when the rein was so slack, and no familiar voice spoke to her. William recovered sufficiently to tell them that he was driving along home, he had just been passed by a couple of fast cars, when he felt queer. He twisted the reins round his hand and remembered no more. He wished Richard could come home. He wanted Dick. He had a lot to tell Dick. But he knew he'd see Dick soon. He wasn't afraid. He was all right. He'd be downstairs in a few days, and out in the fields. Whatever they did, they must all take care of Shepherd's Fields.

He died, and was buried next to Charity and Timothy, and next to another old grave, whose letters were rubbed and worn, Matthew Woodiwiss and Martha his wife. The old farm received him into the company, and remembered the days of his childhood, and the shadows welcomed him to the vast company of the unremembered, unknown dead, who had once tilled the land, and harrowed the fields and served the farm. He was welcomed with rejoicings, and he sat with them, and heard their tales, and told his own, and shared their busy life, and the house's secret life.

He had been very tired the last years, and now he was free from all pain, and his feeling of youth was restored. He was glad he hadn't to go away from the house of his childhood. Heaven would be lonely without those fields and lands he knew so well.

The house was radiant, it kept its secret, it hid the troop of shadows running tiptoes through its rooms, laughing and chattering, kissing one another, as old friends met, sitting at the table, drawing up chairs to the fire.

Virginia knew they were there. She rattled the latch to warn them she was coming, and stayed a moment on a doorsill, lest they should be incommoded by her presence. Then the shades disappeared, they sprang from the chairs, they rose from the hearthstone where they had been sitting warming their toes, then flew into the corners and disappeared into their own world, but sometimes the rocking chair went on rocking, the curtain gave a twitch as a skirt whisked behind it, the looking-glass gave back the reflection of another face, a wrinkled, pointed, smiling, brown old face when she peered at the glass, instead of her own warm rose-tinted skin and the startled eyes. Then she turned swiftly round and looked behind her, but always she was too late to catch the laughing phantoms. A wave of knowledge swept through her, the earth had granted her a favour, the certainty that the life of the house went on to eternity, that through her love for it, her own love was returned.

Days were hard, with no master in the house, and Hetty had changed after William's death to an old woman. She hated everything that reminded her of him whom she had loved so passionately that she had borne with all the troubles and anxieties of the farm for his sake. Now he was gone, and nothing remained for her.

"I'd sell up and go away now, if it wasn't for Dick," she told Virginia. "How can two women keep going?"

"There's Ben. He's doing his best, taking the milk to the station, and managing the bull, and the heavy churns. We've got a man, Aunt Hetty, and I don't think we ought to grumble," Virginia's throat contracted, she could hardly speak for she was afraid that Hetty would go.

"He'll marry you when he comes back," said Hetty. "Oh, you needn't blush and turn away. I know it. It's been writ all over his face, ever since he was a boy. I've known it. Why, when you got married and went away, he was like somebody stricken down. I'm his mother and I knew all the time, but I said nothing, for what could I do?"

"I didn't know," faltered Virginia. "It's only lately that I've grown to love him, Aunt Hetty."

"You ought to have found out earlier. But it doesn't matter now. Perhaps he won't come back at all. I'm in daily fear of getting bad news. There's Tom Dowland, at the Smithy, gone, and Jack Snowball, and Bill Stone, and Ralph Wildgoose, all killed."

"Oh Aunt Hetty. Don't talk like that. We must hope and pray. Dick is coming home, and Shepherd's Fields will look fine on that day. We'll have such a welcome."

"Without your uncle here? How can you say such a thing?"

There was no pleasing Aunt Hetty, and nobody to say a cheering word when things looked bad. Dick's letters were the holds on sanity, the letters that told nothing, for Dick had never been a writer. He had hated school, and he held the pen with stiff fingers, saying little, so that Virginia had to read between the lines, and imagine what he wanted to tell her.

She had the refuge of the fields, the barns, the little old room to which she had returned to sleep. She had only to stand and wait, and gradually the sounds around her dimmed, cocks and hens, horses, and rustling leaves faded, and out of the silence shadows came, glowing shades from the dark spaces of another time; voices rose from the timeless world where everyone dwells, voices talking, singing, whispering, laughing, childish voices, shrill and sweet, warm voices with rich intonations, mellowed by death, generations of them.

"Abigail. You've taken my top, my lovely humming top. Give it me. I want to spin it on this bare bit of barn floor."

"Tabitha. Come, sit on my lap, and hearken to a tale."

"Let me try first, Timothy. Oh, lookye how it spins! Hark how it hums! Like a swarm of bees in orchard, isn't it?"

Yes, there was a clear musical humming sound, and Virginia would see flashes of the red and blue top whirling round the barn pursued by long-skirted little girls with eager faces and fat rosy cheeks.

"Anthony's taken my Dutch doll. See—he's hung it on the ladder. Oh my doll."

"Childer, don't 'ee quarrel. Little birds in their nesses agree. Come sit ye down on this hay."

"Mother. Tell us a story. Tell us about the great big bear that was shut up here. Tell us."

"Once upon a time. Once upon a time——"

The voices murmured on, soft as drifting leaves, quiet as the fall of the spider's thread or the boring of the wood beetles in the great oak beams.

But Virginia's own voices of memory were talking there and she listened intently as they grew louder and clearer than the others.

"Jinny. Jinny. You like me best, don't you?"

"Of course I do, Dick."

"Jinny. Come here. I've summut to show you. See, a swallow's nest. That bird comes all the way from Africky to our farm."

"Dick, lift me up on the cart shaft. Oh Dick! Does it know our names?"

"Yes. It's twittering Jinny! Jinny!"

"Stand and face your lover, as you have done before," warbled a tiny voice, high in the roof.

Then the voices died away, and Virginia could hear Hetty calling, from the house door.

"Jinny! Time to go milking. You'd best be sharp. Now shape yourself. You've been a long time out there, doing nothing I'll be bound."

Summer went by, autumn faded to winter, and somehow Richard seemed nearer on winter days. Robin was walking now, and Virginia had a companion to take her hand and help to feed the cattle, and sip the new milk.

One afternoon, when the glow of a frosty sun filled the yard, she went out to the troughs for buckets of water. There was a thin sheet of ice over all the troughs, cracked where the cattle had drunk, but already freezing again in a delicate layer, with slender trees and geometric patterns inlaid. She stooped to the drinking trough and skimmed off the thin layer. She held it up and viewed the bent grasses and the hoary moss through it. It seemed to change them, to magnify and distort them to something even more beautiful. The trees were laden with ice, crystal shells that clicked and clattered as the wind beat them together. Then the ice layer melted in her hand and fell with a scurry of splinters against the side of the trough. Ice, snow, these would return for ever, and she knew she would return to play with them, the treasures and toys of both worlds, the visible and the invisible.

The oak tree beyond the gate of the farmyard, where Charity had passed her last hours, was very still under its glistening burden of ice crystals. The swing hung nearly motionless, but a sudden wind caught it and started it swaying as if an invisible girl were sitting there, clasping the ropes, in the ice-blue air. Backward and forward it went, and Virginia stood fascinated, lost in her imaginings, dreaming of Richard's words.

"Let's have a swing, Jinny," he had cried the last day of his leave. "You've not been on the swing for many a day, I'll bet."

"That's true. I never swing nowadays. There's no time, and I'm getting too old," she confessed.

"Come along now. Grandmother Charity used to swing a bit even when she was eighty. I remember her sitting on the seat, going to and fro, with a Bible on her knees. I couldn't help laughing at her, but she didn't like me to mock."

"I remember too, Dick. I read *Herne the Hunter* there, and thought this was his own oak tree. I'd like a good swing, high up to the boughs, just as I used to have."

"Do you remember when you fell off?" he asked.

"Do I remember? I do, and you picked me up."

"All bloody you were, and I thought you were dead· You didn't cry at first, your eyes were shut. You were plucky."

"I cried enough afterwards. I was sorry for myself," laughed Virginia. "I've got the scar now." She took his fingers and held them to the back of her head, but instead of touching the deep weal, his hands caressed her hair, lingering on the nape of her neck, sending tremors through her body, and he hadn't spoken.

She sprang away and stood on the seat, grasping the long iron chains, and he stood opposite her. Away they went, knees bent, and straightening, pulling higher and higher till their heads were in the leafy branches, and the tree groaned and the chains creaked with the strain.

At last she cried, "Stop. Enough," and the swing's amplitude lessened, the earth came up to meet her, and she waited until she could spring to the ground. She was dizzy and she swayed unsteadily for a moment, clutching at Richard's coat.

"I told you I'm getting old," she laughed, breathless and dazed. "I never used to feel dizzy after a swing. It's like going right off the world, up into the sky."

"I'd like to get away from earth for a while and then come back to see what it's like," said Dick, staring at the distant hills. "Yes, I'd like that."

"Don't say that. You might be taken off, and not be able to return," said Virginia. "Don't want to get away from the earth, Dick," she pleaded.

"I'd come back somehow," said he confidently. "If it was only to see you I'd come back."

"I'd come back," said Virginia quickly. "The house would draw me back, just like the chains of the swing draw you."

"You can only love on earth," Richard was looking now at her, deep into her eyes and she couldn't meet his gaze. "You can only love on earth. It says so in the Bible. So I'd come back. If I'm killed in France, Virginia, remember this. I didn't want to tell you, not so soon, but I must, lest I'm taken away. You can only love on earth, Jinny, my dear."

"Not us. We should go on loving wherever we were. If we couldn't love in heaven, we'd be ghosts in the fields here."

"I know no place better than this. No place as nice," said Richard. "I don't want to go anywhere else."

"Nor do I," laughed Virginia. She had gained her composure. It was only Dick's lighthearted way of talking, the simplicity of outlook that she had always loved. He didn't mean anything. They had always been great friends. It was comforting to know that whatever happened he would be with her till the end of time. Maurice she loved for ever, he was in her mind; Ronnie, her childhood friend was here too, but Richard was part of her, indivisible from her.

That was all, but she thought of his words many times, and most of all that day as she crouched at the troughs, forgetting what she had gone for, looking at the world through the thin glass of ice.

She thought of him, climbing the highest tree, stepping upward, trying to climb out of the world to gaze down at the warring nations, stepping higher, through the air on stairs invisible, airy steps reaching upward to heaven. She looked up at the sky, at the little white clouds, and an aeroplane flying with faint roar of engines. The barren boughs of the trees knocked together, the stirks moved with their silky hair ruffled by the wind. She shivered and drew her scarf close. A robin flew down very near, and spoke to her, cocking his tail, staring with round beady eyes, singing his shrill song then waiting, head aside, for an answer. Like a human being he wanted a reply.

But Virginia was looking and listening to something else, for the robin's song faded, the leafless trees were still, the sound of the river was muffled in a cloth, and the tinkle of the water trough was lost and forgotten.

The bare trees, the water spring, the earth, she was part of them, and she knelt on the cold ice-sprinkled stones waiting for whatever should come.

"Jinny. Jinny," somebody called, very far away, faint as from another world.

Then the sounds of life returned, the spring flashed into the troughs, with a sweet chuckle and drip, and the river across the fields murmured on its way. Virginia looked round at the house, standing serene and mysterious in its clustered buildings. What was it doing? Had it fair company which she could not see? Had it called her? She longed to creep up to a window and surprise it, to catch the laughter and tales within, but there would only be Hetty ironing the clothes, wondering where she had got to as usual.

Snow began to fall, crazily, carelessly, sideways fluttering and swinging like white butterflies in the gusts of air. Virginia filled her buckets and walked quickly back to the house.

"The house just keeps on. You and me, we die, as our grandmother and all of them died, but the house keeps on."

"Virginia. What's that? How can you talk like that?" cried Hetty banging down the iron. "What have you been doing? You'll get your death of cold and leave me to manage alone."

"No, I won't, Aunt Hetty. I'm sorry I've been so long."

Down fell the snowflakes, down to the yard, hiding the stone doorsills, covering the manure heap with a silky cloth, dropping white feathers on the few fowls that hadn't taken shelter. Virginia went to the window, while Hetty talked, but her eyes were following one flake larger than its companions, swaying and floating there.

"If it alights on the wall, then he will come back. If it drops on the path, he won't return," she said to herself, using old primitive tricks of divination. The snowflake was caught by a light air and fell out of sight.

There was another tide running, beyond the temporal one, and she was swept along in it. She knew part of what was coming, but not all. She had been behind the curtain, watched the edge lifted, and seen the crumpled body, and the loved face. The last night, in sleep she had had a dream from which she awoke in a sweat of fear. Richard lay there, in the mud. It was a little scene, round as a locket, framed in ebony, illuminated with queer intensity. She, an onlooker from a distance, had watched him, filled with compassion, unable to help.

Now it came again, as she watched the wreaths of snow drifting down the yard. She felt again that emptiness of body, that lightness like wings, and the cessation of all sound. Out of the nothingness came the same picture, blue-shadowed with dusk, and Richard lying there. This time he raised his head and stretched out a hand blindly, and she broke through and knelt in the mud and took his head on her knee.

"Thank God you came, Jinny. I've been calling you ever so long. I thought you'd never hear me. I think I can make it now you're here. Take care of Shepherd's Fields. Long acre. Top Meadow. Barley Leas. Jinny——"

"I'm with you, Dick," she had whispered, but her voice made no sound. He knew without words.

"Yes. I can see you all right. I'm glad you've come, Jinny."

239

The scene faded, she tried to hold it, to hear more, but she couldn't stop the disappearing vision. It moved rapidly into the snow, and was gone. She felt sick and worn, something had gone out of her, she had lost strength. She swayed towards the table and Hetty alarmed, put out a hand to save her.

"I'm done up, Aunt Hetty. I'm sick. I must lie down," she stammered, and she went out to her attic room and flung herself on the bed.

She thought that many years had fled away, that all she knew were dead, that she was terribly and intensely alone in a timeless world of the future. She saw herself climbing the stone walls, running in desperate haste, her foot making no sound, her heart beating in terrible urgency, to get there. Where? She was panting in her desire to arrive in time. She saw the house waiting, waiting. She raced across the yard, under the pale cold moon, she pushed open the door, she flung out her arms to cling to the warm kindly body of—whom? She didn't know. There was nobody there. The house was empty. Cobwebs and broken windows and only the wind whistling through. Dark corners and moving shadows. It was a shell. The phantoms flooded the rooms unheeding her. They wouldn't take her in.

"Richard!" she called, and her voice rang down eternity, echoing among the dead stars. Then house and herself dissolved, and only a field of moonlight and a broken heap of stones remained.

Shaking with passionate tears she dropped to the floor, and there Hetty found her.

"You're ghastly white, Jinny," cried Hetty. "I'll get you an egg-cupful of brandy. What's done it?"

"It was a touch of snowblindness I think. I get it when the snow comes. I shall be all right," said Virginia, but to herself she moaned, "Dick? Dick? Are you alive or dead?"

The news came that Richard had been wounded. He lay in the mud, and only after two days had he been rescued and taken to the Base. He was in danger, for a time in the hospital, but at last he was sent to England, and discharged. He had shell-shock, they said, and only time would cure him.

"I was calling you, the doctors said," he told Virginia. "I felt that if you didn't come I should be burned to death. I thought I was in the stable, and it was on fire, I could see the flames coming nearer, all round me, and I couldn't get out. I yelled and yelled for you to save me. I shouted so loud for you, I shouted the world over. Then you came, and held me, and took me to the stable door, away from the fire. Just you. They said I suddenly stopped shouting and went to sleep."

He was very quiet, gentler than usual, with long silences, unaware of anything going on around him. Gradually he began to recover. The old house took a share in this. It talked to him, it answered his own troubled thoughts with sanity and strength. It brought him out of the death shadows and led him slowly to a new life. He began to take an interest in the farm, he worked with his hands, and walked over the land. Virginia and Hetty nursed him, Hetty with a devotion and solicitude and patience that astonished all who knew her.

One day Virginia was alone in the kitchen, working at the table, washing eggs, counting them into the baskets, arranging the white cloths over them, and getting them ready for the market cart. Footsteps came across the yard, and it seemed that life stood still, and music drifted down from the ceiling. A shadow fell on the floor and Richard entered. She turned slowly towards him, she knew what he was going to say. He was part of her life, she had known from her childhood. It had been settled long ago. Other music had come between them, but now there was nothing to hold them apart. Love for Maurice had been a flame, burning up in an intense fire. Love for Richard was something steadier, like love for England, and love for Shepherd's Fields. It had always been there. It was deep as the earth, strong and unchanging with devotion undying.

"Jinny," said he. "Do you know what I want to say? Can you guess?" He spoke slowly as if time didn't matter any more. "Can you guess what I've known ever since you were a little 'un?"

"Yes, Dick. I know."

"I love you, Jinny. I've always loved you. I wanted you long ago, and I waited to be sure, and I missed my chance. Can you think of me in that way? Is it too late."

"I've always loved you, Dick. You know that."

"You'll marry me? Soon? Need we wait?"

"I've always loved you, Dick."

They stood together, and a minute was like a hundred years, and perhaps a hundred years passed in that minute. They were both outside time. The grandfather clock stopped suspended with its old brass pendulum hanging in the semi-curve, defying gravity, waiting while he held her in silence, to resume its motion after long years of happiness had passed, but behold! it registered only a second on its burnished face. So time stayed, at moments of agony and bliss, at birth and death. Nothing could destroy this reality stolen out of infinity. The clock had stayed while Charity died, it had waited while Charity stepped across the threshold to heaven. Now it stopped again and sustained Virginia in a dazzling, blinding light of love. They had something that could not be destroyed nor measured. They were both part of each other, and no death could divide them.

All the sweet joys of life, remembrances of the sun and moon, of harvest and Christmas, were part of the unconscious life they shared together, for now Richard knew that inner life. He had been present in the spirit, for he was herself, and she lived in his heart. Perhaps there would be another moment like this when the door of eternity opened, and they looked through it together. Not until life's end, when the door opened for her soul to slip through, would she know again the happiness and taste the ecstasy that swept over her.

The house rejoiced for here were the two whom it had blessed long ago, whose fate was bound up in its own. So Virginia was married to Richard, and he too shared the old room of Grandmother Charity, and listened with his wife to the murmurs of the house. Calm and content, slow and steady-handed, he shaped and fashioned their lives together. With one hand on the old and another on the future, he steadied time itself and accepted the strength that came to him.

Chapter 20

Night and day the old house kept watch on the seasons. Night and day it kept guard. It knew when wild storms were on the way from the North and it spread out its skirts to shelter its children. It didn't need the weathercock on the roof to warn it of tempest and gale. It felt the wind change, it heard the words of its shrill voice, and saw its beating wings. The house hunched its shoulders and sang its own wild challenge as the gales swept round its corners and tore down its alleys. House and wind fought together, but the house rooted in the deep rocks was unharmed. When the oak tree where Charity spent her last hours was uprooted, the house gave an answering cry of farewell to an old companion. Ice crystals formed in the upper atmosphere, snow descended, frosts bound the earth with heavy chains. The house stared up from its white shawl at the wheeling stars, and pierced with its keen vision the great circling paths of the heavens. In winter its eyes were like those of an eagle gazing round. In summer it was a dove, resting on the earth, brooding, half-asleep, caring for those who lived within its walls, sheltering all who had made the place their dwelling.

Years passed, children were born, a boy and a girl, life was renewed in house, in stable and byre. Servant men came and went, only old Ben remained for he was the link with the old days, he would die in the farm's service. He never accepted the new order. He was full of grumbles and rheumatism. Nothing suited him, but his devotion was given unstintedly, as he tried to understand the changes in the world. Falling prices, cheap goods flooding the country, sheep not worth rearing, calves sold for less than their value, carefree townsmen walking through the fields jingling their money in their pockets, asking many questions, and laughing at the answers, were commonplace. There was foot-and-mouth disease at a neighbouring farm, and deep anxiety lest the herd built up by Richard would have to be slaughtered. Men walked carefully, straw was laid down, and there was the hush of death about the farm. No visitors came, it was like ruin waiting outside the gates, but the trouble passed. A great weight was lifted from their hearts. Then other troubles came, one after another, but even then there were small joys to compensate. Virginia was able to keep her son Robin at the Grammar school and give her little daughter Susan education at the school where she had gone for night classes. David, the youngest, had no desire for learning. He was like Richard, clever with horses, he could ride as soon as he could walk. He would follow Robin to his school, and then come home to the farm, it was all arranged. So it was all planned, between schoolmaster and parents and the house listened and shook its head and smiled.

The years went by, and there were other changes. Now there was a Ford car to take the milk to the station, and new machines in the old barns. Now there was a pole fastened to one of the chimneys and music came through the air, strange grand music and jazz to try to outdo the old tunes that the barn sang. The house was unconcerned, even when Robin got married at the age of twenty. Virginia welcomed Janet, who was a country-bred, simple girl. She was as much a daughter to Shepherd's Fields as Virginia's Susan. Robin was like Maurice, a boy with no farming instincts, a lover of machines, and an engineer.

Old Ben came in one night, struck with amazement at the new order of the Universe. He threw back the door and stood in the kitchen waiting for somebody to notice his distress.

"What's the matter, Ben?" asked Virginia.

Ben heaved a deep sigh and pointed to the sky. He was deeply agitated at his awful discovery.

"Have ye noticed how the stars are, how there ain't as many nowadays as there used to be, Missis Jinny?" He always gave that name to Virginia, for the real Missis was Charity and no other. "I mind the nights when the sky was bung full of stars, all twinkling and winking up there, Orion and Charley's Wain, and the Lady and all of 'em. Now it's different, surelye. They don't shine as they used to do. They've gone away from this old world, and no wonder with things as they is. Countries all fighting and quarrelling, and queer goings-on everywhere and no religion and football on Sundays. No keeping the Sabbath. It isn't what it used to be. That's why they don't shine down on us. They were grand in my time. Why, I 'member seeing 'em so bright like a lot of fires up there, all twinkling like mad. This 'ere old world has fair sickened 'em."

Virginia tried to console him. She took his aged arm and showed him the stars, even her own star up there, blinking down at her with that watchful look she knew so well. It was part of eternity, moving through life and death for ever onward, but he wouldn't agree. Even Charley's Wain was different, not so shiny. Things were wrong, with wireless and all. "Mark my words, Missis Jinny," he concluded. "There'll be summat up soon."

There was, for war came again. Silver-winged planes flew over the hills, and in one of them was Robin. The house watched day and night, it never went to sleep. It was strangely roused, it knew there was danger in the air. Watchers came again to the hill where there was a look-out post. It was the height where Charity had gone as a little girl to seek the lost sheep, for she could see every field and pasture for many miles. It was there she had gazed at the house, and seen it as a being with life and soul of its own. It was there Virginia had watched the chimneys to read the message the spirals of smoke sent up in the air. It was the hill where the Beltane fires had burned long ages ago. Men were on guard among the bracken and heather watching the sky day and night, as they had done in the Napoleonic wars, as they had watched in Elizabethan times when the Spaniards were coming up the Channel. Now other ships were sailing on sea and in the air. The old house remembered all these times of danger, but never had the waiting been so tense, or the peril so great.

Robin had joined the Royal Air Force, and Janet was staying near his camp. Virginia was looking after her first grandson. The servant man had already left, and Richard was struggling alone with old Ben, tottering and ancient, and with young David.

Long white fingers stabbed the sky, pointing up from the horizon, crossing and recrossing the blue bowl as they blindly sought the enemy. They came from the old familiar places in the hills and Virginia and Richard called them by name, as if they were lamps lighted at a well-known farm. There were now no lights from the houses of friends across the valley. There was such a darkness as had not been known for a hundred years. Then Old Ben said he had been mistook about those stars. They had come back now old England was fighting the Germans. They'd come to help her, he said. It all went to show that the Right would win in the end.

Down below, crouched in its hollow of the valley among apple trees and walnut trees, with cattle and horses and human beings safe in its arms, the old house kept guard too. Like an ark it sailed through storm and tempest, an island in the little island called England. Storms swept the land that second winter of war, the winds grew shriller than ever, and the snow was deep in the farmland, nearly cutting it off from the villages. That was another omen, said Ben. The wind whistled on a higher note like the screech of the siren, shrill as a witch's scream. Virginia looked up from her mending, as she sat by the kitchen fire at night, with the shutters tightly closed and the door locked and barred. She thought it was a spectre high in the air, rattling its bones, summoning all the skeletons in the distant churchyard to dance with it.

"Some day I may be called away by such a cry," she thought, looking round quickly in alarm lest anyone had divined her thoughts. Richard smiled at her from the other side of the hearth, where he was reading "Instructions for Invasion".

"We'll make a fight for it, Jinny," said he. "We could hold 'em

245

off a bit with rifles and pitchfork and pole-axe, and even that old blunderbuss on the wall."

Virginia laughed. She was glad he couldn't read her mind as easily as she read his. He knew nothing of the pain that she had in her heart, she had kept it concealed from him. He thought she was more easily tired, that was all. She had been to see a doctor in the market town, a stranger to her, who would keep her secrets. He had been grave, giving her a warning to take things easily, her heart was affected. With care she might live for years, but if she didn't—well—— He thought she would be afraid of the truth. Instead she was transformed. Fear had been defeated, each day was precious as a radiant pearl. She knew where she was going and who would welcome her. That was in the winter. Virginia drove home along the quiet lanes, and gazed about her at everything as if she saw it for the first time. Yet every time was the first time for her. Nothing in all her life had ever palled on her, and now everything showed its inner beauty and called to her as never before. While Richard unharnessed the mare, and Susan made the tea, ready for her, Virginia lingered in the yard, with her burden of knowledge clasped to her, aware intensely of the livingness of every object there. The fields, the big gate, the stone walls, even the frosty sun shining red as blood, and the young moon thin as a ghost were alive and real as were Richard, and Susan, her daughter, and Robin and David. They were more real than anybody in the village for they were nearer, they spoke a tongue she could understand. The doctor was a ghost, his words were dreams.

That little curl of a moon, she bowed to it three times, and spoke a word of welcome. Then to the house she turned. It was beautiful that evening, it had done its hair and brushed its eyebrows, and it wore a dull red frock, reflections from that blazing sun. She smiled up at it, and waved her hands to the invisible ones, and they waved back.

"Oh God, how happy I am," she thought. "Is it wrong to be happy like this, when I have my beloved on earth, and yet I can feel no fear?"

Since then she had had six months of bliss, such as seemed scarcely possible, except for the pain, and that had been dulled. Perhaps it had forgotten, perhaps not.

One summer's day Virginia was sitting in the chimney corner. The queer pain was tearing at her, she sat very still waiting till it lessened. Gradually she came out of the shadowy plains, the curtain of darkness moved, and she stepped back into the light once more. The beech trees were radiant, the mossy walls seemed so strongly endued with life she half expected them to speak as she watched them from the window. The house walls were listening, the house knew of her private agony of body, it comforted her as it had cheered women and men through countless years. Her grief and happiness seeped into the walls, it drifted like smoke out to the yard, to trees and rugged walls, to water troughs and fields. The sorrow and joy was stored in the barn walls, and benches and wooden bins, to remain till somebody came with mind attuned to tap it and feel it again, and Virginia tried to send happiness there for others. All sweetness and grief was waiting, the songs and happiness of centuries, and to the store each added his own small portion. The old house held this grand load to its head, and the forgotten dead came back through its emanations. Currents of thought, of love and endurance, ran like gold threads through the house and entered the receiving mind. So Charity had sent her own valiant spirit out to help all who came after, and Virginia received this help, and gave out her own portion of faith and love.

Now and then she leaned forward to get a glimpse of the field away on the hillside, where Richard was working with a tractor. Machinery had come to the farm, and they had all welcomed it, and made a cartshed free to hold it. The sun shone on Richard's broken straw hat. He moved with the ease and grace of a young man. There was never a grey hair in his head. He seemed to have regained his youth after his long illness. The house had blessed him and saved him, but Virginia had aged and suffered in his stead.

There was a whirr and the machine stopped, and he climbed down and began to tinker. They could hear the note of iron like a bird's song in the distance.

"There I declare! It's broken down again, Susan. Your father will be vexed," cried Virginia. "That tractor isn't worth its keep. Our lands are too stony. Those great rocks will smash anything. It's the foundation of the world itself we get to when we goes down a bit. Stands to reason no tractor can manage it."

"You and Father insisted on getting it," Susan reminded her. She was a brown-haired girl, with Virginia's deep blue eyes, tall as her father, serious and independent.

"That was when Robin was here to deal with its tantrums,"

said Virginia. "It's going to plough up Nick's Corner, and that will be the test. All rocks and bushes, and never been under the plough since Shepherd's Fields was born itself."

"Born!" cried Susan. "How can a house be born?" But Virginia only laughed, "I was wrong. Immortals aren't born," said she.

"Where's little John? she asked, presently, looking through the door. "Is he all right? I can't see him in the garden. Don't let him get into trouble with the bull, or fall in the water trough or break his neck dropping from the steps."

"He's out there, Mother. He's with Bess. He's riding on the old mare."

There was a clatter of hooves in the yard, a jingle of chains and a heavy-footed old mare came through the gate, throwing out her feathered feet in fine manner. A small figure was seated on her bare back. The boy waved a bunch of flowers and clutched the mane.

"Hey. Can you see me, Gran? Can you see me?" he piped in a shrill voice. Ben led the mare before the window, past the open door, and Virginia tapped at the glass with her knitting needles, and then went to the door.

"That's the way to ride! Good boy," said she.

The child's fair head shone like gold corn, his eyes were blue as speedwell. They were like Charity's eyes, thought Virginia with a sudden tug at her heart. Charity would have liked this boy. He laughed loudly and kicked his heels against the smooth fat sides of the mare. His brown legs were nearly the colour of her beautiful skin.

Ben lifted him, but he struggled down alone and ran hurriedly into the kitchen.

"Gran, I rode all the way from Nick's Croft on Bess's back. I did. And Ben never held me, and Bess trotted fast and galloped a bit, and I never falled off. I'm going to have a mare of my own some day. Can Bess be my mare?"

"Yes dear. You shall have Bess for your own."

"For my very own?"

"Yes. I give her to you with my love," said Virginia looking at him with infinite love.

"Mother. How absurd. You can't give a carthorse to a little child like John." Susan was startled by Virginia's nonsense.

"I can! Bess is my own mare. I reared her, I broke her in, and I can't take her with me when I die. It will be good for John to

248

have a stake in the farm, something living, a real personality like Old Bess. I know Bess very well. She came into the kitchen once."

Virginia laughed and the little boy flung his arms around her neck.

"See what I've brought you," said he, thrusting the crumpled petals into her face, cool against her lips.

"You come to the garden with me and we'll pick a bunch of very little tiny flowers and make a peepshow. Yes, we'll make a real peepshow and then you can say, 'A Pin to see a Peepshow' and everybody will give you pins."

The two went into the garden, to find the azure petals of larkspur, the yellow-eyed pansies, and Bachelor's Buttons. As they walked they chattered, Virginia showing the boy the secrets of earth, the webs and insects, and hidden treasures. Susan hurried off to the dairy, where there was plenty of work waiting. Virginia seemed to have forgotten about the work. She took John to the barn, and there she sat on the stone bench, making the peepshow, while the child watched her. After a while he played on the steps, jumping from one to another.

"Take care, you'll wear them out," warned Virginia, and she stooped and touched the hollowed stones, those steps worn by the feet of poor men and women, going and coming with burdens and cares since the time of the Elizabethans. Gay little feet had run down them, and heavy feet had walked up. Children had slid from step to step of the hard stone with peals of laughter as they bumped along, children in smocks, in leather breeches, in wool and homespun. Old men had dragged their weary feet one step at a time, with a hand on the rough wall to steady themselves, with trailing cloak of sacking and thick coat of frieze. Those who followed in the future would have different hopes and fears, but they would be made in the same pattern, youth with its joys and hopes, age with its regrets. A mechanical age could not alter the fundamental web of life.

"What are you thinking about, Gran?" asked John, dragging at her hand. "I'm thinking of all the people in this barn," and Virginia arose and went back to the house.

"There's been a bad raid on London, Mother," said Susan when Virginia returned. "Ben's just brought the paper. It was left at the bottom gate. The boy's too lazy to come up with it."

"We must get the wireless put right. We need a new battery when Father drives to the village."

"A pity we can't get electricity here."

Virginia turned the peepshow in her hand, and cut the window in the paper concealing the flowers.

"Electricity?" she echoed vaguely. "Yes. It's a grand thing. I learned about it at night class. Positive and negative electricity. All the world is made of it, they said. Strange I remember quite a lot of those lessons we had with that funny little science master long ago."

"At Youlgrave's Farm the cowsheds are lighted with electric light, and they've got an electric cooker, and the farm lighted up, and milking machines. Charlie Youlgrave was telling me," said Susan, and she blushed as she spoke. "He's going to get his commission, Mother."

"Youlgraves have plenty of money. Always had. Ron Youlgrave had a sixpenny dinner every day," said Virginia, who knew all about Charlie Youlgrave and Susan. "But Shepherd's Fields would look grand with electric. It might make the shadows hurry away, but they'd come out again all right. The house would be proud as Punch to be lighted up like a ship sailing in the valley."

"We shall have it soon, Charlie Youlgrave says. As soon as the war is over they'll bring it to the houses outside the village and then we can get it, only it'll cost a lot."

"There's my hundred pounds," said Virginia happily. "I've planned many a thing with it, but we've always managed not to spend it. Even the tractor didn't take it, though it was a near squeak."

"It would be a fine thing to spend it on," said Susan. "I should like us to be as grand as the Youlgraves."

Virginia looked at her proudly. Susan was going to college, to learn all those wonderful things that Virginia had tasted and left. She was going to be a teacher.

"There goes Charity Woodiwiss, the schoolteacher," sang the kitchen. "There goes Virginia Dale, the schoolteacher. There goes Susan Dale, the schoolteacher."

She would go out into the world, but Shepherd's Fields would hold her by a cord that would never break. Besides, there was Charlie Youlgrave to draw her back to the hearthstone of his farm. Susan belonged to the land as intimately as Virginia and Richard.

The old house awoke that night and waited. There was an air of brooding excitement, the house was alert with foreknowledge.

It held its breath, it listened to the warnings of the winged ones, it heard the stars cry out. Its ancient heart beat with distinct rhythmic blows like the beating of a distant drum. It held itself in readiness, crying, "Here is the supreme test." It stretched its roots down to entwine in the rocks, and it took courage from the heart of the world itself. The phantoms swept in like mists, they encircled the walls with their arms outstretched, they folded the house in their love and made it inviolate.

Virginia lay in the four-poster bed, with Richard asleep at her side. His arm was flung across her, and she felt his slow even breathing and the warmth of his body. Her thoughts went back to a night long ago when she had been brought to her grandmother in this same room. She remembered it as clearly as if the scene had been photographed upon her mind. The candle shining and guttering, the beads of sweat on her grandmother's face, the white nightcap with its lace edge and strings, the queer smell of medicine and embrocation, and something else, undefinable. She remembered too that strange sound which had risen above the surge of wind and the beat of fire, that deep throb that had shaken her heart.

"Surely I can hear it now?" she whispered. She lay listening, her senses widely aware of every motion in the air, her sub-conscious mind aware of other things, voices soft and murmur-ous, shadows flowing out of the walls, sometimes a face she knew, Charity for a brief moment looking at her with loving eyes, Maurice smiling there, even Sam the crooked-mouthed, holding up his arms to shield the roof beams, and William standing for a moment, his back bent, a ripe pear in his cupped hand. Snow and rain, sunshine and frost, moved in quick succession, the years rolled back, far beyond her own lifetime. The feeling of those others who had striven and worked and died for so little flooded her mind. She thought of the women and men of other centuries, which seemed like yesterday, and thinking of them she became them, she was those who had lived in farms and villages, work-ing, talking of their husbands and children, sighing for grief, and weariness, laughing for the joy of life, carrying water from the springs and troughs, working in the fields. She knew their joys and pains, as if the waves of their thoughts, their sorrows and delights remained on earth and swept over her and permeated her. They were part of her, she was a shell filled with their lives, the echoes of their minds.

The house, always haunted by old loves and hates, by strength of character and indomitable will, by fierce and stormy religious beliefs, sent its emanations through her. The past surged from the walls, and filled the hearts of each generation, so that they were changed, made wiser, influenced by something they couldn't define.

Virginia gently removed Richard's arm. "Darling," she whispered, and slipped softly from the bed. She drew her dressing gown around her and pulled the thick curtain from the window. A searchlight stabbed the sky, far away, like the finger of God. Then another rose and crossed it, moving slowly and deliberately among the stars. The searchlights were pointing to the Great Bear, catching one of its stars, as if some unearthly being were playing a game. There were the stars, and the moon, and somewhere among those heavenly bodies flew demons from hell.

"Not for the first time either," thought Virginia. "Gran used to say there were devils abroad, flying with black wings, and angels fighting them, all invisible to us. I was frightened by the thought, less the devils should swoop down and catch me on my way home from school."

She opened the window and looked down at the sleeping farmyard, illuminated by the exquisite silver of the moon. This was the time for ghosts to appear, filmy wraiths of farm people who would go out to visit the fields, to stare at the new tractor, and wonder at Nick's Croft, ploughed up and sown with oats. They would talk to one another about all they saw. She shivered slightly and drew her dressing gown closer. She pressed her hands on the stone windowsill. Once before she had received the imprint of a rough sill upon her palms, long ago, in a dream. Her hands were wrinkled now, worn and curved. Maurice had said they were beautiful hands. That had been surprising. Whoever noticed people's hands? He had held her long fingers and slim palms with a hollow in them that he had found and kissed. That was a long time ago, and Maurice was dead, but to-night he was alive, smiling up from the yard as he rode off on his motor-cycle with a rose she had picked stuck in his coat. There was Ronnie too, going off with her pincushion in his pocket. Charity was there, walking across the yard, leading a horse to the troughs and William, sowing the corn, harrowing, rolling, ploughing, working in that dim invisible world that runs parallel to the visible.

"Virginia. Whatever are you doing? That plane was very near. It was a German I'm sure," cried Richard suddenly awake.

"They say one can't tell the difference," said Virginia, drawing the curtain over the window and returning to bed. "German planes won't get here. They'll never find this little house." The broken rhythm of the plane sounded close, the plane was swooping like a black bird of prey.

Richard caught her cold hands in his. "My girl, you're frozen. Come to me." He clasped her to him for a moment and then he sprang from the bed in a great hurry as a plane roared near.

"There's the hell of a row. Bombs dropping somewhere not far off."

Richard drew on his clothes. "You must get up, Jinny. It isn't safe to stay there. There's something on to-night. Listen."

There was another crash and the sound of guns over the hill.

"No, Richard. I'll stay here," said Virginia slowly, and her voice was soft as a dream. Richard hesitated a moment in the doorway.

"Be sensible, Jinny my lass. Be sensible. Come along," said he urgently.

"No. I'll stay here." She was quite firm this time, there was no moving her and he had to hurry away.

"Jinny. If the house is hit, we shall have to hunt for your body," he shouted.

"It won't be hit, Dick. It's not caring."

"Very well. I'm going to the stable to quieten the horses. There'll be some incendiaries dropped perhaps. We must be ready for 'em."

"Take care of old Bess. She won't like this," called Virginia. Richard picked up the flashlamp and ran downstairs.

There was a hurried sound of doors opening, and candles tumbled on the landing. Then Susan came in with the little boy excitedly clutching her skirts, and John ran in to his grandmother. The servant-girl was already running downstairs. Her feet clattered noisily and shrill nervous laughter came from the passage.

"Mother! Oh dear! Do come down. I'm sure it's a German and it's such a bright moonlight night, it can see us. The noise is terrible," cried Susan.

"Robin's somewhere up in the sky to-night. We are quite safe," said Virginia dreamily.

"Mother. You say ridiculous things. He isn't anywhere near here, you know quite well."

The fiendish shriek of the plane as it seemed to swoop to the farm was deafening, but mingled with it, deep below was another

sound, the cry of the house itself, defiant, age-old, the voice of
centuries, the immortal voice of all those who had lived there.
The room vibrated with the sonorous organ note. The dark
shadow of the plane passed over the farmyard, the barn's angle
tipped with quicksilver was cut, the jet black moulded eaves, the
old stones of the wall with the glittering milkchurns ranged along
the top, chequered with moonshine, all were cut for an infinitesi-
mal time by that sinister shadow of evil.

Susan screamed and ran downstairs, without noticing the little
boy who stayed behind.

"I want to stay with you, Gran," whispered the boy, pushing
close to her, but Virginia took his hand and led him downstairs
and stood by the kitchen door, where the oaken pillar rose.

There was a roar of engines, as the plane dived over the farm,
machine-gunning the yard. There were flickers of light from
incendiaries, and then an earth-shaking explosion which threw
them to the floor. The house seemed to quiver, the windows
splintered, the plaster fell around them. They picked themselves
up, and Virginia brushed the dust from the child's face with
trembling fingers. Her heart was beating too fast, and she held
tight to the great wooden post, notched and scarred and blackened with smoke of years. It was firm as a rock, and the panic
died down. A column of smoke was rising from the ancient part
of the farmhouse, the little building which the shepherd had built
five hundred years ago was burning, but the bomb had fallen in
the field. There was a rumble and groan from the house, and a
cry of triumph, as the plane rocked drunkenly and swept away.

"Ah! The apple-chamber's afire." Richard and Ben and David
were already carrying water, and pumping upon the fire.

"The plane's coming down. It's come down yonder,"
shouted Richard, and he waved his hand towards the fields at
the back of the farm. They ran up the look-out steps, carrying
water, and from the platform they could see it. Over the meadows,
beyond the little wood a fierce flame shot up, with a great explosion.

"It's burning in Nick's Croft," cried David.

"Then let it burn. There's no water over yonder, we can do
nothing for them. We must look after this place. The farm is safe,
thank God. Only that little bit harmed. Lucky there was nobody
sleeping there. There's a hole in the roof, and the floor gone, but
the fire's out."

Virginia stared at the gaping wound in the little old building, where the small chamber was smoking.

"It was my own little room," said she.

"I never knew, that," said Susan. "Did you really sleep in that little loft?"

"Yes. For years it was my bedroom. Grandmother Charity gave it me. I'm sorry it's gone."

"Better that than the house, or the stables. We're lucky. We've had a wonderful escape. The old house still standing and only that bit harmed. We can get that mended."

"Thank God Himself," whispered Virginia. "The house has won. It has triumphed." Aloud she said, "I think if it had been all burned down it would have gone on. The house has a soul."

"You go back to bed, Virginia. You look overdone by the shock. Take your mother to bed, Susan, and look after John."

"I'm all right," said Virginia. "Only tired."

She climbed wearily to bed and drew the blankets up to her chin. She heard the deep breathing, and there seemed to be a rumble of laughter in the house, a chuckle of the ancient stones. The house drew the shadows around it, and whispered to them. It spread out its voluminous skirts and shielded all within. It took the darkness as a cloak and wrapped it round its ancient head. Then it crouched low between its two mothering hills, with its foundations deep in the freestone rocks.

Virginia lay still. A fierce pain gripped her, tore her heart so that she could scarcely breathe. She lay still, hearkening to the words of the house.

"Courage and Life," it said. "Courage and Life."

Her thoughts ran fleetfoot from room to room, visiting each, taking comfort from the dear shapes she saw as invisible she fled, scenting the smells of each distinctive room, dairy and parlour, pantry and kitchen, stable and bedrooms, she entered every one of them, touching the walls, the furniture, the stalls, the benches, holding the household gods with sensitive fingers, her body lying prone in old Charity's bed. The pain got worse, and she shut her eyes, but she saw even more clearly. A heatless flame leapt high in the empty fireplace, and the room was lighted by it. It was welcoming, it beckoned, and called to her. There was a grand friendliness. Shadowy arms were outstretched to embrace her. A hundred years, a thousand, those pointed flames would dance, the room would murmur and call, as Virginia's spirit would return to the secret light with the others to warm her hands, to laugh and sing in the soft dim radiance of that unearthly fire with all those who had once lived there.

Her thoughts slipped backward to childhood, as she saw them waiting for her. Good luck and bad luck, but always strength to go on, a store upon which to draw, as one draws water from the earth's springs. Happiness, days of sunshine and snow, Christmas, Midsummer. They were happening again, those days. Richard! Ah Richard!

She lay very still. Even when Susan opened the door and came close to her, she didn't wake. The candle had gone out.

"Mother! Mother!" cried Susan. Then she called in sudden alarm. "Father, come here. Oh Mother!"

But the old house only smiled as it welcomed the latest of its lovers to its warm company of shadows. Its great heart beat so loudly that it seemed to be a pulsing rhythm flowing out to the fields, rising to the hills, shaking the sky itself. It breathed deeply, and a peal of laughter came from its antique roots. No bomb could hurt the soul of the house, for it was immortal. It opened wide its eyes and gazed at the deep night sky, where the planes flew under the wheeling stars, and the fingers of the search-lights glided through the Great Bear. Slow-moving stars and illimitable sky were part of its own life.

The beautiful shadows trooped down the stair and out into the yard, the ditchers, and cowmen and shepherds who had loved the farm and shared the life, the people of no account who had laboured for generations, tending the flocks on the hills, building the walls in true fashion, serving the land, giving much and taking little, these people who were the servants of the earth, friends of the ancient homestead. Back they went, stepping lightly across the kitchen floor. Through the doorway they flowed to see the little old building, and with them, a radiant happy ghost, went Virginia.